SPINNING OUT
THE BLACKHAWK BOYS

SPINNING OUT

THE BLACKHAWK BOYS

New York Times Bestselling Author
LEXI RYAN

Spinning Out © 2016 by Lexi Ryan

All rights reserved. This copy is intended for the original purchaser of this book. No part of this book may be reproduced, scanned, or distributed in any printed or electronic form without prior written permission from the author except by reviewers who may quote brief excerpts in connection with a review. Please do not participate in or encourage piracy of copyrighted materials in violation of the author's rights. Purchase only authorized editions.

This book is a work of fiction. Any resemblance to institutions or persons, living or dead, is used fictitiously or purely coincidental.

Cover © 2016 Sarah Hansen, Okay Creations
Interior design and Formatting by:

E.M. TIPPETTS BOOK DESIGNS

www.emtippettsbookdesigns.com

For Kai

About SPINNING OUT

Once, the only thing that mattered to me was football—training, playing, and earning my place on the best team at every level. I had it all, and I threw it away with a semester of drugs, alcohol, and pissing off anyone who tried to stop me. Now I'm suspended from the team, on house arrest, and forced to spend six months at home to get my shit together. The cherry on top of my fuckup sundae? Sleeping in the room next to mine is my best friend's girl, Mia Mendez—the only woman I've ever loved and a reminder of everything I regret.

I'm not sure if having Mia so close will be heaven or hell. She's off-limits—and not just because she's working for my dad. Her heart belongs to someone else. But since the accident that killed her brother and changed everything, she walks around like a zombie, shutting out her friends and ignoring her dreams. We're both broken, numb, and stuck in limbo.

Until I break my own rules and touch her.

Until she saves me from my nightmares by climbing into my bed.

Until the only thing I want more than having Mia for myself is to protect her from the truth.

I can't rewrite the past, but I refuse to leave her heart in the hands of fate. For this girl, I'd climb into the sky and rearrange the stars.

THE BLACKHAWK BOYS, an edgy, sexy sports romance series from *New York Times* bestseller Lexi Ryan. Football. Secrets. Lies. Passion. These boys don't play fair. Which Blackhawk Boy will steal your heart?

Book 1 - SPINNING OUT - Coming May 3rd (Arrow's story)

Book 2 - RUSHING IN - Coming mid-2016 (Christopher's story)

Book 3 - GOING UNDER - Coming late 2016 (Sebastian's story)

PROLOGUE

MIA

Before midnight. New Year's Eve. Black sky. Black clouds. Headlights. New moon.

My mother always told us that change happens at the new moon.

They're arguing. Brogan's drunk—not himself. Nic's pissed—too much himself.

"Nobody raises his hand to my sister." Nic spits in Brogan's face, and Brogan swings. Then the sickening sound of fists connecting with flesh. My brother's fists. My boyfriend's. They're going to kill each other.

"Stop!" I beg, my voice like breaking glass. "Nic, just take me home." Sleet pelts my face, coming at me the way the guys go at each other. I pace, my arms wrapped around myself, my fingers numb. It's so dark out here, and the only light comes from the headlights of the boys' cars, facing each other on the side of the road.

"Get in the car," Nic growls at me without taking his eyes from Brogan. It's the third time he's given the order, and I refused, as if my presence could keep them from hurting each other. This time I obey, climbing in and shutting the door behind me. It's warmer in here without the sleet and relentless wind, but I can't stop shaking. Cold. Scared. Fucking night from hell. I wait for my brother, but he doesn't follow. He shoves Brogan into the street, and Brogan falls, then scrambles. Nic kicks him before he can get up.

"Just take me home!" I scream. My stomach cramps, folds, convulses around itself. It wasn't supposed to be like this.

I turn the key in the ignition and look at the clock as if it might be ticking down to the end of their ugly shouts and angry punches. 11:59. How is it *still* 11:59? Will this night never end?

As if answering my mental plea, the clock ticks over, and I hear screeching tires.

Black sky. Black clouds. Headlights. New moon.

My mother always told us that change happens at the new moon. She was right.

PART I. AFTER

April, three and a half months after the accident

MIA

"What is she doing here?" Arrow's words are spoken in a hard whisper that crawls up the walls and under the wooden nursery door. They creep into my sanctuary and claw at my heart. The murmurs of his stepmother's reply float up behind the hate, but I can't make them out.

"You couldn't find any-fucking-body else to play mom to *your* baby?" No more whispering. Words directed like knives intended to hurt us both—her for being an unfit mother by hiring a nanny, me because he wants me to know how unwelcome I am.

The dull thud of toppled furniture—maybe a dining room chair, maybe an end table. Heavy footsteps. The echoing, house-shaking boom of a slamming door.

I shift baby Katie in my arms and cross to the window. Between the slats of the wooden blinds, I watch Arrow. The sight of him climbing into his electric-blue Mustang GT steals my breath. The engine purrs, and he tears out of the driveway.

Breathe, I remind myself. I close my eyes and focus on the cool air filling my lungs, the warmth of the newborn curled into my body, the hum of the ceiling fan almost whispering the reminder: *Breathe in. Breathe out. Breathe in. Breathe out.*

Gwen's heels click on the hardwood planks of the hall, and I know she's heading my way before she knocks.

"Come in."

She opens the door slowly and steps into the room, bringing with her a cloud of expensive perfume and a reminder of my anxieties. She looks every bit the part of the stereotypical trophy wife—from her blond hair and perfect body to the single-carat diamond studs in each ear.

At twenty-six, Gwen is only six years older than me, five years older than her stepson. She married Arrow's father a convenient eight months before she gave birth to Katie, making her husband a father to his second child at the age of sixty-five. I don't judge her for marrying Mr. Woodison, a man nearly forty years her senior. We all have our reasons for taking paths for which the world will judge us.

"I'm guessing you heard that," she says.

I nod and tell my racing heart to steady. If she asks me to leave, I don't know what I'll do. Get a job at Walmart, maybe? The pay cut would be a bitch, but it would be *something*. Of course, then there'd be no school next fall, and the fact that Mr. Woodison pays me enough that I'll be able to afford my tuition at Blackhawk Hills U is definitely the sweetest part of this arrangement.

"He hates you so much," she says. The words hit me with the dull force of a blow to the heart. "Why?"

Because I destroyed everything. "I don't know."

She extends her arms for Katie, and I hesitate. Seeing Arrow again—even for only the ten seconds it took him to climb into his car—has left me feeling ugly and guilty. The baby's warmth is a soothing balm to my battered conscience, but I hand her over.

"I don't know what we're going to do about him," Gwen says. "But if that's a taste of what's to come, it's going to be a *long* six months." She shakes her head and peers between the slats in the blinds. "I can't say that I'm happy with him serving his sentence here, but it wasn't my choice to make."

"He's not that bad." When she cuts her gaze to me, I wish I'd kept my mouth shut. If I'm going to keep my job with the Woodisons while Arrow is home, I need Gwen as my ally.

With a sigh, she releases the blinds and turns back to me. "I won't live in a house with you two at each other's throats. So as long as I'm stuck with him here, you're going to have to fix it."

"I'm sorry?"

"Whatever is wrong between you and Arrow. *Fix it*. Or I'll have to find someone else to help me with Katie and the house."

My heart plummets, and I reach out and grab the edge of the crib. "I'll talk to him." Not that talking will help. The best thing I can do for Arrow is avoid him. He won't be so angry about me being here if he doesn't have to look at my face.

"Between you and me," Gwen says, her lips curling into a perfectly painted snarl, "I'm hoping he'll slip up and start using again. I'd rather see his spoiled ass spend the next six months in jail than have him under my roof."

"*Start using again.*" I never thought those words would be connected to Arrow, and hearing them is a slap in the face. Because Gwen might be clueless, but everyone else in this town knows why Arrow's life spun out of control this semester, and anyone who's honest knows I'm to blame. I wasn't driving the car. I wasn't throwing the punches. But I was the catalyst. If I'd stayed home that night . . .

I keep my mouth shut, and I'm rewarded with a smile as Gwen hands Katie back to me.

Fix it. A simple command delivered by a woman who's grown accustomed to having her demands met. Only she doesn't know she's asking for the impossible.

No one can fix this.

ARROW

The house is dark and quiet when I get home. Maybe everyone is sleeping, but that's unlikely. At eleven, Dad's probably drinking his first scotch. Maybe screwing his nubile young wife.

And Mia? Is she sleeping? Studying? Maybe she's rocking the baby to sleep and humming a lullaby.

I climb the stairs and head straight to my room, each step feeling like another click of the invisible shackles of my house-arrest sentence. Tonight was my last night of freedom, and I spent it sitting in my car alone by the lake. Because apparently I'm a fucking masochist who wanted to wallow in his memories for a while. As if having her in the room next to mine for the next six months isn't going to be reminder enough.

I can't decide if her nearness is a gift or a curse—if seeing her in the hall and catching her scent will be heaven or hell.

Pausing at the door to Mia's room, I press my palm to the

wood. I swear my pulse triples at the thought of her on the other side.

"Wrong door."

I spin around at the sound of her voice and find myself face to face with Mia Mendez, my stepmother's goddamn nanny, my best friend's girl, and a reminder of everything I regret.

Her dark hair is piled in a sloppy knot on top of her head, and soft tendrils curl at the base of her neck. She's wearing some sort of oversized, wide-necked T-shirt that's slipped off one shoulder, exposing a dusting of freckles I know too damn well continue down to her bra line. Her feet are bare, her toenails painted pink, and her legs . . . *Christ*.

She swallows and stares at my chest, like she can't look me in the eye anymore. *Join the fucking club.* "That one's mine," she says softly.

"*Yours?*"

Her head bobs as she nods, and anger flares in my stomach, a hot flash over the lust that sucker-punched me the second she appeared. She's ashamed of me. Or disgusted. It would only be worse if she had any idea what being this close to her does to me. "This isn't *your* room," I say. "It's just where you're staying while you work."

She lets out a breath and shifts her gaze to the door. "Whatever."

I give her another once-over, all the while telling myself the ugliest lies I can about her. Anger is so much easier to deal with than this soul-stealing desire. No. Desire would be easy. It's basic. Practically juvenile compared to what I feel for Mia. This is something else. Something more. "You make a habit out of walking around my dad's house like this?"

She arches a brow. "Like what?"

I shift my gaze down her torso and let it linger on her thighs just below the hem of her cotton sleep shorts. "Half naked?"

Shaking her head, she pushes past me and into her room. The shorts shift with each step, and I simultaneously wish they were longer and pray they might become shorter. Because *this*—the view of the caramel skin at the back of her thighs and the memory of how she whimpered when I rolled her onto her stomach and put my mouth there—*this*, without the gratification of seeing the curve at the bottom of her ass. *This* nightmare my life has become—having her so close and knowing she can't ever be mine. *This* isn't heaven or hell. It's fucking purgatory.

She nudges the door closed, but I catch it before it latches and push into the room. Coming in here is impulsive and foolish, but the instinct to get closer to Mia has been there since the day I first looked into her big brown eyes. Some things never change, even if we wish they would.

She throws up her hands. "Sure. Come on in. Make yourself at home." She gives me her back and heads over to the basket of unfolded laundry sitting on the bed. The room is tidy, and except for the stack of books on the dresser and the laundry on the bed, it's not much different from how it looked when it was the guest room. You'd think she'd decorate—put a poster on the walls or pictures of her and Brogan on the nightstand—*something*.

"Did you need something?" she asks, as I close the distance between us.

"I don't like you being here." Part of me hopes she'll understand why I have to say it. I want her to know me well enough to see through my bullshit. I'm only trying to convince myself it's true. But she flinches at the words, and I feel like the asshole I am.

"I'm here to watch Katie. It's not for you to like or not like. It's my job." Not bothering to look at me as she speaks, she takes a new item of clothing from the laundry basket.

I snatch it from her hands. Red lace and spaghetti straps—there isn't much to it. *"Watch Katie?"* I hold the garment by the straps for inspection. "Maybe you're being more than the stand-in mom. Maybe you're also the stand-in screw."

She swings, her open palm coming toward my face, and I don't bother to duck. I let it land and relish the sting of her fingers connecting with my skin. I've been numb for months, but it's no surprise that Mia's the first to make me feel something.

When I open my eyes, her nostrils are flared. Her chest rises and falls with her heavy breaths.

"I don't even know who you are anymore," she says in a sharp whisper. "Stay away from me."

"I'm the guy you fucked behind your boyfriend's back." I scrape my gaze down her body and back up before throwing the red lace nightie on the bed. "And probably the one you think about when you wear that piece of trash."

Her breath leaves her in a rush, and she bends at the waist as if I threw a punch to the gut.

The words *I'm sorry* sit heavily at the back of my throat, choking me. I want to bury my face in her chest and whimper my apologies like a four-year-old, but she wouldn't understand what I was apologizing for, and I don't deserve her forgiveness. I'll say whatever horrible things I must to make sure she never tries to give it to me.

I leave her before she can reply and before I can say anything worse. Apologies won't change what happened on New Year's Eve. They won't fix Brogan, and they won't bring her brother back from the dead.

MIA

Gwen told me to fix whatever's wrong between Arrow and me, and I slapped him.

Good going, Mia.

I pick up Gwen's lingerie, carefully fold it, and add it to the pile with shaking hands. My job with the Woodisons goes beyond watching the couple's infant daughter. That task isn't nearly enough to warrant my generous paycheck. I also do the laundry, cook the meals, and keep the house clean. For two months, it's been going just fine. I tend to Katie. I scrub the toilets. I cook dinner and make sure there are fresh flowers in the dining room.

I should have made the extent of my duties clear to Arrow, but for some reason I couldn't stomach him thinking of me as the maid. Uriah Woodison's last maid was my mother, and I don't want Arrow equating me with her. Not tonight, when his return still stings like a sticky bandage repeatedly ripped off a wound. Does he really think I'm fucking his father, or is he just trying to drive a bigger wedge between us?

I want to be angry with him. To hate him for the things he said tonight, and worse, what he didn't say, the comfort he didn't offer. No one but Arrow can understand how empty I've felt since the accident. No one but Arrow can understand the weight in my chest that is equal parts grief and anger.

But I can't blame him when I'm almost relieved to have animosity as a buffer between us. I've always had a soft spot for Arrow Woodison. Maybe that explains why I betrayed Brogan for one night in his arms.

"Quit acting like you were cheating when you were broken up." I can practically hear my best friend Bailey's voice in my head. It's a lecture she's recited enough times. I'm sure we both have it memorized. But it doesn't change how I feel about the things I did and the decisions I made.

My phone vibrates on the nightstand, and Bailey's name scrolls across the screen as if she knew I was thinking about her.

I snatch it up. "Hey, you."

"How's it going, lovely?" Bailey asks. "I hear the prodigal son returned home today."

"Yeah." I risk a glance toward the door, but I'm still alone. I walk over and close it quietly.

"So?" she asks. "Did you get the scoop? What is *up* with him? The only one of us who had a sure ticket out of this fucking town, and he screwed it up. I just don't understand."

"I don't know," I murmur. But it's a lie. I understand why Arrow spun out of control like he did. He wasn't the type to drink to excess and never touched drugs. Then on New Year's Eve, our worlds went to shit, and he lashed out.

"I envy you," Bailey says. "I wish I got to spend my summer watching Arrow shirtless at the pool."

Bailey is convinced that working for the Woodisons means a life of leisure, as if they hired me just so I could sit at their pool drinking mai tais all day. So far from the truth, but I'd be lying if I acted as if it were a rough gig. The hardest day at the Woodisons' is easier than the best at home. Of course, if my dad knew I was working here, he'd lose his shit, but I've made sure he won't find out.

"I thought you were working tonight," I say, changing the subject.

"I'm on a break. You're coming to my party tomorrow, aren't you?" she asks. "You never come out anymore. I want to get drunk with my girl."

"I'll think about it." Another lie. I haven't been to a party since New Year's Eve. Just the scent of alcohol makes my stomach churn. The last thing I need is to be surrounded by a bunch of drunk people.

"Oh, crap. Mia, wait a sec, okay?" I hear the muffled sound of her talking to someone with her hand over the receiver, then, "Your dad's here."

I wince. Bailey works at a strip club, and Dad thinks strip clubs are an abomination. He's been known to drunkenly stumble the quarter-mile between the trailer park and the Pretty Kitty to tell the dancers they're "tempting good men." I'm sure his eyes never stray to the girls on the stage. *Yeah, right.* "I'll be there in ten minutes."

I pull on a bra under my tee and trade my sleep shorts for a pair of cutoffs before heading downstairs to find Gwen. She's stretched out on a chaise by the pool, sipping a glass of wine and staring into the distance.

"Gwen?"

She startles at the sound of my voice, then surreptitiously wipes at her cheeks. "Mia, what can I do for you?"

My heart aches a little for her. It's not like we talk—we don't have that kind of relationship—but I know she's been unhappy since Katie was born. She spends so much energy trying not to show it, so I pretend not to notice. I've considered speaking up a few times, worried she's suffering from postpartum depression, but in the end I keep my mouth shut. Gwen's not the type to appreciate life advice from anyone she deems "the help."

"Is it okay if I leave for a couple of hours? My dad . . ." I don't want to finish, even if she deserves an explanation.

"Sure. No problem. Katie's sleeping?"

I nod. "She just finished a bottle and drifted right off. She should be set for a few hours, but I'll be back as quickly as I can."

She waves a hand. "Take your time. Despite what my husband may have led you to believe, I'm perfectly capable of getting out of bed to tend to my daughter."

"I know you are."

She nods toward the front of the house. "Go on, then."

"Thank you." I take a few steps toward the gate and stop to

turn back to her. I know what it's like to be isolated, to suddenly find yourself in a world where you don't belong, and I feel like I should say something, like I should let her know she's not alone.

She speaks first. "Please don't tell Mr. Woodison I was crying. I was just having a moment. Hormones. You know."

"Of course." Again, I want to speak up, tell her there's no shame in getting help.

She stands, her eyes glittering in the low light from the lamps lining the pool deck. "A piece of advice, Mia?" she says. "Tempting as he might be, you'd do best to keep your legs closed."

I open my mouth but have no idea what to say. I'm not sure if I'm more surprised that she's offering this piece of wisdom, or insulted that she thinks that's the kind of advice I'd need. Who is it she thinks I need to be warned away from? Arrow, or her husband?

Not trusting myself to reply, I press my lips together and rush to my car.

I don't let myself think about what Gwen must think of me or why, and I definitely don't let myself think about how much I hate driving the curvy roads into Blackhawk Valley at night. I'm going to do the same as I've done for the last four months—whatever is necessary. Just because Arrow is home doesn't mean anything has changed.

When I open the door to the strip club, the smoke and pounding music hit me in the face. Nobody cards me or cares that I'm underage. In this kind of place, boobs are more likely to get you through the door than a valid ID.

SPINNING OUT 19

The place is packed with college guys tonight. They all look the same to me—white boys in jeans and fitted T-shirts trying to act the part of grown men by gawking at bare tits and drinking too much overpriced beer. Once, I told my brother, Nic, that I just didn't *get* strip clubs. Here are all these good-looking guys, many of whom already have a girl at home, paying to see what they could have for free.

Nic just laughed and told me getting into a girl's bed might be easy, but getting out is another matter. *"Strip clubs mean boobs without expectations."*

My brother was such a sexist asshole. I'd give anything to have him back.

I scan the faces at the tables and by the stage, but I don't see my father. "Fuck," I mutter, pushing my way through the crowd.

A guy at the bar shoots his hand out and grabs my arm. "Hey, beautiful. You work here?" His thumb strokes the bare skin above my elbow, and the touch makes my skin crawl.

"No."

"You should," he says, his words slurring together. "You're prettier'n the rest of 'em."

"Hands off, dirty." Bailey appears at my side and pulls the guy's hand off my arm. "You touch another girl tonight—stripper or not—and I'll have your ass thrown out of here."

She pulls me away from him, and I mutter a weak, "Thank you."

"I swear, Mia, the creeps see you coming from a mile away. It's a special gift."

"I'll be sure to add it to my résumé," I say. "Where's Dad?"

"I stuck him in the GM's office. Found him in the ladies' room asking the girls to go home with him."

"Seriously?"

She rolls her eyes. "Says he wants to save them. Take them to church. Show them there's a better way to live."

My father. World's biggest hypocrite.

She gives me a sympathetic squeeze on the shoulder, and I follow her through a set of doors and into the back hallway that runs behind the stage. The doors swing closed behind us, and the music drops to a dull roar.

She opens an office door and says, "He's all yours."

Dad's slumped in the chair beside the desk, eyes closed, spittle dangling from his bottom lip. *Way to be a cliché, Dad.*

"I convinced my manager not to call the cops, but you've gotta get him out of here."

I sigh, nodding. "Of course. Thank you." I turn to her and force a smile. "For everything."

She wraps me in a hug and squeezes tight. "Anything for you, chica." When she pulls back, she offers a half-smile. "You good? Everything okay at Palace Woodison?"

I shrug. "It's a little tense since Arrow came home." *Tense.* Considering I slapped him less than an hour ago, that's probably an understatement. I need to talk to him and soon. But what is there to say?

"You know what fixes tension, don't you?" She cocks her head, waiting for my guess, then grins when I stay silent. "*Fucking*, Mia.

A well-fucked man is rarely a pissy one."

I roll my eyes. "Bailey!"

"Give it a try and tell me if I'm wrong." Her grin rockets up a notch. "Scratch that. You had your chance with Arrow and decided he wasn't worth the trouble, so I'll take care of it for you. I'm a saint like that, making sacrifices for my friends."

I know she's joking. She's never been interested in Arrow.

She tilts her face to the ceiling and sighs. "And with Arrow's body, I might just sacrifice again and again. And again."

I can't help it. I burst into giggles, and my dad stirs in his sleep, grunting something. *Back to reality.* "Come on, Dad." I slide my hands under his arms and help him up.

He's unsteady on his feet and blinks at me. "You're working here now, too? I won't have a daughter of mine working in a strip club!"

"I don't work here, Dad. I'm here to take you home." I duck under one of his arms. The weight across my shoulders feels like a thousand pounds, but I take a deep breath and lead him forward.

"Got him?" Bailey asks, following us out of the office.

"Yeah. He's fine."

As we head back through the club toward the front doors, I immediately feel eyes on me—people staring as I lead my drunk father to the door. I'm not embarrassed anymore. Someone needs to take care of Dad, and with Nic gone, that falls to me.

"Have a good night," I tell Bailey.

"Oh, I will," she says. "There's a table of BHU guys over there who are going to pay for my fall tuition if they keep it up with the tips." She winks at me and saunters away.

Dad jerks his head up and stops walking. "Where's Nic? I need Nic to take me home. I need my son."

I'm waiting for the day that hurts less, but the words slice through me every time. "Nicholas is gone, Dad. Remember? We lost him."

"Good riddance," says a man a couple of tables away. His eyes are on the tits of the shirtless girl grinding on his lap, but I know he's talking about my brother.

"Too bad he had to take one of the good ones down with him," another man says in a low rumble. The night my brother died, he'd been clean for months. Not using. Not selling. But nobody cares. If your last name is Mendez, you don't get a second chance. Not in this town.

Ignoring them, and the ache in my chest their words threaten to wake, I say a quick prayer that my dad's too drunk to process their words.

"Come on, Dad." I urge him forward, knowing we have an audience and determined to keep my chin up.

"Why'd God have to take my only son?" my father whispers. I hear the tears in his voice and move my feet faster. I need to get him home before he breaks down.

No one here is going to have any sympathy for him if he starts wailing about losing Nicholas. All they see is how the accident hurt one of their own, Brogan Barrett. And in my brother's death, all they see is a scapegoat, an easy way to answer the unsolved mystery of the hit-and-run. Even the local paper was happy to report the accident as "likely gang violence" without any real evidence to support such an assertion.

The second I ease Dad into the passenger seat, he closes his eyes and his head lolls to the side. I buckle him in and take the short drive in silence.

A dark SUV passes me and makes me do a double take. It was a dark SUV that flew over Deadman's Curve and hit my brother and Brogan on New Year's Eve, and every time I see one, my gut twists with too many emotions.

I don't bother with the radio. I wouldn't be able to hear it over the clamor of my heartache anyway.

ARROW

I slam a third cabinet door shut and open another, looking for the fucking skillets.

Mia left.

Did I piss her off that much, or did something else call her away? I stood in my room and watched her car roll down the drive and cautiously through the gate. I'm going to have to make my peace with her working here. And I can. I will. Fuck. It just took me by surprise. I came home from rehab mentally prepared to serve my house-arrest sentence. The judge acted like he was doing me a favor by letting me serve time here. He obviously doesn't know what it's like to be Uriah Woodison's fuck-up son.

I thought I was prepared—for Dad's disapproval, for his anger and disappointment—and then Gwen launched the curveball at me.

Mia Mendez is living here while she helps with the baby.

Mia Mendez is eating in my kitchen, sharing my shower.

Mia Mendez is sleeping on the other side of my bedroom wall in a cotton sleepshirt so thin it makes my hands itch to slide under it.

I yank open another cabinet and finally find the skillets. Christ, I just want some food, but I'll be fucking damned if I'm going to eat any of the meals in the fridge. My stomach clenched when I saw them—perfectly balanced, prepared meals labeled in Mia's neat handwriting: *quinoa and chicken, peppered flank steak and green beans, fajita frittata.*

She's not just helping with the baby. Dad has her doing his meal prep. As if she's the Alice to his Brady Bunch or some shit. So fucking twisted. Count me out.

I put a skillet on the stove, pour a little olive oil in it, and look around while it heats.

Gwen remodeled this space while she was pregnant. Contractors came in and ripped out the cherry wood cabinets my mother had chosen and replaced them with a stark white variety that feels so sterile you almost expect the place to smell like bleach and commercial disinfectant.

It's everything my mother's kitchen wasn't—cold to the warm, white to the dark, showpiece to the functional. It's as if she ripped the heart right out of my house.

"That's fucking dramatic," I mutter to myself.

I grab the eggs from the fridge and crack them against the side of a bowl, dumping the egg whites and tossing the yolks in the trash. I chop fresh basil and beat it with the egg whites before pouring the mixture into the skillet.

My phone buzzes, rattling against the white marble countertop.

> **Keegan:** *Someone told me they saw Mia Mendez walk into the manager's office at the Pretty Kitty. I'm heading that way. If there's a god, she'll be on stage tonight.*

My fist tightens around the phone, but before I can do something stupid like throw it against the wall or, worse, let Keegan know exactly what I think about his hopes for the evening, it buzzes again. And again. Two, three, four messages all coming in at once, making me realize this wasn't a text he sent just to me but one of those mass-group texts that guarantees to keep my phone rattling for the next half-hour.

I read through the conversation as I stir my eggs.

> **Mason:** *You fucking wish, loser. Mia wouldn't strip.*
> **Trent:** *If you love me, you'll tell me if this happens. But I heard she was working at the Woodisons'—that true, Arrow?*
> **Mason:** *Not that I object to the idea in theory. Because damn.*
> **Keegan:** *Why work for the Woodisons? Ass like that and she could make BANK stripping.*

Chris: *You're all so low. This is Brogan's girl you're talking about. Show some respect.*

Brogan's girl.

I stare at those two words for so long that time drops away. Brogan's. Girl.

I draw in a breath and my throat burns with smoke. *Shit.* I throw the exhaust fan on full blast so my burned eggs don't set off the smoke alarm and wake up everyone in the house. I toss them into the trashcan and put the pan in the sink to soak. Not wanting to embark on another failed cooking attempt, I grab a protein shake from the fridge.

Chris's mention of Brogan predictably silenced the conversation, but I turn off my phone anyway, shutting it down before I can say something I'll regret, or worse—find out that she really is stripping.

I twist the cap off my drink, sink into one of the living room couches, and turn on ESPN out of sheer habit.

"Let's talk biggest draft disappointments," the announcer says to his co-host. "Give me your top five."

The broad-shouldered black man taps his papers on the desk in front of him and pushes his glasses up his nose. His name is Craig Jennings, a retired running back for the Indianapolis Colts. When I was in seventh grade, he was my hero. He was the reason I told the coach I didn't want to play quarterback, even though half my friends were dying for the position. No. I wanted to be Craig. I wanted to power down the field, zigging and zagging like

Craig. Finding the holes and making impossible plays. He was the reason I loved football, and that stubborn declaration was just the beginning of a long list of careful decisions that pulled me to the top of my sport at each level.

Craig looks at the camera, lips pursed, eyes serious, and says, "My list starts with Arrow Woodison. And I put him as the number five instead of number one only because he hadn't yet decided if he'd be entering the draft at the end of this year or playing his senior year at BHU. But even as a long shot, my boy Arrow is nothing short of a *profound* disappointment for any team who believed they might be able to pick him up this year or next."

"Fuck you, Craig," I whisper. I made my decisions. I knew what I was doing every step of the way. No one forced me down the path that led to my house arrest.

But when you idolize someone—whether it's a parent or a football star—you want him to *get* you. You want him to understand that the terrible choice you made was the best you could do.

I didn't think I even cared about football anymore, but Craig's words make me feel claustrophobic. Stuck. *Profound disappointment.* They kick at the dead dream and remind me I buried myself these last few months, not just my football hopes. But wasn't that the point?

I grab the remote, but even though I know I should shut off the television, I only turn up the volume, lean back on the couch, and listen to what else the man has to say about me.

MIA

When I pull into the trailer park, my tires crackle on the gravel road. I park in front of my childhood home and cut the engine. The windows are draped with dark sheets and part of the roof has been covered with a piece of rotting particleboard. The air-conditioning unit hangs from the bedroom window, but it hasn't worked for years. As I climb out of the car and walk around to get my father, guilt washes over me, just like it does every time I visit. Tonight—and every night this summer, if Arrow doesn't get me fired—I'll sleep in the air-conditioned comfort of the Woodison mansion, a feather pillow under my head, cool, silky sheets wrapped around my legs, and Dad will sleep in this hot trailer, sweating through his sheets.

"Come on, Dad," I say, sliding my arm behind his back. "Time to get you inside." He's out cold and doesn't stir when I tug on him. "Dad. Wake up." Nothing. Not even a grunt. "Crap."

"Here," someone calls behind me. He shuffles down the steps

of the trailer beside Dad's and saunters toward me before I can answer. I don't know him, but his thick arms and broad shoulders indicate he's a much better candidate for the job of maneuvering my fifty-year-old father inside than I am.

I step aside and let him help, holding the door as he leads my half-conscious father into the house.

"Take him to bed?" he asks.

"Please." I point to the back of the trailer and follow him, watching as he settles Dad onto the unmade bed. I remove Dad's scuffed work boots and pull a blanket over him as the stranger fills a cup of water from the tap and puts it on the table next to him.

"Thank you," I say as we head back out.

The man holds the door open for me this time, but he doesn't speak until the screen door clatters to a close behind us. The porch light illuminates the sharp angles of his cheekbones and a neatly trimmed beard. He's tall and broad-shouldered with an aura of *bad boy*. Tattoos peek out from under the sleeves of his T-shirt. I make a mental note to tell Bailey about him. He's absolutely her type.

While I lock Dad's door behind me, the stranger dismisses my gratitude with a shrug. "If I hadn't been here, someone else would've helped."

He's probably right. The trailer park never really sleeps. Not many people who live here work bankers' hours, so there's always someone sitting outside, smoking or taking in the night air. Nighttime promises blazing porch lights and the rumble of unhappy car engines. It's such a dramatic contrast to the dark, silent acres of the Woodison Estate.

"You lived here long?" I wish he could help me keep an eye on Dad and his drinking, but I'm too ashamed to ask.

"Grew up in Blackhawk Valley and came back this fall."

I nod and look at my feet. "You see my dad much?"

"Some. He tells me he used to work for Woodison?" He can't be too much older than me, and I wonder if he has a job and where. I wonder if he understands that my dad isn't rational when it comes to Uriah.

How Uriah Woodison screwed me over is one of Dad's favorite subjects. "He was let go a few years ago. Hasn't been able to find anything else." *Hasn't tried.*

"Woodison." Turning his head, he looks across the gravel lane. "There's a fucking asshole."

That asshole is buying Dad's groceries and keeping his lights on—not that I'd tell Dad that. "Well, I need to get going. Thanks for your help tonight."

"I'm Sebastian Crowe." He doesn't offer a hand, only studies me. "You must be Mia."

"Yeah, sorry. Mia Mendez. Nice to meet you."

"You're even prettier than they say."

"Who?"

He shakes his head, dismissing my question. "How's your boyfriend doing?"

"Brogan?"

"Do you have *another* boyfriend?"

"He's . . . No change." I force a smile, refusing to let him see how unnerving it is to have this guy know so much about me when I don't think I've ever seen him before. "Thank you for asking." I wander toward my car, wishing he hadn't brought up Brogan, wishing he weren't looking at me like he knows my secrets. "You sure know a lot about local news for someone who just moved to town."

"In this neighborhood, it's about all they talk about."

Yet another reason I'm glad to be staying somewhere else. "Well, thanks again. For tonight."

"Don't be such a stranger." He tucks his hands into his pockets, and I sense his gaze still on me, even if I can't tell in the darkness. "I'd like to see you around more often."

Oh, shit. I don't have the energy for this tonight. "Listen, I hope I didn't give you any ideas by accepting your help. I'm not looking for . . ." I've always sucked at these conversations. Whether I'm trying to flirt or let a guy down gently, it never comes as naturally to me as it does to Bailey. "My life is kind of complicated right now."

He arches a brow and rocks back on his heels. "I just asked about your boyfriend, and you think I'm coming on to you?"

"I . . . well . . ." I roll a piece of gravel under the toe of my sandal. "I'm sorry. A lot of people think that since Brogan's accident, I should . . ." I hate this, but I force myself to lift my chin and meet his gaze through the darkness. Away from the porch light, I can't make out his features at all, but I'm questioning myself now. Maybe he does look familiar. Maybe I've seen him around before. Not here, but where? "I just didn't want there to be any confusion."

"Your dad needs you. You should come around more *for him*."

Nodding absently, I climb into my car to dodge the guilt trip I don't need. I'm doing all I can for my father. At Nic's funeral, Mom tried to talk me into going back to Arizona with her. In the years since she left, she's gotten a teaching degree and now has a good job teaching Spanish at a high school out there. She told me I could live with her and go to college there. She practically begged me, and I declined—not just because my relationship with her is screwed up, or because I didn't want to be that far from Brogan. Part of me relished the idea of running away after that horrible night, but I could never leave my dad alone.

No, I don't need a guilt trip. Guilt is a constant for me.

I pull away from the trailer park as quickly as I arrived. I've had to take unscheduled hours off from the Woodisons four or five times in the two months I've worked there. Thus far, Gwen has been accommodating when it comes to my absences, but I don't like to push it. Besides, there are too many memories here. Too much pain.

When I pull into the Woodisons' circle drive, the floodlights click on, cutting through the darkness of the country night. I take the spot next to Arrow's Mustang, throw the car into park, and climb out. I close my eyes and take a deep breath of the clean country air. The old neighborhood suffocates me. Or maybe that's from being around my dad. My guilt and frustration with him get so tangled that I don't even know whom I'm angry with anymore—myself for leaving him to live in that hovel, or him for doing nothing to pull himself out.

Dad and I aren't so different. We both want to escape our lives. The difference is the path we take. I'm searching for freedom through school and work, and Dad finds his escape in booze.

"Way to feel self-righteous, Mia," I mutter. But that's why I took the job with the Woodisons, isn't it? Dad would rather see me dealing drugs like Nic than have his daughter work for Uriah Woodison. I knew that, and I told Dad I was living with Bailey and took the job anyway, telling myself that Uriah owed me this, that I was doing what I needed to do to help Dad and get myself through college, promising myself that what my father doesn't know won't hurt him.

But were those my only reasons? Or did part of me hope this might get me closer to Arrow?

Before tonight, he hadn't spoken to me since our fight on New Year's Eve. He came to the hospital the evening after the accident, but the only indication that he even knew I was there was the moment his eyes skimmed over the bloodstains on my white dress. He sat in the waiting room with his teammates and didn't say a word to me. Not *I'm sorry about your brother* or— what I really needed to hear—*It's not your fault.*

I stare at Arrow's Mustang and fight to keep my breath as grief threatens to rip it away. Arrow might be angry with me, but I'm disappointed in him. I needed him after the accident, and I thought he was better than this. I didn't expect happily-ever-after. *Cinderella* is a fairytale, and this is real life. But even though I didn't expect him to be Prince Charming to my Cinderella, I expected him to be the friend he'd become. The friend I needed when my world was at its darkest. I thought he was a big enough man to forgive me for New Year's Eve. I thought he was a *good enough* man to comfort me when I lost my brother, to stand by my side as I watched Brogan fight for his life in the hospital. Instead, the steadfast Arrow I'd known disappeared.

Before I realize what I'm doing, I reach out, touching my fingers to the window of the Mustang. I squint, trying to make out something in the back seat that isn't there. I can almost see us on the other side of the glass—desperate, greedy hands fumbling with my clothes, trying to work faster than my conscience. But when I blink, the apparition is gone, fizzled out in the floodlight of reality.

I enter the house, locking the door and enabling the alarm behind me. I'll let Gwen know I'm back and then go to bed. I might be able to catch a couple of hours of sleep before Katie wakes for another bottle. If I'm really lucky, she might skip that feeding like she does sometimes.

Voices from the television murmur in the great room and I head in that direction, hoping to catch Gwen before she goes to bed.

It's not Gwen but Arrow who's on the leather couch. I stop before he sees me. He's sitting with his legs spread, his elbows on his knees, the remote in his hand. ESPN is on the television, but he's not looking at the screen. He's hanging his head.

When I catch the name "Brogan" coming from the speakers, I look up and my heart breaks all over again. For myself. For everything I lost that night. But also for this powerful and talented man sitting helpless in front of me as he listens to the announcer.

"I've spoken with Woodison's coach," the announcer says. "He's known Arrow since the young player's elementary-school days. This kid was the kind you never had to worry about. He wasn't one to party or drink or mouth off on the field. He was one of those rare finds—humble, hardworking, with a coachable attitude and the drive to be his best on and off the field. He knew what he wanted, and he was going to make it happen in all the right ways. But then his best friend, also a BHU player, was injured, and Woodison did a one-eighty."

"It's heartbreaking," the co-host says. "And I wonder if it doesn't speak to some weaknesses in our sport on the collegiate level. Do we talk enough about depression? What *are* we doing for players who have mental health concerns? Woodison was the last player you expected to see tangled up in hard drugs."

"I agree, but whether we expected it or not, it happened. And now instead of preparing for training camp with an NFL team or for his senior year with BHU, he's just been released from rehab and is going to spend the next six months on house arrest."

"Any word from Woodison about his choices this last semester?"

He shakes his head. "He's not talking to the press. Representatives from the school are saying he needs space to think about his actions and get some counseling."

"Can we talk about what Woodison's football season could have looked like if he hadn't fallen down this rabbit hole? If he'd stayed straight and entered the draft?"

I don't understand why Arrow's torturing himself by listening, but I can't handle another minute of their pseudo-empathy and exploitive speculation. I walk around to the front of the couch, grab the remote from Arrow's hands, and turn off the television.

His head snaps up and his eyes narrow. "What do you think you're doing?"

I swallow and shrug. "You don't need to hear that."

The corner of his mouth twitches with a smirk. "So, you're not only playing nanny to my little sister, you're playing nanny to me, too? Planning to tell me what I can watch on TV and when to go to bed?" He grabs the remote from my hand. "Thanks, but I'll pass."

"Arrow . . ." I search for the words as his grip tightens on the remote, his knuckles whitening, but the television remains silent and dark.

"I heard you were at the Pretty Kitty tonight." He doesn't look at me. He keeps those dark eyes focused on his hands. "My dad not paying you enough? You need another income stream?"

I lift my chin, my aching heart pounding, but I refuse to answer. It's not my job to make Arrow like me again. It's my job to take care of his home and his baby sister. "Can I get you anything before I go to bed?"

His head snaps back, and he glares at me. "You're not my fucking servant, Mia. If you don't want to piss me off while you're working here, don't try to wait on me."

Nodding, I turn on my heel and head toward the stairs. I don't know this man, this angry and hateful version of the boy who once held me while we watched the sunrise. I feel his gaze on me and desperately want to know if there's any regret in it, but I don't turn around.

ARROW

It shouldn't physically hurt to watch her walk away from me—God knows she's done it enough—but it's a punch in the solar plexus every time.

I grab my phone off the end table and power it back on. There's a text from Chris, but this one's just to me, not the group.

Chris: *Keegan's a fucking idiot. You okay?*

I stare at the screen, trying to think of a casual response and coming up empty. I'm not okay. I'm so fucking tired, I just want to close my eyes and be done with this shit. But I don't have the courage for sleep. There are too many demons lurking there. Too many questions and never any answers.

"Fuck it," I mutter, tossing the phone down. Chris will live without a response.

I go to the kitchen to find my doctor-prescribed sleeping pills. They took away the illegal shit I was buying from the hipster from my dorm but were happy to pump me up with all sorts of shit they prescribed themselves—sleeping pills, anxiety meds, antidepressants.

I open the bottle, tap a sleeping pill into my hand, and stare at it. On good nights, I take it and everything goes black until morning. I crawl into bed and am out like the dead, and if I have dreams, I don't remember them.

On bad nights, I slip into the same familiar nightmares, and sleep pins me down, holding me in my own personal hell until the meds wear off. The dreams are variations on a theme. I'm yelling at Brogan, shoving him against the wall, telling him he's a fuck-up, threatening to tell Mia the truth. Then I'm at Coach Wright's house, and he's sitting in front of the TV with blood on his hands and tears in his eyes. Sometimes, I try to talk to him but I can't open my mouth. It's as if my lips are super-glued together. Other times, I open my mouth to scream, and the Sahara desert pours out onto his living room floor and Coach is drowning in it, fighting his way to the top for air. I reach for him, shovel sand away, but everything I do to help pushes him deeper.

Sometimes, it's the deer that haunts me. Its big, glassy eyes watch as I scrub the garage floor with bleach rags. Then I'm scrubbing at Mia's tears—a flood of bloodstained water surging up to drown me as I hear the message she left on my voicemail. *"Brogan. My br-br-br— We're at the hospital. So sorry. So, so sorry."*

I glance toward the stairs and put the pill back into the bottle. Not taking meds means I'm guaranteed nightmares, but at least if I'm not medicated, I can escape them.

MIA

I wake to a thump and sit up in bed. It's three in the morning and my room is dark, but there's more thumping. Someone's kicking the wall between my room and Arrow's.

My heart clenches as I picture him on the other side having wild sex with some girl. Maybe some old fuck buddy came over after I went to bed. Hell, for all I know it's Gwen visiting her stepson's bed.

I dismiss the idea as quickly as it comes. Arrow can't tolerate Gwen, and he may have changed, but he's never been one to fuck girls he can't tolerate.

There's another thump, then I hear Arrow's voice. "No. Don't." Rough, choked words. And more thrashing. "Why?"

I throw off the covers and run to his room, opening the door without a thought.

I don't know what I expected to find. Arrow is sleeping alone, tangled in his covers.

Frozen, I stare at him. Moonlight spills in through the open curtains and casts shadows across his face. Sweat glistens on his forehead, and his face twists in a grimace.

I step closer. I could touch him, but I shouldn't. "Arrow?"

He kicks. His arm flies out and hits the wall.

"Arrow," I repeat, louder this time.

He grabs my hand at the wrist and flies upright in bed as his eyes pop open. He's breathing hard, and anguish is all over his face. For a minute, I feel like I can see inside him—all the terrified, vulnerable parts he hides from the world. I can see inside him and I know exactly what I'm looking at, because my dreams make me feel the same way.

"What are you doing here?" he asks in a low whisper. The anger from earlier is gone from his voice.

"You were having a nightmare."

His eyes rake over me—greedy, hungry, desperate. "What? No red lace nightie? Or do you save that for my dad? Like mother, like daughter?"

I gasp before I can stop myself. Why doesn't he just punch me? His fist to my face would hurt less than those words.

I yank my hand away, spin on my heel, and walk toward the hall. As I reach for the knob, he's behind me. He slams his palm against the door, and it closes with a violent *thunk*. "I'm sorry," he whispers behind me, his breath on my neck. "I'm sorry I said that."

I keep my gaze on his hand. Arrow has the best hands. Big, strong, beautiful. And the first time they touched me . . .

I squeeze my eyes shut at the unwelcome memory, and shrug. "I need this job," I say slowly. "Your stepmother has made it clear that she'll fire me if we can't get along, and we both know your dad will fire me if you ask him to. But please don't. Please don't screw it up for me."

"Mia," he says softly, and I feel him step closer, the heat of his body against my back. The rough pads of his fingertips brush the hair from my neck, then his breath, hot and sweet, tickles against that tender skin.

I'm frozen, divided between the wish for his kiss and the fear of it. "I'm sorry," I whisper. Hot tears roll down my cheeks, and I don't know what I'm apologizing for. For taking this job? For going with Brogan that night when Arrow asked me not to? For entering his life to begin with?

Yes. All of that. More. "I'm so sorry."

He drops one hand from the door and the other from my neck. My body grows cool as he steps away.

"Stop apologizing," he says.

I turn the knob and head to my room. I don't look back.

ARROW

I go down to the kitchen to grab breakfast. Dad and Gwen are sitting at the breakfast table having coffee. Gwen's dressed in heels and a pink strapless dress, looking more like a girl ready for a night on the town than a young mother preparing for a day with her family. She sweeps her sleek blond hair over one shoulder as she looks through interior design catalogues. On the opposite side of the table, my father is dressed in jeans and a polo shirt—what I've come to know as his weekend golfing attire—and is reading the *Blackhawk Valley Times*. Now more salt than pepper, his thick hair has always made him look younger than he is, no matter how much it grays. Even so, a stranger walking in the room might guess them to be father and daughter.

"Coach is going to send over a workout schedule for you," Dad says, not bothering to put down the paper and look at me. "I expect you to train just as hard as you would if you were in the weight room with your teammates."

Train for what exactly?

I want to ask, but I don't. I'd work out anyway—I feel like shit when I don't—so I might as well use Coach's program. "Yes, sir," I say, pouring myself a cup of coffee.

Mia comes down with the baby, and I stop the mug halfway to my lips. She's wearing a yellow sundress with her hair tied back at the base of her neck. Her backpack is slung over one shoulder, and the baby's cradled in her arms. She looks so natural with my little sister. It's weird to see her more a part of my family in that way than even I am.

She looks so damn beautiful that I expect that old sparkle to be back in her eyes, but when she meets my gaze, I realize I'm only anticipating what I hope to see. Her stare is vacant and cold. The old Mia still sleeps somewhere, not facing a world without her brother, not accepting a world that would do this to Brogan.

"Here's your mama," she says, handing Katie over to Gwen.

"Good morning, baby!" Gwen says to Katie. She settles her into her arms and looks to Mia. "When do you think you'll be back?"

"The usual," Mia says. She gives Katie a kiss on the forehead. "Just call if you need me sooner. It's not a big deal."

"Of course," Gwen says.

"Good morning, Mr. Woodison," Mia says, nodding to my father.

"Morning, Mia." Dad folds his paper, lays it on the center of the breakfast table, and pushes his chair back. "I'll be in my office if anyone needs me." He leaves before any real conversation can begin, which is typical of my father. He's more comfortable working than talking to his own family.

Mia looks at me and then cuts her eyes away. "You have a good day too, Arrow," she says.

I keep my mouth shut and just incline my chin in acknowledgment.

I can't help but watch her go, my eyes drifting to the sway of her hips as she heads to the front door. I listen for her car and drain half my mug of coffee when I hear her pull out of the drive.

"Where is she going?" I ask it out loud without meaning to. It's more a stray curiosity than an attempt to make conversation with Gwen, but my stepmother smirks at me.

"The same place she goes every Monday, Wednesday, Friday, and Saturday—to Indianapolis to visit her boyfriend." She pushes back from the table and shifts the baby in her arms. "I imagine you'd know something so important, but I guess you were too busy doing *drugs* to know how your friends spend their lives."

Damn, I hate this woman.

But four days a week? It shouldn't surprise me, but it hurts a little to imagine her sacrificing that much time—sacrificing so much of her check for gas—for Brogan. I wonder if she believes he wants her there. That seeing her makes his days better.

Hell, maybe it does. I haven't said a civil word to her since I got home, and seeing her sure as hell makes *my* days better.

"Damn," Keegan says. "You're one lucky son of a bitch, Woodison.

What kind of punishment is this, anyway? You don't have to go to class, don't have to have Coach bitch at you every day, no suicide drills, no nasty-ass dorm showers."

I smirk and add, "No social life, no degree." Then the smirk falls off my face as I think, *No football.*

A half a dozen guys from the team came over tonight and a few brought girls with them. Since having Mia so close is making me lose my mind, I was grateful for the distraction.

Keegan cracks open a beer. "You really expect me to feel sorry for you?"

I follow his eyes to the second-story picture window where Mia folds sheets, her back to the window, her ass filling her denim cutoffs. My jaw tightens as I turn back to Keegan.

He laughs. "You're gonna try to tell me you're not hitting that?"

Beside me, Chris groans.

"She's Brogan's," I growl.

Keegan smirks. "Like that ever stopped you before."

One second, I'm standing there, my hands clenched at my side, and the next, Keegan's flying into the pool, fully clothed, beer in hand.

Chris grabs my arms and pulls me back before I can jump in after Keegan, and I'm grateful, because with the anger pulsing through my veins I'm not sure if I'd punch him or drown him.

Keegan comes up sputtering. "What the *fuck*?"

"Don't be an ass," Chris tells him.

Keegan smirks. "I'm just telling it like it is."

Fucker must have a death wish. I lunge, but Chris holds me tight.

"Not worth it," he murmurs.

"Get out of my fucking house," I call as Keegan climbs out of the pool.

He's sopping wet, his T-shirt clinging to his torso, his soaked jeans hanging precariously at his hips, his beer can floating in the water. He glares at me then turns to leave, lifting one hand and extending his middle finger as he pushes through the gate.

Only after he's disappeared from view does Chris let me go. "Since when do you let Keegan's bullshit get to you?"

I squeeze my eyes shut and focus on breathing. The humid air fills my lungs, and I hold it in for a beat before I exhale. Adrenaline buzzes through my veins, begging for release.

I've been home a week and I don't know how to talk to Mia. Don't know how to live with her so close to me. The last four months have been a haze of apathy and numbness, and I don't know what to do with everything I've felt since I came home.

I lift my eyes back up to the window and catch Mia staring at me, her lips parted, shock on her face. For a moment, our gazes lock, and something nearly tangible pulses between us. Regret. Frustration. Desire.

She turns away, and it feels like someone has sliced off a piece of my heart.

"Christ," Chris mutters. "You can't look at her like that and expect assholes like Keegan to keep their mouths shut."

MIA

There are so many things rich people have and take for granted. It's not just the big houses and the flashy cars. It's not the decadent vacations or the security of knowing you have a safety net if today's job disappears tomorrow. It's also the little things. Like fine linens. Thick, plush towels that hug your skin and smell like flowers. Sheets so soft they caress your skin as you slide between them. A stocked fridge. Fresh fruit year-round, and never the crap from cans. Air conditioning.

I fold the last of the towels, relishing the smell and the feel of them, and then begin my journey throughout the Woodisons' house to put them away. I learned quickly that rich people don't just have nice towels. They have different sizes of each towel—guest towels, hand towels, bath towels, bath sheets, and swim towels. And the Woodisons have different colors designated for each bathroom. In fact, Gwen's a little OCD about her towels. I think she fancies herself an interior decorator or something.

Since Arrow has friends over, I head to the bathroom just off the pool first. The door to the back patio is open, and music and laughter float into the house.

I roll the towels and position them in the baskets the way Gwen likes them. My eye catches on the group gathered on the other side of the porthole window. Half a dozen guys from the Blackhawk Hills University football team gather around the pool, girls hanging on the arms of a couple of them. In the middle of the semester, I heard the coaches told the guys to stay away from Arrow, but here they are. Bailey said that rumor has it the judge thinks his team is the positive influence he needs to turn his life around.

As I start to turn away, I spot a broad-shouldered blond laughing at the pool-house bar. My heart squeezes hard, refusing to beat for one painful breath, then a second. You'd think I'd become accustomed to these moments when the world stops and I have to scramble to remember where I am in time and space. I grasp for my footing in the present, like forcing myself awake from a good dream and finding myself in a nightmare. The guy turns around, and I have a better view of his face, and just like that, I'm body-slammed back into the present—the nightmare. No. Not Brogan. Of course not. He won't be joining his friends tonight.

"Oh, hey, Mia!"

I shake myself out of my reverie and turn to see Christopher Montgomery standing in the doorway. The BHU quarterback, Chris has soft blue eyes and one of those dimpled smiles that makes a girl feel like a princess. His chest is bare, and his shaggy mop of brown hair is wet from the pool and slicked back from his face. He's not a loudmouth like some of the other guys, and he's got this Southern accent to go with his striking good looks. I imagine he's melted countless panties since he hit puberty. "Hey, Chris. I'll get out of your way." I shove the rest of the towels into their spots and grab my laundry basket.

"What are you doing with all that?" He frowns at the towels. "Why aren't you out back with everybody else?"

I shake my head and try to pretend it doesn't matter. "Gotta work."

He steps to the side, blocking my escape, and cocks his head at me. "I guess the rumor was true. You are working for the Woodisons."

"There's a rumor about it?" I tell myself I don't care, but my stomach's sudden summersaults say otherwise. "I had no idea my employment status was fodder for gossip."

"It's not like that. Just with Brogan, we all . . ." He shrugs. "We all worry about you."

Sure they do. They worried enough to show up to my brother's funeral—an endless line of broad shoulders in black waiting to shake my hand and avoid my eyes. And after that? Nothing. "You could visit him, you know."

Chris flinches and averts his eyes. "It's just . . . hard."

"You should visit." I stare at him until he meets my gaze again. He nods. "Yeah. You're right. Okay. We'll go this week."

Satisfied, I nod and turn to leave. "Excuse me."

"Go put that basket in the laundry room and put on your swimsuit. Join the party."

"I couldn't. Arrow wouldn't . . ." The rest of the words fizzle away as Arrow walks up behind Chris, his hands in his pockets, his eyes on me.

"Arrow wouldn't what?" he asks, making Chris turn.

"Nothing." I take advantage of the moment to push out of the bathroom and past both men.

Chris says something to Arrow, but I can't make it out. I keep walking.

I'm hanging clean towels in the master bathroom when I sense someone behind me.

"Come to the party," Arrow says, his voice low.

"I'm working." I keep my head down. I can't look at him. For the first time since I took this job, I feel shame for being the hired help. Which is bullshit. I work hard and pay my own way. Always have. Always will. That's nothing to be ashamed of.

"You're the nanny, not the maid."

I open the cabinet with more force than necessary, and the handle clacks against the wall. "What, are you in charge of my job description now?" From the baby monitor clipped to my hip, I hear Katie fuss. "I need to check on the baby. Go back to your friends, Arrow."

I don't turn until I hear him leave, and then I stop in the doorway and lean my head against the wall, breathing deeply. Even though I just gave Chris a hard time about never visiting Brogan, I've been relieved not to have to face the team. Having so many of them here is too much of a reminder of how things used to be. Before. And it's too easy to give in to the game of *what-ifs*. What if I hadn't asked Nic to come get me? What if I'd told Brogan the truth? What if I hadn't left with him that night? What if I hadn't let Arrow comfort me when I was hurting?

I hate that game. It's painful and pointless.

ARROW

The worst part of having a party at my house is that I can't just leave when I'm done with it. I was done with this party about twenty minutes after everyone arrived. Not a *party*, I mentally correct. I'm not allowed to have *parties*. But the judge encouraged me to "keep company" with people he deems a good influence. Namely, the guys from the team. The ones I let down.

I don't even know how to be around people without being trashed anymore. House arrest comes with those fun little piss tests, though, so my using days are behind me. Drugs and booze never offered the oblivion I was looking for anyway. Some demons can't be escaped.

Keegan came back not long after I kicked him out, and I took his apology with a silent nod. "You can talk shit about any of us," Chris told him, "but Mia's off-limits." And I was grateful he said it so I didn't have to.

"Lemme stay," Trish says now in a drunken slur. She smells like whiskey and is dressed in a skimpy bikini top and a pair of jean shorts that show more ass than they cover. She's always tried a little too hard around Brogan, but it's like I'm her substitute now, and lately she uses any excuse she can to get close. Like tonight when she tagged along with Keegan, making him think it was a date until they arrived and she changed her tune.

"Not a good idea," I say, taking a half step back.

She snakes her hand into my shirt and curls her lips into a smile as her fingers skim across my abs. "You won't be sorry." She lifts onto her toes and presses her mouth to my neck, and I want so badly to feel something, *anything,* that I knot my hand in her hair and yank her head back so I can press my mouth to hers.

Moaning, she slides her tongue against mine and hitches one leg around my waist. She circles her hips in a way that promises just what would happen if I let her stay.

The kiss is sloppy and reminds me of New Year's Eve in a flash that brings on a wave of nausea I stomp down out of sheer determination.

"Woodison!" Chris barks.

I tear my mouth away from Trish's just in time to see Mia at the foot of the stairs, hurt all over her face. It's not there long. She lifts her chin and covers her face in a mask of disinterest. But I saw it, and I'm the world's biggest asshole.

I thought she'd gone to bed. *Fuck.*

Because it wasn't just any girl I kissed. It was *Trish.* Worst fucking choice possible. And it shouldn't matter, but it does. What

Mia thinks of me and how I make her feel will always matter. No hangover could change that, no high.

Chris gives me a hard look. He doesn't know what happened between me and Mia—no one does, unless you count us and Brogan, I guess. But Chris is a good guy, astute on a level these other guys wouldn't get. He sees things. Always knows more than he has reason to.

"Need a ride back to campus, Trish?" Chris asks.

Her fingers slide under the waistband of my jeans. "Do I?" she asks. After seeing the look on Mia's face when I pulled away, the nausea is back, and I just want Trish to stop fucking touching me. Now and forever. "Or should I stay so we can be alone?"

"You need a ride," I say, forcing a straight face. "Sorry. Sex is prohibited by my probation, and I'm afraid you'd be too much of a temptation."

Mason chokes on his beer, and Chris bites back a smile.

Trish, however, buys it, and her hazy eyes go big. God, why did no one notice how much she was drinking? "That's *inhumane.*"

"I'll have sex with you, Trish," Keegan calls.

She attempts a smile. "Nah. That's okay."

Keegan sighs heavily. "Women never want guys from the O-line. They all want the men with the glory positions."

"Whatever," Mason says. "I saw that girl doing the walk of shame from your door this morning."

"Oh. Right," Keegan says, nodding. "Good point. Damn, she was hot."

"Come on, you guys," Chris says. "Pile your drunk asses into my car. It's time to head out."

I follow them and help Trish into the back seat. She's really the only one who's had too much to drink, but I'm still glad they carpooled tonight.

"We're planning to go to Indy to visit Brogan next week," Chris says as I shut Trish's door. "Want to come?"

The sound of my best friend's name brings my walls down, and any humor I felt earlier flees. "I can't. House arrest, remember?" I lift my foot and tug on my jeans to show my ankle monitor.

Grimacing, Chris shakes his head. "Right. Sorry. We'll tell him you said hi."

Nausea crashes over me, threatening to break through my walls. I've gotta get away from this conversation, and Chris clearly feels the same. No doubt Mia was the one who guilted him into visiting Brogan. She primps and fusses before each visit up there as if she's getting ready for a date.

Mason climbs into the passenger seat, and I watch as Chris pulls out of the circle drive. When I head back in, I spot Mia through the French doors off the living room. She stacks the dirty dishes and throws away the beer bottles.

I should go to my room and get away from her, but I hate the idea of her cleaning up after me and the guys, so instead of what I *should* do, I head back out there. "You don't have to do that."

She hesitates for a beat before continuing to gather trash. "It's no problem."

"From what I can tell, this job is all you do. Do you go out? Spend time with your friends?"

She won't look at me. "I'm not a hermit, if that's what you're asking. I get out plenty." She heads to the other side of the pool, and I follow.

"Visiting *him* doesn't count as getting out." The words scrape my throat, and I didn't even say his name. I *can't* say his name. The man she visits isn't the Brogan I knew. He isn't my best friend. Not anymore.

Mia has gone still. It's too dark out here, but I wish I could see her face. I want to know if talking about him hurts her as much as it hurts me, and then I want to wrap her in my arms and do anything I can to ease that pain away. "What do you want from me, Arrow?"

I want the hope I feel when I look in your eyes. The feel of you in my arms. The forgiveness I don't deserve.

I want to go back to the day we met and kiss you—claim you before he can.

Everything.

I want everything.

"Nothing. Go to bed. I'll clean up the rest."

PART II. BEFORE

October, Fifteen Months Before the Accident

MIA

Something came up and I can't meet to study with you tonight. Call me and we'll reschedule.

Hastily, I sign my name and add my number to the bottom of the note. Bailey lost her cell phone this morning and has been borrowing her roommate's. I highly doubt she has my number memorized or written in a book somewhere. She's not that organized.

I pin the note to the corkboard on her dorm-room door, hoist my bag over my shoulder, and head to my car. I was supposed to help Bailey study for her calculus test tonight, but someone called needing a sitter, and I don't like to pass up easy cash.

My phone buzzes as I climb into my beat-up '97 Escort. The screen shows a text message. It's a local number, but not one I know.

Unknown: Is this the girl who just left a note on Bailey's door?

I frown at my phone, running the number through my memory to see if it rings any bells. It doesn't.

Me: Yes. Is everything okay?

I step out of my car and am halfway back to Bailey's dorm when the next text comes through.

Unknown: Not exactly.

My heart surges into my throat.

Me: What happened?

In the few seconds it takes for the reply to come through, I imagine countless horrible scenarios involving Bailey. An accident at the crosswalk on the way to class; assault; alcohol poisoning. When the text comes through, I have to read it several times.

Unknown: I fell.

Fell? I blink at my screen and stop walking.

Me: *Who is this?*
Unknown: *I'm a guy on Bailey's floor. I've never met you before. I think we need to remedy this ASAP.*

Shaking my head, I sink down onto a bench and type out a reply.

Me: *I thought you said you fell?*
Him: *For you. I mean, a little bit. I see you studying in the library. Not like in a creepy-stalker kind of way, but I noticed you—enough to text you and risk you thinking I'm desperate.*

I bite back a grin. I have to give him credit. He's the first guy to come on to me through an anonymous text. Before I can decide whether or not to reply, my phone buzzes again.

Him: *I swear I've never done this before. You're just . . . insanely beautiful. Please don't think I'm a creep.*

The next text has my phone buzzing in my hand just as I finish reading.

Him: *That ship's sailed, hasn't it?*

I actually laugh out loud, and even as the rational part of my brain tells me I should ignore these texts, I find myself typing a reply.

Me: *Lil bit.*

My worries about Bailey put to rest, I head back to the car. My phone buzzes again as I walk.

Him: *Shit. I have no game. No, worse than that. I have so little game that I walk into a room, and every dude around me has less game just by my nearness. But I'm told I have a real nice personality.*

I can't help but laugh. I'm entertained—as much as one can be by creepy texts from random guys. I'm still smiling when the next text message comes through.

Him: *Can you just erase this whole conversation and come to my party tomorrow night? We can pretend we're meeting for the first time? Bailey will be there. She's dating my roommate Mason.*

Bailey already invited me to that party, and I declined. This guy may think he wants me, but the truth is nobody wants a townie at their college party.

Me: Thanks for the invitation.

Him: That's you turning the creep down nicely, isn't it? Please, tell me you're hideous under your clothes. Maybe you have a few extra nipples, and I don't have to kick myself for blowing this?

Me: No extra nipples, sorry.

Him: That's okay. I'm pretty sure I'd still think you were hot, even with a couple of extra nips. What about foot fungus?

Me: Not last I checked. But seriously, foot fungus would be a deal-breaker for you?

Him: You're right. I'd just buy you some ointment. What about an incurable STD?

Me: Not that I'm aware of.

Him: Throw me a bone. There has to be something unappealing about you.

Me: I'm an insomniac.

Him: FAIL. Now I'm thinking of you lying in bed.

Him: And now you're thinking about me thinking about you lying in bed, and I'm at least twice the creep.

Me: I'm afraid of geese. Like, irrationally so. They terrify me.

Him: That's a little weird. Okay. What else ya got?

Me: I have to get to work. I'll think about it and get back to you.

Him: I look forward to it.

I can't help but grin on my way back to my car. Whoever this guy is, he makes me laugh. Creepy introduction aside, that appeals to me, and by the time I get the kids at my babysitting job in bed that night, I'm still thinking about him.

I settle into the couch with a glass of water and grab my phone.

> **Me:** *I'm just a townie. Thought you should know.*
> **Him:** *A Blackhawk Valley native?*
> **Me:** *Sorry to say.*
> **Him:** *Me too. Born and raised.*

I bite my lip. I didn't expect that. Sure, a handful of Blackhawk Valley kids stick around and go to BHU, but it's tough to get admitted, and most of us can't afford it anyway. The dorms are full of East Coasters whose rich parents think the rural college will keep their kids out of trouble, and city kids who are here on athletic scholarships.

> **Me:** *You never told me your name.*
> **Him:** *No way. When I meet you and sweep you off your feet, I refuse to have you connect me with the creep who stole your phone number and tried to pick you up with a text message.*
> **Me:** *So you're going to meet me and never give me your number?*
> **Him:** *I'll give you my number, but first you have*

to delete these messages. You haven't done that yet, have you?

Me: *You're pretty funny for a creep. I'll give you that.*

Him: *Here's the deal. You come tomorrow, and I promise I'll tell you my name. I'll tell you anything you want to know.*

I can't believe I'm actually considering it, but I don't reply. No need to get his hopes up only to disappoint him when I come to my senses.

Four days later . . .

I find myself at Bailey's side as we knock on the door to the suite down the hall. She said she left her books here and needs them to study. But Mason opens the door and doesn't bother with a "hello" before he drags Bailey in the room and kisses her.

"Books, Bailey," I remind her firmly. "We're here for *books*."

I'm not sure if they're dating or just fucking. Bailey hasn't specified. I'm not sure she cares. She isn't looking for a meaningful relationship. Living down the hall from her with his hard body, dark skin, and seductive green eyes, Mason is exactly the kind of guy Bailey likes—readily available and sexy as sin. The first time I met him, I couldn't look away.

"We'll be right back," Bailey manages before dragging Mason

to his room and shutting the door behind them.

I groan and frown at the closed door for a minute. *Rookie mistake.* What did I think was going to happen if I followed her here?

I head into the suite, plop down onto the couch in the shared living area, and pull out my English homework. All of BHU's dorms are set up like this—two doubles sharing a bathroom and common living space. I'm green with envy that Bailey gets to live in a space like this while I'm stuck in the trailer with Dad, but it's not like she doesn't make sacrifices to live this life.

I have my legs folded under me and my notebook in my lap when someone sighs dramatically.

I look up and see a tall, broad-shouldered guy scowling at the red necktie hanging around Mason's doorknob.

"Jesus, Mason," he mutters, and my mouth goes dry. Mason is hot, but this man is freaking *divine*. I can't help but watch, transfixed, as he drags a hand through his dark hair and his biceps bulge against his fitted T-shirt.

Mason's roommate. I bite my lip, recalling our exchanged text messages. I haven't thought about my mystery texter in a couple days. I should have prepared for this. Will he be mad that I blew him off? Will he even remember me?

He turns into the living room. "Hey, I didn't see you there." He grins and slides his honey eyes over me. "I'm Arrow. Mason's roommate."

Right. Didn't he say he wanted to act like we hadn't met? How do I even know it's him? "How many of you are there?"

He points a thumb toward the door. "I'm the only one lucky enough to be locked out of his room while Mason indulges in sex marathons, if that's what you mean. Lucky me."

"I'm . . . Mia?" I smile awkwardly.

Arrow lifts a brow. "Is that a question?"

My gaze drifts down the length of him. I can't help myself. Arrow is beautiful in the hard-bodied way of a man who pushes himself to the limits on a daily basis. When I lift my eyes back to his face, he's frowning at Mason's door again. For someone who was so eager to meet me a few days ago, he seems oddly uninterested now. Maybe he's insulted by the way I blew him off. Or maybe I'm not as pretty to him this close.

I shake my head, trying to make my insecurities scatter. It doesn't matter what Mr. Adorable Texter thinks. I'm not interested.

I'm also a liar.

"Any idea how much longer I should expect to be locked out of my room?" he asks.

"They just . . . um . . . got started." I move my backpack from beside me on the couch and slide my books into it. "I'll get out of your way."

He turns back to me. "You don't have to do that." The sound of moaning comes through the walls, and Arrow drags his hand over his face. "In fact, please don't go anywhere. I spend more time than I'd like to admit sitting here alone while they . . . do what they do. It's starting to make me feel like a pervert."

I laugh softly. I know what he means. Bailey isn't exactly

quiet.

"Want a drink?" He strolls over to the mini-fridge under the window and sinks to his haunches.

I shake my head. "I don't drink."

He grabs something out of the fridge and stands. Turning, he quirks a brow and tosses a bottle of water onto the couch beside me. "You must be pretty damn dehydrated."

"Oh. Thanks."

Arrow takes a seat in the chair just as the rhythmic *thunk-thunk-thunk* of the headboard hitting the wall comes from his bedroom.

I'm hypnotized by the movement of his throat as he drains his water. Hypnotized. By his *throat*. I'm so pathetic. Maybe I should have gone to that party.

He leans forward, his elbows on his knees. "I can think of a lot of awkward scenarios for meeting a beautiful girl, but this one takes the cake."

My cheeks burn. *Beautiful.* He just called me *a beautiful girl.* My stomach is a mosh pit of butterflies flailing to the beat of my hammering heart. I search for a clever response but come up empty. God, he even smells good.

Bailey screams out, and Arrow chuckles. "Think if we started being as loud as them, they would feel as awkward as we do?"

"Knowing Bailey, she'd just cheer us on."

His eyes shift to the door then back to me, but his annoyance has faded, and now he looks amused. "What year are you, Mia?"

"I'm not. I mean, I don't go here." He must not have

understood what I meant when I said I was *just* a townie. I was trying to explain that I didn't go to BHU.

"Oh, are you visiting? Where do you go to school?"

"Terrace Community College," I say reluctantly. Blackhawk Hills University is a great school, and I'd love to graduate from here, but I can't afford it. Unlike Bailey, I'm not willing to strip to make it happen. I don't judge her for her decisions, but I know my limits. So I'm taking one or two classes a semester at the community college and working on an associate's degree in criminal justice. "Do you play football too?" I ask just to move conversation away from me. He's gotta play some sport. That body. Those big hands. Sweet mother of Jesus, a girl could go into shock from an estrogen overdose looking at those hands. My body pumps out the hormones like the survival of the human species depends on giving this man my babies.

"Are you joking?" he asks.

"Um, no. I know Mason's on the team, and I thought maybe you were, too."

He smirks, obviously amused by my question. "You don't follow sports much, do you?"

"Not at all," I admit.

He nods. "Yeah, I play ball." He points to the door opposite his own. "So do Brogan and Chris."

"Are you all friends, then?"

"Oh yeah." He grins. "In fact, initially Brogan and I were bunking, but Chris couldn't stand Mason's busy—er, *social* life." He drops his gaze. "Sorry."

"Why are you apologizing?"

"Bailey's your friend. You probably don't want to know about her new guy's bedroom activities prior to her."

I shrug. If that did indeed bother Bailey, she'd have no room to talk. "That's between the two of them."

Bailey cries out again, and the headboard thunking grows faster.

Arrow's eyes cut to the door, then back to me. His cheeks are the tiniest bit pink. "So if you don't go to BHU, I'm guessing you know Bail from high school?"

"We go back further than that," I say. "Bailey's been my best friend since we were four, and I caught her stealing my Barbie from the baby pool on my deck."

He laughs. "Interesting start to a friendship."

"I didn't have a choice," I say, grinning. "I said I was going to tell on her, and she said I couldn't and I had to be her friend. Or so goes the story Mom told me. I honestly don't remember a time when Bailey wasn't my best friend."

"Brogan and I are the same way," he says. "Well, minus the Barbie."

"I'm surprised we've never met before," I say, remembering from our texts that he's from Blackhawk Valley too. "I'm guessing you didn't go to high school at East."

"Westside," he says.

Our eyes lock. There's something about his eyes. They're not quite brown but not hazel, either. More like the color of rich honey. They're warm eyes. Kind eyes. But maybe a little haunted.

Too mature for his age.

I swallow as his gaze drifts to my lips and lingers there for a minute.

The moment is broken when Bailey screams, "God! There! Yes!"

A few months ago, I accused her of being loud only because she likes the idea of people hearing, and she just laughed, neither confirming nor denying. At this moment, I'm confident in my hypothesis.

Arrow bites back a grin. "You wanna get out of here? Go for a walk and let the porn stars finish their business?"

"Please. I'd love that."

He opens the door and waves me through. "After you."

I follow him to the elevator and out the dorm's side door.

In promotional materials, BHU boasts it has one of the most beautiful college campuses in the country. That might be true. The pedestrian campus is covered in paved walking paths that weave over and around the wooded green hills and between the historic brick buildings.

Autumn is just starting to make her presence known, and a light breeze rustles through the trees, showing flashes of the first red, yellow, and orange leaves.

Arrow cuts his eyes to me as we walk. "So, *Mia*, that's a pretty name."

I laugh. "A guy named Arrow is asking me about my name?"

He arches a brow. "It's Spanish, right? Does it mean something? I took Latin in high school, so I'm pretty much useless in the foreign-language department."

"*Mia* means *mine* in Spanish."

"So you essentially walk around with people calling you *theirs* all the time?"

Laughing, I shake my head. "I never really think about it. It's just a name."

"Do you speak Spanish, then?"

Sometimes when people ask me this it feels like a politically correct way for them to ask if I'm Mexican, but for some reason the question doesn't seem so calculated coming from Arrow. "My mother was born in Mexico, and I grew up with her speaking Spanish at home." The admission comes with an ache that resides in the center of my heart. I miss that—the sweet cadence of my mother's voice as she chattered on about her day in her native tongue.

"I always thought it would be amazing to speak another language," he says.

"So, logically, you took Latin."

He stops walking and squats to pick up a smooth purple leaf from the ground. He grins up at me as he rubs it between his fingers. "Dad thought it would help me get into med school if the whole football thing doesn't work out." He stands and hands me the leaf. "It matches your sweater."

It's a redbud leaf—purple and heart-shaped, and probably the sweetest thing a boy has ever given me. "I love autumn." I keep my eyes focused on the leaf, too embarrassed by my own reaction to risk him seeing what it means to me.

"Football, bonfires, parking by the lake and watching the leaves float on the water in the moonlight." He swallows, as if the description brings back painful memories.

I instantly imagine experiencing exactly what he described but in his arms, wrapped in a blanket, our bodies pressed close to stay warm.

His Adam's apple bobs as he swallows. "I used to love the fall."

"Used to?"

He shrugs and shifts his gaze back to the trail as he starts walking again. I follow alongside him and wait for him to explain. Instead, he says, "You *really* don't follow football?"

"Sorry." To me, following sports always seemed like a luxury reserved for rich people with too much time on their hands. Intellectually, I know that's not true. Bailey grew up in the same neighborhood I did, and she's obsessed with sports—well, her obsession is really with athletes and the way they look in their tight pants, but it's more or less the same thing. "I've tried to watch the Super Bowl a couple of times, but I don't understand anything that's happening on the field."

"Do you want to learn?" The melancholy I thought I detected in him when he talked about the season is gone, and now he sounds almost hopeful. It's cute.

"If I had the right teacher, maybe."

We've stopped walking, and I lean against the side of the library. After his text messages, I expected he'd be more forward with me. He seemed like the type who'd crack jokes all the time, always working to get a laugh. Instead, Arrow's reserved, and though it's obvious we're attracted to each other, it's almost as if he's not sure what he wants to do about it.

His gaze drifts to my mouth again and his lips part. He has a great mouth. Full and firm. I'm not sure I've ever noticed a guy's *lips* before. Or wondered, just minutes after meeting, how they would feel on my skin.

"I want to get to know you," he says softly.

That simple line steals my breath. Not just the words. Any guy can say the words. It's the look in his eyes, as if he really means it. It's the crease in his brow, as if he's surprised to feel this way. It's that he's looking at my mouth like he wants to kiss me, and he totally could, but he's talking to me instead. "What do you want to know?" I ask.

His eyes lift to mine and burn into me. "What's the thing you want so desperately that the idea of having it makes you as sick to your stomach as the idea of never having it?"

I blink at him, because that's exactly how I feel about singing. I haven't told anyone, not even Bailey, but I dream about singing my songs on a big stage. I love it so much that the idea of someone giving me a chance to do it for an audience makes my stomach tangle into tight, painful knots.

But I'm not going to be a singer. It's not practical, and I can't afford the requisite "starving artist" years. Instead, the second-best choice will get all my energy. I'm going to be a lawyer. Guys like my brother need someone who cares enough to defend them. They need someone who understands that, while the law might be black and white, right and wrong, the real world is not.

Law school is expensive, and I'm lucky if I can afford my car insurance, so that's going to be enough of a struggle. Still, it's a dream that's within my grasp. And maybe one that won't destroy me if I try and fail.

But when I think about never getting the chance to sing professionally, my stomach cramps.

Arrow grins.

"Why are you smiling?"

He gives a lopsided shrug. "Because you have a *thing*. It's all over your face. You have something you want with all your heart and soul. Something you want so much you're scared to have it."

"Doesn't everyone?"

He shakes his head. "No. Not everyone, Mia. Most people are happy just to survive, to let the days pass. But you're like me. You want it and you'd fight for it. Now I just want to know what *it* is." His gaze drops to my mouth again and he doesn't step closer, but his body sways ever so slightly in my direction, as if there's a magnet pulling us together.

I can't breathe. He's going to kiss me. I've been kissed before, lots of times. But I've never wanted to be kissed as much as I want Arrow to kiss me.

My phone buzzes in my pocket and shatters the fragile moment to bits. I'm ready to ignore it when Arrow steps away.

"You gonna check that?"

I fumble for my cell to read the text.

Bailey: *Sorry about that. We're done.*

When I look back to Arrow, he's turned away, his hands tucked into his pockets. "That was Bailey," I say. "We can go back."

He nods but remains withdrawn. *Nice to meet you, Mr. Mixed Signals.*

When we make it back to the dorm room, Bailey and Mason are in the living area, snuggled together on the couch in some sort of post-coital bonding that makes me reevaluate their relationship.

Bailey looks at me, then Arrow, then back to me, and wriggles her eyebrows. "And where have you two been?"

Arrow shrugs. "Someone told us about a place where we could go listen to people having really loud, athletic sex. We had to check it out, since that's our favorite way to relax."

"Isn't it everyone's?" I add.

Bailey doesn't even blush. She winks at Arrow, and for a second I'm so jealous of her self-confidence, I'd become a thief if it meant I could steal it.

The door to the other bedroom opens, and the guy who steps out does a double take when he sees me. "Mia?"

I frown. "Yes?"

Tousled blond hair and broad shoulders. He's cute. Handsome, even. If I hadn't been staring at Arrow for the last half-hour, I might even go so far as to call this guy sexy. He grins and shoves his hands into his pockets. "God, you're even prettier up close."

Arrow stiffens, and his gaze bounces between me and the blond guy. "You know Brogan?" he asks me.

"I . . ." *I'm not sure what's happening.*

"We texted a little." Brogan flinches and turns to me, holding up his hands dramatically. "No, we didn't. Forget I said that. That fool with no game doesn't live here. I'm Brogan, and totally charming, and not at all a creep."

Fool with no game. Oh, crap. *Oh, no.* I open my mouth to speak and have to force the words out past a tangle of emotions. "I . . . I thought you said you were Mason's roommate?" I say to Brogan.

Brogan gestures to the common space. "We're all roommates." He steps toward me and smiles. Charming. He's so *very* charming. And so *not* Arrow. "I'm glad you came. We were gonna grab some dinner. Wanna come?"

Disappointment crashes in around me. Brogan is sweet. Goodness radiates off him. I liked him from his first text, and I *like* him now. But I don't *want* him. How could I when every drop of *want* in my body has been newly dedicated to Brogan's roommate, the sexy, mysterious Arrow, who has a *thing* he wants so much it makes his stomach hurt?

"Let's go," Bailey says. "Come on, Mia, it'll be fun."

Brogan slides his arm through mine and looks at Arrow. "You wanna tag along, too? Call your girlfriend—we'll triple-date."

ARROW

*F**uck. Fuck. Fuck.* Mia's eyes widen and her face pales. She looks as if she's been blindsided. I know how she feels.

"I'm sorry," Mia says. "I can't go to dinner. I really need to do some homework."

Brogan's face falls. Dude can't hide his feelings for anything. "Another time?"

"Sure," Mia says. I've known her less than an hour, but even I can tell her smile is forced. And that's my fault. I'm the one who screwed this up. She grabs her backpack off the couch. "I'm gonna get going, actually."

"You're too good," Bailey objects in a whine. "Everyone needs to play hooky once in a while."

Mia shakes her head. "What I need is to ace this test."

"Are you sure?" Bailey asks.

"Positive," Mia says. She nods at Brogan. "Nice to meet you." She doesn't look at me as she says bye to the group and turns to the door.

When Mia's gone, Bailey's gaze locks on mine. I can't answer any of the questions she asks with her eyes.

Brogan drags his hands through his hair, frustration wiping the ever-present smile from his face. Turning on his heel, he goes into his bedroom and swings the door shut. I catch it before it latches, and follow behind him.

He tilts his head back and stares at the ceiling. "Why do I suck with women?"

"You don't suck."

He opens his mouth to reply then snaps it shut again. It seems my best friend is at a loss for words, which I think I've seen happen to him once in my whole life. Brogan always has something to say. Always.

"You've got it bad, huh?" I ask. I want him to say no, that Mia's just a girl, but I know better.

He rubs his forehead and blows out a slow breath. "Yeah."

My gut twists. *Fuck. Fuck. Fuck.* "Because she's hot?"

"She's afraid of geese, and she thinks I'm funny," he answers, and I get the message. This is about more than a slammin' body. "She studies in the library," he finally explains. "I'd seen her there a few times when I was leaving study tables. She tutors high school kids sometimes, and I've watched her."

"Creep much?"

"Shut the fuck up. I mean when I was stuck at study tables and she was a few feet away helping some idiot kid pass Spanish. There's just something about her. Then when I realized she was

Bailey's friend . . . You know her too?"

"Not really. We met today. She's"—*so fucking special I want her for myself*—"nice."

After a few minutes, everyone's getting ready to go to dinner, and I make up an excuse to skip it and head to the library. I find her tucked into a corner in the basement, legs curled under her, textbook open on the table.

When I spot her, I have to stop for a minute and catch my breath. Because she steals it. When I first saw her in my room today, I felt like I'd been punched in the gut. She's that kind of beautiful. She has caramel skin, big brown eyes, full lips, high cheekbones dotted with the most adorable freckles, and long, dark hair that falls in soft waves around her shoulders. And her body? If she works at the strip club with Bailey, she's gotta make a killing. But I already know she doesn't. This isn't the kind of girl who'd be comfortable taking off her clothes for money.

It's hot in the library, and the sweater she wore earlier is draped over the back of her chair, leaving her in a soft gray tank that shows her freckled shoulders.

She lifts her head from her book, as if sensing my appraisal. Our eyes lock, and my stomach flips.

I swallow. "I didn't know you had something going with Brogan."

"I didn't know you had a girlfriend."

"I—" I snap my mouth shut. I'm not going to insult her by pretending nothing happened between us today. We may not have touched, but we connected, and if Bailey hadn't texted, I would have kissed Mia. I still haven't decided if I'm grateful for or resentful of that text. "Not so much a girlfriend as a girl I've been seeing."

"And does she have a *thing*?" Mia asks.

"What?"

She cocks her head. "A thing she wants so desperately that the idea of having it makes her as sick to her stomach as the idea of never having it?"

And that, ladies and gentlemen, is my heart. Right there in the teeth of the woman my best friend has fallen hard for. "No," I admit. "She doesn't have a thing. Most people don't, Mia."

"Does Brogan?"

I close my eyes. "I couldn't be best friends with someone who didn't."

"You're best friends." She chuckles softly and shakes her head. "Of course you are."

I take the chair across from her, spin it around, and sit. "Mia?" I like saying her name. I like how it rolls off my tongue, how it suits her, and how her lips part just a fraction when I say it. *Mia. Mine.* But she's not mine, and any connection I felt to her today is meaningless if she has feelings for my best friend. "What are you going to do? Are you going to give him a chance?"

With pursed lips, she closes her book. Her mouth is perfect. Pink and soft. I bet she doesn't even wear that sticky gloss crap that girls seem to like so much. "I don't even know him," she says.

"He's a really good guy." I'm underselling it. Brogan isn't just a good guy. He's the best. He's been there for me like no one else has. "He's the kind of guy a girl like you should want."

She looks at my fingers, and I realize I've settled my hand on the table less than an inch from hers. "Is that why you're here? To convince me to go out with your best friend?"

"I'm not sure why I'm here." My pulse beats in my throat. I could shift forward and touch her. Are her hands as soft as they look? Is her mouth as sweet? "Except that I keep thinking how Brogan deserves a girl like you."

"A girl like me?"

Sweet. Vulnerable. Passionate. Someone who makes his heart hammer in his chest like you do mine. "Yeah."

She turns away and sighs. "I don't really have anything going on with Brogan. He found my number on a note I left for Bailey, and we texted a few times. Honestly, I'm embarrassed because when I met you, I assumed you were the guy I'd been texting. And to be fair, I may have read you a little differently if I hadn't been thinking his words were yours."

"You liked him?"

She lifts a freckled shoulder, and the side of her mouth quirks up in a crooked smile. "He's sweet. He made me laugh."

The words are a punch to the gut and they fill me with an emotion I've never felt toward Brogan. *Jealousy.* I want to be the one to make her laugh. The one she calls sweet. And I hate the idea that any chemistry between us today was created—even in part—by the things he said to her.

"I was with my last girlfriend for five months before I found out Brogan had a thing for her. He'd asked her out before we started dating, but I'd been clueless. He never told me because he thought she was special, and he didn't want to get in the way of me being with someone like that. He's that kind of guy." It sucks by way of an apology, but when she lifts her eyes to mine, I know she understands. "So you see, this is the part where I'm supposed to tell you to give him a chance. I want to be the guy who's good enough to give you that speech."

She tugs her bottom lip between her teeth. "But that's not why you're here."

Fuck. Fuck. Fuck. Brogan's the closest thing I've ever had to a brother. I'd never pick a girl over him, and definitely not one I don't even know. And yet here I am. I drop my gaze to my hands. "If you have feelings for Brogan . . ." What? I'll watch them be together? Act like I don't care when he holds her hand? When he kisses her?

"What happened with her? The girl Brogan liked?"

I lift my head and meet her soft brown eyes. "I realized later she only wanted me because I'm a Woodison. Brogan's family never had enough money for her to give him a second glance."

Something changes in her expression. Her eyes seem to harden, and she leans back in her chair as she stiffens. "You're a Woodison? As in Woodison Pork. Woodison Farms?"

Figures. She doesn't recognize me as the star football player, but she knows of my dad. "Guilty." That's the worst part about going to college here. Everyone knows my dad's business, or at least knows of it. You can't miss an empire that powerful in a place as small as Blackhawk Valley.

She shoves her book into her bag and shakes her head as she stands. "Don't worry about this, Arrow. I'm not going to ruin a friendship just so I can be the townie who got to go on a few dates with a football player."

She starts to walk away, and I stop her with a hand on her shoulder. "What just happened?"

She shrugs. "I won't be choosing between you and Brogan. I don't want anyone. I don't have time for that in my life right now."

When she steps out from my grasp, I let her. I watch her walk away, and even though my brain is telling me it's for the best, that getting involved with her would be a mistake, my stomach plummets, and it's all I can do to trap the word on my tongue: *Stay.*

MIA

I wander around the trailer park under the light of the street lamps, one hand in my pocket where my knuckles brush the leaf Arrow gave me. *"It matches your sweater."*

"Hey, sexy!"

I spin around to the sound of Bailey's voice and manage a smile for my friend.

"So did you talk to your boy, Brogan?" She cocks her head, and a lock of her long blond hair falls across her forehead. "Or is it Arrow?"

Sighing, I roll my eyes. "It's neither."

She slings an arm over my shoulders and bumps her hip against mine as we walk down the gravel lane. "Do you want to talk about it? Or do you want to pretend that having two insanely sexy men drool over you is no big?"

I nudge her with my elbow. "No one was drooling. It was a big misunderstanding."

The gravel crunches under our feet as we walk. "Brogan told me about your texts over dinner. He's so cute when he talks about you. If you can call any guy with shoulders that broad *cute*. Damn, girl, will you just hit that and tell me about it?"

Cutting my eyes to her, I shake my head. "The last thing I need right now is a relationship with a BHU jock."

"Who said anything about a relationship? Use him for his body. You're young."

"You're sick."

She gapes at me. "Using an acquaintance for sex is a rite of passage! A time-honored tradition men have participated in since going off to college became a thing. Hell, probably before that." Her smile falls from her face, and she sighs. "I went back to Mason's room after dinner hoping to get something out of Arrow, but he was studying and tight-lipped, and moodier than my mom was when she was going through menopause. I wanted to ask him about your little walk, but Brogan was there, so I decided not to."

"I appreciate your restraint."

"Come on, Mee. Spill. I'm dying here only knowing half the story."

I shrug and rub my leaf between my fingers. "I thought Arrow was the guy who'd been texting me. Like I said, it was a big misunderstanding, and now it's cleared up."

"There was something in your eyes when you came back from that walk. Will you please admit you like him?"

I fold my arms. "For one, I hardly know him, so any feelings

I may or may not have had today were completely superficial."

"Whatever. Insta-love's a thing. I've watched Disney movies."

"*Two*," I say, ignoring her objection, "he's a Woodison. Uriah Woodison's son. He's literally the son of my father's worst enemy."

"Like *Romeo and Juliet*!" She throws her arms in the air. "So flipping romantic."

"Why does everyone think those idiots were romantic? Shakespeare wasn't writing a romance. He was writing a *tragedy*. Do you remember how it ended?"

She cocks her head thoughtfully. "Something about *et tu, Brute*?"

"Dork," I mutter. She tries to pretend she's dumb, but I know better. And I also know how much she hated the ending of *Romeo and Juliet* when we read it in high school. I had to listen to her rant for a solid twenty minutes about what a selfish, immature idiot Juliet was. That might not seem like a long time, but it's probably the longest single block of time I've ever witnessed Bailey focus on anything that doesn't involve a hot guy.

"This isn't Shakespeare," she says, her voice softening. "It's your life."

"Exactly. And I'm not stupid, selfish, immature Juliet."

"So that leaves Brogan. The sexy, goofy, charming Adonis."

"And Arrow's best friend."

"Fair enough." She sighs. "So does this mean neither Blackhawk boy will be initiating you to the pleasures of being a young woman?"

"Sorry to say, but I really appreciate your concern for my

sexual health."

She bumps my hip with hers again, and I giggle.

"Speaking of sexual health and relationships . . ." I clear my throat. "You want to talk about what's happening between you and Mason?"

She arches a brow. "I think you already know what's happening between us. We weren't, um, *quiet* about it, as you and Arrow pointed out."

"What's going on *other* than the hot monkey sex?"

"It's just fun. He knows that."

"Bail."

She kicks a piece of gravel with her purple Chuck Taylor. "What?"

"This isn't about Nic, is it?" I shake my head. "Don't throw away a chance with a great guy because you're waiting for my loser brother to get out of prison."

"I didn't say anything about waiting for Nic."

"You didn't have to," I whisper. I find her hand at her side and squeeze it. "I love my brother, but he's made his own choices, and they weren't good."

"I know." Her jaw has gone tight, just like it does every time we talk about Nic.

"I don't want to see his bad decisions drag you down."

She tilts her chin and studies the sky. Her eyes sparkle in the light of the three-quarter moon. "I know, Mee. And I'm trying to move on. I promise."

Two weeks later...

When I park the car at the quarry south of town, I can already hear the laughter on the other side of the rocks. The sound makes me tense, but I promised Bailey I'd come if she got an A on her calc test. Because she's way freaking smarter than her grades would indicate, I knew she could do it if she put her mind to it. So here I am.

It's not that I'm antisocial. I actually love hanging with Bailey. But since she started going to BHU this fall, I cringe at the thought of her group gatherings. I don't fit in with her friends from the university. While she might not care how they view a townie from the trailer park, I can't ever get past what different worlds we come from. I tried to bring it up with Bail once, and she suggested—very politely, because she is my best friend—that I get over myself.

With a deep breath, I tuck my phone in my pocket, climb from the car, and begin navigating the rocky mound that separates the gravel lot from the old quarry. An autumn chill hangs in the air, and I'm glad I dressed in jeans and a sweatshirt. Because of the water and privacy, this spot is an old favorite for parties anytime the temp's above freezing. Bailey said she and Mason are building a bonfire by the water tonight. It should be nice, actually. Assuming I can *get over myself.*

"Oh. Hey."

I look up toward the deep voice and see Brogan standing on a rocky ledge that overlooks the lake. He's dressed in a BHU Football sweatshirt and jeans that hug his narrow hips, and his smile falters as he takes me in.

"You didn't know I'd be here, did you?" He tucks his hands into his pockets. "I told Bailey to let it go, but she's . . . determined. I wouldn't have come if I'd known. I don't want to make you feel awkward."

"No, I didn't, but . . ." I glance around to take in the group and recognize Mason, Chris, and a couple of girls I've seen hanging out on Bailey's floor in her dorm. He belongs here more than I do. "I'm not avoiding you. I'm sorry if I made you feel that way."

He grins, showing off his straight white teeth. He really is handsome. "Can I get you anything to drink? We've got beer and vodka, and some fruit that's been soaking long enough that it'd probably knock you on your ass."

I shake my head. "I'm driving."

His grin mellows to a softer smile. "Bailey said you were very responsible."

I arch a brow. "Is that a bad thing?" Well, crap. Now I sound defensive.

"Do you have any idea how many drunk girls I see on campus every weekend? And that's fine. We're young. I get it. But I don't know." He shrugs. "It's refreshing, honestly, to meet a girl who doesn't think she has to drink half a bottle of cheap vodka to make friends."

"Thanks, I guess."

He opens his mouth, but his reply is cut off by Bailey's scream from the other side of the fire. "She's here!" She hustles over and wraps her arms around me, squeezing. "I'm so glad you're here. Brogan's here, too, but I see you already saw that."

"Are you trying to play matchmaker, Bail?"

She grins and shimmies back toward the fire. "No idea what you're talking about." Mason grabs her from behind and wraps her up in his arms. Squealing, she spins and kisses him in that long, open-mouthed way that makes you wish you weren't watching.

Sighing, I look to Brogan. "Are they like that all the time?"

He makes a face. "Pretty much. I mean, we've all started walking around the dorm room with our eyes closed and earplugs in, so I can't tell you for *sure*."

I laugh. "God, no one could blame you." We walk toward the fire, and I take a seat on the grass close enough to hear the crackling of the burning wood and feel the heat, but not so close that I'll feel like I have a sunburn. I pat the patch of grass beside me and look up at Brogan. "Wanna keep me company? Looks like Bailey might be otherwise occupied tonight."

He grins and drops down to sit by my side. "It would be my pleasure."

I tilt my head to the side. "Thanks for being nice to me."

He frowns. "Why wouldn't I be?"

"I've kind of been a bitch to you."

The corner of his mouth twitches as he bites back a smile.

"What?" I ask. "What's that look for?"

"No offense, Mia, but I don't think you know how to be a bitch. And besides, there's nothing bitchy about turning down a guy who doesn't interest you."

I frown. "Who said you didn't interest me?"

He lies back on the grass and threads his fingers through his hair as he stares up at the sky. "This conversation is awkward. You know that, right?"

Sighing, I lie beside him, shivering a little when my shoulders hit the cold grass. "Totally awkward."

"Tell me something about yourself." He rolls his head to the side so he's looking at me. "Anything."

"Is this you asking about foot fungus again?"

He chuckles. "No. It doesn't have to be something bad. Just something I don't know."

"I sing." The words take me by surprise, and I bite my lip while I try to figure out how much I want to say about it. "It's not a secret or anything. I go to open-mic night at the Vortex a couple of times a month. I've always loved it. I don't remember a time it wasn't something I looked forward to."

He turns onto his side and studies my face. "I bet you're amazing. Are you going to school for music?"

"Terrace doesn't exactly have a music department." I shake my head, suddenly embarrassed that I shared this much. "It's just a hobby. It doesn't mean anything."

He grunts. "I know all about that lie, Mia. It's like when I tell people football isn't a big deal to me, that it's just a way to get part of my tuition paid while having fun. But nobody works this hard for something they don't care about."

"It's your thing."

He grins, and my stomach does a little flip-flop at what a good smile he has and how it feels to have that smile directed at me. "Yeah. It's totally my thing. And singing is yours, but I'm not going to be that guy who tells you to go after the dream. I know it's more complicated than inspirational posters make it out to be."

After talking to Arrow and seeing the intensity in his eyes when he talked about his *thing,* it's a relief that Brogan understands. As a Woodison, I'm sure Arrow's never given a second thought to whether or not he should chase his dreams. We're not all that lucky.

"My high school brought in this motivational speaker my senior year," I tell Brogan. "He was all about walking the tightrope without a safety net. He said if you have a net, you'll need it. You'll use it. But if you want to make yourself reach your dream, you have to take away the net so you have no other choice."

"I don't know if that's a metaphor for bravery or suicide," Brogan says.

"Exactly! I kept thinking only someone who's always had a safety net would preach something like that. Maybe he didn't have a career to fall back on, but he had family who would step up. Some place to sleep when he didn't have money for rent, food when there's no money for groceries. No one relying on him to keep the lights on."

"So you sing," he says. He reaches out and toys with a lock of my hair. "But you're majoring in something practical."

"I don't know about practical. Criminology. I want to go to law school. That's enough of a stretch, I think."

"Ah, the money path. Not a bad plan. Then you can be the safety net for your kids, and they can grow up to believe they pursued their dreams without one."

The butterflies in my stomach swoon. "That's pretty much the plan," I admit.

"Law school." He nods as if he's mulling the idea over. "You're smart enough."

"How do you know?"

"I'm the creepy guy who watched you tutor kids at the library, remember?"

"Right. I forgot about that." I grin and he grins back, and we lie there in the cool grass with the sounds of the party carrying on around us. "Turns out you have some game after all, Brogan."

"Why do you say that?"

I shrug and scoot closer. There's a connection between us I can't deny. It might not be that sizzling attraction I felt with Arrow, but maybe it's safer than that. Warmth without the fire. "Because I'm lying here thinking about how much I like you."

"I'm told I'm a very likeable guy. It's a curse. I'm intimately familiar with the friend zone."

"Hmm, and yet I'm wondering how I can get you to kiss me."

He props himself up on one elbow and scans my face before his gaze drops to my mouth. "For real?"

The butterflies recover from their swoon to flutter wildly.

"Oh, yeah."

Slowly, he leans over me and sweeps his lips against mine. Once, then twice. I've been kissed before, but Brogan's kiss is different. Most boys kiss like they're trying to rush to the next event. The kiss is nothing more than an irritating prerequisite to the activities they're truly interested in. Brogan's kisses are an effort to slow down time, to memorize the shape and taste of my lips. Under his mouth, I'm not some townie crashing the college kids' party. I'm something to be cherished.

He doesn't climb on top of me or try to snake his hand up my shirt. And when I part my lips, he only briefly touches his tongue to mine before pulling away and drawing in a ragged breath. "I'd love to hear you sing sometime," he says, and I blink at him for a minute before my eyes can focus on his blue ones. "Would you mind?"

"I think I'd like that."

Grinning, he finds my hand and laces our fingers together. "It's a date."

PART III: AFTER

May, four months after the accident

MIA

Mrs. Barrett meets me at the door and wraps me into her arms before I have a chance to say hello. She's a large woman—as tall and as broad as her son, and her hugs bring my face right into her bosom. "Have you been praying for a miracle, Mia?"

"Every day," I whisper. "Every single day."

When she pulls back, her eyes are filled with tears, but a hopeful smile covers her face. "He's having a good day today," she says, leading me to the back of the house. "You know how much he loves sunny days."

"Spring is his favorite."

The click of her heels against the dull hardwood floors echoes off the ceiling. Mrs. Barrett and I don't talk about the past. We don't talk about the fact that before the accident, she wouldn't acknowledge me as Brogan's girlfriend—that she objected to his dating someone she deemed so beneath him, and regularly thwarted his attempts to be with me. We don't talk about the nasty things she once said to me.

We're bonded by this tragedy and our love of Brogan. If she blames me for being there that night, she's never said so. And if she doesn't blame me . . . well, I'm sure she'd be the only one.

She opens the doors to the three-season room and motions me toward the big, sunny space where Brogan sits during the day. He's strapped into his wheelchair, eyes at half-mast, mouth hanging open.

"I'll be in the kitchen if you need me," she says, before leaving and pulling the doors closed behind her.

I walk over to him and touch his face. It's swollen from the edema, distorting the features I once loved so much. His body is gaunt after months of muscle atrophy have eaten away at the solid mass of a man he once was.

"Good morning, handsome." I press a kiss to his cheek before picking up his hand and holding it in both of mine. "I saw Arrow this morning." Hanging my head, I squeeze my eyes shut, remembering my argument with Brogan on New Year's Eve, the betrayal in his eyes. *You think I don't see the way you look at him?* But even as angry as he was with his best friend, I know Brogan wouldn't want to see Arrow destroy his life. He'd want better for him. "It's good. His house arrest will keep him out of trouble. It'll help him get his head on straight."

Swallowing hard, I lift my hand to Brogan's jaw. "I think we're all screwed up. And I know we all miss you." My eyes burn with unexpected tears. Seeing Brogan doesn't normally make me cry, but now that Arrow's back, I feel like someone who's never known she was blind and was suddenly given sight. Seeing Arrow makes the world too bright and loud and painful. All I want is for the dark numbness to return. It's easier that way.

I sit with Brogan for almost an hour, holding his hand and thinking, avoiding my return to Blackhawk Valley. When I can't put it off anymore, I go to the kitchen to find Mrs. Barrett.

She wipes down her already-clean counter. The house is modest, but always spotless. After the accident, the Barretts sold their house and moved to Indianapolis to be closer to his doctors. Caring for Brogan in the home like they do has exhausted their savings, and I'm sure they're racking up more debt by the day, but the Barretts never complain about money.

"Have you remembered anything else about that night?" she asks.

I shake my head. "I'm sorry."

"The police are sick of hearing my voice." She releases a humorless laugh. "I keep calling to see if they have any new leads, but I don't think they're even working on the case anymore." She settles her hand over mine. It's cold and clammy. "Don't you want to know who killed your brother?"

I did, once. Now all I want is for Brogan to wake up. The doctors tell us not to hold out hope for that, but it's happened before. I've read books about men who've woken from PVS—medical speak for *persistent vegetative state*—and could recite everything that was said to them during their days trapped inside their own minds.

I would go the rest of my life without having answers about that night if I could have a miracle for Brogan.

But I don't say that. I open my mouth and force air into my reluctant lungs. If I've learned anything in the last three and a half months, it's that sometimes the best and only thing I can do is to take the next breath.

"I wish the police would do more," she says.

"Me too." The police chalked the hit-and-run up to "gang violence" quickly. They had nothing to go on, and everyone was satisfied with the answer but the Barretts and me. I told the police all I could, but they didn't have much to form any sort of investigation if they'd even cared to—and they didn't. It was dark. A big, dark-colored SUV came speeding up over the hill and killed my brother and destroyed the better part of Brogan's brain.

Mrs. Barrett wants answers. The only ones I have she wouldn't want to hear. His drunken pleas. His anger. His refusal to let me out of his car until I promised not to leave him. The bruises he left on my arm because I tried to leave anyway. Then Nicholas's fists when he came to rescue me. A grieving mother shouldn't have to know any of that. "I'm sorry," I whisper.

Her cold hand squeezes mine. "It's not your fault."

If only that were true.

ARROW

"We saw Brogan yesterday," Chris says, eyeing me as I put the burgers on the grill. Dad invited the team over to celebrate the end of finals week, so now it's my job to entertain them and pretend everything's normal.

"How's he doing?" I have to force the question out and pretend it doesn't hurt like a bitch.

Chris shrugs. "Not good."

"He doesn't even look like himself anymore," Keegan says. "He's skinny and pale and he just sits there with his mouth hanging open and . . . What?" he asks when everyone turns to stare at him.

"A little delicacy?" Mason suggests.

Keegan lifts his palms. "What? It is what it is. No one here really thinks he's coming back from this. Am I wrong? Except maybe Mia, but she's inside."

"You're such an asshole," Mason mutters.

Chris takes a breath, and we exchange a look. Chris comes to stand at the grill by me. "Ignore K," he says, so only I can hear.

I swallow hard. "He's not saying anything I didn't know, right?"

Chris nods and shoves his hands into his pockets. "I still hate hearing it. Brogan was one of the good ones."

"The best," I say, and my voice cracks on the word *best* as if I'm going through puberty all over again. Fuck these regrets. If I could take back the things I said to him that night—if I could change everything . . .

"Don't do that," Chris says.

"What?"

"Don't paint him as a saint because of what happened. We all love him and what happened sucks, but don't beat yourself up for fighting with him that night. He cheated on Mia. *He wasn't a saint.*" Chris's jaw is hard, and I get the impression he's been waiting awhile to have a chance to say that.

"My shrink wants me to visit," I admit. "I'm stuck in this fucking house all the time, but she got my probation officer to agree to let me go see Brogan."

"That's great," Chris says.

"I don't think I'm going to. I saw him in the hospital and visited a few times before the Barretts moved to Indy. The doc thinks I'm more likely to start using again if I don't resolve shit between me and Brogan." Grunting, I shake my head. "As if we can have a conversation or something."

"Mia thinks he knows what's going on around him, and from

what I've read about PVS, I'm not sure, but . . ." He takes the spatula from my hand and flips the burgers before I burn them completely. "It's for you as much as him. You need to say your piece."

I lift a shoulder. "We'll see."

"His mom says hi," Chris says. He tilts his head. "She told me to tell you thank you, said you'd know why. Keegan overheard and made jokes all the way home that you probably tapped her. But I'm guessing you talked your dad into helping with some of Brogan's medical expenses after all. That was cool, man."

"It's just money. It's no big deal."

Chris grunts. "Yeah, maybe, but we all know how your dad is. I'm sure it wasn't easy talking him into that. What's he getting out of it?"

Shrugging, I adjust the flames on the grill. My dad's such a penny pincher, he wouldn't help another family with their medical bills even if he'd get the Nobel Peace Prize for it. All I did was convince my father to let me tap into my inheritance. The Barretts assumed I got the money from Dad, and I let them. My father thinks I sold him my soul to get that money early, but the joke's on him. It's not mine to sell.

"There's Mia," Chris says, and I snap my head up, thinking she's joined us on the patio. Instead, he looks toward the kitchen windows where Mia's standing with her head bowed, probably doing dishes. "I'm worried about her."

"Me too." I've been home almost a month, and she walks around like a robot. Katie's the only one who gets her rare smiles, and as far as I can tell she only leaves the house to see Brogan and check on her dad. She's not living. She's surviving.

"Bailey said she never goes out anymore, and she's not herself. I'm sure all this hasn't been easy on her, but since you two both live here, she thought you might know more." He studies me, and the questions in his eyes are more complicated than the ones coming out of his mouth. "You think she's okay?"

"I don't know," I say, but the truth is, I don't think she's okay at all. And it's eating at me every day.

"I wish she'd join us. Want me to go talk to her?"

I hand him the platter for the burgers and shake my head. "No. I've got this. You feed the savages; I'll talk to Mia."

"Good."

The inside of the house is like a different world. Cold to the hot, quiet to the loud. With the boys here, everything turns chaotic and messy out back, but in here everything is white and sterile. The inside of a tomb.

Mia's sitting at the kitchen table with a book, the wine glasses she just washed air-drying in the dish drain. She's in a short pink sundress that hides her curves but shows all that caramel skin of her long legs, and her bare feet are propped up on the chair beside her.

"Hey," I say softly, but she still jumps and looks up at me with wide eyes.

She puts her book down. "Do you guys need something? I didn't want to be in the way."

"We need you to come outside."

"To cook the food or—"

"To be with your *friends*."

"No thanks," she says, picking her book back up.

"Mia, Katie's not even here right now. You can take an hour off to talk to other people your age."

"No," she says without looking up.

I tear the book from her hands and want to rip it in half when I realize what it is. *I Can Hear You: One Man Wakes From PVS and Shocks the World*. "What is this shit?"

"It's called a book." She avoids my gaze and reaches to retrieve it.

I hold it out of her reach and skim the description on the back cover before turning back to her. "Is this what you're waiting for? You're just going to put your life on hold and wait in case he snaps out of it one day? Haven't they told you how it works?" I shake the book. "*This* isn't what happens. *This* was a fluke. Brogan isn't coming back."

She keeps her gaze cast on the floor, and even though I know I'm right, I wish she'd argue with me, scream at me for giving up on him, or yell at me for not believing in miracles. Something. *Anything* to prove to me that she isn't phoning in her life.

"You want this book back?" I ask, tucking it into the back of my pants.

"Yes, please."

"It's yours. All you have to do is stop ignoring the rest of the world and come outside."

She springs from the chair, eyes wide, hands on hips. "You

don't own me, Arrow Woodison."

I almost fucking smile. It feels so good to get a rise out of her, to see the anger flicker in her eyes and tinge her cheeks pink. "I never said I did."

"Then leave me alone."

"I'd be happy to if you ever did anything but work and study."

"It's none of your business how I live my life."

I step forward, stalking toward her, but with each step I take, she takes one in reverse. "I don't care how you live your life. I only want you to *live* it, not hide from it."

Her back hits the wall and she lifts her eyes to mine, her mouth set in a stubborn line. "I'm not hiding from anything."

I take a final step, and her breasts brush my chest. Any closer, and her whole body would be pressed into mine. My mouth goes dry, and my nerve endings seem stretched to their limits as they ache for contact that isn't quite there. "You are. You're hiding from everything. From everyone. Brogan's gone, and you want him back. I get that. But you're here. Live your life, Mia." My voice trembles slightly on the words. Does she notice? Does she care?

"What life?" she whispers.

I want to kiss her, suck her bottom lip into my mouth and bite down until she feels the pain and pleasure of being flesh and blood. I want to take her upstairs and strip her, put my mouth to her most sensitive bits of flesh until she screams with life. "You didn't die that night."

She swallows. "No. Death would have been easier."

MIA

This time when the banging against my wall wakes me in the middle of the night, I know what it is.

I sit in the darkness for as long as I can stand it, but I can't just listen to his torment and do nothing, so I climb out of bed, grab the baby monitor, and pad softly into his room.

I don't know what I think I'm doing. Chances are, waking him up isn't going to go any better than it did last time. I slowly shut his door behind me and set the monitor on his dresser before walking over to his bed.

The curtains are parted, and a sliver of moonlight cuts across his face. His brow is damp, glistening with sweat, and his jaw is tight.

"Mia," he says. Or at least I think that's what he said. His head thrashes side to side, and my stomach tightens.

I sit on the edge of the bed and skim my fingers over his forearm. "Arrow, wake up." My words are too soft, I know, but

I'm afraid I might startle him and make the nightmare worse. I speak a little louder this time. "I'm here. It's okay."

He moans softly, and some of the tension leaves his shoulders as his head stops thrashing and lolls to one side. With each inhale his breathing grows steadier, and his face relaxes until I feel like the nightmare has passed and I can leave.

Removing my hand from his forearm, I stand.

"Mia," he murmurs. This time his eyes flutter softly. "Don't leave." He reaches out and his fingertips brush mine before dropping back to the bed.

I don't know if he's awake at all or if he'll remember this in the morning, but I can't resist the pleas of a defenseless Arrow, so I lower back down to the edge of the bed.

"Thank you," he says. When he wraps his arm around my waist and guides me into bed with him, I don't resist. My heart practically trembles with every beat, and tears surge into my throat at the feel of his warm chest against my back and his arm around my waist. But when I give myself permission to let him hold me, to stay and close my eyes, I find sleep is closer than it's been in months.

ARROW

What am I supposed to do?

Mia is in my bed and in my arms, and I have no idea what the fuck I'm supposed to do about it.

Vague flashes from last night come back to me. The nightmare. Mia's soft voice. I'd taken a damn sleeping pill and thought I'd dreamed her. Why else would she have come so willingly into my arms?

But here she is, and this is definitely not a dream. This is me with a fucking hard-on holding the girl I can never have.

I prop myself up on an elbow and look down at her. Her face is cast in shadows, and I wish there were more light so I could make out all her features, so I could memorize the shape of her lips and the flush of her cheeks as she sleeps.

It's a dark, clear-sky night. The kind of night when I like to go out behind the barn and away from the lights of the main house and stare up into the stars until I forget I have a body.

Until I dissolve and am nothing but this emptiness floating in the infinite space between here and forever.

But with Mia in my arms, I don't want to become nothingness. I want to be here, to relish the feel of skin touching skin, to hear her moan and see the flash in her eyes before she gives over to the pleasure and comes apart.

Not trusting myself, I remove my hand from her stomach and back away as much as I can without shifting the mattress. It would be so easy to touch her right now. In my bed. In the darkness. I don't need light to memorize her. I'd use my tongue to trace the shape of her lips, my open mouth to explore the curve of her hip.

The darkness is the devil on my shoulder, whispering permission to do everything I can't. To wake her and kiss her. To hold her hands and look into her eyes as I slide into her. I'm haunted by the catch of her breath, the arch of her neck as she moans, and I want it all again. Touching her would give me wings that could pull me from this hell.

But the reprieve would be temporary, and when I fell back down, I'd drag her with me.

I trace the length of her neck and swallow hard. "Mia." Her name is a strangled sound tearing from my throat. "Mia, wake up."

She jerks upright and the blankets fall to her waist.

Don't go. "You need to leave."

"I'm sorry. You . . ." She shakes her head and climbs out of bed. "You asked me to stay."

Because I need you. "I was dreaming."

"Right." She stumbles toward the door, taking all the warmth from my bed with her, and I feel so fucking weak because I'd swallow my pride whole to call her back to my bed. To beg her to give me one night. One hour. One minute in my arms.

But Brogan will never be able to ask her for that again, so why do I think I have the right?

"It's not your job to check on me in the middle of the night," I say. "Don't confuse me with my baby sister." When she opens the door, she's a silhouette against the hallway light, and I roll over in bed so I don't have to watch her leave.

"I don't blame you, you know."

That word. *Blame.* That word makes my chest ache. It weakens the barriers that keep all my thoughts trapped inside. I swallow and slowly roll back to face her. Her back is to the hall, and her arms are wrapped tightly around her stomach. "Blame me for what?"

"For hating me," she whispers. "I know you hate me and I don't blame you, but I wish . . ." She turns her head.

"You think I hate you?"

She shrugs. "You don't have to pretend otherwise. We just need to find a way we can live together when—"

I throw back the covers and leap out of bed, stepping forward, moving closer before I can stop myself. Then another step, because I'm drawn to her scent and her heat, crave it like a marooned man craves water. "I don't hate you," I growl. I should stop there. The wall between us is for her more than me. But I can't stop thinking about her response when I told her she didn't die that night. *"Death would be easier."*

The words stole my breath and trapped my lungs in a vise—a feeling I relive again and again every time I remember them.

"You don't have to lie," she says. "I see it in your eyes, Arrow."

"I don't hate you," I repeat, grinding the words between clenched teeth. "I *want* you."

Her gaze jumps to mine and her breath catches, her lips forming a little O of surprise. "You . . ."

"I want you." My eyes have adjusted to the light, and I rake my gaze over her—the dark tank top with the skinny straps that fall off her shoulders, those little cotton sleep shorts that make me crazy, those dark brown eyes full of more goodness than I deserve. I can't have that goodness. I shouldn't even stand this close. Mia deserves more than a fuck-up, more than this ugliness I'll never escape, and yet— *"Death would be easier."*—I step closer. "I lie here and think about you on the other side of my wall. Do you have any idea how hard it is for me to leave you to sleep alone in that bed? I want to climb in beside you."

In the back of my mind, I hear my counselor from rehab. *Don't expect more from your willpower than it can handle. You're human. You have weaknesses. Stay away from the things you crave, and you'll never have to be stronger than those weaknesses.*

Drugs were never my weakness. But Mia . . .

Her tongue darts out, leaving her bottom lip wet. I take another step forward and skim my knuckles against her waistband. "I want to slip my hand into these fucking mind-scrambling cotton shorts you sleep in and remind you that you're still alive."

"Arrow." She breathes in my name like it's air, and I want to be closer so she can breathe in all of me. I'd give her my last breath if it would fix this.

"I want to take off your clothes." I grab a fistful of her shirt, then release it. Now that I've started, it's like I can't stop. "I want to spread your legs and see if being inside you could possibly be as incredible as I remember."

She draws in a ragged breath and lifts her arms to the side. "Then do it."

I flinch. She offers her body while her mind is full of sadness. "I can't," I say. "Because more than any of that"—I swallow hard—"I want to be worthy of half the attention you give a dead man." *But I'm not.*

I step back, and she grabs my shirt in her fist before I can retreat another step. "Don't," she says.

"Mia . . ."

"Don't say things like that to me and then walk away."

"I shouldn't say things like that at all. We both know it." I close my eyes and take a deep breath, drawing in her sweet scent, leaning into her heat. "And I have to walk away. Just like I should have that night at the lake."

She releases my shirt. "You are worthy," she says, and rushes from the room.

You are worthy. I hold my breath because out of Mia's mouth, the words feel true, and I want to cling to that feeling as long as I can.

MIA

"Where are your books?"

Bailey plops down on the couch next to me and leans her head against my shoulder. We used to sit like this all the time. For one semester, I kind of felt like a normal college student, living in this apartment with Bailey, attending classes at Terrace, going out with Brogan. But death is expensive, and any emergency fund I had was drained by Nic's funeral, and then there was the issue of tending to Dad. The day after we buried my brother, Dad's lights were turned off for nonpayment, and I found out he hadn't paid rent on the trailer lot in almost a year.

I had to move out, and Bailey had to get a roommate who wasn't panicked by the prospect of rent and utilities.

Bailey sighs. "I lied."

"What?"

"There's not a test I need help studying for. Finals were last week."

My stomach sinks. The semester is over. A whole semester since the accident, and I've been hiding at the Woodisons', marking time. Waiting for Brogan to wake up. "I should have known that, huh?"

"You have a few things going on." She gives me a tentative smile. "I just wanted to see you, and the only way you make time for me is if you think you're helping me out."

I flinch. "Am I that bad?"

She grabs my hand and squeezes it. "I worry about you. You look more stressed than usual. What's up?"

That's a loaded question. What's up is that I slept in Arrow's arms last night. What's up is that I can't stop thinking about him since he told me he wants me. What's up is that I offered myself to him, and he sent me away.

"Do you ever think about who was driving the car?" I ask. I don't have to explain what car or when. The accident never strays far from either of our minds.

"I don't believe Nic was dealing again," she says. "It's bullshit. And even if some of the thugs he used to run around with decided to get rid of him, how would they know to look for him on Deadman's Curve in the middle of the night?" She shakes her head. "I don't buy it."

"Me neither."

She lowers her gaze and worries her bottom lip between her teeth. "I used to spend so much time thinking about who did it," she says. "I couldn't sleep. I'd sit in the parking lot of the Pretty

Kitty and catalogue every man who climbed into a dark SUV. Turns out that's a pretty fucking popular car choice around here."

"Whoever it was hit two grown men," I say.

"I know. And the fucker walked away." She shakes her head. "It's not right."

"No, I mean, Brogan and Nic weren't small guys. They had to have done damage to the car, right?"

She shrugs. "Yeah. I'm sure." Then she sits up. "The list of folks around here driving dark SUVs might be impossibly long, but the ones driving banged-up, dark SUVs . . ."

I nod. "Or the ones who got body work done on their dark SUVs . . ."

"But surely the police already went through this?" she says.

"They say the investigation is ongoing, and they won't tell me what they've done. But you know how the police work in this town." I wrap my arms around my waist. I can't stop thinking about what Arrow said about me acting like I died that night. Maybe if I had some answers, living my life wouldn't feel like betraying Brogan. "What if they're trying to protect someone? An officer, or the kid of an officer or something?"

"I've wondered about that myself."

"I made some calls this morning," I admit. "I called around to different body shops in the area to see if they'd give me some information on cars matching that description that had body work done."

"Any luck?"

"I got a 'Nice try, lady,' a 'Quit wasting my time,' and a 'Just who do you think you are?' So I stopped calling."

Bailey points at me. "That's where you went wrong. You gotta do this shit in person. With cleavage."

I arch a brow. "You really think boobs are going to make people give us answers?"

"We're not talking about *people*. We're talking about men."

We start at the most popular body shop in town—Crowe's Automotive. We walk in the front door and wait at the front desk. To the right of the waiting area is a glass wall that overlooks that shop. I remember when this place was built. Everyone thought it was the coolest thing they'd ever seen.

Bailey steals a mint from the bowl and pops it into her mouth before ringing the bell. "You know what's sexy?" she asks around her candy.

"What?" I ask. I'm not really interested in her answer, but when she points, I have to look.

"That," Bailey says with a sigh. "*Him.*"

There, standing on the other side of the glass in low-slung jeans and a tight white oil-stained T-shirt, is Sebastian Crowe.

"I know him," I say.

She cocks her head and folds her arms. "I swear, you have some sort of muscle magnet embedded in you. The more muscle they have, the faster they come." She snorts. "That sounded dirtier than I meant it, but that's probably true, too."

"I said I *know* him. Like, I met him once. He helped me get

Dad inside after I picked him up from the Pretty Kitty a few weeks ago. I think he lives in the trailer park."

"No shit? I thought mechanics were supposed to make good money."

I shrug but don't get the chance to answer because Sebastian pushes through the swinging glass door that separates the service bay from the waiting area.

His gaze lands on me first. "Mia. Are you okay? Does your dad need something?" He's already grabbing a set of keys from a hook on the wall behind the counter.

"Muscle magnet," Bailey murmurs beside me.

I nudge an elbow into her side. "Dad's fine. Actually, we're looking for some information about, um, the services you provide."

Bailey gives me an exasperated look. "Amateur." She tugs on the hem of her shirt, and the already-low scooping neckline falls an inch lower. Propping her elbows on the service counter, she leans forward and grins at Sebastian. "I'm doing research for my marketing class. We're supposed to analyze local markets, and I chose body work." She drags her gaze meaningfully down his chest. "You know, on cars."

Sebastian grunts, and I can't help but like him more for not being impressed by Bailey's act. An older man with Sebastian's dark hair and eyes pushes into the waiting area, and Sebastian's eyes shift to me, questioning.

"We're looking for information about the people who've gotten body work done here since the beginning of the year," I explain. "Everything from a tiny dent to serious damage."

The man I assume must be Mr. Crowe rolls his eyes. "Who sent you? Denny's place? I told them we're not sharing our info. These young business owners today with all this secret-shopper bullshit."

"We're not secret shoppers," I assure him. "We just want the names of people who—"

"You want the *names* of my customers?" the man says. "Give me a fucking break. Denny sent you. Trying to poach my customers. What's he gonna do? Call and tell them I did it wrong so he can redo it? You tell him that if he did good work, he wouldn't have to have you girls in here lying in a pathetic attempt to get business."

"No, really. I—"

Sebastian lifts a hand and holds my gaze. The warning is there loud and clear: *Stop while you're ahead.* "Don't worry about it, Dad. I'll see if I can help the girls with their *marketing project* without sharing any of our customer information." He comes out from around the counter and goes to the front door. "Come on," he says, looking at us over his shoulder. "I'll walk you to your car."

"Thanks," I say to his father. Bailey and I rush to the door, escaping the rapidly mounting awkwardness filling the waiting room.

"What do you think you're doing?" Sebastian asks me when the door closes behind us. "And don't give me that bullshit about a marketing project. The semester just ended, and you two don't even go to the same school."

Bailey props her hands on her hips. "Well, aren't you creeptastically familiar with our lives, Mr. Muscles."

Rolling his eyes, he drags a hand through his hair. "Please tell me this isn't about the accident."

Bailey shifts her gaze to me and drops her hands from her hips.

"It was an SUV," I say, looking Sebastian in the eye. "Big and boxy, so probably not a recent model. It hit two grown men. There had to have been some damage."

"What makes you think it was someone local?" he asks. "Or that they got the work done here? Could have been another body shop or, hell, if I was trying to cover something up I might go to a place in Indy or Louisville. Not the place the crime happened."

"I know," I say. "I know all of that. But I just have to do this, okay? I have to look."

Sebastian shifts and glances over his shoulder toward the shop. "You want names?"

"Yes. I won't tell anyone where I got the information."

"I'm not promising anything, but I'll see what I can do."

ARROW

I fucking hate the treadmill. I love running. I love pushing my body and churning my legs so fast my lungs burn. But I hate being stuck on this treadmill. I want big sky, not ceiling. I want the give and take of a real hill and the rise and fall of the earth, not the whirring of the mechanical incline. After five miles, I do sprints, pushing my body and my legs until my heart pounds so hard and my breath comes so fast that there's no more room for my thoughts.

It's after ten by the time I leave the basement gym and climb up the stairs. The house is dark, but the patio lights are on. I grab a protein shake from the fridge and go outside. Even as humid as it is, the night air is refreshing. I take another step out to look up at the stars, but my eyes catch on the figure swimming in the pool and never find their way to the sky.

She's in a modest black one-piece and doing laps, pulling her arms through the water, her dark hair streaming behind her. She looks like a goddess.

I don't know how long I watch her. Ten laps. Twenty. Thirty. Her body and her movements hypnotize me. When she surfaces, she clings to the edge of the pool and takes desperate gulps of air. I'm not the only one running from my thoughts tonight.

"How long have you been standing there?" she asks without looking at me.

"Not long," I lie.

She hoists herself out of the water, and for the two breaths it takes her to grab her waiting towel, I'm treated to the sight of her curves. Those tight, toned legs, her hips, the modestly covered round of her ass, the curve of her breasts. She wraps the towel under her arms in her best attempt to hide from me, but my mind remembers everything. So do my hands.

"It's all yours," she says with a nod toward the pool. "Enjoy."

"Mia, I . . ." But she keeps her head down and disappears into the house, leaving me alone.

I hit the patio lights and stand in the darkness for a few minutes. When I head back to my room, the shower is running in the bathroom across the hall. My heart thuds and stumbles at the thought of Mia nude under the spray. She doesn't have to hide her curves from me. Every inch of her skin is branded on my brain like the roadmap to salvation. I lean against the wall and wait my turn. There are other showers in the house, but I want to use this one. And I want to see Mia one more time before I climb into bed and surrender to my nightmares.

I close my eyes and listen to the sounds inside the bathroom, but my plans are shattered when my cell rings and the name Coach Wright flashes on the screen.

I answer reluctantly. "Hello?"

"I'm at your door but don't want to wake the baby with the bell. Come let me in."

I squeeze my eyes shut. I don't want to talk to anyone tonight, but especially not my football coach. We used to be close. He noticed my talent when I was young and made sure everyone who needed to along the way did, too. Then when it came time for college, he made sure I not only had a spot on the BHU team but that I actually got the chance to play. He's always had my back and pushed me to be my best, but I can't look him in the eye these days. I've let him down, just like everyone else. "On my way."

I head downstairs and see the silhouette behind the front door. I open it, and Coach wraps me in a hug I don't want. I stare at his black Cherokee parked in the circle drive instead of thinking about what his hug means, how worried he is about me.

When I pull back, I catch the disappointment in his green eyes before I turn to lead him down to the basement.

"I talked to the other coaches today," he says as he sinks into one of the dark leather sofas in the rec room. He adjusts the collar of his polo and bows his head of gray hair to smooth invisible wrinkles in his jeans. "We agree there's no reason you couldn't train with the team again after your house arrest, assuming you pull your grades up during your online courses. Train with the team and then enter the draft next spring. Only one season out before you're back in the game."

I don't sit. I cross to the opposite wall and study the collage of baby pictures Gwen has on display.

His face looks older suddenly, as if his wrinkles have deepened in the last few months. I did that to him. "You *do* want to play again, don't you?" The hitch in his voice hints at exasperation, as if this is such a simple question.

I hang my head. Football has been part of my life since the day I was born. My dad's NFL dreams were crushed by an early college injury, and he didn't *hope* his son would have the career he'd missed—he expected it. And I never minded, because carrying a football was as natural to me as breathing. It's just that since the moment I walked into the hospital and saw my best friend had become a vegetable, I haven't much wanted to breathe, let alone play ball. They all expect me to follow my dreams while Brogan's wither right alongside his body.

"It's okay," Coach says. "We'll get you through this and back on track. In a couple of years, you'll be playing professionally, and all this mess will be behind you."

"I can't do it," I whisper. It's the first time I've said it. In our dozens of talks since New Year's Eve, I've thought it a thousand times but I've never said it out loud. "I can't do it anymore. It's too much."

"Arrow, don't. We have to put the past in the past, focus on your future."

I spin to face him. "And what about Brogan? Does he get to focus on his future?"

"Do you think *this* is what he'd want for you? Spinning out of control, self-destructing?" He pushes off the couch and stares at me for a long minute. When I don't answer, he sighs and starts climbing the stairs. I watch him go, hating this new distance between us but needing it to defend myself from the sympathy in his eyes.

When he reaches the top, he stops. "You're like a son to me, and I'd do anything to protect you. You can hate me if you want, but I only want what's best. You deserve a good future, whether you believe that or not."

The basement door clicks shut behind him, and I listen for his footsteps and the sound of the front door opening and then closing again. Vibrating with frustration turned rage, I swing, barely registering the pain that radiates up my arm when my fist shatters through the glass of a picture frame and into the wall. I scream. From the pain burning my hand, from the frustration of living this life, from the agony of enduring these secrets.

I sink to the floor, my fist drawn to my chest, and barely register the shuffle of feet on the stairs.

"Oh my God. What have you done?"

I blink up at Mia. Impotent rage clouds my eyes, and my fingers are hot and sticky with blood. "Don't." I pull away as she reaches for me, but it's too late. The blood is already on her hands.

"You can't play if you can't hold a ball. Why are you trying to throw your life away?"

I shake my head and push myself up. Glass crunches under my feet. The world spins with the kind of pain I haven't felt since I broke my collarbone in high school. I lean against the wall for support, and the world rights itself. "I don't have a life. I'm just a fuck-up. Ask my dad. Ask Coach. Ask anyone."

She tries to take my hand again, and when I hold it out of her reach, she steps closer until she has to crane her neck to look up at me. Her mouth is so close, so tempting. "Let me help, please."

I blink as her words slingshot me back in time. To my car. To her fingertips brushing under my waistband. *"Let me. Please."* I want to go back to that night and stay there. Never leave the lake. Never let her leave my arms. "Do you remember that night, Mia? Do you remember letting me touch you?"

Something flashes in her eyes but she closes them, locking the emotion away before I can read it. "We need to get you to the hospital."

"Can't," I whisper. The world's going fuzzy, the edges blurred with pain. "House arrest."

"I think you broke your hand. I'm pretty sure your probation officer will forgive a trip to the ER."

"Do you remember?" I ask again. My voice doesn't sound like my own. "I need to know."

She nods, and there's so much goddamn sadness in her eyes that I should hate this, but I can't. Because she's close. And when she's not, the air isn't fit to breathe. "Of course I remember," she says. "Do you?"

"Yes." *Every single moment.*

Her gaze drifts to my mouth and her lips part. "I'm sorry." She lifts her hand to my jaw and skims her fingers over the stubble there.

"Why would you say that?"

"Because you regret it," she says, "and I should, too."

I close my eyes, telling myself this is only a moment. I'm so caught up in the pain and the memory, I can allow myself this touch. This contact of her skin with mine that makes me want so much I can never have.

"I don't regret it." My voice breaks on the words, and I step away before I can say more. Before I can admit that memory is all I have. It's the only thing that reminds me I'm alive. The memory of Mia's mouth, her touch, the way she tastes—that was all that kept me from following her brother to the grave I put him in.

PART IV: BEFORE
May, eight months before the accident

ARROW

I usually avoid off-campus parties. They're always more trouble, alcohol, and drama than they're worth, but my teammates ganged up on me, and I agreed to come to this one.

When I pull up, the street is lined with cars, and music pours from the house. The front porch is crowded with people drinking from red cups and smoking, and I decide I'm going to make an appearance and head back to the dorm. I can already tell this party is trouble.

I head in and spot Mia in the kitchen, and I pause. *Trouble.*

I'm slammed with that push-pull of want and guilt deep in my gut. I shouldn't even think of her as Mia. I should think of her as *Brogan's girl*. But she'll always be Mia to me. She'll always be more to me than I can admit to anyone.

God, she's beautiful. Her long, dark hair is down tonight, hanging in loose curls around her bare shoulders. Her black shirt fits snugly against her body, displaying her curves more blatantly than her typical choice of clothing.

She laughs, and Bailey hands her a shot glass. Mia shoots it back like an old pro.

Bailey throws her hands in the air. "Yes!" And promptly pours another.

What the fuck?

I head to the kitchen and wrap my hand around Mia's wrist before she can bring the second shot to her mouth. "Slow down, champ."

My eyes lock with Mia's, and time skids to a halt. The room grows silent around us—or seems to—because it's still there. At least, it is for me. She's been with Brogan for more than six months now, and I'm still jarred by an electric current every time we touch.

I'm horrible and despicable. I'm broken. I shouldn't be thinking about electric currents in the context of my best friend's girl.

"I thought you didn't drink," I say.

"What are you, Arrow? Her dad?"

I ignore Bailey's soft punch to my shoulder and keep my eyes on Mia. "What's up?"

Mia avoids my gaze and traces the rim of her shot. "I just want to let loose a little." The words come out with a tremble. Nerves? Something else?

Bailey's loud guffaw pulls my attention from Mia. Her grin stretches across her face. "She's trying to relax so she can rid herself of her V-card."

"*Bailey*," Mia says, her eyes going wide. Bailey throws her hand over her mouth, and Mia looks at me. "Ignore her. She's drunk."

Her V-card? "You're a virgin?" Oh, hell. Somewhere there's a list of questions you don't ask your best friend's girl when you secretly want her for yourself. That one's gotta be somewhere near the top. There's also a list of questions that you shouldn't care how your best friend's girl answers, and it's probably number one on that list, too.

Mia glares at Bailey. "Why do I tell you anything? Why?"

"She's a virgin," Bailey says. "*For now.*"

And she plans to end that tonight? With Brogan? My stomach twists into knots but I manage to keep a straight face as I pull the shot glass from Mia's hand. "If that's the case, you probably shouldn't get trashed tonight."

"Where is Brogan, anyway?" Bailey says. "Didn't he say he was here when he texted you?"

"He had to leave," Keegan says, stumbling over to us. "His grandma's in the hospital."

Mia sets the shot glass on the counter and slips her hand into her purse to retrieve her phone. Her fingers tap quickly at the screen. "I had no idea. Crap."

Bailey frowns. "I guess this means you aren't going to give it up tonight. Bad timing, Grandma."

Mia frowns at her. "You are the actual worst, you know that?"

"Sorry. I suck at serious conversations. Tell Brogan I'm sorry or whatever it is I'm supposed to say." She bites her lip and cuts her gaze to me. "I'm really not a bitch, I swear. I'm just bad at life."

Mia's phone rings and she swipes the screen and puts it to her ear. "Where are you?" She nods, listening. "I'm so sorry, sweetie. I can get a ride and be there in . . . Oh. Okay . . . right. No, of course. Please don't worry about it. I understand . . . yeah. Okay. Well, call when you have a chance but don't worry about me . . . Okay. I love you." When she hangs up the phone, all the giddy energy that buzzed around her when I first walked over here is gone. "His grandma had a stroke. She's in the hospital."

"Are you going to go?" Bailey asks. "I bet Chris hasn't been drinking. He could probably drive you."

Mia shakes her head. "No, it's just family right now." She forces a smile. "I'll let you know when I hear something, but I think I'm going to go out back so I'm somewhere with less noise when he calls again."

"Okay," Bailey says.

Mia excuses herself, and I watch her push through the crowd and out to the backyard.

When she's gone, Bailey turns to me. "Brogan's mom is a fucking cunt."

"Bailey!"

"Don't *Bailey* me! I guarantee you she's the reason Mia's not welcome at the hospital. *Family only.* Mia is family, or should be, but that woman's determined to keep her out."

I stare at the doors to the back. "Are you going to go talk to her?"

"Nope. Because I'll call his bigoted whore of a mother a *cunt*, and that will only upset Mia." She smacks me on the back. "This is a job for you, I'm afraid."

I frown. "Why me?" But she's already gone, swallowed up into the mob as she makes her way to the crowd dancing on the other side of the room.

"Hey, Arrow," Trish says. She scans the room. "Have you seen Brogan?"

"He's not here, Trish." *And he wouldn't want to be with you if he was.* Not that I don't sympathize with her. Unrequited love is a bitch.

Shaking her off, I head toward the back, but I don't find Mia on the deck where half a dozen people are smoking and another dozen are making out.

I head down the steps and into the yard and finally spot her sitting behind the big oak tree by the back corner of the fence. I sink to the ground and take the seat beside her. "Hey."

She wipes her cheeks with the back of her hand. "Hey. What's up?"

"Wanna talk about it?"

"Nope."

"Wanna talk about something else?"

"That would be amazing." She folds her legs under her and studies the grass, combing through it with her fingers.

I clear my throat. "Things must be pretty serious between you and Brogan, huh?" It's a stupid question and not the full change of subject I promised, but I can't stop thinking about her plans to give him her virginity tonight.

"Do you think I'm a hypocrite?"

"Why would I think that?"

"Because I was doing shots and hoping to hook up after a college party. Typical basic bitch, right?" She draws in a long breath. "But don't worry. I learned my lesson."

"I don't think you're a hypocrite," I say softly. "And you couldn't be basic if you tried."

"Maybe I am. I tell myself I'm not like those girls who go to parties, get trashed, and hook up." She laughs—if you can call it that. There's no humor in the sound. "And look at me tonight. That's exactly what I was trying to do. Big fat fail."

"Mia, I don't think sleeping with your boyfriend constitutes a *hookup*."

She tugs on a blade of grass, then another and another, making a little pile in front of her crossed legs. "I was going to do it for him. He . . . It's important to him."

"Not to you?"

She shrugs. "I'm Catholic, Arrow. I was raised to believe a girl should save herself for marriage, that the purpose of sex is procreation, so if you don't want a baby, you shouldn't do it."

"And do you still believe that?"

"No. I don't. But that doesn't mean I'm going to jump into bed with the first guy who shows any interest."

"Obviously not," I mutter.

She scoops up the tiny pile of grass and throws it at me. "What's that supposed to mean?"

"Come on, Mia. If you wanted to lose your virginity, all you'd have to do is walk into that party and announce it. You'd have dozens of eager volunteers before you could finish the sentence."

She laughs again, but this time I hear her smile in it. "I'm being delusional if I think this thing with Brogan is going anywhere—his mom hates me so much she won't even invite me to Sunday dinner. And now she won't let me come to the hospital to comfort him when his grandmother might die."

"His mom is . . ." I swallow, feeling guilty about saying anything bad about the woman who often acted as my surrogate mother after Mom died. "She's not easy to win over, but when she gets to know you, she'll love you."

"Arrow, I'm a Mexican from a trailer park. My father's a drunk, and my brother is a convicted drug dealer."

"Is that seriously the sum of how you see yourself?"

"Isn't that what you see when you look at me?"

"No." My heart hammers as I look at her, wishing we had more light so I could see her eyes. "I see you, Mia. Just *you*." I want to say more, to tell her how bright she shines, to explain that her family is half of what leaves me in awe of her. I'm not blind to my privilege. I get how lucky I am, how much has been handed to me from the day I was born. But Mia doesn't have any of that. Everything she is and has, she earned without help from her family. And yet she's constantly doing everything for her dad and writing letters to her brother in prison. I've never met a person as selfless as her.

She shakes her head and lowers her voice. "She'll never love me, but before tonight I was optimistic enough to believe she might accept me someday. I've been fooling myself. Hell, maybe I should make use of your idea and go in there and see if some kind soul would rid me of my virginity."

"I'd tackle you before you reached the door."

She laughs again. "Why do you care so much?"

Because I've thought of you as my own since the day we met.

"Right," she whispers. "Brogan." She groans. "I'm so disgusted with myself right now. His grandmother just had a stroke, and I'm here making it about me."

"You have every right to be upset."

She scoots away from the tree and leans back, stretching out on the grass and looking up at the leaves. "What would you do if you were me?"

Dangerous territory, my brain warns. *Tread carefully.* "That depends. Does he make you happy?"

"I hate that question. Generally, I'm opposed to the whole idea of someone being responsible for someone else's happiness."

"You're dodging. How do you prefer I ask the question?"

She sighs. "I love my time with him. He's so funny and he makes me feel . . ."

I wait for her to finish even though I want to take the nearest exit from this conversation, even though I want to show her how much *I* could make her feel. *Not in the cards, asshole.*

"I love how much he loves being with me. Does that sound self-centered? He makes me feel so precious and valued. No one's ever made me feel like that before. No one's ever said the things he says to me and made me believe them."

It's like she handed me a blade and I can't help but cut, can't help but slice into the wound just to watch it bleed. "Like what?"

"It will sound stupid." She's still staring at the leaves overhead.

"I doubt it."

"He said I make him want to walk without a net."

"What does that mean?"

She shakes her head and sighs, a halfway smile curving her lips. "It doesn't matter."

Good. I don't know that I want to hear much more about the Great and Incomparable Brogan and the sweet nothings he whispers to Mia. "What are you looking at up there?"

"When I was a little girl, Mom would lie with me like this if I couldn't sleep. The wind would blow, and the starlight would peek between the leaves. She told me the light was dancing fairies." She swallows hard. "She told my brother and me that we had to be quiet or we'd scare them away. So we'd watch in complete silence, Mom lying between us, and we'd fall asleep like that."

I swing around and lower myself to lie on the grass beside her and watch the starlight peek between the leaves. We're the only people on the backside of the lawn, and even though I can hear everyone who's hanging out up by the house, it feels like we're alone. Just Mia, me, and the dancing fairy light.

"Your mom sounds amazing," I whisper, as if speaking too loudly really will scare away the fairies.

"She was. Sometimes I miss her so much. It feels like she took a piece of my guts with her when she left, as if I've never functioned properly since."

I know exactly how that feels. "What happened?"

"She left my dad and moved away. She doesn't visit."

"Does she call?"

"A couple of times a year, but it's always so awkward that I hang up wishing she hadn't." Then she bursts into giggles. Not sardonic laughter or chuckles, but giddy, nearly maniacal giggles. It's a sound that brings a smile to my face. I can't imagine anyone could hear Mia laugh and not smile.

"What?" I ask. She rolls to her side to face me, and now we're close enough that I can see her eyes. When they lock on mine, I have to swallow hard and will myself to stay put, to resist the instinct to close the distance left between us. *Not mine.* But the pull I feel toward her is as consistent as the gravity keeping us on the ground.

"Oh my God, Arrow. I am the biggest buzzkill of the century."

"I wasn't buzzed, so you couldn't be a buzzkill."

"Seriously, though, you should go back to the real party. My pity party is no way to spend your Friday night."

"I'm not going to leave you unsupervised until I'm positive you're not going to offer up your virginity to the first fool willing to take it." *Unless that fool is me.* Fuck, I don't even know what I'm doing, but I can't stop. I roll so we're facing each other. A lock of dark hair has fallen across her cheek and brushes her lips. I want to smooth it away with my fingers, lean in and taste those lips for myself. "Mia . . ." *Not yours, asshole.*

She brushes the hair away before the impulse to do it myself can win me over. "You really think I'd do that?"

"No." I smile. "But I do think Bailey might do it for you if she thought she could get away with it."

"Probably! God, please don't mention it to her. The way she goes on about Mason's skills, she'd probably ask him to do the honors, and Bail and I are close but I don't know that I want to share lovers with her."

I draw in a ragged breath and feel as if I'm about to step out onto ice I know is too thin to support me. "I know we're just joking here, but can I say something in all seriousness?"

Her face grows serious, and her gaze drops to my lips. "What?"

"Don't throw it away on some asshole who isn't one hundred and ten percent worthy. And that includes Brogan. If you're not doing it because *you* want to, don't do it at all."

"You don't think he'll leave me if I make him wait?" Her voice is small, as if she's afraid to speak the secret fear too loudly.

"Any guy who sees you for as special as you are will wait until you're ready."

MIA

October, three months before the accident

"I can't go to the Cavern," I tell Bailey as she drags me out of the car. "I'm not twenty-one."

She rolls her eyes. "Look at you. No bouncer in his right mind is going to card you." Stopping, she grins and pulls something from her back pocket and shoves it into my hands. "And there's this."

"You didn't." I study the fake ID with my picture and name.

"Consider it your birthday present. Come on! They have karaoke. It'll be fun!"

I follow her into the Cavern, a popular hangout for preppy college kids who fancy themselves craft-beer aficionados. She leads me to a big U-shaped booth in the back that's already filled with the usual suspects—Chris, Mason, Trent, Keegan, and Trish, a girl who always seems to show up at these get-togethers, whether she's invited or not. The only two missing are Brogan and Arrow. Brogan's out of town with his family for a couple of nights, so I know he won't be joining us.

I was supposed to go with him. Until his mom found out about our plans.

I shove the thought from my mind before it can latch on. It's my birthday. I'm not going to turn tonight into a pity party.

"Hey, Mia."

And there's Arrow. The sound of his voice murmuring my name sends chills up my spine and makes the butterflies in my stomach do a little dance.

Pretty much, I hate myself.

I take my seat in the booth and Bailey positions herself on the side opposite me. When Arrow slides in beside me, I smile at him, as if sitting next to him here is no big deal, as if I haven't spent the last year avoiding being this close to him.

"You could have sat by me, Arrow," Trish says from the other side of the semicircle.

Snorting, Bailey cocks a brow at her. "And have you molest him under the table?"

Chris props his elbows on the table and leans forward. "Where's Brogan?"

"His cousin's getting married tomorrow," I say. "But don't worry. He'll be back for the game on Saturday."

"Right, the wedding," Keegan says. "But I thought you were gonna go with him? Make a weekend of it or something?"

"Didn't work out," I say quickly.

"I bet he let his mom talk him out of it," Keegan guesses with a nod. "What a fucker."

Arrow looks away, pretending to watch the guy who's setting up the karaoke machine at the front of the bar, but I know he agrees with Keegan. Brogan didn't come out and say his mom told him he had to change our plans. He said he was worried he'd be too busy with wedding and family stuff.

"It's a family thing," I say, dismissing Keegan's concerns with a wave of my hand. "And anyway, I'm working tomorrow."

Chris frowns at me.

"And on that note," Bailey says, "let's drink."

ARROW

Mia looks so fucking beautiful tonight I almost swallowed my tongue when I saw her. Her hair is down, and she's wearing this black shirt that's fitted at her waist and hangs loose around her neck. When she shifts forward, the shirt moves with her, exposing the soft swell of the tops of her breasts. The sight literally makes my mouth water, and I have to swallow hard and remind myself she's not mine.

She's never been mine.

I'm so pissed at Brogan, I almost didn't come tonight. I read him the riot act when he told me he canceled plans with Mia because his mom didn't like the idea of Mia coming to a family wedding. He said I was overreacting. Making more out of it than there was. The idiot's in denial. His mom doesn't like Mia—which is absurd—and Brogan wants to pretend that it's not about Mia, that she wouldn't like the idea of him getting a hotel room alone with any girlfriend.

"Karaoke?" Trent groans, eyeing the guys setting up speakers at the front. "Seriously?"

"Yeah," Trish says. "A little lame, isn't it?"

Bailey rolls her eyes. "Not as lame as *you*."

The girls stare each other down for a minute, then Trish huffs. "Whatever. I'd just rather be dancing. Wouldn't you guys?" She glances around the table and is met with a chorus of "Not really," "Not a dancer," and "Nope."

I keep my mouth shut, but I'm with them. I'm not one for singing karaoke, but I don't mind it, either. The music is never as loud as the bars with the live bands, so we can still talk, and I'm not much of a dancer.

"I like karaoke," Keegan says. "Hot girls drink too much and then proceed to do something that makes them insecure. And that's when I step in."

"You're disgusting," Bailey says.

"Are you going to sing?" he asks her.

"Fuck yes," Bailey says. "And if y'all are lucky, so will Mia."

She tenses next to me then gives her friend a stern scowl. "Probably not, Bail."

A waiter sidles up to the table with a tray full of shot glasses filled with amber liquid. He winks at Bailey and slides the tray onto the table. "I have specific instructions to keep these coming."

"That's right, you do," Bailey purrs. She shoots the first back even as she slides another across the table to Mia, who grins at her friend the way one might at a wild-mannered toddler.

Her phone buzzes in her purse between us, and when she

pulls it out to look at the display, her face changes.

"Is everything okay?" I ask.

She grimaces as she swipes the screen to accept the call. "I need to take this."

I climb out of the booth so she can go, and watch her rush to the door, phone pressed to her ear.

Bailey comes to stand beside me. "Shit. That's probably her mom doing her obligatory happy birthday call. If she really cared, she'd leave Mia alone."

"Should we go talk to her?" I ask. "Make sure she's okay?"

Bailey's frown covers her whole face, and for someone who never takes herself seriously, she looks formidable. "First Brogan, and now this. Fucking shit birthday if you ask me."

"So what do we do?" I ask. On the other side of the glass entrance, Mia has a hand tunneled into her hair, her face tilted to the sky, her eyes closed.

I want to give her the kind of birthday that makes her feel special and loved. The kind that makes her look forward to the next year and makes her grateful for the friends she's made in the last.

Now Bailey has turned her frown on me. "You can't fix it, Arrow. Girls like Mia don't need to be fixed. They need someone who can accept them and their fucked-up lives. Just be her friend. That's what she needs tonight." She points to the booth. "So sit back down."

I'm not sure what that speech is supposed to mean, but I nod and take my seat. The guys have started arguing about next week's game against Allegiance, but I can't think football when my head is full of Mia.

Bailey said to be her friend, and that's what I've done for nearly a year. Friendship means I get to make her smile. It means I get to crack jokes that I know will make her giggle, or send her texts wishing her luck on the exam she studied for all weekend. It means I get to sit next to her at a bar and never lean over to whisper just how beautiful she looks. It means I get to ignore the pull I feel toward her that's so relentless I don't know how she doesn't feel it, too. It means I get to put her happiness—*Brogan's* happiness—over my own selfish needs.

I stare at my phone, scrolling through Instagram and pretending to be busy so I don't have to chime in.

Less than two minutes later, Mia slides into the booth next to me, a smile plastered on her face as she reaches for not one but *two* shots from the tray.

"Whoa." I put my hand on top of the second as she tosses the first one back. "Slow down, sailor."

"It's my birthday," she says, yanking the shot out from beneath my hand. "I don't have to slow down."

"That's what I'm talking about." Keegan slaps his palm against the table. "How about another round?"

Bailey presses her open hand to Keegan's face, pushing him back in the booth. "What did she say?" she asks Mia.

Mia rolls her shoulders and tilts her head from side to side like a boxer getting ready to enter the ring. "My *mother* said happy birthday. And that—get this—she'd like me to come down to visit so I can meet my new stepdad."

"Your *what*?" Bailey's lip curls in disgust. "She got married and didn't even tell you?"

Mia nods, and the bravado falls from her face. "At least she's happy, though, right?"

"Fuck, fuck, fuck," Bailey says. "And to think I spent my childhood idolizing that bitch."

"That would make two of us," Mia mutters. She ducks her head and avoids all the curious eyes at the table.

"Talk!" Bailey says, scowling at us. "About anything but negligent mothers and pussy boyfriends."

"Bailey!" Mia says, glaring at her best friend.

Bailey shrugs. "Calling it like I see it tonight. Sorry, Mee."

Mason jumps in. "Okay. Who can tell me the dirtiest joke they know?" That does the job, and the guys go around the table exchanging raunchy jokes while Mia composes herself. I know that's what she's doing. I can practically hear her counting out her measured breaths, and she relaxes little by little. The tequila probably doesn't hurt, either.

I don't know what to say. When my mother died, I felt as if I was being ripped in two, but she didn't have a choice. Mia's mom did, and she left anyway. Maybe it wouldn't have sucked so much if she hadn't been a great mother, but I know from the few stories Mia's shared that the woman was the kind of mother daughters adored. The kind they clung to.

Mia cuts her eyes to me and whispers, "You're staring."

Of course I am. She's fucking beautiful. Not looking at Mia

when she's right next to me is like not stepping into the sun after a month of rain. "You want to get out of here?"

She holds my gaze for so long, I expect her to say yes. Instead, she shakes her head and slides out of the booth. "I want to sing."

Bailey snaps her attention away from Keegan's ridiculously raunchy joke and hops up to stand next to Mia. "Fuck yeah, you do!"

Mia snakes her arm through Bailey's and the two make their way to the little stage, and a minute later, the guys at the karaoke station cue up a song. Mia looks happily buzzed as she takes the microphone and begins filling in the vocals to the beat. The screen shows a picture of Adele and the lyrics run across it, but Mia doesn't look at the screen. She simply holds the microphone and uses her voice to show her heartache to every person in the bar.

"Holy shit," Mason says. "Girl's got lungs."

She has more than lungs. She has serious talent. As she sings "Rolling in the Deep," I'm captivated. She sings like no one else is in the room, holding nothing back as she nails every note, using her whole body as she comes to the climax of the song and belts out the chorus.

I don't look away once. I'm not sure I breathe. And when it's over, everyone applauds. She grins at Bailey and hands off the microphone as if she was just playing around and not ripping out her own heart. But I know. This is it. Her *thing*. Mia sings.

Bailey picks a lighter pop song, and Mia stays by the stage while she sings.

"I didn't think it was possible," Keegan says, eyes on the stage, "but Mia Mendez just got hotter."

"*Dude,*" Mason says.

"What?"

"You don't say that shit about your friend's girl." Mason shakes his head. "There's a code."

Chris makes Mason move out of his way so he can get out of the booth, then he comes around to my side and takes Mia's spot. I have to bite my tongue to keep myself from telling him to move. There's no reason I should insist on Mia sitting next to me. Like Mason said. There's a code.

I'm able to successfully move my attention back to my friends while Bailey takes her turn, but when Mia takes the mic again, it's as if they all disappear.

"Do yourself a favor," Chris says under his breath, "and stop staring. You're only torturing yourself and giving these assholes ideas."

I tear my gaze off Mia. "What?"

Chris raises a brow, but doesn't say anything else. In fact, he doesn't bring it up again for the rest of the night. Mia and Bailey come back to the table between songs only to return to the stage. Sometimes they sing solo; sometimes they sing duets. Some other girls take a turn every couple of songs, but mostly, it's the Mia and Bailey show.

When Mia's on stage, Chris asks me questions about our game this Saturday or about our next physiology test. He doesn't bring up Mia again or warn me about the way I look at her, but

I know his every effort to take my attention from the stage is a favor.

I'm just not sure it's a favor I want.

MIA

Arrow: I can't stop thinking about what you did at the Cavern tonight. I had no idea.

My stomach flips when I get the text from Arrow. It's not like I hide my singing from my friends. It's a hobby. Something I love and do for fun. But I'd never done it in front of Arrow before, and I should have known he'd see right through me. He'd know it meant more to me than just some silly thing I do with my friends.

> *Me: I was drinking. It was a mistake.*
> *Arrow: Was it? It didn't feel like a mistake.*
> *Me: We're not talking about this again.*
> *Arrow: Okay, but I'm at your door. Come open it so I can give you something.*

I frown at the clock. It's after eleven. When the last of my tequila buzz left me, I pleaded fatigue, and Mason offered to drive me home. Bailey came too, and the two of them locked themselves in her room a few minutes after we got here.

I put down my phone and go to the door to check the peephole. Sure enough, Arrow's on the other side a few steps back from the door, head bowed, hands tucked into his pockets.

I release the chain from the lock and open the door. "What's going on?"

Bailey and I moved into this apartment at the beginning of the semester, and as far as I know, Arrow hasn't ever been here before. It's odd enough for him to text me—he's had my number since we were planning a surprise for Brogan's last birthday, but he rarely uses it—but to call his showing up in the middle of the night a surprise is an understatement.

He swallows hard and shrugs. "I forgot to give you your birthday present." He leans over and picks up a gift bag I didn't notice before.

"You didn't have to do that."

"You're right," he says. "I didn't have to. But I wanted to." He extends the bag.

"Thank you." I exhale slowly. This is awkward, and it shouldn't be. The only reason it would feel awkward to have a friend visit me in the middle of the night is if he were more than a friend. And he's not. He's my boyfriend's best friend.

At least, that's all he's been to me for months. Then tonight, he leaned over and whispered in my ear, asking if I wanted to leave, and all those old feelings came back full force, like a train racing into the station without brakes.

"Do you want to come in?" I ask, pulling the door open farther.

He holds my gaze for a long beat before shaking his head. "I don't think that would be a good idea, Mia."

My stomach squeezes and then flips. What's that supposed to mean? Is it a bad idea because people would get the wrong idea about us? Or is it a bad idea because he felt it tonight, too—that connection that sparked to life the first day we met and seems to sit there, waiting like two potent chemicals that are safe alone but explosive when mixed? I could ask, but there's no answer that would be okay, so I pick up the bag and nod.

"But how about a walk?" he blurts out. "It's a beautiful night."

"Um." I shrug and set the gift bag just inside the door. "Sure. Why not? Let me grab my phone."

I slip my phone into my pocket in case Brogan calls and then follow Arrow out to the street. The night air cools my burning cheeks. Bailey and I got an apartment close to campus, so it's a nice area with well-lit sidewalks, but tonight the streetlamps are aided by the moon and the stars that shine so brightly above us they seem closer than usual.

"You have the most beautiful voice I've ever heard." The words are so soft—such a scratchy rasp of low sound—that I might mistake them for the breeze rustling through the drying autumn leaves. But he's looking at me and watching my reaction, so I can't pretend I didn't hear.

I can't pretend I don't care that he thinks I'm good. "Thank you."

"You love it. I could see it. You came to life on that stage."

Stop saying sweet things. "You make it sound like I normally walk around half dead."

"Or maybe you walk around pretending that part of you isn't important when it's not just important—it's everything."

"It's a hobby."

"It's a gift."

He hasn't looked at me with this much intensity since the day we met, and I simultaneously want to soak up every bit of his attention and beg him to stop. But tonight I'm tired and a little weak, so I walk along beside him, enjoying his attention and letting the silence stretch out between us.

"I'm sorry you had a crappy birthday," he says, as we turn the corner.

"It wasn't that bad. I was being a little dramatic earlier. I'm fine now."

"Your mom left you and married a guy she didn't even tell you about. I don't think it's dramatic to be upset about that. And Brogan..."

"What about Brogan?"

"Does he make you happy?"

He makes me feel safe. He makes me smile. "That question again?"

"Yeah. I guess so." He drops his gaze to the sidewalk and watches our steps until we reach the end of the block. When we reach the crosswalk, we both stop, as if we need a minute to decide if we're going to go any farther. He watches me, ready to follow my lead.

ARROW

I've never felt as exposed as I do in this moment, waiting for the girl I want to tell me she's happily in love with my best friend. It's not a question I have any right to ask. Brogan might be a pushover when it comes to his mother, but he's a good guy, and all signs indicate that he makes Mia happy.

But I need to hear it from her.

She steps off the sidewalk and into the row of trees. After toeing off her shoes one at a time, she sinks her bare feet into the grass growing beneath the locust tree.

When I came to her apartment, I was going to give her the gift and leave. When I declined her invitation to come inside, she looked baffled, and I was so afraid I'd hurt her, I blurted out that we should go on a walk. I imagine what Chris would say if he knew I'd invited her out here and dared to ask about the state of her and Brogan's relationship. He probably wouldn't say anything. He'd just give me that look that speaks more disappointment than any words can.

"You don't have to answer," I say. "I know you don't like that question, and anyway, it's none of my business." *You wanted him and not me. You chose him, and I don't get to make you happy even if he's failing.*

Sighing, she leans against the locust and steadies her gaze on her bare feet in the grass. "When I was a little girl, my mom would tell me stories about the way Dad swept her off her feet. It was as if they met and fell in love in an instant. She was eighteen and in Chicago visiting some cousins, and one night, Dad showed up at a party. She said the way he looked at her lit her soul on fire. They married less than a month later, despite the objections of my grandmother. She was already pregnant with Nicholas."

Set her soul on fire. I take a breath, fighting to regain the wind I just got knocked out of me. Fuck, that hurts. I don't want him to be the one who sets her soul on fire. "That's how you feel about Brogan."

She meets my eyes for a beat and then looks back down before continuing on with her story. "As we got older, Mom slowly added details to the story. She'd been engaged to a boy back home. A boy who was quickly becoming a man. A good man who made her smile and kept her safe. She said he was the steady, reliable warmth of the sun, and my father was the flash and heat and passion of the fire."

My gut knots because I think I know where she's going with this and I don't like it.

She tugs her bottom lip between her teeth. This time when

she lifts her gaze to mine, she holds it. "Mom didn't leave a good marriage. Dad was moody and jealous. Their life was never half the things he promised her it would be. I knew that any fire they'd had between them had burned out years ago. The day she left, she told me she'd been greedy. She'd been content with her boy back home, her steady warmth, but she'd met my father and was seduced by the excitement of the fire. She said the best thing I could do for my life was choose the steady warmth. The sun isn't going anywhere, but eventually the fire runs out of fuel. I'm not saying that Brogan is perfect, but no one is."

"That's a nice metaphor," I say softly, "but you're not your mother, and Brogan isn't some sweet kid you left behind in Mexico. Does he make you happy, Mia? It's not a hard question."

"It's not his job to make me happy. It's my job."

"But are you?"

"Why are you pushing this?"

Because I'm in love with you, and I need to know I'm not making a mistake by keeping that to myself. "I'm pissed at him," I say. I'm a fucking coward. "I told him as much myself when I found out he canceled on you this weekend. And don't stand there and tell me it doesn't matter when you and I both know it does. I was there last spring when his grandma died, remember? I remember how it made you feel when his mom didn't want you at the hospital."

She pushes away from the tree and wraps her arms around her middle. "I want to go home now."

Fuck. I pushed her too much. Too far.

We walk back in silence, and she doesn't look at me until we reach the door to her apartment. She turns to me and leans against it. Her hair falls over one shoulder, and her cheeks are pink from the wind. I want so badly to step closer and kiss her that my stomach aches with it.

"Thanks for coming over, Arrow. I do appreciate your concern for me. You're a good friend."

A good friend. "Just . . ." I have to look away. How am I supposed to look into those deep brown eyes and not fall harder? "I'll always be here for you. If you need a friend."

The door clicks as the deadbolt releases. Mia steps forward, and the door cracks open. Bailey peeks out at us, her hair tousled, her eyes squinting against the light in the corridor. "What the hell are you two doing out here?"

"Arrow just stopped by to give me a birthday present," Mia says.

Bailey raises a brow and opens the door the rest of the way. "Is that so?"

Mia steps inside and grabs the gift bag, lifting it up for Bailey's inspection.

Bailey looks at me then Mia. "What is it?"

"I haven't opened it yet," Mia says. She opens the bag and pulls out the tissue paper.

I flinch. I didn't really want her to do this with an audience. "You don't have to—"

She pulls the small canvas from the bag, and her jaw goes slack and her eyes soften.

"Oh," Bailey says. "It's a painting. It's—"

"Dancing fairies," Mia says, skimming her fingers across the words in the bottom corner of the canvas. "Where did you find this?"

One of my mom's best friends is an artist, and after the night last spring when I lay under that tree with Mia, I got the idea to commission her to paint this.

"It's like the stories your mom would tell us when we were kids," Bailey says, studying the painting of the stars peeking through the moonlit tree branches. "Wow."

"This is the most thoughtful gift anyone—" Mia bites her lip, as if she won't allow herself to finish that thought. I want to revel in the moment and enjoy Mia's reaction, but I can't with Bailey standing there, scowling at me, seeing too much.

She doesn't like that I gave this gift to Mia. She doesn't like that I showed up here in the middle of the night when Mia was having a rough day. Maybe she thinks I'm encroaching on Brogan's territory.

Maybe she's right.

"I don't know what to say, Arrow," Mia says. "Thank you."

"You're welcome." I shift awkwardly under Bailey's scrutiny. "I should go."

Bailey nods. "Night, Arrow."

I can't take my eyes off Mia and the way she holds my gift. As if it's the most precious thing she's ever received.

Bailey clears her throat and gives me a hard look. "Drive safely."

"Happy birthday, Mia."

When I get back to the dorm, Chris is awake and sitting in the common area between our rooms. "You okay?" he asks me. His voice is low, but with Mason with Bailey and Brogan out of town, there isn't anyone to overhear.

I frown. "Why wouldn't I be?"

"Because." He tosses his magazine on the end table before turning back to me. "I see how you look at her."

I shake my head. "No. She's just a friend."

He gives a sad smile. "And yet out of all the girls in the bar tonight, you didn't even have to ask which I was talking about."

Fuck. I study my shoes and shrug. "It doesn't matter."

"Just be careful."

PART V: AFTER

ARROW

I'm not prepared to see Brogan again, but here I am.

I'm not sure what made me decide to come. Maybe it was busting the shit out of my hand and breaking a couple of bones. Maybe it was hearing Mia tell me she doesn't regret the night we spent together in October when I thought I was nothing more to her than a regret. Maybe it was my dad's endless lecture on the way to the ER—how foolish I am, how this could screw up my football career. I wanted to tell him there are things that matter more than football. I thought of Brogan.

Whatever the reason, this morning, with a fresh cast and a bottle of painkillers I won't take, I came here.

I told myself not to expect any change, braced myself to see him looking as bad as he did months ago, shortly after his parents had taken him home. But I wasn't prepared for him to look worse. Smaller. A shadow of the man he used to be.

"Thank you again for coming," Mrs. Barrett says behind me.

"I'll leave you two alone."

I don't know what to do with myself. Brogan sits in his wheelchair, strapped in so his body doesn't fall forward. His eyes are open, his jaw slack.

My stomach suddenly feels completely empty of anything, and acid crawls up my throat. And my eyes—I blink—I'm *not* going to fucking cry right now.

For a while, I was grateful Brogan didn't die that night, grateful he had a chance to fight. But seeing him like this, I know he got the worse fate.

He was a proud man, and I hate to think how he'd feel about Mia seeing him like this every time she visits.

When Mrs. Barrett opened the door, she asked if I've prayed for a miracle today. Every time I see him this way, I say a little prayer that God will have mercy on this proud man. After more than four months as a vegetable, I pray he'll be allowed to die. Before, the prayer was blanketed with shame, guilt that I'd wish for such a thing. But not today. Mia believes Brogan is conscious and aware of his world, but I don't. I think he's gone. Nothing but a brainstem keeping Brogan's body alive with the assistance of a feeding tube. But I'm here anyway. In case I'm wrong.

"I'm supposed to talk to you," I say quietly. "It's supposed to bring me closure."

He doesn't respond. Of course. He can't. God, wouldn't it be nice if Mia were right? If Brogan could have the same fate as the guy who woke up after being in a persistent vegetative state for twelve years? If Brogan could be the miracle Mrs. Barrett asks everyone to pray for?

I could say, "Hey, remember that fight?" and he could say, "Yeah, I was a fucking idiot. And so were you." Then we could hug it out like a couple of teenage girls.

What would that be like for him? Waking up and finding himself in this body? Learning to walk all over again? He had so many broken bones and torn-up ligaments and tendons that even before they were sure about the state of his brain, they said he'd never play football again.

I hang my head. "I won't be playing ball next year. I got out of it the only way I knew how. Wouldn't have been right to be on the field without you." I sigh. "But you know Dad. He's already pulling strings right and left to try to get me back in the game as soon as possible."

A robin lands on the bird feeder outside the window, and I watch it peck at the food.

"I'm worried about Mia. We all lost so much that night, but it's like she was a casualty, too, and nobody noticed."

The bird flies away, and I put my good hand on top of Brogan's, testing the feel of his too-pliant flesh against my palm. This is the part where I'm supposed to say sorry. I'm supposed to apologize for not being a better friend, for getting in the way, for every dumb-ass decision I made that night.

But I can't. It doesn't seem right to force-feed him an apology he won't be able to reject. I don't deserve his forgiveness.

Mrs. Barrett walks into the room and gives me a sad smile. "Thought I'd check and see if you'd like some coffee."

I wonder if she knows she's rescuing me from myself right now.

I release Brogan's hand and nod as I stand and follow her to the kitchen. "That would be nice."

"He looks good today, doesn't he?" she asks over her shoulder.

No. He looks broken and empty. A shell of a man.

I smile instead of answering, and she shakes her head. "Sorry. I'm used to Mia's visits. Saying what she needs to hear." Her hands shake as she pulls two mugs from the cabinet and picks up the coffee pot. "I'm not blind. I do know how he really looks."

She hands me a steaming mug, and I take a sip, letting the hot, bitter liquid scald my tongue. "Mia's not handling this very well, is she?"

"No." Mrs. Barrett wraps her hands around her mug and stares into it. "I wasn't very kind to her while she and Brog were dating, and now I feel a little responsible for her. I should have been a better mother. Accepted her instead of worrying that he could have been with someone better." She shakes her head, and her eyes fill with tears. "Sometimes the price of perspective is just too high."

I don't know what to say, so I steal my therapist's words, rewriting them to work for Mrs. Barrett. "You loved Brogan. You were the best mom you knew how to be." I'm almost surprised when the words fit between us, right where they need to go. When the doctor said them to me, they felt like just another platitude. "Let the rest go."

"His kidneys are failing." Tears wet her mascara-caked lashes and spill onto her cheeks, bringing smudges of eye makeup with them. "I keep praying that God will show me the way, but I don't know what I'm supposed to do. The doctors don't really think we should begin dialysis, but if we don't . . ."

Let him go. The words sit trapped in my throat. *Please, let him go.*

"I think maybe it's time for Brogan to join Jesus."

Let him. I stare at her, willing her to feel the words I don't dare speak. Would Mia hate me if she knew I felt this way? If she knew my greatest wish was for her boyfriend's death?

She clears her throat and wipes away her tears. "We haven't told Mia yet. I just want to be sure before I break her heart. Can you keep this secret?"

I nod, but I don't dare speak. My throat's too thick, my heart too full of secrets to carry another.

MIA

"This dinner is important to Uriah," Gwen says, smoothing an invisible wrinkle in her skirt. "Make sure everyone's wine stays full and their dinners are served while hot." She takes a deep breath, and I almost feel sorry for her. It must be hard having to play the part of the perfect trophy wife all the time. But then she ruins it. "And try not to look at Arrow like he's your celebrity crush, okay?"

My jaw clenches. "Not a problem. When will Katie be back?"

"Mom's going to keep her all night. I don't know how long Uriah's guests are going to stay, and I didn't want you distracted by your duties tonight with a fussy baby."

"Right." Damn, this job was easier when I liked Gwen, but she's been increasingly bitchy since Arrow's been home.

"You said your friend was going to help you?"

"Bailey's in the kitchen. She has lots of experience serving, so don't worry." I don't mention that most of that experience took place behind the doors of the Pretty Kitty.

The doorbell sounds at the same time as the buzzer rings from the kitchen.

"Let's do this," Gwen says. Her hands tremble slightly and she smooths her skirt, letting me peek at the insecurities beneath her bitchy façade for a split second.

When I step into the kitchen, Bailey already has the oven open. "The hors d'oeuvres are ready." She pulls out the pan and wrinkles her nose. "What is this shit?"

"Shh!" I look over my shoulder to make sure no one else is in here, but of course, the guests are just arriving and oblivious to Bailey's potty mouth. Loud, forced laughter carries in from the foyer and across the hall. "It's escargot wrapped in bacon," I tell Bailey, grabbing the glass serving platter I'll present them on.

"Escar— That's snail, isn't it? That's just the fancy-people way of saying *snails*."

"Can't get anything by you, Bail."

"Just looking at them makes me want to gag. No way would I put something that disgusting in my mouth."

"Never stopped you before," a deep voice says from the hallway door.

Bailey spins around to put a face to the asshole, but her glare softens when she sees Mason. Bailey can take razzing from Mason because she knows he doesn't mean it. Anybody else would probably have a knee in the balls by now.

"I made a one-time exception for you," she says, batting her lashes.

"Don't think I don't appreciate it." He looks over his shoulder toward the dining room, then shuts the door behind him and lowers his voice. "What the fuck happened to Arrow's hand?"

The question kicks at my heart like a couple of shock paddles.

"Do you remember? I need to know."

"I don't regret it."

Bailey and Mason both stare at me, and I realize I haven't answered. "The idiot punched a picture frame, but it was hung on a stud, so instead of busting right through the wall, he broke two bones in his hand."

His dad came out of his room while I was trying to get Arrow upstairs, and he took over. It was pathetic how much I wanted to be the one to take Arrow to the ER. Would he have kept talking?

"Ouch," Mason says, massaging his own knuckles. "That's . . ." He shakes out his hand. "His *hand*."

"His hand is his hand?" Bailey asks. "Aren't you the genius?"

"You know what I'm saying. How's he supposed to play ball with his hand all banged up? I know he's out for this season, but he could have fucked it up long-term."

"It's like that's the point," I whisper. I hate the way he looked at his busted hand—as if it were inconsequential.

"If you're in the kitchen, you have to help," Bailey tells Mason, and I'm grateful for the change in subject.

Mason grins and unbuttons the cuffs of his gray Oxford, the one that makes his green eyes even dreamier than normal and his dark skin look like melted chocolate. He rolls up his sleeves.

"Honestly, I'm more comfortable serving than being served. Put me to work."

"Mason," I say. "We can't let you help. Gwen would kill us."

Bailey presses the palm of her hand to my chest, gently pushing me away from Mason. "Mia, the sexy man is offering to do the dishes. Let him, please?"

I roll my eyes. "Get out of here, Mason. Gwen would be horrified to know the staff was fraternizing with one of her guests."

He arches a brow. "The *staff*? That's not seriously how you see yourself?"

"That is literally what we are." I nudge him toward the hall. "So get out of here."

Mason turns pleading eyes on Bailey. "Don't make me go out there, Bail. They're talking about the year of the wine, and I can't pretend to care."

"Who's out there anyway?" Bailey asks. "We were told it was a party for some of Uriah's friends."

He grunts then drops his voice to a whisper. "Mr. Woodison is kissing ass. This dinner is all about sweet-talking Coach. I'm just here to make it less awkward, but Arrow's mood is so foul you could have the whole team at that table and it would still be uncomfortable as fuck."

I snap my gaze around to Mason. "Arrow's in there?" Gwen's comment about not looking at Arrow should have tipped me off, but I just thought he'd be *around,* not at the table. I don't know why I assumed he'd stay in his room. He's on house arrest, not solitary confinement. But I don't want to have to look at him tonight. I don't want his angry eyes watching me while I serve dinner and refill their drinks.

"I'd better get out of here," Mason says. He gives Bailey a final once-over that's so suggestive it makes *me* blush. "Stay out of trouble, sexy."

"Fuck, he's hot," she says when he's gone.

I should totally take this opportunity to give her the third degree about Mason. This time last year, they were still screwing like bunnies and insisting their relationship was "platonic."

Everything changed after Nic was released from prison and Bailey's head got all screwed up about him again. Now Nic's gone, Mason seems as interested as ever, and I'm the world's worst friend because I honestly don't know where she stands with him.

I check my tray to make sure the snails didn't slide around too much when I dropped it, and when I take a breath to broach the subject, Bailey smacks me between the shoulder blades. "I won't ask you about Arrow if you don't ask me about Mason."

Our eyes meet and she gives me her special *I've got your back* smile. It's not like the brazen grin she gives the world, and it doesn't meet her eyes the way a smile should, but it's the smile of the girl I've known since I was a child. The one who taught me to practice kissing on the inside of my hand. The one who left half her dinner on my deck when times were tight. The one who'd throw a punch to anyone who looked at me funny. It's the smile of a friend who wants you to know she's still there, and even when everything else changes, your friendship won't.

"Thanks," I whisper.

"Let's get this over with."

ARROW

"Where's Trish tonight, Coach?" my father asks. Coach shifts his gaze to mine before meeting my father's eyes again. "She had plans with some friends, I'm afraid."

"We would have loved to see her, but I understand. Kids are busy these days, aren't they?"

I guess I should count my blessings. The only thing that would make this night more awkward for me would be trying to eat dinner while having my dad play matchmaker. I've gotten the lecture already. He saw the pictures from New Year's Eve. He's on Facebook like everyone else.

"If you're going to fuck around with the coach's daughter, you'd better be planning to buy the girl a ring."

It was never about Trish. Dad's not that kind of guy. It was about football and how my relationship with Trish might be a politically risky move for my place on the team. My best friend was fighting for his life in the hospital, and my dad thought I needed lectures about keeping my dick in my pants.

A tall, bearded guy joins us in the dining room. Sebastian Crowe. He was my quarterback my last year at West High School. A year younger than me, he always had a chip on his shoulder. He spent his first year of college playing running back at Purdue. Recognition must flash across my face, because Coach gives me an apologetic wince.

"Uriah," Coach says, his hand on Sebastian's back. "This is Sebastian Crowe. He's the transfer from Purdue, and we're excited to see what he can do on offense next year."

"Nice to meet you, Mr. Woodison," Sebastian says, taking my dad's hand.

My father is hosting a meal for the BHU coaches and a few of the starters for next year. I'm grateful to have Mason here, but seeing Sebastian Crowe is a kick in the nuts. And that's exactly what my dad wanted it to be.

Sebastian transferred in this fall. Something about being close to his grandma, but rumor is he couldn't get along with the coach at Purdue and mouthed off one too many times during his freshman year. Of course, NCAA rules state that players can't play the first year they transfer to a new team, so he had to sit this year out. Brogan was worried sick about Sebastian's move. It wasn't likely Coach was going to give Sebastian my position, but Brogan's had always been up for grabs. I told him not to worry about it. I wouldn't have had half the yards I did last year if Brog wasn't blocking for me, and anyone who knows what they're looking at can see that on the film. But now neither of us is playing next year, paving the way for Sebastian to step in and be the hero.

Whatever. Football is the least of my worries. It doesn't even seem important in the light of everything else. But that doesn't mean knowing someone can replace me doesn't gnaw on something in my gut.

There are awkward smiles all around as we find our seats at the dining room table.

Sebastian takes the seat across from me and inclines his chin. "Hey."

I nod. "Hey."

His gaze settles on my cast-covered hand resting on the table. "What happened?"

"I got into a fight with a wall. I lost."

Sebastian grimaces. "It's your *hand,* man."

I set my jaw and return Sebastian's worried stare with my cold one.

He shifts his attention to Gwen. "Thanks for inviting us to dinner, Mrs. Woodison."

She beams at him. "We love having company. You're welcome anytime."

Dad opens his napkin and positions it on his lap. "We just want to make it clear that the BHU football program has our full support. Even though Arrow's not playing this year, we still want to be a part of making the season a successful one. That means exactly what it did last year—the boys can watch film in the theater room anytime they want, and of course the team will get my usual monetary support."

I want to kiss your ass and make sure Arrow still has a spot on the team when he comes back, I mentally translate.

I eye the door to the kitchen, willing Mason to reappear. He's my ally tonight. Chris is visiting his mom in Texas and couldn't come, though I don't think I'd care for watching my QB bond with my replacement.

Gwen follows my gaze and shifts uncomfortably. "The appetizers should be out anytime," she says. "I apologize for the delay."

"Can I interest anyone in a drink?" Dad asks, scanning the table.

Sebastian takes a drink of his water. "I'm good, sir."

"I have a nice Syrah or a single-malt scotch," Dad offers. "Arrow won't be drinking tonight, of course. He lost that right." He laughs awkwardly, and I want to punch him in the face just so I don't have to hear it anymore. "What do you say, Coach?"

Mason emerges from the kitchen and takes the spot beside me, but I don't have the chance to be relieved before Mia and Bailey follow behind him, trays of appetizers in their hands.

"There they are," Gwen says. Her cooing tone is contrary to the sharp disapproval in her eyes.

Mia avoids my gaze as she places the tray in the center of the table. "Escargot wrapped in bacon," she says, pointing to her tray. Bailey settles her tray next to it, and Mia points to it and says, "And bacon-wrapped dates."

"Woodison pork all around, of course," Bailey says with a smile that's a touch too forced.

"Can I get anyone anything before I serve the entrees?" Mia asks. Her eyes scan the table and freeze when they land on Sebastian. I swear I can see her tense. "Sebastian?"

He grins and shamelessly slides his gaze over her, from her white button-up shirt to her black skirt and down her bare legs. "Hey, Mia."

My stomach knots. This fucker isn't just taking over my position on the team; there's something proprietary about the way he looks at Mia. And she's looking at him like . . . like she has a secret and he's holding it for her.

"Do you know each other?" my father asks, directing his question to Sebastian.

"Not really," Mia says at the same time as Sebastian says, "Sure do." He hasn't taken his eyes off her since she walked into the room, and he narrows his gaze now, his lips quirking.

"Mia's our live-in help," Gwen says. "She's made herself quite useful since my Katie was born."

I don't trust myself not to glare in Gwen's general direction, so I drop my gaze to my hands. *The help.* I hate hearing Mia described like that, and I hate watching her act like it.

"You work here?" Sebastian says. "That's interesting." He finally takes his eyes off her and looks at my father. "I know Mia's father. He lives by my gram."

"What are you doing here, anyway?" Mia asks him.

"Mia!" Gwen says. "Forgive her rudeness, Sebastian.

She typically cares for the baby. She doesn't understand the appropriate way to act in these situations."

"I apologize," she says quickly.

Sebastian grins. "Nothing inappropriate about her question, ma'am. Mia probably doesn't know I'm on the team." He shifts his gaze to me. "I haven't been traveling in the same social circles as the rest of the guys, since I wasn't playing last season."

"Well, that's about to change," Dad says. "Seriously, the boys are welcome here anytime, and that offer stands for you, too, son. I forget you were raised in Blackhawk Valley. Is it good to be home?"

"It's always good to be close to family."

Bailey busies herself filling water glasses, and Mia bites her lip and stares at Sebastian. For the first time it occurs to me that maybe she didn't tell her father about working here. Her old man would probably go on a tear if he knew. Does *Sebastian* know that?

"You should probably go check on dinner," Gwen says to Mia.

Mia nods and scurries out of the room, Bailey not far behind.

MIA

"Did you know Mr. Muscles was on the team?" Bailey asks. "Because *damn*. Sebastian Mother-May-I? And the way he was looking at you? I think he would have tried to devour you whole if he didn't have an audience."

I pull the broiling pan from the oven and sprinkle the filet with blue cheese crumbles before sliding the pan back in to let it melt. "You have an overactive imagination. He was looking at me like that because he knows how my dad would feel about me working here. Not everything is sexual."

"Not *everything*." She cuts a slit in each of the foil-wrapped potatoes and then positions them on the plates lining the counter. "But *most* things, and definitely the way he was eye-fucking you."

Sebastian definitely wasn't *eye-fucking* me—he was looking at me like a guy who knows how my father would feel about my job—but there's no use arguing any such thing with Bailey. She sees what she wants to see.

We work in silence for a few minutes, then she sighs heavily and turns to me. "Ask me about Mason."

"What? Why?"

"I've been good. I don't ask questions. I don't demand you tell me things normal best friends tell each other. So ask me about Mason so I can talk about the damn elephant in the room."

I fold my arms. "Fine. What's going on with you and Mason?"

"Nothing. I broke it off when Nic got out of prison."

"I remember." She fed me some bullshit excuse about things getting too serious between the two of them, but I knew the truth. Nic was home, and she needed to be available.

"Mason has been nothing but a friend for me since," she says. "Trust me, I wanted more after Nic died, but Mason says we can't be just sex anymore. He said we're in too deep for that, so he's holding out. No sex unless I'll be his *girlfriend,* and you and I both know I'm not in a place to sign up for that. So. Your turn."

"Wait. Slow down. Mason won't sleep with you?"

"Selfish motherfucker, isn't he?"

I bite my lip. "I kind of respect his restraint. He cares about you, and he wants more. It's sweet."

She narrows her eyes. "It's sexual blackmail." Grabbing the potholder, she opens the oven, pulls out the steaks, and begins adding them to the plates. I follow behind her with the green beans.

"Let's get these on the table before they get cold," I say, grabbing a few plates.

We serve dinner and refill drinks. Sebastian watches me with undisguised curiosity the whole time, but we're able to escape the dining room without another awkward conversation.

"The elephant!" Bailey says when we're back in the kitchen.

"What's the elephant?"

She grabs my hand and pulls me into the living room and out the French doors. "Arrow. I'm going to be honest, I was hoping him coming home might be good for you. Good for you both." Her eyes are soft and gentle, and I know all I have to do is say that I don't want to talk about it and she'll let it drop.

"I'm the reason Brogan was in the middle of the street in the middle of the night. Arrow should hate me for that. How could being around him be good for me?"

She tilts her head and squeezes my shoulder. "I thought maybe he'd help you live your life instead of hiding from it."

"I'm not hiding." The words come out sharper than I intend.

"Don't be mad. I'm being selfish. I never see you anymore. I miss you."

"You're not selfish." I drop my gaze to my hands. I hoped the fresh air would do me good, but the night is hot and I can't breathe much better out here than I could in there. "And you're not the first person to say I'm not really living. Arrow has said the same thing." If I've been avoiding my life it isn't a conscious choice, but I understand why they see it that way. I didn't think it mattered. Who cares if I just go through the motions? Who cares if I never feel sincerely happy again?

I know Bailey cares. And I guess Arrow does, too. I'm not

sure what to make of that.

"Do you ever wish you'd picked Arrow?" she asks softly.

Lifting my head, I study the wispy clouds floating across the starry night sky. "I don't know. All I know is that I wish we hadn't been out there that night. I wish Brogan could still laugh and Nic could still be my overprotective big brother. I don't think of what would have happened if I'd picked Arrow." I swallow hard, pushing down tears before they surge too high. "I think, what would things be like if I'd stayed away from both of them like I said I would when I met them? Brogan would be himself. We wouldn't have been out there that night. And Nicholas would still be alive."

"Are you okay, Mee? I mean, do you need to talk to someone?"

"I'm talking to you."

"You've been through a lot. No one expects you to be Wonder Woman. I'm just saying . . ." She finds my hand and squeezes. "If you ever think not living would be easier than living, call me first, okay?"

"Okay," I say. I swallow hard. I remember talking to her about *Romeo and Juliet* the night I met Arrow. We laughed, remembering what an idiot Juliet was. I never understood her before. Not really. But now I can imagine what it was like to wake up in that tomb and see Romeo dead beside her. The guilt. The grief. I'm not looking for a dagger, and I don't want to die. But there are days—maybe more than I want to admit—when I don't want to live either. "I'm not Juliet," I whisper. "Don't worry about that."

"Damn straight you're not," she says, "because you've got me. You wake up from the poison and instead of grabbing the dagger to stab into your heart when you see Romeo is dead, I drag your ass out of there and point out that the friar is pretty fucking fly, too."

"The friar?" That is *so* Bailey it makes me laugh, only it's not the forced laugh I've been pushing through my lips for months. It's real, and something brightens inside the darkness in my chest. "If only Shakespeare had given Juliet someone like you."

"Would have been a better play."

We grin at each other and settle into silence. It's so pretty out here with the stars and the lights reflecting off the pool.

"Dinner was great," someone says behind us, and just like that the moment of tranquility fizzles into thin air. Sebastian closes the doors behind him and takes the steps down to the patio. "But I have to admit, you were the last person I expected to see here tonight."

I shrug. "Now you know how I feel. Why did you let me think you were a mechanic?"

He unbuttons his shirt sleeves and rolls them to his elbows. "Because I *am* a mechanic, Mia. Dad's owned the shop all my life, and I practically grew up there."

"You made me believe—"

"You assumed," he says, his voice gentler than the truth. "Not all of us are like Woodison and get to play our way through college and have everything we need handed to us."

I tense. "He's not like that."

"And how much do you know about what Woodison is and isn't like?" He turns his head and scans the brick façade of the backside of the house. "You two must be pretty cozy living here together."

"Oh, fuck off," Bailey says. "Don't act like you have to work for your meal ticket and then judge her for taking a really fucking great job."

He turns. "I don't think I was talking to you."

Bailey leans against the side of the house and rolls her head from side to side. "When you're out here trying to shame my girl? You might as well be talking to me."

"Bailey, it's okay." I turn to Sebastian. "There's nothing going on between me and Arrow, but please don't tell my dad I'm working here. He would freak."

"And yet here you are," Sebastian says.

"Somebody's gotta pay the bills."

I expect more argument—that there are other jobs in town, that this isn't the only choice I have—but I don't get any. Sebastian nods slowly. "I get that."

"Crap," Bailey says. She wipes the back of her hand across her sweaty forehead. "Mrs. Woodison is in the kitchen. I bet she's looking for us."

"I've got it." I start in that direction, but Bailey grabs my arm and shakes her head.

"No. You and Mr. Muscles here go ahead and finish whatever it is you need to talk about. I'll take care of Trophy Wife."

"Bailey," I say, warning in my tone.

She holds up both hands. "*Gwen*, I know. *Gwen*. I'll behave. I promise."

She disappears inside the house, and I give my attention back to Sebastian. He watches me, his head tilted to the side, his eyes narrowed slightly.

"What?" I ask.

"Is it true you're waiting for Brogan?" he asks. "That's the rumor, you know. That you were already committed to him so you're his until he dies."

I look longingly toward the pool. It's so hot out here. I can't wait for everyone to leave so I can dive under the water and swim so hard and long there's no more room for thoughts in my head. No room for wondering how Arrow feels about me. No room for the guilt and regret and constant second-guessing of every decision I made that night.

I swallow hard. "That's the rumor?" I hate the idea of people talking about me, but I suppose what they're saying could be worse.

"Seems a little dramatic. You're so young. I know you love him, but . . ."

I was trying to break up with him that night. That's why we were arguing. That's why he wouldn't let me out of the car. That's why I had to get my brother to come save me. That's why they were in the street . . .

Sebastian studies me, and I wish I could turn off my thoughts rather than risk him seeing them on my face. "There's also a rumor that you were pregnant with his baby and that's why you haven't left his side." His gaze drifts to my stomach and then back up. "But I imagine that would be noticeable by now if it were true."

I release a dry laugh. "No truth to that one, I'm afraid."

"You see," he says, "I look at you and I see a gorgeous young woman who has her whole life ahead of her." He takes a step back and tucks his hands into his pockets. "I see someone I'd like to get to know, someone I'd like to make smile when she's ready to smile again. But I can't decide if your little research project is going to help you move on or if it's going to trap you in the past even longer."

I stare at the patio, not sure what to say and too tired to try.

"Yeah, so that's where I am," he says. "If you were wondering. That's why you don't have your list yet. Because I like you, and I don't want to do anything that's going to make you hurt longer than you already have."

I close my eyes and hear him walk away. His steps across the patio, the click of the French doors opening and then closing.

Alone, I look up into the night sky. By warning me off this search, Sebastian's trying to protect me from some faceless demon. He doesn't understand the demon already has me in its claws.

ARROW

"Is Mia going to join us?" Sebastian looks over his shoulder to the light coming from the kitchen window.

"I told her to come out here," Bailey says with a huff. "Miss Antisocial doesn't even have the baby as an excuse tonight."

Since Katie is with Gwen's mom, Coach Wright insisted on taking Dad and Gwen out for a drink, and after Dad gave me a long, hard stare that told me he thought I might bust up the other hand while unsupervised, they left. Mason and—unfortunately—fucking Sebastian hung around, and everyone moved to the patio to play cards. Everyone except Mia.

I push my chair back and stand. "I'll get her."

Bailey arches a brow. "Yeah. Good luck with that."

Ignoring her skepticism, I head inside and find Mia in the kitchen sterilizing bottles.

She jumps when she sees me. "Arrow." Ever since the night she accused me of hating her and I told her I wanted her, she's been like this any time I'm around. As if she's afraid of me. Except for the night I broke my hand. She wasn't afraid of me that night.

"Because you regret it and I should, too."

"Do you need me to do anything for you?" Mia asks.

My back teeth slam together. I fucking hate when she acts like my servant. "Yeah. Actually, you can."

Surprise registers on her face but she tries to hide it with a plastic smile. She pulls the last bottle from the steaming water, flips off the stove, and turns to face me, her back against the counter. "Great. What's that?"

"Take the night off. Katie's gone. Gwen's not even here. Come outside and hang with us, and anything on that list of yours that you don't get done, I'll help you with tomorrow."

She opens her mouth—probably to object—and then closes it again.

"Please," I whisper, stepping closer.

She sneaks a look out the window and tugs her bottom lip between her teeth. "I don't know how to do it anymore."

"Do what?" I take a final step and stop, because if I step any closer we'll be touching.

She keeps her eyes on the window. "Be like them."

A puff of laughter escapes my lips, and she looks back to me, frowning. "You were never like them, Mia. And I don't think that's what you mean at all."

Her eyes search my face. "Then what do I mean?"

"You don't know how to *live* anymore."

"What's the point, Arrow?" She shakes her head. "I can't even feel anything."

God, this woman's going to break my heart. "Close your eyes." At first, I don't think she's going to do it, not with as tense as things have been between us, but then she does.

I take half a step closer, brush the hair off her neck, and lower my mouth to her ear. When the scent of her fills my senses, time skips like an old record hitting a scratch and backing up to a better song. I'm back in the car with her, watching the morning sun stretch out over the water, her body tucked into mine.

"What are you doing?"

"Reminding you," I say against her ear. My hands find her waist first, settling at the top of her hips and waiting for permission. It comes in the slightest shift of her body toward mine, the barest arch of her neck to give my mouth better access to her ear.

It's so easy to slip my hand under the hem of her skirt. So natural to put my hand between her legs. She gasps, but instead of stepping away, she drops her head to my shoulder, wraps one arm behind my neck, and uses the other to brace herself against the counter. Just this—her letting me touch her, her responding to my touch like this—is enough to have me hard and aching against the fly of my jeans.

"I wonder if you have any idea how often I think about this." I scrape my teeth against her ear and chase the guilt away by telling myself this is for her. I can't stand seeing her moving through life like the walking dead, and if all I can give her is this . . .

I tug her panties down so my fingers can explore the sensitive flesh between her legs. Again my brain treats me to flashes of the night at the lake and the next morning when I spread her out on her bed and put my mouth between her legs.

"Do you feel that?" I ask as I take her clit between two fingers. And I know she does, because her hand tightens around the back of my neck, her nails biting into the skin. But I want an answer, so I graze my thumb along that swollen piece of flesh and ask again, "Does the numbness go away when I touch you?"

"Yes." She lifts her hips, pressing into my hand in a wordless plea that I'm helpless to resist. I slide a finger inside her and hear my own groan as her tight heat envelopes me.

She takes a fistful of my shirt as she tries to pull me closer, and I focus on the sounds of her breathing, the slick heat of her body as I stroke her. Maybe, just maybe, I'm pulling air deeper into my lungs than I have in months. Maybe my blood's pumping harder, sending sensation buzzing through nerve endings that have gone numb with disregard. Maybe she's not the only one waking up.

"You're beautiful," I say. "I don't even know if I deserve to look at you, but some days it feels like you're the only piece of beauty left in the world."

She draws in a ragged breath and circles her hips in one last effort to control her need before she fully fucks my hand, grinding against me, pushing my fingers deeper. I tug her earlobe between my teeth then drop lower, latching on to her neck and sucking hard until she moans. With every sound, her movements grow more frantic, as if I woke her and she discovered she's been sleeping underwater and is now desperate to swim to the surface.

"You are beautiful," I repeat, my face between her breasts now. I straighten so I can look into her eyes. I want to see Mia undone. I want to know I can still do that for her. "And you're alive."

"Only when you touch me." Her nails bite into the back of my neck, and her sex squeezes tight around my finger. She arches her back and sinks her teeth into her bottom lip, and I can only watch in awe as she comes.

Beautiful isn't the word. It's grown too weak with overuse. Mia is something greater than that. Bigger. Brighter. More important.

I remove my hand from between her legs and swallow hard as I back away. She opens her eyes and brings her fingertips to her mouth. Because I didn't kiss her there? Because she wishes I did? Or because she said something she wishes she hadn't?

"I need this job," she whispers. Her big brown eyes sparkle with tears.

"No, you don't. Quit, Mia. I have money. I'll pay whatever my father's paying you."

"Would it be worth it? Just to get me away from you?"

"It would be worth it to make you stop hiding from your life. You didn't die with your brother. You aren't brain-dead like Brogan. Stop acting like you lost your life that night. You don't have to live in this purgatory you've created for yourself."

"Me?" Her eyes go big. Too big. Angry. Outraged. "Look who's talking, Arrow. You had *everything,* and you threw every bit of it away so you didn't have to face the pain of living your life without Brogan by your side. I know you feel responsible because of what happened between us, but *I* was the one who decided to tell him. *I* was the one who broke up with him. I was the one who texted my brother when Brogan wouldn't let me out of the car."

I squeeze my eyes shut. It's easier to think of Brogan as a saint who was wronged than a jealous man holding Mia hostage and demanding her heart as ransom.

When I open my eyes, Mia's brimming tears finally spill over and course in rivulets down her cheeks. "Maybe I'm living in purgatory," she says, "but that's only because I deserve worse."

Mia blaming herself for *my* crime is buckshot to the soul. "Don't say that." I thread my fingers into her hair and cup her jaw. Maybe if I can hold her together, I won't fall apart. And the fact that I even care about myself is a revelation. "You didn't do anything wrong."

"Didn't I?" She reaches up and wraps her fingers around my wrist. "Thank you for not blaming me. But if you want to help me forgive myself, you have to stop being a casualty of that night. Seeing your life fall apart too is nothing more than another punishment for me."

"Don't let it be. You were never the one I was trying to punish." I close my mouth and swallow back words before more can rush out. I've said too much already.

Releasing my wrist, she lifts her hand to my face, tracing the edge of my jaw, then my lips. Even after what I just did to her—*especially* after that—the touch feels like the most intimate one we've exchanged. I turn my face into her hand and press a kiss to the center of her palm.

"I don't understand what you want," she says. "You send me away and then you come in here and touch me."

"I don't want to be your mistake." I don't know if I'm talking about tonight or last October, or maybe there's no difference. She said she doesn't regret October, but tonight . . .?

She opens her mouth as if she wants to reply, but then she stops herself, darts her tongue out to wet her lips. I need to taste her there. It's as much a choice as taking the next breath.

I lower my head to kiss her, and she draws in a soft breath, sways into me. Just before our lips brush, I hear footsteps and pull away.

"Whoa," Trent says. I spin around, and it's evident on his face that he saw us. He clears his throat and holds up his hands. "Listen, man, I'm not judging. I mean, it's not like Brog is dead yet or anything, but go ahead, help yourself to his woman."

"Fuck," I mutter. This was careless. Foolish. Trent's words were intended to hurt, but they dug into all my open wounds even more than he could know.

I start after him, but Mia stops me with a hand on my arm. "Don't." Her eyes are wide. Is she upset we were discovered, or that I touched her at all? "There's nothing you can say."

MIA

I can't look out back when the guys are all here. It hurts to see them cruising along with their lives. I know tragedies happen and the world keeps turning, or at least I know intellectually, but seeing it firsthand is a hot iron poking at my grief. It seems like there's always someone from the team here now that school's out.

Then there's Arrow, watching me when he thinks I won't notice. Tiptoeing around me since that night a week ago when he slid his hand up my skirt and made me feel things I didn't believe my body could feel anymore.

I'm not sure if I'm supposed to feel guilty or satisfied or pissed at him for not explaining what it means. *He didn't even kiss you, Mia.*

I'll get these dishes done and spend the day upstairs. It's better that way. I remind them of Brogan, and judging by the laughter coming from around the pool, they don't want to think about him today.

"Mia." I turn from the sink at the sound of Sebastian's voice. He closes the patio doors behind him and comes into the kitchen and around the island. "How are you?"

"I'm fine."

He tucks his hands into his pockets. "I've been wanting to talk to you about something."

Tensing, I put the dishrag down. "Is my dad okay?"

"You think I'm only going to talk to you if your dad needs something?"

"Of course not. I—" I shake my head. "What do you need?"

I spin around, but with him on this side of the island, my turn puts us uncomfortably close. He leans against the thick slab of granite, legs wide and leaving me almost standing between them.

"Do they ever give you a night off?"

"Sure," I say. "I'm not a slave, and contrary to what my dad may have told you, Uriah is actually a very good employer."

His lips twitch. "Good to know. So does that mean you're free to join me for dinner some night? Maybe a movie? It's gotta get old hanging around this place all the time."

"Um." I dry my hands on my apron. I'm stalling. Sebastian is incredibly handsome, and this was what Bailey was talking about, wasn't it? She said I've been letting life pass me by, and I feel like if she were here, she'd be jumping up and down, nodding. She'd also probably make a few inappropriate sexual innuendos about what could happen at the movies. "It's just that . . ." I drop my gaze to my hands, now wringing the apron.

"Isn't this cozy," Arrow mutters.

When I swing around to the sound of his voice, I stumble forward. Sebastian catches me. After I right myself, he doesn't bother to take away the arm around my waist.

"Hey, Woodison," Sebastian says, unfazed as I step out of his embrace. "Thanks for inviting me. I was looking for an excuse to see Mia again."

I shoot Sebastian a warning glare, and he meets it with a smile.

Arrow's gaze ping-pongs between me and Sebastian. Emotions I can't identify flicker through his eyes, and I wait for him to say something nasty—about me or Sebastian, I'm not sure—but instead he gives a sharp nod, turns on his heel, and goes out back.

He had his hand up my skirt a week ago, and he just walked away at the sight of another man holding me.

"So that movie?" Sebastian sidesteps around the island. I have to give him credit for understanding that giving me space increases his odds here.

"I don't think so." I flick my gaze up to peek at his expression but find myself drawn in by his dark eyes. It's not as easy to look away as I'd like. "I'm just not ready."

"And is that because of Brogan?" He lifts his chin and points his gaze out the window behind me. "Or because of Arrow?"

I stiffen. "Don't act like you know me. You don't."

"No, Mia. I just want to. And when this world is full of people who want to take advantage of us more than they want to know us, I like to think that's a good thing." When I don't reply, he sighs, fishes in the pocket of his low-slung jeans, and comes up with a folded slip of paper. "Here."

I take it from his hands and frown. "What's this?"

"It's a list of everyone who had body work done on an SUV this winter. We're not the only place in town, so it's only a small piece of the puzzle, and you can't tell anyone I gave that to you, but I hope it helps."

I unfold the paper and scan the list. "Coach Wright's here."

Sebastian shakes his head. "Yeah, I worked on that one myself. Not what you're looking for. He hit a doe coming out of his driveway."

"Okay." I press the paper to my chest. "Thank you. This means a lot."

"I know you think you want answers," he says, his gaze steady on the men on the other side of the window, "but before you dig too deep, make sure you're really ready for them. Answers to these kinds of questions rarely bring us the peace we seek."

"And what do you know about it?"

He gives me a sad smile. "How are you holding up? I overheard Coach talking to Mrs. Barrett today. She told him the news about Brogan. I just wondered how you were taking it."

"News?" The only thing that's been consistent in my life since the accident has been Brogan. When it comes to him, nothing changes. No matter how hard I pray. "About what?"

"His kidneys. Since they decided not to do dialysis. Don't you . . ." He flinches. "Shit. You didn't know. Why haven't they told you?"

"What about his kidneys?" I ask, but he just shakes his head and doesn't have to say more. Suddenly, I'm in the dark again, the sleet biting into my skin as I climb from the car and rush to the boys. I'm in the dark feeling for a pulse. I'm in the dark punching numbers into my phone, watching with detached fascination as blood smears across the screen.

"Mia? Mia?" I open my eyes, and I'm on the floor, the cool tile pressing into my back. Sebastian leans over me, his hand on my face. "Look at me. Breathe. Okay?"

"What happened?" Arrow's voice. "Jesus, is she okay?"

Arrow crouches down next to me and brushes the hair from my face. Sebastian shakes his head. "I'm sorry. I didn't know they hadn't told her."

"Shit," Arrow whispers.

"I'm fine." I smack away Arrow's hands and sit up. And I am. I'm . . . just fine.

ARROW

Eight hours later, I still want to punch Sebastian Crowe in his smug face. I want to kick him in the balls and tell him to never touch Mia again. But I can't. She deserves to be happy. Whether that's with Sebastian or someone else, I'm not going to stand in the way.

"Mrs. Barrett?"

I sit up in bed when I hear her voice on the other side of the wall.

"Yeah. It's Mia. Sorry I'm calling so late." Her voice is broken. She sounds upset. "I was calling to see how Brogan's doing . . . Yeah. I'm coming tomorrow. I—"

I close my eyes and mentally fill in the gaps of the conversation. Is Mrs. Barrett talking about the squirrel they watched running across the backyard today? Or has she, in her grief, resorted to her old cold attitude toward Mia?

"Can you just tell me?" Mia asks. "Is he dying?" A pause.

"Isn't there anything they can—" A broken sob. "But can't they just . . .? I know."

I don't need the other side of the conversation to know what's being said, or to know that Mrs. Barrett is breaking Mia's heart all over again. They decided not to do the dialysis. This is good for Brogan. I know this, but . . . *shit*. Poor Mia.

"Why didn't you tell me? Yes, I understand. It's just . . . Okay. Yeah. I'll be there tomorrow." She sniffles a few times, and I hear her soft tread as she paces the floors. "You too."

After that, there's nothing but silence for a long time. No footsteps. No miracle-man book being thrown against the wall for giving her false hope. Just her silent grief on that side of the wall. Mine on this side.

And when I think I've heard the last of her tonight, when I think she's fallen asleep: "Damn you, Brogan." Then the sobs begin. They come from her, but they might as well be coming from me, might as well be torn from my chest. Each one is a piece of my heart sawed off with the dull blade of regret.

How many times has she come to me and saved me from the nightmares?

I don't have to think about it. I don't knock. I go into her room, and I don't stop myself, because she needs someone right now. Maybe she needs someone better than me, but I'm the only one here.

She's sitting on the bed, her knees drawn up to her chest, her gaze centered on the floor at my feet.

When she lifts her head, the tears welling in her eyes stream down to join the ones already wetting her cheeks. "He's dying."

"He's already dead, Mia."

Her face crumples at this, her shoulders shake, and no longer do I hear her heart-wrenching sobs. She's folded in on herself, wrapped the pain up, and her cries are silent and so powerful they rock her whole body.

I climb into bed behind her, wrap my arms around her, and pull her back against my chest and let her cry.

"I needed him . . ." She's struggling to talk around her tears. "I needed him to wake up."

"We all wanted that."

"No, but I needed . . ." She draws in a ragged breath. "Arrow, I needed to apologize."

Fuck. "You don't need him to wake up to hear your apology. You don't even need him to be in the same room." She doesn't owe him an apology, but there's no point in saying that. It won't make her believe it. "You're going tomorrow?" She nods, and I press a kiss to her hair. "Apologize then. Maybe your book's right. Maybe he can hear you. Maybe he's just trapped and he can hear you, and you're gonna go and you're gonna tell him what you need to tell him. Then you're going to *let him go.*" The words hurt. They're emotional suicide. "The Brogan we knew, the Brogan we *love,* does not deserve to be trapped in a body he can't use."

"I'm selfish. Wanting him to wake up, wanting him to hang on, wanting his parents to give him dialysis treatments. I know. It's so selfish."

"No." I stroke her hair with my good hand and use the other

arm to hold her close. "You're just *dealing*. We all do the best we can. We just deal however we know how."

I hold her for a long time, talking nonsense about saying goodbye and letting him go, and the next thing I know, I'm not talking about Brogan anymore. "I'm sorry for how I acted on New Year's Eve," I say. I should have said it a long time ago. I should have said it that night. "What you said took me by surprise. But it never changed the way I felt about you. I came to you that night because I knew Brogan was screwing around on you, and I thought you deserved better." I draw in a long, ragged breath. "God, was I pissed at him. He was my best friend my whole life, and I'd never wanted to hurt him until that night. But he was right. He said my ego couldn't handle being second choice. He knew me better than I knew myself."

"I don't understand. What did him cheating on me have to do with you?"

I lay us on the bed, rolling so we're on our sides, our bodies pressed together, our faces inches apart. "That was when you were mine. In the one night between his betrayal and his apology, you were mine, but only because you couldn't be his." The memory hooks its claws into my aching heart and tugs.

"It wasn't like that at all," she says.

I swallow hard. "I never hid my feelings, Mia. You knew that very first day that I didn't want to step aside for Brogan. It's true even now." My voice drops to a whisper. "You're in my arms, but you're still his. And I can't blame you for that. I don't."

She tries to smile, but it looks more like a grimace. "I loved him, Arrow."

I roll to my back and squeeze my eyes shut against the pain those words bring. Even now I'm jealous of him, jealous of what he had from her. And I hate myself for that. "I know."

"He was easy to love. So kind and funny and generous."

"I know," I say again, still not looking at her.

"I've been selfish from the beginning. I wanted to love Brogan. He was my safe place, and I wanted to be in love with someone like that."

"He loved you, Mia. He fucked up a lot—I'm not denying that—but he loved you."

She's quieter now. Her body has stilled, and the tears and sobs seem to have broken, but I know there's more grief to come. We've only reached the calm center of the storm. Not the end of it. "And I thought that if I could focus on that, if I could nurture that easy love, I might be able to drown out the hurt."

Slowly, I open my eyes and turn to her, blinking. "He shouldn't have hurt you to begin with. He shouldn't have—"

She shakes her head and studies me, dark eyes intent. "That's not the hurt I'm talking about. I'm talking about the ache that burned in my chest every time I looked at you and knew we couldn't be together. I'm talking about the terrible self-loathing I'd feel when I'd catch myself comparing Brogan to you. He was good and kind and more than I deserved, but he was never you. You could never be second choice, Arrow. Because I never allowed myself to consider you a choice at all."

I press my open palm to the ache in my chest. I can't do this anymore. "Mia, you need to know. About that night—"

She presses two fingers to my lips and shakes her head. "Don't. Please? I don't want to talk about New Year's Eve. If you want me to remember that I didn't die that night, you have to promise me you won't talk about it anymore."

"Don't make me make that promise," I say. Because I can't.

"Just tonight, then. Don't talk about it tonight."

"Okay." I pull in a breath and realize I'm shaking. Would I have said it if she hadn't stopped me? Would I have spilled it all out? And then what? She'd hate me, and what would happen to Coach?

"I need to apologize to him," she says.

I bury my nose in her hair and inhale slowly, my shaking subsides, and my feet come back to the earth. "Tomorrow. You can apologize tomorrow." Reluctantly, I release her to climb off the bed. "Lie down. I'll tuck you in. You need a good night's sleep."

"No." She reaches for me and drops her hand just before her fingers brush my bare stomach. "Don't go."

I don't know if I can do it. Hold her without touching her. Spend a night soothing grief I'm responsible for. "Mia, we—"

"Don't go." She bites her bottom lip and cocks her head to the side. "Please? I'm scared to sleep alone."

I can't do it. I can't walk away from her. "Okay." I climb back into the bed and pull her back to my front. "Do you want me to give Katie a bottle if she wakes up?"

"No, I can do it. I can get her."

"Okay. Just go to sleep now, okay?" I reach over her head and click off the light, and we lie in silence for a long time.

I close my eyes, knowing I won't sleep but hoping she can. She'll need her rest for tomorrow.

"Arrow?" she asks, long after I think she's fallen asleep.

I don't answer. My heart is too raw to talk more tonight; my need to tell her *everything* is too strong. I keep my eyes closed and my mouth shut so I won't tell her what I can't.

"I loved Brogan," she says into the darkness. "But I couldn't *fall* for him. That stupid difference between loving and being in love. I never thought it mattered. But I couldn't fall *in love* with Brogan. I could only love him." She finds my hand where it's wrapped around her waist and pulls it up to rest on her heart. "Because I'd already fallen for you."

I force myself to breathe. If I hold my breath, she'll know I heard her confession. If I squeeze her tighter, she'll have to deal with her secret being out there. If I roll her under me and kiss her like every cell in my body is begging me to, she'll know. But I didn't realize until this moment how long I've been waiting to hear it. How much of me has been waiting since New Year's Eve to know that the girl I love loves me back.

So I breathe and promise myself that soon I'll find a way to tell Mia the truth without ruining Coach's life.

I'll find a way.

PART VI: BEFORE

October, two and a half months before the accident

MIA

When I show up to the house party, half the people there are already drunk. I had to work late and I missed the game. *Bad girlfriend.* Bailey texted me updates at every time-out and between each quarter. The Blackhawks won in overtime. I didn't think I'd even be able to make it to the party, but I wanted to surprise Brogan. He hates that I have to work so much, and he really hates when I miss his games.

Things haven't been right between us since my birthday, and I can't figure out if that's my fault or his. Did my heart-to-heart with Arrow leave me looking for fault in Brogan, or has he really been more distant and moody since he came home from the wedding last weekend?

Keegan is in the kitchen, pouring a drink for a pretty, fragile-featured girl with dark pixie-cut hair. His eyes go wide when he sees me. "Mia. I thought you couldn't come tonight."

"I got off early. Have you seen Brogan?"

"Um." His loud swallow gives him away. Keegan is a shitty liar. "I think he left?"

"He's upstairs," the girl says. "I saw him head up there with—" She stops speaking at Keegan's hard glare. A weird sickness immediately fills my stomach at what she didn't say. I'm already pushing past them to the stairs at the back of the house. He hasn't just been moody. He's been secretive.

"Mia," Keegan calls. I hear him on the stairs behind me, but I rush forward anyway.

Don't be that guy, Brogan. Don't be that guy.

I throw open bedroom doors, one after another, until I find them.

Brogan's sitting on the edge of the bed, one hand buried in the hair of the girl sucking him off.

"Brogan." I don't mean to speak. It just comes out. All my disappointment and heartbreak in that one word.

He's slow to respond. *He's drunk,* I tell myself. *He doesn't know what he's doing.* But God, it hurts. *He's drunk. He's stressed. He's upset that his girlfriend doesn't show up to half his home games.* My mind scrambles to pile on excuses—like putting pressure on the wound to stop the bleeding—but his betrayal bleeds through.

When he opens his eyes, the way the shock rolls over his face is almost comical. The way Trish snaps her head back, his dick popping out of her mouth, is almost comical.

"Mia." Keegan's hand closes around my shoulder, and I shake it off.

Brogan pushes Trish away, and in his haste to get his pants zipped, he catches his dick in the zipper. "Fuck," he growls.

"Karma works quickly," I say softly. Then I shake my head, because part of what I always loved about Brogan was that I trusted him. I believed he'd never hurt me. "I'm done. This is over."

I don't scream or shout or even shed a tear. It's like I flip the switch I found after Mom left and shut all that off. I turn and push past Keegan, who looks so guilty you'd think he was the one caught with his pants down.

"Why'd you let her up here?" Brogan shouts at him.

"You're an ass," Keegan replies.

I don't hear any more because I make a beeline for the door. I don't bother with my car but keep walking until I get to the dorms. I'm not even sure what makes me go to Arrow, but that's where I am before I can even think it through. He opens the door to his quad, and as soon as he sees my face, he knows.

"What did he do?" he asks, his voice deadly and low.

I bite my bottom lip. "House party. Trish."

ARROW

"We broke up."

I swallow hard and squeeze my eyes shut. If I could spend a year watching her date my best friend, I can certainly spend another fucking thirty seconds to take a breath before I pull her into my arms.

When I open my eyes, she's worrying that bottom lip between her teeth and twisting her hands. "I probably shouldn't be here," she says, but instead of heading to the door, she opens the door to Mason's and my room. "I just didn't know where else to go, but it was stupid to come here. He's your boy and I—"

"What are you doing?"

She's on her hands and knees, searching for something under Mason's bed. She pulls out a bottle of tequila and gives me a sideways smile as she unscrews the cap. "It's Bailey's stash." She takes a long pull right from the bottle and squeezes her eyes shut as she swallows. "Crap, that burns." She wanders around the room with the bottle in her hand, taking sip after sip as she paces. "I never worried about Trish, you know that? I knew she liked him, but it didn't occur to me that he might like her, too."

"Do you want to tell me what happened?" I ask cautiously. I don't like how quickly she's draining that bottle.

"There's not much to the story, Arrow." She plops onto my bed and takes another swig. "I showed up to surprise him, and Trish was already sucking his dick." She snorts, and a long stream of giggles slips past her lips. "Oh my God, it's so absurd."

"Mia—"

"I give *great* head," she says, bringing the bottle to her chest.

I rub my temples. Do I really want to be the sweet guy friend who can sit here and listen to her talk about giving Brogan blowjobs? *Hell no.*

"I mean, I do all the things you're supposed to do, and he sure seems to like it, but what do I know? Maybe I suck." She snorts again. "Get it? I *suck*?" She takes another drink, and I walk across the room and pull the bottle from her hand.

"Yeah, I get it, Mia." I put the bottle on top of the dresser.

She stretches out on my bed, arms above her head. "Why do guys cheat, Arrow? Are they programmed that way, or is it me?" Her BHU T-shirt raises up to expose her navel and the smooth skin of her stomach. "I bet it's the blowjob thing. I bet I'm no good."

Mia. On my bed. Talking blowjobs.

I clear my throat. "Do you want to get out of here? We could go for a drive?"

She sits up and nods, but suddenly tears pool in her eyes and stream down her cheeks. *Fucking Brogan.*

Maybe I should want this. A clean break for them so Mia and I can finally . . .

Fuck, I don't even know. But I'm not happy. I'm not relieved or feeling the slightest bit victorious. Instead, I want to take a swing at him for hurting her. And since beating the shit out of my best friend for cheating on the girl I love makes next to no sense, I'll settle for finding a way to make her smile tonight. Because that's what I do. I'm the friend. I'm the shoulder to cry on, the promised smile. That's why she's here. Nothing more.

She follows me to the car, and I open the door of my blue Mustang and watch her climb inside. Her jean shorts bunch around her hips as she sits. I fist my hands at my sides. *Don't be a fucking asshole.*

"Where are we going?" she asks when I climb into my side and buckle my seatbelt.

Anywhere that doesn't involve looking at you in my bed. "Well, obviously this calls for ice cream first and foremost."

There it is. The first smile of the night. Or partial smile, because it doesn't meet her eyes. But I'll take it. I'll have her grinning outright in no time.

"I want one of those massive sundaes," she says, buckling her seatbelt. "The ones with all the crap that's so bad for you and, like, two thousand calories each. I've always wanted to try one of those, and I think it's time."

I turn the key in the ignition and feel the car purr to life.

"You're telling me you've never had a big ice cream sundae?"

She shrugs. "A cone's bad enough. I work hard trying to get my ass to shrink. Don't need ice cream to make it an even more impossible battle."

I bite my tongue against saying something inappropriate but then decide *fuck it*. Brogan cheated on her and they broke up. I don't need to censor myself out of respect for him anymore. "I'm pretty fond of the size of your ass, Mia."

Her eyes go wide and her jaw drops a fraction, and she stares at me as if she truly can't believe what I just said. When I just wink at her, she smacks me in the arm with the back of her hand.

"What?" I ask.

"You can't say that stuff to me."

"Why not?"

"Because . . . Arrow, we're friends. That's important to me above all the other petty shit. You don't say stuff like that to your friends."

"Are you sure?"

"I'm sure."

"Hmm. I don't know. I think you're thinking of *mean things*. You don't say *mean things* to your friends. What I said definitely doesn't qualify. If you'd like, I can elaborate, and you'd know just how kind my feelings about your ass really are."

"Ice cream." She points at the road and bites back a grin, but her eyes are already smiling. "Stay focused."

I'm so proud of myself for making her smile, it's all I can do not to give a little victory fist pump. "Yes, ma'am."

We go to the Dairy Maid drive-through, and Mia orders a four-scoop chocolate and peanut butter sundae with the works. I order a turtle sundae of similar size so she won't feel self-conscious, but I know I won't be able to eat it, not when my stomach is in knots over having her by my side. *Single. No longer Brogan's.*

And fuck it. It's not like I don't know there are rules. You don't go out with your best friend's ex. Maybe it would be acceptable after a respectable period of time passes, like, say, three or four years, but most definitely not the night she dumped him.

I'm not going to do anything. Nothing but make her smile. Make her laugh.

"Where do you want to go?" I ask as I pull out of the Dairy Maid lot. "We could watch B-grade horror flicks at the dorm or maybe play laser tag?"

At a stop sign, light from the streetlamp illuminates her face. Her cheeks are still pink from the tequila. She arches a brow. "Laser tag?"

"After we finish our ice cream. Sure. You could pretend the opponents are all Brogan and Trish and shoot them repeatedly."

She laughs. Really laughs. A bright, beautiful sound that seems to fill the car. "No, thanks. Not sure I'll be able to button my jeans after I'm done eating this, let alone run around in them."

"Fair enough," I say, but I have to grip the steering wheel a little tighter and try very hard not to think about activities that involve Mia unbuttoning her jeans. Because *damn*. "So, how about the movies?"

She pokes at her ice cream with her spoon. "Could we just . . . go somewhere private and talk? Not my apartment. Brogan's probably looking for me, and I'm not ready to face him."

"The dorms?" It's more a horrified question than a suggestion. I don't know how much more Mia-on-my-bed I can handle without acting on seriously poor judgment.

"I don't think so," she says. "There are always people coming in and out of your quad, and I don't feel like pretending to be okay tonight."

Private. Private sounds dangerous. "Whatever you need." I go to the light and pull a U-turn, heading back out of Blackhawk Valley and toward my father's house, all the while trying to decide if this is the worst idea I've ever had. I've always done my best to be worthy of Brogan's friendship, and I know there's no way I can tell Mia how I feel tonight without being a complete scumbag, which is why I was trying to suggest very *public* activities. But I can't turn her down.

On the way to my dad's property, she pokes at her ice cream, only taking a bite or two and abandoning it altogether when I pull up to the gates and drive into the estate.

Straightening, she sits the ice cream in the cup holder beside her. "We're going to your dad's house?"

"Not exactly." I'm trying to be mysterious, but she's too distracted, her eyes scanning the horizon as we follow the rolling hills to the back of the property.

"That's where you grew up?" she asks, as I drive on past the house.

I shrug. "It's just a house, Mia. A big one, sure, but we had our problems like anyone else."

"Right. Brogan said your mom died when you were in high school. I'm sorry about that." She turns her head and watches as it goes by, but soon I pull onto a gravel road at the back of the property and it's out of sight.

When I reach the lake, I bring the car to a stop near the bank, and she gasps. The lake is irregularly shaped and has fingers that stretch along a lot of the property, but this alcove surrounded by trees is by far my favorite. Water cascades from the creek down the stone-lined wall on the far side, making a little waterfall.

Clouds dim the moon and stars tonight, and my headlights offer the only illumination of the waterfall and alcove.

"I know this place," she whispers. "Bailey and I came here when we were kids." She throws her hand over her mouth and grimaces. "We . . . snuck in. This is yours?"

"My dad's, I guess. It's quiet back here. I like to come here to think."

"And swim, right?" She grins. "Bail and I swam here. God, what I'd give to go back to those days. Life was so much simpler."

"You have no idea how hard I'm kicking myself for not spending more time down here when I was in high school."

She bites her bottom lip and, ice cream forgotten, opens her door and climbs out of the car, rendering me temporarily helpless.

I'm frozen in place. Because Mia is walking toward the lake in the path of my headlights and pulling her shirt off over her head. Her bra is dark. Lace. *Fuck.* She tosses the shirt onto the ground then toes out of her shoes and drops her shorts before running to the end of the dock.

When she stretches her arms over her head and dives into the dark lake in nothing but her bra and panties, I snap out of my stupor and jump out of the car. "Mia!"

She bobs to the surface and shivers. "It's cold."

"No shit? It's October. Get out here before you get hypothermia or worse."

She laughs. "It's been an Indian summer. It's not that cold."

"Come on, Mia."

She answers by diving down again, and the light from my headlights isn't strong enough to allow me to see under the surface of the water. I wouldn't be comfortable with her swimming alone in the best of conditions, but in the dark, buzzed and maybe drunk, it worries the shit out of me.

"Fuck," I mutter. I pull off my shirt and shoes, drop my jeans, and dive in behind her, and *fuck is it cold.* My nuts immediately retreat, trying to draw up into my stomach, I swear.

Mia laughs. "You're so tough on the field, plowing through all those big guys, but put you in a little cold water and you look like you're being tortured."

"You're crazy. The tequila you chugged in my room is the only explanation for why swimming in this could seem even remotely like a good idea."

"You didn't have to get in," she says through her laughter.

Her swimming in the dark makes me nervous as hell and the

water is cold enough it makes my teeth chatter, but it's worth it. She's laughing. Smiling. Her dark hair is wet and slicked back, and the smooth skin of her arms peeks in and out of the water as she wades. God, she's tempting, and tonight is threatening to use up the last of my restraint.

She needs a friend. Yep, I anticipate reminding myself of that ninety times in the next five minutes.

"Why are you looking at me like that?" she asks.

"Like what?"

"I don't know. Like . . ." The smile falls from her face and she swallows hard.

Like I want to kiss you? Like I'm in love with you? "Like I want you to get your ass out of this lake before you make yourself sick?"

"No," she says. "That's not how you were looking at me."

I hold my breath, waiting for her to say more, but she spins in the water and starts swimming toward the waterfall and out of the beam of my headlights.

"You're fucking kidding me!"

"Loosen up, Arrow. It's not that bad."

I follow her through the water, and once I let myself relax a little, I realize she's right. The water still holds on to the late summer heat, and now that my body's adjusted, it feels good to swim with the cool night air above us.

I can't see as well over here, but I can make out her silhouette as she climbs onto a large flat stone next to the fall, draws her knees up to her chin, and wraps her arms around her legs. The rational part of me is grateful for the darkness, glad I can't see the smooth skin of her back or her long legs. The greedy part of me wants full sun on her so I can look at every inch and save the memory for my lonely nights.

"You're shivering." I push up onto the stone and settle down next to her. "You okay?"

"I don't know," she whispers. She shudders. "I don't know if I'm okay at all."

"I'm sorry," I say. I'm glad I won't see Brogan tonight. I'd probably do something I'd regret. Like kicking him in the balls.

"What are you apologizing for? Brogan made his own decisions. You're not responsible."

"I'm sorry you're hurting."

"Arrow?" The word floats into the night air, mixes with the whisper of the leaves and the music of the trickling waterfall, but I hear it as clearly as if she said it right into my ear.

"Yeah?"

"How can my heart be so broken and I want . . ."

The unspoken part of her sentence sends something hard and sharp tugging at my heart and piercing my lungs. I can't breathe. I want too much with Mia, and I don't trust my instincts. I want to believe I'm the thing she wants, but maybe she was thinking something entirely different.

She shifts onto her knees and presses her palm against my bare chest. "Do you ever wonder if things would have been different if you'd kissed me the day we met?" She swallows. "Or if Brogan had never seen my phone number on Bailey's door?"

There's no hiding how I feel when her hand is pressed over

my pounding heart, but I'm ashamed to admit it. All I can do is cover her hand with mine and close my eyes. "He's a fucking idiot for screwing this up. You're the best thing he's ever had."

MIA

I'm a hypocrite. Brogan cheated on me with Trish, and I mentally called him the ugliest names I could think up. And now—hours later—I'm wishing Arrow would kiss me.

We broke up. Sure. But is my being with Arrow really all that different than what Brogan did with Trish?

I love Brogan, and surely my heart hasn't caught up with my brain yet, but it had a head start. I've been harvesting feelings for Arrow for too long, locking them away and hoping they'd disappear. When Brogan let Trish touch him, he didn't just break my heart. He broke that lock.

Arrow's skin is hot, the muscles on his chest so solid I want to map them with my fingers. His hand rests softly over mine, but I want it in my hair, behind my neck.

"I'm sick of feeling guilty about being attracted to you." The words surprise me. I didn't mean to tell my secret, but without the lock on my heart, I don't have the strength to hold it in.

"Mia." His voice is rough, gravelly, and carries more than words.

If there was a moon tonight, I'd be able to see his eyes, read what he's feeling, but maybe I don't want to know. There's so much unsaid between us that I've started mentally composing his thoughts without even realizing it. What if I've been wrong about how he feels?

The answer is delivered in the form of his kiss. I've wanted this for so long without admitting it to myself, and I hold my breath as he lowers his mouth. He tilts my chin up as his lips sweep over mine in that first forbidden touch. He sweeps a second time, more of a brushing of skin than a kiss, and when our mouths finally press together, I'm a contradiction of emotions. I want to melt with the longing and want and the heat of a long-held secret fantasy fulfilled. And at the same time I want to freeze with the horror of what we're doing. My mind travels too fast, jumping the cart miles ahead of the horse and zipping through thousands of outcomes, none of them good.

But when Arrow's tongue traces the seam of my lips and touches mine, I don't care about outcomes anymore. The cold, hard rock under my knees roots me to this moment, and darkness erases every moment before and beyond this.

Arrow's kiss is soft and tentative. His fingers trace along the side of my neck. His calloused hands send goosebumps racing up my arms and something else altogether pooling low in my belly. When they slip back into my hair, he cups my jaw in his big hand

and sighs against my lips.

It's the sigh that undoes me. As has always been the case with us, so much is spoken with what's unspoken, and this moment is no different. The sigh tells me he's waited for this as long as I have and that maybe, just maybe, the touch of our lips is twisting him up inside as much as it is me.

I let my hand drift from his chest to the waistband of his boxer briefs. He breaks the kiss and draws in a sharp breath as he stops me with a hand around my wrist.

"Let me," I whisper. I pull from his grasp and graze my fingertips against the skin just above his waistband. "Please."

"Mia." He rubs his hands down my arms. Goosebumps cover my skin, and his warm hands simultaneously heat it and remind me just how cold I am. "You're freezing. Let's go to the car."

I don't want to leave. I want to stay right here. On this rock. In this moment where Arrow kisses me and I have the courage to touch him. But he's already slipping back into the water, taking my moment away.

I follow him, and we swim in silence to the dock and gather our clothes off the shore before heading to the car.

Suddenly too aware of my near-nudity, I step into my shorts and clutch my shirt to my chest. "I don't want to go home," I tell his back as he reaches the Mustang. And he can take that however he wants—like I'm some brazen hussy or like I'm avoiding Brogan, who will undoubtedly be looking for me at the apartment. Maybe both are true.

Arrow nods, opens the driver's-side door, and pops the

trunk. He grabs a blanket and wraps it around my shoulders. "So we'll stay here and watch the sun rise."

Taking his hand, I climb through the front door into the tiny back seat of Arrow's Mustang while he turns on the heat, kills the lights, and turns on the dome light. There's not enough room back here for him to sit comfortably with his long legs, but he follows me anyway, pulling the door closed behind him before wrapping an arm around my shoulders.

I settle into him, leaning my head against his chest. "I don't understand you," I say, peeking up at him through my lashes.

"What don't you understand?"

I take a breath and let it out slowly. "One second I think you like me, I think maybe you want me, and the next . . ."

He squeezes his eyes shut, and I watch his throat move as he swallows. "You've been drinking."

"I'm not trashed. I know what I'm doing."

"I'm not sure that's true."

"Okay," I admit. "I don't have a clue what I'm doing. Only what I want." But that's not completely true either. I know what I want *right now*. But tomorrow? Next week?

"You've been drinking," he repeats, but he softens the words by following them with a kiss on top of my head. "Are you warm enough?"

I nod against his chest, then wiggle the blanket off one shoulder so I can wrap it behind him. Now we're both under the blanket together.

"Tell me something," he says.

"Like what?"

He swallows. "Something about your childhood. A good memory."

"I have a lot of those. I had a good childhood. Nic pestered me mercilessly as big brothers do, but we had fun." I let my eyes float closed, remembering the good days. "Mom would take us to the park and on these long hikes through the woods. She'd tell us stories about Prince Nicholas and Princess Mia and the adventures they had trying to save their kingdom from various villains. We thought she was the smartest woman ever, and we'd beg for her to tell us more stories, so she'd use them to get us to do our chores. She'd tell us stories while we folded the laundry or helped her with dinner."

"That sounds nice."

"It was." I smile remembering it. She wasn't just a good mom. She was amazing. "I didn't know we were poor. I mean, it was clear the other kids at school had more stuff and nicer clothes, but I was probably in fourth grade before I realized that was something worth envying. When my mom was around, life at home was better than good. It was rich. Anything felt possible." And then she left and took that away. My heart squeezes with the ache of that loss.

"My mom was like that, too," Arrow says. "I've always been surrounded by people who believed in me, but Mom believed in me without expectation. There were never any strings to her affection. She just wanted me to be happy."

He hardly ever talks about her, and I want to know as much

as he's willing to share. "When did she die?"

"Five years ago this weekend. The end was tough. I was glad when she finally let go. When did your mom leave?" he asks, rubbing my arm under the blanket. I wonder if he even realizes he's doing it.

I shift against him and wrap an arm around his waist, as if his nearness could protect me from the pain of talking about my mother. "She left the summer before I started high school, so just over five years ago." I frown at the coincidence of both of us losing our mothers around the same time.

"Did she say why?" he asks.

"I think it was all too much for her. Dad was sober more often back then, but he was still a lazy misogynist. She did everything. She worked nights at the dry cleaners, got us to school every day, cleaned the house, did the shopping, cooked the food, picked up side work as a maid anytime she could for extra cash. She was just done. So she left."

"Why didn't she take you with her?"

I spent so many years avoiding asking that question out loud. Asking a question means you're willing to hear the answer, and I didn't think I could handle someone telling me what I already believed in my mind. *She didn't want us.*

"I'm sure she wanted you," Arrow says, as if reading my thoughts. "She had to have made the decision for a reason."

"I don't know. Maybe she thought it was my father's turn to do all the work and child rearing. She never said. She didn't even say goodbye if you don't count the note. She couldn't have known that her leaving would drive Dad to drink. She couldn't have known that he'd lose his job, and Nic and I would be left fending for ourselves."

"I'm sorry, Mia."

"I wish you'd quit apologizing for my life. It's embarrassing."

"You deserve better than what you've been given. Better than a mom who leaves without explanation, better than an alcoholic father, and better than a boyfriend who sleeps around on you."

"What makes me so deserving?" I pull back to look at him. He's watching me with cautious eyes. "Doesn't everyone deserve all that?"

"No, Mia. Some people don't deserve shit. But you . . ." He touches my face, tracing my jaw and skimming his thumb across my lips.

"Do I deserve you?"

He draws in a breath. "What happens tomorrow? After I take you home and Brogan calls? What happens after your buzz wears off and you remember you don't want to be with me?"

"Why would you say I don't want to be with you?"

"Wasn't that the decision you made when you decided to date Brogan? You didn't want to be with me because of who my father is, and so you chose him," he says. "I don't blame you, but I'm asking what happens tomorrow when you remember all of that."

"I don't know." I remove my hand from around his waist and find the dark trail of hair I know from memory starts just above his navel and travels down under his shorts. "I'm sick of making decisions based on tomorrow. I've been doing that since I was fourteen. I want tonight. For once."

He releases a long, slow hiss of breath. "You're sure?" he asks, his voice low and husky.

I nod, move to straddle his lap, and let the blanket fall off my shoulders.

His lips part and he stares up at me in a way that makes me feel like a goddess granting his greatest wish. I release the clasp on my bra, and he watches as I toss it to the floorboards.

Cupping my jaw gently, he leans forward to trail soft kisses down my neck. His mouth opens, and his hands go to my sides. His thumbs brush the undersides of my breasts.

He strikes me as absolutely vulnerable in this moment. He touches me with such tenderness that I'm melting from the very center of my core all the way out to my fingertips.

"You're beautiful, Mia." He dips his head to my breast and draws a nipple into his mouth.

I moan involuntarily and arch into him—his touch, the stroke of his tongue, the wet heat of his open mouth latched onto me. His hands slide down my body and find the button on my jean shorts. I push them down, along with my panties, and kick them to the side. He takes my hips, squeezing them tightly.

I let myself dissolve into the moment. Into the feel of his tongue on my breasts. Into the heat of his mouth on my skin. I roll my hips, slide my fingers into his hair. For once in my life, I stop worrying about what I'm supposed to be doing and how I'm supposed to be acting. I just feel. Arrow makes me *feel*.

He responds to every sound that comes out of my mouth.

Every move I make. Every time I moan or shift my hips to press our bodies closer. His breath catches and his hands grip me tighter, showing me how much my response turns him on.

Nothing is simple between us. Even if I never return to Brogan, he'll always be between me and Arrow. Even if my dad can forgive me for falling for a Woodison, Arrow's family will always be something between us. I'm not fooling myself into thinking that another girl sucking Brogan's dick suddenly made my affection for Arrow less complicated. All I'm doing is allowing myself this night. This moment.

"I have condoms in my glove compartment," he murmurs in my ear. "If you're sure."

I'm not sure. I'm scared. Not scared that it'll hurt—though it might—or that he won't be gentle with me—I know he'll define gentle. I'm scared what this means to me. I'm scared that I've had months and months with Brogan and so many opportunities to do this with the man I'm supposed to love and I've found every excuse to avoid it. And here I am in Arrow's arms at the first opportunity.

I'm scared of how much it means to me that he was there tonight—alone in his dorm room after a win, as if he were waiting for me instead of going to the party. I'm scared of how I'll feel after. When I've given another piece of myself to the guy who had me from the first. But mostly I'm scared that this night might slip away before I can stretch my wings and fly.

"I'm sure," I say, and before I can chicken out, I climb over the seat, pop the glove compartment, and pull out the box. It's new. Closed. Sealed on all sides. That shouldn't matter. It doesn't necessarily mean anything more than that his last box is gone. But I don't want to be just another condom in a half-empty box, so I like that I have to open it.

Arrow helps me peel his shorts and briefs from his hips, and I hand him the condom in its wrapper. He puts it on, splitting his attention between me and the latex covering his shaft.

I straddle him. He cups my jaw and his eyes lock with mine as I position my body over him and slowly work my way down. He gasps, and I bury my face into the side of his neck so he can't see me grimace. It hurts more than I expected.

"Dear God, Mia. You're so . . ." One hand squeezes my hip and the other falls from my hair to find my hand. He laces our fingers and holds them to his chest.

I stay still for a minute, letting my body adjust to his size, to this intrusion of someone inside me, until the pain gives way, edged out by pleasure. I pull back enough to look at our intertwined fingers, my skin against his, my knuckles against his pounding heart.

"Are you okay?"

Swallowing, I nod. "I'm good." The emotion clogging my chest makes the word come out too thick, and I'm afraid he knows just what this means to me. Afraid he'll take it back if he understands the magnitude of this moment.

He strokes my cheek and skims his thumb over my bottom lip. "Beautiful." He holds me behind my neck and leads me forward to his kiss. His kiss is gentle and his lips are warm, and I feel so safe and good.

Any pain from the beginning is gone as I slowly rock into him. Experimentally, I lift my hips and slide down along his length. He sets his jaw and squeezes his eyes shut, so I do it again, and his breath rushes out of him.

I'm ashamed to admit to myself that I've imagined this before. Tonight isn't the first time I've thought about making love to Arrow. I'm sure it could have been more romantic. I'm sure he would have rather been with me for the first time in a bed. But there's nothing about this I'd change.

Every move we make feels sweet and so poignant, as if he's found my heart unlocked and is carefully retrieving it.

I don't know how long I move over him before the look on his face changes. He goes from sweet and tender to something a little more desperate. From careful and controlled to something wild. Watching him lose that careful control is somehow sweeter than every tender touch before.

"Did you?" he whispers, his voice hitching.

Tonight means too much for me to taint it with a lie, so I shake my head. "It's okay."

"Mia," he murmurs. Then, like he can't handle it anymore, he buries his face in my neck, grips my hips tight, and shifts his hips under me. He rocks into me with more force than he's used to touch me all night long, and it hurts a little but I love it. I offered myself to him, and *this*—his pleasure, the rough sound at the back of his throat, his jerky movements—*this* feels like he's taking me. Making me his.

He holds me tight as he groans, and I feel him swell inside me, feel the long rush of his exhale against my neck as he comes. Then he's still. Fingers in my hair. Lips trailing up and down my neck.

"I've waited too long," he says, and I'm not sure what that means, so I just nod.

We find some tissues to clean up after, and before things can get awkward, he gathers me against him and covers us both with the blanket and holds me in a cocoon of warmth. I close my eyes for just a moment, and the next thing I know, he's whispering my name in my hair.

"The sun's rising."

I sit up, and sure enough, orange stretches out behind the trees on the other side of the lake. The sun is rising, and I'm here in Arrow's arms.

I wake up to someone kissing the back of my thigh. Soft, open-mouthed kisses on that tender skin just below the curve of my ass. Arrow's mouth. Arrow's kisses. Deft and skilled and guaranteed to make men fall short for the rest of my life.

Moaning, I start to roll over, but he places a hand on my back to hold me still. "I'm really just getting started if you don't mind." His voice is low, gravelly with sleep—the little we got—and it stirs something low in my belly.

After watching the sun rise, we came back to my apartment this morning, locked the door to my room, climbed into bed together, and napped. Or at least I did.

I look over my shoulder to where he's kissing his way up my back. "Why can't I roll over?"

He grins and cups me between my legs with one big hand. Heat pools there fast and tight. "Because." Then he doesn't need to say anything more. He strokes me, and at the same time his mouth is on me again, trailing down my back and over the curve of my ass. He kisses the backs of my thighs, then follows the path up with his teeth and tongue, all the while working his fingers over me. The angle of his touch is different than anything I've ever felt before, and the skin he teases with his mouth so much more sensitive than I could have imagined. I suddenly feel like Brogan left half my body unexplored.

The thought of Brogan makes me tense, and Arrow must notice because he lifts his head and stills his movements. "This okay?"

"Yeah. I . . ." I swallow. "It's good."

He nuzzles my inner thigh and groans. "Damn right it is." He guides my thighs farther apart, slides his hand out of the way, and replaces it with his mouth. Pleasure stabs through me—the sudden heat, the angle, the scratch of his stubble—and his lips move over my most private spot, and everything inside me coils tight and hot and needy.

When he pulls back, it's only long enough to roll me to my back and position his face between my legs again, but he just looks instead of kissing me.

"Arrow," I whisper. I want his mouth again. His hand. Both.

More.

He flicks his gaze up to mine and grins. "I woke up with you and for a second I forgot last night. I thought I was dreaming." He leans forward, and I gasp as his tongue runs the length of my clit. "When I remembered . . ." He watches me as he licks his lips. "Well, I hope you don't mind if I kiss you here for a while."

His words steal my breath and make something greedy and achy coil tight between my legs. I don't have a chance to respond before his mouth is on me again, longer this time. Slower. He spreads me with his hands and explores me with his lips and tongue. And it would feel good no matter what, because he seems to know just how to touch me—how to alternate soft and hard and where to suck—but when I force my eyes open and witness the fantasy of *Arrow* in my bed, *Arrow* kissing me like this, it only adds to the pleasure.

I'm halfway there when he slides a finger inside me, and even tender from last night, I can't help but lift my hips off the bed and get his mouth closer to my aching clit. He groans and rewards me by sucking. Ever. So. Gently.

And then I'm gone. Slipping. Falling. Melting.

"*What's your thing*, Arrow?" The clock reads ten a.m. We're still in bed, and I'm in no hurry to go anywhere. My phone flashes at me from the nightstand, but I don't want to see a bunch of missed calls from Brogan or face reality after these amazing hours with Arrow. I will. Just not yet.

"My thing?"

I feel stupid for a minute. That day we met was so much to me. Maybe he doesn't even remember it. My curiosity wins out over my pride. "The thing you want so desperately that the idea of having it makes you as sick to your stomach as the idea of never having it?"

His eyes lock with mine, and I know he remembers. His Adam's apple bobs as he swallows. Tearing his gaze from mine, he rolls to his back and stares at the ceiling. "It used to be football."

I always presumed it was football, but then he never said one way or another. "It isn't anymore?"

"Football's been playing second string in my wishes for a lot of months now. My life was easier when football was my everything."

"What is it now?"

That's when he looks at me again, his eyes dark and tormented, his body tensed beside mine. The silence grows thick with everything we never say. "You."

My heart squeezes and my breath catches. There's so much in that word. A promise of what he'll be to me if I let him. A question of what tomorrow will hold. And I'm not sure what I think about either, so I just take the answer as the gift it is and remind myself to breathe.

I don't want to speak his name and break this spell, but someone pounds on the door, breaking it anyway. I pull from Arrow's touch and sit on the edge of the bed.

"Ignore it," he says, wrapping an arm around my waist.

"Mia Maria Consuela Mendez!"

"That's my brother. Shit." Nic's only been out of prison a couple of weeks, and neither of us are used to it yet. I forget that he can stop by anytime he wants, and he forgets that I'm not five anymore.

"I know you're home," Nic calls. "Your neighbor told me she saw you come in this morning."

Arrow sits up and drags a hand over his face.

"I'm sorry," I whisper.

"It's cool." He scans the room, probably knowing how bad this looks, considering I was his best friend's girlfriend this time yesterday. "Tell me what you want me to do."

I swallow. "Hide?"

"Mia—"

"I'm serious," I hiss. "Nic is not going to like seeing you here, and I'd rather you leave with your face intact. Get your clothes and hide in the closet."

"I'm not scared of him."

"Do it for me," I say as Nic pounds on the door again. "Please."

"Right. Okay. Fine."

While he gathers his clothes, I hurry and dress myself. I grab a button-up shirt and a pair of jeans.

"Mia, I fucking swear!" Nic calls.

"I'm coming," I say. "I was sleeping."

"It's important," Nic says. "Dad's gone on a bender and he's gotten out the gun."

My fingers pause halfway up the buttons. *This is reality, Mia.*

This is your real life. Not Arrow saying sweet things to you under the stars or waking you up with kisses. This. Your dad and alcoholic benders that make him wax poetic about suicide.

I hurry with the last few buttons as I rush to open the door. "What does he want?"

"He's flipping out about talking to you," Nic says.

Since all he's cared about for the last eighteen months was Nic getting out of prison, this surprises me. "Why?"

He shrugs. "Just come home so we can talk him down."

I nod and cast an apologetic glance to the closet where Arrow's hiding. I hate leaving him like this, but I don't have a choice. Maybe he needs the reality check, too.

When we get to Nic's car, I hesitate with my hand on the door handle.

"Get in!" my brother calls.

I fold my arms across my chest. "Let me see your eyes."

"I'm clean. For Christ's sake. You *know* I'm clean. Hell, you're probably the only one who does know."

I can see in his eyes he's telling the truth, and I trust him to be honest. He knows how I feel about riding with him when he's stoned—or anyone, for that matter. Not happening.

When we get to Dad's trailer, he's sitting on the edge of the bed, crying—blubbering, really—a handgun hanging from his fingertips.

Nic and I exchange a look, and he nods. I'm hoping in our silent communication he's thinking that he'll get the gun while I distract Dad.

"Daddy?" I step closer slowly. The last thing I want to do is startle him.

Dad's head snaps up and his jaw hangs open for a minute as he takes me in. "My daughter," he says. "My daughter. Tell me it's not true."

"What's not true?" Another step closer. A shallow breath. A silent prayer.

"Frank told me he saw you with the Woodison kid at the Dairy Maid last night. Tell me it's not true. Tell me they're not going to take *you* away from me, too."

"No one's taking me away, Daddy. I'm right here." Another step, and then I jump as the gun hits the ground with a *thump*.

"They can't have you, too. Not my daughter. It's bad enough that they took Isabella."

Nic grabs the gun off the floor. I try to catch his eye and fail.

"Who took Mom?" I ask. "What are you talking about, Dad?"

"Tell me it's not true," Dad says. "Tell me you aren't letting a Woodison ruin you."

Ruin me. Dear God, do I hate that expression. "No one is ruining me." I wrap my arms around his shoulders and hold him while he cries.

Nic and I work together to calm him down and get him into bed, and when the trailer is quiet, I follow my brother outside.

"What was that about?" I ask.

"He fucking hates Woodison. The dude fired him. You know that." But Nic still won't look me in the eye.

"What aren't you telling me?"

When he meets my eyes, it's with a resigned sigh. "There are things little girls shouldn't have to know about their moms, Mee."

"Then it's a good thing I'm not a little girl anymore. Tell me."

Nic pulls a pack of cigarettes from his back pocket, taps one out, and lights it, and I watch his every move. After his first, long drag, he says, "Mom had an affair with Woodison before she left town. She'd been fucking him for months, and Dad found out and threatened to kill him."

For a hysterical, panicked moment, I think he means Arrow, and then my brain kicks in. "Uriah Woodison?"

"Yeah." He grunts and shakes his head. "Mom knew she couldn't live with Dad after that—that he'd make her pay for it every day—so she left."

An iron fist closes around my throat. "Mom and *Uriah Woodison*? Are you sure?"

Nic nods. "He has a right to hate the fucker."

A car roars into the trailer park. Gravel sprays out as the red Jetta screeches to a stop in front of me and Nic.

When Brogan climbs out, I'm still hung up on what I just learned, and for a minute I forget what he did last night. In the same moment, I forget what *I* did last night.

"Mia!" His eyes are swollen, bloodshot, and his face is pale. "I've been looking for you everywhere. Where have you been?"

I blink at him, but I can't register anything when my brain keeps playing my dad's sobs on a loop. *"Tell me they're not going to take* you *away from me, too."*

My mother was having an affair with Arrow's father. I knew

my father hated Uriah Woodison. I knew he wouldn't like the idea of me dating Arrow. But now that I understand why, I know he'll never be okay with it.

"You're not talking to me," Brogan says, and I realize I haven't answered his question. "Okay, I deserve that, but will you hear me out? Please?"

Nic narrows his gaze on Brogan, then looks to me. "What did he do?" He steps forward. "Did you hurt my sister? I told you I'd fucking ruin you if you hurt her."

Brogan holds up his hands in surrender and shakes his head. "I was drunk. I saw the texts on your phone, but it's okay. I can forgive you. I *do*. But I need you to forgive me. I'm an idiot and I was jealous and pissed and I thought he was stealing you away from me."

I don't know what he's talking about, can't think about anything but the bomb Nic just dropped.

"Please," Brogan says. "Talk to me."

"What did he do, Mia?" Nic asks. He takes another step toward Brogan. "Want me to kick his ass?"

"Come at me," Brogan says. "I fucked up, but I love your sister, and if you want to beat the shit out of me for that—"

"*Stop*," I bite out. "I can't deal with either of you right now." I turn to Brogan. My sweet, sweet Brogan, and for the first time, what I did with Arrow last night crashes into me like a thousand shards of glass. How can I feel so guilty now when those moments with Arrow felt so right? So *destined*? "Go home, Brogan. You're not making sense, and it doesn't matter. I don't have anything to say to you and I don't have any interest in hearing your excuses." Stopping, I take a breath and realize I do have one thing to say. "I hope Trish is worth it."

"But—" he begins, but he stops when I hold up my hand.

I turn to Nic. "Take me home. Please."

Nic's jaw is hard and a muscle in his neck twitches. Oh yeah, he'd give anything to take a swing at Brogan right now. Nic's a fighter. He's never known how to navigate the world without his fists. But for me, he'll tamp down that urge and let Brogan go unharmed.

"Get out of here," Nic says.

Brogan shakes his head and tries again, more softly this time. "Let me drive you home, Mia. Please."

"My sister told you to *leave*," Nic growls.

With one last desperate look at me, Brogan nods and climbs into his car.

"You want to tell me what that was about?" my brother asks, as I climb into his rusty pickup. I slip into the passenger side and buckle my seatbelt, and Nic gets in and says, "So?"

"No, Nicholas. I don't want to talk about it. Just take me home."

That muscle twitches in his neck, and his dark knuckles go white around the steering wheel, but he finally starts the car, and we head toward my apartment in silence.

"I'm sorry you had to find out that way. About Mom. She should have been the one to tell you."

I wince and drop my gaze to my hands folded in my lap. I'm

still processing. "Do you think she loved him?"

"Woodison?" Nic barks out a sardonic laugh. "Sure she did. He had her fooled. But you can guaran-damn-tee that he didn't love her. She was his maid at that oversized house of his. Keeping the place clean while his wife was dying. Nothing but an easy piece of ass to him. When Dad found out and started throwing around threats, Woodison didn't do shit to make it right."

Outside my window, hawks scavenge the Dumpster behind my apartment, and I stare at them while my mind flips and flops these mismatched puzzle pieces and tries to find a story that makes any sense to me at all.

"She was so beautiful," I whisper. "When I was a little girl, I wanted to grow up and look just like her. She made me believe . . ."

When I don't finish my thought, Nic reaches over and squeezes my hand. "I know, sis. Me too."

"Don't hurt Brogan. He's just . . ." I take a deep breath and exhale slowly. "He's trying so hard to be who he thinks he's supposed to be that sometimes he makes stupid mistakes." I hate myself for how much that explanation undercuts Brogan's betrayal. Then again, he's not the only guilty party on that count.

Mom was an adulteress. A cheater. *Like me.*

Sure, we were broken up, but a breakup hours before sleeping with Arrow feels more like a technicality than an out.

"Is it true?" Nic asks.

"What?"

Nic squeezes the steering wheel and sighs. "Were you with

Woodison last night? Is that who was in your apartment this morning?"

"No one was in my apartment this morning."

"Come on, Mee. I'm not an idiot. There were two sets of feet running around before you answered the door." He studies me for a beat before shaking his head. "You know what we are to people like them, don't you? Worker bees. Drones. Whether we're fucking them or carving their swine. They'll never see us as one of them."

The words hurt in part because they come from my brother, who's supposed to believe I can rise above, and in part because they tap into the fear I've carried ever since Arrow told me his last name. "Arrow's not like that."

"And do you believe that enough to convince Dad?"

I bite my lip hard and dig my nails into my palms. "Dad doesn't need to know. I don't have anything with Arrow. He's a friend. Last night he was just . . ." *Claiming my heart. Once and for all.*

Nic snorts. "He was what? Comforting you? Isn't Brogan his boy? Jesus. That's a Woodison for you. Take whatever they want. Fuck everybody else."

I'm too tired to have this conversation, too unsure to defend Arrow to my brother, so I open the door. "Thanks for coming for me this morning. Let me know when Dad wakes up later."

"Will do."

I step out of the car and am about to close the door when Nic calls, "Mia?" and I stop. "Don't sell yourself short. All those things Mom taught us were worth believing in. Even if she wasn't."

ARROW

Brogan came by. My best friend came by his girl's apartment to talk to her. Knocked on the door. Pleaded through it. Begged for her forgiveness when I was the only one here to listen.

I suck. *Goddamn do I suck.*

There's a guy code, and then there's just common fucking sense. I crossed lines last night, and maybe crossing those lines was inevitable, but it all happened too fast. Too soon. And now I have to find a way to explain it to Brogan that won't make him hate my guts forever.

By the time Mia gets back to her apartment, I've mentally rehearsed ten different ways to tell Brogan what happened, showered, dressed, made a pot of coffee, and, after searching her cabinets for real food and coming up empty, eaten a Pop-Tart.

When she closes the apartment door behind her, she's deflated. Every piece of this morning's joy has fled, and the energy in the apartment shifts from nervous to ominous.

"Everything okay?" I ask. Stupid fucking question, considering what had her running out the door.

"Yeah." She avoids my gaze and heads to the coffee pot. "Dad's asleep now. He'll be okay. Just a rough night."

"Brogan came over. I didn't answer the door, of course, but he was here. We need to talk about what we're going to tell him."

She dumps some of that powdered creamer junk into her coffee and stirs, staring at her spoon as if this takes careful focus. "Nothing. We're not going to tell him anything."

"Right. So you think we should wait a few weeks and keep this quiet for a while?" My stomach knots at the idea. I don't keep secrets from Brogan. And yet I did. I've kept my feelings for Mia a secret for nearly a year. I nod. "You're right. We'll give it some time."

She turns slowly, abandoning her coffee on the counter and folding her arms as she looks at me. Her face is blank, nothing like the woman in my arms this morning. "We aren't going to tell him at all, Arrow. Not now and not in a few weeks. I saw him at my dad's this morning, and he's already a mess. There's no reason to hurt him more."

My breath leaves me. "You're going back to him. I thought..." I look away. God, this hurts like hell, and I deserve it. I slept with her the night they broke up. I knew better and I did it anyway. And now I'm nothing but a mistake to her. A dirty secret.

"I'm not going back to him." My relief is short-lived. Her words are cold, her face stony. All the passion and emotion from last night has been hidden, locked away tight somewhere. "And that'll hurt him enough. Please don't hurt him more by confessing our betrayal."

"You were broken up," I whisper, even though her description of what we did is an echo of my own thoughts. "You can't betray someone you aren't committed to."

"You and I both know that's not true."

"We can't keep this secret forever. I want to kiss you in public and hold your hand, and I'm willing to wait a couple of weeks, a month even, but eventually it needs to come out, and it's better if it comes from us."

Her stony face falters, but then she closes her eyes and her walls go back up. "There is no *us*, Arrow. There can't be."

I feel like she punched me in the gut with a set of brass knuckles. I fucked this up. "What happened? Did Brogan say something to you? Something about me or..." *Or is guilt gnawing at you the way it's gnawed at me all morning?*

She drops her head and studies the floor. "You were right last night. You said that when I decided to date Brogan, I was choosing him. That I did it knowing I couldn't date you. It was true then, and it's still true now."

"So last night was..."

"I'd been drinking. I was emotional. It was a mistake."

"Right." Fuck. My first concussion was more enjoyable than this. I look around for my keys, grab them off the counter, and head for the door, where I have to stop because leaving her literally hurts. It tears me apart from the inside.

"I'm sorry, Arrow. You're a good guy. I just..."

"You just made a mistake." I attempt a smile, but even I can feel it twisted on my face—half plastic smile, half painful grimace. "For what it's worth, last night wasn't a mistake on my side. Not even a little."

MIA

My apartment is on fire.

I rush to unlock the door when I see the flames flashing on the other side of the glass. My hands shake and fumble the keys, and before I can find the right one, someone pulls open the door.

Brogan.

And the apartment isn't on fire. Candles glow from every surface, flickering under the breeze created by the ceiling fan.

"Surprise," Brogan says, taking my bag from my arm.

"What?"

"This is a birthday redo," he says. "I shouldn't have missed it. Tonight I'm going to make up for that."

I don't relish celebrating my birthday. I find the whole idea weird—people focusing on me and doing something just because I happened to leave my mother's womb this day years ago. And frankly, I hate being the center of attention.

Brogan told me he'd change that. He said he'd teach me to enjoy the spotlight. And then he canceled our plans and left me at home while he went out of town.

It's not even my birthday anymore, but here he is and I'm afraid I'm a lost cause, because after the day I've had, I don't have the energy to dodge his well-intentioned romantic advances.

"Brogan." I sigh. "I told you this morning I didn't want to talk to you. What are you doing here?"

He holds up a hand. "I know I'm probably the last person you want to see, but just hear me out."

"Fine." I fold my arms across my chest as he leads me into the apartment and to the kitchen. It smells great in here, like chocolate and fresh bread, and I realize I haven't eaten today. I don't usually forget, but my mind is so crowded with everything that's happened, even remembering to eat seems like too much.

I sit at the table, where he's laid out a feast in chocolate: chocolate pastries, chocolate-covered strawberries, chocolate chunk cookies, and, of course, in the center of it all, a three-tiered chocolate cake already topped with flickering candles. "Why'd you do all this?" I shake my head.

Brogan isn't like Arrow. He doesn't have an endless bank account at his disposal. Sure, he grew up in a house nicer than mine, but as far as I can tell, his parents are up to their eyeballs in debt—choosing to buy their way into a higher social class even if they can't afford it. "You didn't have to, Brogan. I don't need it."

"You deserve it." He takes the seat beside me but sits sideways on the chair so he faces me. "Do you remember telling me that you wanted to grow up and marry a guy who made you feel special every day?"

"Everyone wants that," I say. But maybe not as much as I do. Other girls expect it. I, on the other hand, grew up watching the way my father treated my mother—as if she was the hired help or expendable. For me, it's not an expectation—it's something I only dare to hope can be. Something I'm not sure I believe is real.

"I've always believed that guy would be me, but I saw he was texting you and freaked out."

"Guys aren't allowed to text me now."

He swallows hard and bites his lip. "Trish told me that you and Arrow had a thing. She said I was stupid if I couldn't see it and that you'd leave me in a second for him."

This is the part where I'm supposed to say, "And you believed her?" But I don't. The question is as good as a lie. So I choose a different one. "Why didn't you talk to me about it instead of unzipping your pants?"

"Because sometimes I'm a coward." He bites his lip and grimaces before meeting my gaze. "And it was easier to look at your phone."

He said something about texts this morning, but I was too distracted by what Nic told me about Mom to fully register anything. "I still don't know what texts you're talking about."

"It doesn't matter. I shouldn't have looked." He draws in a long breath. "I knew you were friends, but seeing it like that just seemed to confirm everything she'd said. And I already know how much he makes you smile."

"Brogan—"

"I warm the bench while I watch my friends compete in a sport I've dedicated my life to. I only get to go in when they need someone to block for Arrow or to do kick returns. Playing second string means there's someone better. I didn't want to be second string to you. And I panicked because I thought I was. What I didn't realize was being your second string trumps not being your anything. Every day of the week."

"I never thought of you as my second string," I say, and suddenly I don't care what he's done or who betrayed whom. I want to curl into his strong arms and let him hold me. I want to listen to him talk to me about the future and let his dreams be mine. Brogan isn't Arrow, and that's a good thing. Arrow and I can't be. Not after what I learned from my brother. Not even before. But Brogan? He's a good guy. Sometimes his insecurities motivate him to make terrible decisions, but I could say the same of half the people I know.

"I'm so sorry. Let me prove myself to you, Mia. I know you don't owe it to me, but I'm asking anyway."

"I can't promise we can come back from this, Brogan." But I want to try, I realize. Maybe I'm scared to be alone. Maybe I can't stand to see him hurting this much. Or maybe I'm selfish and need a buffer between me and Arrow.

"We'll take it slow. Tonight, let me feed you. This weekend, maybe you'll let me take you out. We'll start over and you can decide . . ." He draws in a ragged breath. "You can decide if I'm worth the kind of forgiveness it'll take to get us through this."

"And what happens the next time you feel insecure, Brogan? What happens when I laugh at another guy's jokes or don't at yours?"

"I remind myself that I'd rather play the bench than not at all. Because it's true, Mia."

"That breaks my heart," I whisper.

"Why?"

"Because I don't want you to see yourself as playing the bench with the girl you end up with. I want you to believe you're the star. You're worth that."

His mouth opens and then closes, as if he can't figure out what to say. And then he leans forward and presses his lips to mine.

For a fleeting, ridiculous moment, I wonder if he can taste Arrow there. If he can feel the memory of another man on my lips. But then I let go of that ridiculous thought and part my lips for his kiss, welcoming its warmth.

Tonight I'm lonely, chased into the empty corners of my mind by the ghost of my mother and her decisions. Brogan chases the ghost away, and the loneliness fades. And for that, for now, I'm grateful.

He breaks the kiss, breathing hard, and leans his forehead against mine. "I'm going to take that as a yes."

"Take it as a maybe." I squeeze my eyes shut. *You love this man. This is good.* But part of me screeches a warning in the back of my mind that I'm being selfish, that I'm using Brogan to put distance between Arrow and me in the only way I know how.

I shake my head, pushing the thought away. *This isn't about Arrow.*

"I don't know where this is going," I say, and the words soothe my conscience a bit. "I don't know if what we have can be salvaged."

He cups my face in one big hand and gives me a sad smile. "I do, Mia. In this, at least, I have enough confidence for us both. We're good together."

"Well hello, romantic evening!"

Brogan and I turn to see Bailey standing in the doorway to the kitchen, her hands on her hips. I saw her this morning after I kicked Arrow out and told her everything. I was grateful to have someone I could tell the truth, and I'm grateful to see her now.

"Fucking A, Brogan," she says, "you planning to win her back through sugar alone?"

Brogan blushes and shrugs. "If that's what it takes."

Bailey saunters to the table, grabs a cookie off a plate, and takes a big bite. "Sweet, delicious, sinful carbs, Batman. God, you want to date *me*? Because keep this shit coming and I will spread my legs, honey."

"Bailey!" I laugh, then so do Brogan and Bailey, and then we're all laughing and it feels damn good. Until the humor leaves Brogan's face completely and his jaw goes hard.

I follow his gaze to see Arrow standing in the doorway, a bouquet of yellow roses in his hand.

I watch as Arrow takes everything in. The candles, the food, Brogan by my side, and then finally the betrayal marring Brogan's beautiful face.

"Who are the flowers for?" Brogan asks. His voice is hard, and all the softness from his earlier expression is gone.

Bailey gapes, taking two seconds to look at me then Arrow. "Me," she says, walking toward him and snatching them from his hand.

Arrow plasters on a smile as Bailey wraps her arms behind his neck.

"Thanks, sexy," she says, rising onto her toes.

And even though I know she's trying to help me, even though I know there's no future for me and Arrow, something inside me breaks at the sight of her lips against his.

"You ready to go?" he asks when he pulls back, and the sexy raspiness of his voice and the way he smolders at her—yes, *smolders*—is so believable that I, for a ridiculous, panicked second, really don't know for sure that he *didn't* come for Bailey.

Brogan clears his throat and shifts. "Does Mason know about you two?"

"Why?" Bailey asks. "You think Mason owns me or something?"

"Um . . ." Brogan looks to me, and I shrug. I don't claim to keep up with Bailey's revolving door of boy-toys, but I didn't think she'd slept with anyone else since she started messing around with Mason.

"Mason and I are history," she says.

"Bailey?" I say, and she gives me a hard look. If she and Mason broke up, it's because of Nic, but this isn't the time or the place to talk about it. Not that she'd want to hear what I have to say about her pushing Mason aside for my brother.

"You two coming?" Bailey asks. She looks at Arrow. "You're treating us to sushi, at the place uptown, right?"

He looks to me and Brogan and our joined hands. All of his smolder—pretend or otherwise—fades, but he plays along. "But these two probably want to be *alone*."

"What do you say?" Brogan asks. "Sushi sound okay to you?" He leans forward, his lips skimming the shell of my ear. "Or would you rather stay in?" he asks, so only I can hear.

Stay here with Brogan? Maybe hang out in my bed where Arrow touched me so intimately just hours ago? Even if I wanted to, my heart couldn't take it.

ARROW

Well, dinner was fun. Watching Brogan throw himself all over Mia between dirty glances in my direction. Watching Mia's defenses melt bit by bit until he had her laughing by the end of the meal. Yep. *Barrels of fun.* A close second to having my junk punched repeatedly. Very, very close.

I get back to the dorm before Brogan and settle into the couch in the common area with my physiology textbook and a beer. I've got a test in A&P Tuesday, and if I don't get my head together and study, I'm going to bomb. Twenty minutes later, Brogan bursts into the room and slams the door behind him. All I've managed to accomplish is opening my textbook to some chapter that may or may not actually be covered on the exam, and a detailed mental recounting of everything that happened between when Mia's brother knocked on her door and when she kicked me out of the apartment.

I can't fucking figure it out.

When I lift my head from my book to look at Brogan, he's glaring at me. Fuck. Did she tell him? "What's wrong?"

He folds his arms and his nostrils flare as he sneers. "I take responsibility, okay? What I did last night was fucking stupid, and you can stop looking at me like I'm some dirtbag who doesn't deserve her."

Okay, so we're going to do this. Taking a breath, I put my book down on the couch cushion beside me and stand. "She caught you with your dick in another girl's mouth. You're going to stand there and tell me that she doesn't deserve better than that?"

"I fucking screwed up, but can you blame me?"

"Yes. I can. I do." I step forward, and he throws up both hands and pushes me back. The backs of my legs hit the couch, and I let myself fall into it. "I'm not fighting you just so you can feel better about yourself." She wouldn't want me to, and I have to let her make her own choices.

"I saw her phone. I saw your texts." He drags a hand through his hair and his mouth twists. "You were supposed to be my best friend but you just couldn't handle that I'm first choice for once."

"What texts? What are you talking about?"

He pulls out his phone and taps on the screen. It's a screenshot of my text exchange with Mia from her birthday.

> **Arrow:** *I can't stop thinking about what you did at the Cavern tonight. I had no idea.*

> **Mia:** *I was drinking. It was a mistake.*
> **Arrow:** *Was it? It didn't feel like a mistake.*
> **Mia:** *We're not talking about this again.*
> **Arrow:** *Okay, but I'm at your door. Come open it so I can give you something.*

"I saw it on her phone and took a screenshot. I saved it to my phone so I could decide what to do."

"Why are you looking at Mia's texts?"

He smacks the phone out of my hand. "Fucking stand up, Arrow. Look me in the eye and tell me nothing happened between you two."

But I can't. Of course I can't. Only now do I realize how incriminating those messages look, but I can't say nothing happened, and I promised Mia I wouldn't tell him something did. So I stand, look my best friend in the eye, and say, "You're the biggest fucking idiot. You had a good thing, and you fucked it up over nothing."

"I'm not you, Arrow. I'm not the guy the girls fall all over. I'm not the MVP or the smartest kid in the class. I'm none of those things, but I want them all. And maybe . . . maybe I was feeling like I wanted to be some of those things, even for a few drunken minutes in a dark room."

"That doesn't make any fucking sense. You might not have everything you want, but you had *her*, and you're a fucking idiot for not understanding what that's worth."

He snatches the phone off the couch and holds it up. "Was I

supposed to ignore this?"

"I was texting her because I had no idea she could *sing* like that. You would have known that if you'd asked her, but you assumed the worst. Or maybe you wanted an excuse. Trish has been following you around for months, just waiting for her chance."

Brogan steps back—one step, two—then collapses into a chair. "She didn't cheat on me." He tugs on his hair with both hands and stares at the ceiling. "I see the way you look at her, Arrow. I know she sees it too, and I've spent all these months waiting for the moment she'd figure it out and leave me."

"Figure what out?"

He drops his hands to the arms of the chair and lowers his gaze to meet mine. "Figure out you were the better guy. Why would any girl want me when she could be with you?"

Guilt gnaws at my stomach. I sink onto the couch and lean forward, my elbows on my knees. I can't look at him.

He swallows so hard I hear it. "I was so convinced it was coming that I didn't question it. I just assumed. I don't want to be that guy. I don't want to be the dick, but she kept putting off being with me, and I get that it's her religion or whatever, but it started to eat at me. You know, like maybe it's not sex that's the problem but *me*."

I snap my head up. "What did you say?"

"I don't want to be like that," he says, wincing. "But we've been together for a year, Arrow, and a guy starts to wonder."

"She hasn't . . . You two haven't . . ." Yep, now I'm stuttering.

"Don't look at me like that. I love her, okay? I'm trying to be patient." He throws his head back and groans. "I *was* trying. I screwed up everything."

How long can a heart race without oxygen? Because blood whooshes through my ears but I can't breathe. I can't freaking breathe. She was still a virgin? I assumed in all the time since we talked about it she and Brogan would have . . . But they didn't.

Fuck. And she didn't think that was important to tell me? She never had sex with Brogan, but then one night with me and—

"Arrow?" Brogan calls, and I can tell by his tone that he's waiting for me to answer a question.

"I'm sorry. What?"

"You don't deny it, do you? You have feelings for her. Tell me I wasn't completely insane." The accusation is gone from his tone. Brogan is back. My empathetic buddy who gets that life just isn't fair sometimes, who gets it better than anybody, because life is never fucking fair to him.

Mia was a virgin. It doesn't matter. It shouldn't matter.

Fuck. It matters so much. That means something, doesn't it? But as much as I want to believe it means I'm more to her than she says, I'm afraid it only reinforces what she hinted at the night of her birthday. She thinks what we have is like what her mom and dad had—the hot, fast-burning passion. The impulsive mistake.

Brogan stares at me. Waiting for me to answer his question. No point in denying it. Chris knew; Brogan knew. Clearly it's all over my face every time I look at her.

I swallow hard. "Do you know what we talked about on her

birthday? After I stopped by to give her my present?"

Brogan grimaces. I could always read him like a book, and right now he's trying to decide if he really wants to know or if maybe the truth might hurt even worse than his suspicions.

"We talked about you," I say, putting him out of his misery. "I asked her if you made her happy." When he opens his mouth to say something, I hold up a hand. "I know. That's not the kind of thing you ask your best friend's girl, but I did. Maybe I wanted her to tell me she was lonely with you or that you weren't good to her. I don't know what I expected, but it's not what I got."

He rubs the seam at the end of the chair arm. "What did she say?"

"She compared you to the sun. You keep her safe and warm." I don't want to lie to him at all, so I'm glad I don't have to lie to him about this. I'm glad I don't have to pretend. "It doesn't matter how I feel about her, Brogan. You're the one she wants." *I'm the fire. The danger. I'm the mistake.*

"I screwed up." He turns to me, looking me in the eye for the first time all day, and says, "I didn't believe I was even capable of hurting her. But you should have seen her face this morning. Christ, I didn't even know she cared that much, but when I pulled up at her dad's, she looked like she'd been cut in two." He swallows. "I knew she loved me, but I didn't believe she was *in love* with me. Maybe if I'd believed it, maybe if I had any fucking self-esteem, I wouldn't have assumed the worst from those texts, and I wouldn't have been such an idiot last night."

I stand up. I don't have it in me to sit here and listen to him bemoan his mistakes. I'm all out of sympathy. When I get to my bedroom door, I stop. I keep my gaze trained on the doorknob as I ask, "Have you heard her sing?"

"It's amazing, isn't it?" He sighs heavily. "That's her *thing*, you know? She's just too scared to go after it. Too practical."

"She told you her thing." I didn't mean to say it out loud. But there it is. Standing in the room with us like an unwanted guest who shares your secrets.

"Of course she did, Arrow. She's my girlfriend."

PART VII: AFTER

MIA

"Mia, could you come in here, please?" Gwen calls from the study as I walk by.

I stop in the middle of the text I was writing to Bailey and tuck my phone into my pocket.

Gwen's standing behind Uriah's desk, holding fabric swatches against the dark walnut furniture.

"Can I do something for you, Gwen?" I ask.

The picture of irritation, she flips through the swatches, past a bunch of dark paisley prints that would be a better fit for the gentlemen's club look Uriah has going on in here, and stops when she lands on a pure white swatch the texture of velvet. "I saw Arrow coming out of your room this morning," she says.

Shit. "Gwen, I—"

She holds up a hand. "Listen. I feel like somewhere along the way, you may have gotten the idea that you and I are friends, and I know I'm young, and I know I don't come from money, so maybe you think that makes us twinsies or some shit. But we're not. And you're not my friend. You're my employee. You're not Arrow's friend. You're Arrow's employee. So if you want to make *fucking him* part of your job description, go for it. But if you think you're going to sleep your way into a better position in this house, you can forget about it right now. It didn't work for your mother, and it's not going to work for you."

I flinch at the mention of my mother. How does she even know about them? Uriah? Rumors? I have to clench my teeth to keep myself from talking.

"My husband has plans for his son, and they don't involve marrying trailer trash. Do you understand?"

Straightening my spine, I lift my chin and fist my hands at my sides. "Yes, ma'am."

She drops the ring of swatches to the desk and rakes her cold eyes over me. "How convenient for you that your little boyfriend turned into a vegetable that night. And now you're free to fuck a Woodison, which I'm guessing is what you wanted all along." She sighs dramatically and gives me a cold smile. "Unfortunately for you, Woodison men have figured out what Mendez women are good for, and it ends in the bedroom."

"You can say anything you want about me," I say. My cheeks are hot. My skin burns as if my blood is actually simmering in my veins. "But you say one more thing about my mother, and you won't have to fire me, Gwen. I'll leave, and I'll make sure Uriah knows why he has to scramble to find a new nanny."

The color drains from her face, confirming my suspicions

that her husband wouldn't approve of this conversation.

"Is that what you want?" I turn around and walk out of the room.

I didn't think we were friends, but I did think we were *allies*. And I know she didn't come from the kind of money Mr. Woodison has, but I didn't think her life was a model for how I could improve mine. I didn't respect her enough for that.

Arrow stops me in the hallway. "Is everything okay?"

"Why?" The monitor crackles, and then the sounds of Katie cooing come through. *Saved by the baby.*

He cocks his head to the side. "Mia, you look upset."

I shrug. "I'm fine. I have to go get Katie. It's time for her bottle." I grab a bottle from the kitchen and head to the nursery. I feel Arrow behind me the whole time, but I assume he's going to walk away the second I step into the nursery door, because he seems to want nothing to do with his baby sister.

But he surprises me. He follows me in, and when I stop to place the bottle into the electric warmer we keep by the changing table, he skirts around me and stands by the crib before I can.

"She's pretty, isn't she?" he says, looking down on her. She's on her back, eyes open, baby fists extended toward the farm animals on her mobile.

I stand beside him and feel some of the anger and hurt from Gwen's lecture wash away. "Yes, she is."

"I always wanted a kid sister," he says. "Sister, brother. I didn't care. I just hated being an only child. Mom had to have a hysterectomy after me, though." He lifts his eyes to mine. "That was her first fight with cancer."

"I'm sorry." I draw in a ragged breath because he's *talking* to me. He held me last night. He let me cry about Brogan and stayed in my bed when I told him I didn't want to be alone. But he hasn't said anything to me all morning, and I assumed we were going back to our old dynamic where we don't talk about anything.

He shakes his head. "It's okay. I just always imagined a kid sister who looked like my mom. Katie's beautiful but she doesn't— Obviously, she wouldn't look like my mom." He reaches into the crib and scoops her up, his big hands holding her from under her arms. Her eyes go big and she gurgles happy baby sounds.

"She likes you."

He cuddles her up against his chest. "Hmm."

"You really know how to hold a baby," I say. "You're a natural with her."

"She's not the first baby I've held, Mia." He shakes his head but keeps smiling as he gazes down at his baby sister. "Man, you play football, and so many of those idiots are having kids too early. They're a hotshot on the field so they think they're too good to wear a condom or something. I don't know. But I've gotten to hold a lot of babies." He lifts his head and aims that smile at me, and I feel something in my chest—as if his smile pulls down this barrier that's been protecting my heart.

I swallow. "Gwen thinks we're sleeping together."

His smile falls away, but he keeps his eyes locked on mine for a long minute. Am I supposed to know what he's thinking? Because I don't. I can't tell if he doesn't give a shit or if this information makes him angry. He doesn't speak to me enough yet for me to guess his thoughts.

He walks Katie over to the changing table and begins to change her diaper. "I'll talk to her."

"No, don't, Arrow. There's no point."

He nods, and again I wish I knew what he was thinking. He lets me in his bed, even comes to mine, touches me. Holds me.

I haven't done anything wrong, and I'm not the kind of girl who dreams of marrying her way to financial security. But when I wake up in the middle of the night and Arrow's arms are wrapped around me, I *wish* we were sleeping together. When my brain is still half asleep, my body wakes. I want him to roll me over and make me feel the way he did that night in the kitchen. I want his mouth and hands to chase my numbness away. I want him to use me to chase his away.

Then when my brain wakes, I remember Brogan and my guilt, and I'm so glad I didn't let my body decide. I'm so glad I didn't give in to that need to *feel* something, so glad I didn't give in. Even though there are nights when the fear of never feeling anything again is worse than the guilt and the grief.

"*How convenient for you that your little boyfriend turned into a vegetable that night. And now you're free to fuck a Woodison, which I'm guessing is what you wanted all along.*"

I know she's only giving voice to what others will think. She's probably not the first to think it, and I hate that. It's not fair to Brogan or Arrow.

"It's going to be fine," I assure Arrow. "Don't worry about it."

"Do you think she's going to tell my dad?"

I draw in a sharp breath. *Tell my dad.* I imagine that wouldn't end well for him. "I don't know, Arrow. If you're worried about it, maybe you should talk to him. Let him know what she thinks and set the record straight if you need to. But don't do it for me."

He only fumbles a little as he changes Katie's diaper, but mostly I'm impressed that he knows which way to put it on and how to button the onesie. He's a natural.

He grabs the bottle from the warmer, puts his finger on the nipple, and shakes it as he takes a seat in the rocker.

"You don't have to do that," I tell him.

He cocks a brow. "Maybe I want to. I mean, she seems to like *you,* so I figure she can't be all that bad."

There it is. That tugging in my chest again. But this time it's worse.

After the accident, I felt my heart going into hibernation. After I buried my brother. After they told me Brogan would never be himself again. I could feel my heart wrapping itself up and retreating to the cave where it could hide safely. And I was glad when it did, because it meant I didn't have to breathe around the constant aching anymore. I was glad, but I had no idea how much it would hurt to feel it wake up.

When I pull up to the Barretts' home, I have to sit in the car for twenty minutes trying to catch my breath. How many times did I come here and wish I didn't have to go inside? How many chances did I have to tell him everything I was thinking, and I talked to him about the weather as if he were some stranger passing the time with me in the line at the DMV? I know that with Brogan's current health, I need to treat each visit as if it's the last I get. Because it might be. Suddenly, there's not enough time. I need more time. More quiet minutes to hold his hand. More long afternoons by his side in the sunroom. More opportunities to reiterate the apology that will never be enough.

When Mrs. Barrett sticks her head out the front door and waves to me, I decide my pity party is over, wipe my cheeks, and go inside.

She pulls me into a hug—a little longer and a little tighter than any hug before—and I return it in kind. "Say your goodbyes," she whispers in my ear. "You say your goodbyes today."

"I know." I don't want her to have to coddle me. She's going to bury her son soon, and she shouldn't be responsible for tending to my grief. "I will."

Pulling away, she shakes her head. "We're, um, making arrangements. Just trying to get things in order for the funeral. We'll have it in Blackhawk Valley, of course." The hope has drained from her eyes. The blue irises she shared with her son are empty. "He always talked about how beautiful your voice was, and I think he'd want to hear it when he says goodbye to us. We were hoping you'd sing."

I suck in a breath. *It's not her job to comfort you.* "I don't know."

"You don't have to answer right now. Think about it."

"Okay."

She tilts her head toward the back hallway. "He's in bed. Hospice is coming. We're just trying to make him comfortable now."

Make him comfortable. Those words make it real, and I rush back to the bedroom as if he might disappear before I can traverse the length of the hallway.

Brogan is lying in bed, just like she said he would be. His eyes are closed, and his body doesn't look like his own. It's small and lanky. All bones and weakness. This is no longer the man who begged me to stay with him. He's no longer even the man who whispered my name after the accident. Not even the one who took my shaking hand while I looked for a pulse.

"I'm sorry. I'm so, so sorry."

His last words to me were an apology. And now it's my turn. "Brogan." I sweep his hair off his forehead, and just the touch of my fingertips against his skin makes me want to fall apart. "I wanted to be in love with you. I wanted you to be the one for me. Every girl deserves a guy who can make her laugh the way you did, and I thought if I just held on tight enough, you could be enough."

I swallow hard. I've never stopped regretting my decision to end it with him that night. Never stopped hating myself for telling him the truth about what happened with Arrow. He was being so irrational, and I thought that if I could just *hurt* him, he'd let me out of the car.

Instead, he kept the doors locked, and his last moments were of anger, frustration, and sadness.

"I love you. And I'm so grateful that you loved me." I put my fingers against his soft lips. Those lips that kissed me so many times. The lips that uttered sweet words I came to take for granted. "I never should have ended it like I did. Or tried to end it, or whatever. If I could change the way it all unraveled..."

I close my eyes and listen. As if maybe if I don't look at Brogan's empty shell of a body, he'll be able to talk to me—he'll be able to tell me he understands. But all I get is the ceiling fan—*Whoomph. Whoomph. Whoomph*—and cars spraying water on the sidewalk as they drive down the street in front of the house.

"Of course you would, sweetie." That's not the voice I've been waiting for, and I feel exposed as I turn to see Trish step into the room. How long has she been listening? "We all would," she continues. She's been crying. Her face is red and blotchy, her eyes swollen. She comes to stand beside me, and I'm glad she's there. Something about her falling apart helps me hold it together.

I don't need to feel stronger than her. This isn't about strength. The comfort of shared grief is the antithesis of trying to be the stronger one. This is about understanding that our pain is what makes us human, and allowing ourselves to feel it. I can't feel angry with Trish anymore and can't blame her for Brogan's decisions, not when I see her like this, grief laid out and exposed.

"This sucks," she whispers. "As if it's not hard enough to say goodbye to someone you love—this is all tangled up in the fight you two had." She squeezes her eyes shut. "It's tangled up in our mistakes. I know he betrayed you, but if you feel like you have to blame someone, don't blame him." She takes my hands in hers and squeezes them. Her hands are so cold, as if she's been cuddling with the dead. "I loved him and I decided I'd do whatever it took to get him. *I* screwed up. *I* am to blame." Her eyes plead as she lifts them to mine. "Everyone wants someone to blame, and no one will blame me. I knew he was in love with you and I still . . ."

I turn and wrap her in my arms, and she dissolves into silent sobs against my chest.

"I loved him so much."

"I know." I stroke her hair and take a long, deep breath. *Damn you, Brogan.* He had to have known how she felt, and he should never have messed around with her if he wasn't going to pursue it. He shouldn't have done a lot of things, and the reminder of his flaws gives my grief a jagged edge, makes it hurt more with everything that was left unsaid and undone. No wonder we paint our lost loved ones without flaws. This is harder.

When Trish pulls away, she pastes on a smile I know is for my benefit. "He loved you, you know? He loved you with the kind of intensity that makes teenage girls obsessed with romance. He loved you, and I was just so jealous of that. I wanted to steal it. To make it mine. I'm the one to blame here. And I'd trade my life for his." She holds me by my shoulders for a long time, staring into my eyes. "I want you to know that. I *need* you to know that I'd give my own life to make it right."

She seems so melodramatic, and I grimace. I've probably said the same to someone along the way. I have to believe her, because if I ever said it, I'm sure I meant it, too. "It doesn't work like that,"

I tell her softly.

"Right." She releases me and steps around me to study Brogan. She touches his face and runs her fingers along his jaw. "But if it did..."

ARROW

There are too many people at my house. A quick glance out the back windows and onto the patio and I count a dozen guys from the team and nearly as many girls.

Mia went to say goodbye to Brogan today, and there have been people milling around since she got home, so I haven't been able to get her alone and ask how she's doing.

Trish comes in from the patio and props her sunglasses on the top of her head. She's had them on out back all afternoon, so I never noticed how swollen her eyes are. She looks as if she's been crying for days.

"Are you okay?" I ask. It seems like she shows up here as often as she can since I got home, always trying to get me alone. My irritation with her kept me from registering that she's got to be as upset as the rest of us about the end of Brogan's life.

"I'm not." With a glance to the crowd out back, she grabs my wrist and drags me down the hall and away from the kitchen.

"Trish," I say, the warning in my voice. "I'm sorry if I gave you the wrong idea, but I'm seriously—"

"Shut up!" She pushes me into the study and pulls the door closed behind her. "We need to talk, and I'm sick of trying to get you alone."

"I'm sorry about New Year's Eve." It's an apology I should have given her a long time ago. "I didn't mean to lead you on. I didn't—"

"Fuck that, Arrow. I'm in love with Brogan, not you. That night wasn't about you. It was about him."

"Okay," I say cautiously.

She paces the length of the room behind the dark leather couch. "Do you remember?"

My stomach sinks. I really don't want to do this. "Do I remember New Year's Eve?"

She stops and lifts her eyes to mine. "Yeah."

I swallow hard. "Not a lot, Trish. I mean, I remember us... you know."

She stares at me hard, and I don't know what else to say. How much does she know? Has her dad told her something? Jesus, I don't want to talk about this. "Arrow," she says, holding my gaze. "*I* remember it."

"I'm sorry. I think we were both screwed up that night."

She shakes her head. "No. Not the party. After the party."

"After your dad picked you up?" I ask. Because as fragmented as my memory is, that piece is there—Coach showing up at the party to pick up Trish, because her punishment for her latest screw-up was having to ring in the New Year at home.

"I convinced him to let me stay with you, to let you drive me home. He didn't know you'd been drinking, but I thought it'd be okay. You'd stopped drinking and were trying to sober up."

My stomach turns sour. "What are you saying?"

"I was in the car." She folds her arms and squeezes her eyes shut. "*I* remember it all. The sick thunking sound. The screeching tires. The silence in those seconds after and before we . . . I know my dad covered it up. I wanted you to know that I know."

I just stare at her. I can't speak. There's nothing to be said. She knows about this prison I'm trapped in. And she's been trapped here, too. All this time. "How could you keep this secret? Why didn't you *stop* me, Trish?"

"I'm sorry."

"I don't remember anything after leaving the party." *I don't even remember leaving the party.*

"I know you don't. Consider yourself lucky."

I shake my head. "I hit them and I just . . . drove away? I can't fucking remember."

"Stopping wouldn't have changed anything," she whispers.

I squeeze my eyes shut, as if this new piece of information might make the memory appear in my brain, but nothing's there.

"I'm an idiot," she whispers. "I thought the best way I could get Brogan's attention was to hurt him. I thought the *worst* I could do to him was to be with you. I thought he'd see pictures of us together and hear people talking about how we were all over each other. I wanted to hurt him so he'd wake up and realize he wanted me more than he wanted her."

"This is more than some stupid jealousy!" My voice booms, echoing off the walls of my study, and I have to take a breath. There are people out there who'd be destroyed by this conversation if they heard it. *Mia* is out there.

"That's my point," Trish says. "I thought hurting him like he'd hurt me was so important, and then suddenly none of that mattered. It didn't matter how many pictures there were of you and me on Facebook. Brogan couldn't look at pictures. He couldn't get jealous."

"You were in the car?" I can't wrap my mind around it, and my brain keeps going back to the morning after the accident. I got a ride from the hospital to Coach's house, and that damn deer was hanging in the garage, bleeding all over the place. I grabbed a bucket and some bleach water and scrubbed at the garage floor until my hands were raw, as if I could clean it up, wipe it away, change the thing I couldn't even remember.

"It was a terrible night for everyone," Trish says.

"If you'd just made me stop and call the cops, your dad wouldn't have had the chance to cover it up." I press the flat of my palm to my chest and rub it around, as if it might be able to rub away the hurt. "Why didn't you tell me sooner? You've known what I've been living with."

"Dad wouldn't let me talk to you about it. He didn't want you knowing I'd—" She looks away and shakes her head. "And I was scared. It was awful. You're *lucky* you can't remember."

"I'm sorry," I whisper. Because I see it on her face now—the evidence of torment I should have recognized months ago. The torment of living with a horrible secret that's eating you from the inside.

"I remember it all. The sick thunking sound. The screeching tires. The silence in those seconds after."

"I'm so sorry," I say, because I can't apologize to Brogan's parents. To Mia. To the people who really deserve to hear my apology. "I can't figure out why I would have thought I was okay to drive. I'm not that guy."

"I'm not looking for your apology, Arrow. Stop apologizing." She draws in a breath and straightens her shoulders. "I just wanted you to know that I know."

"Okay."

Mia opens the door and steps into the room with Katie in her arms. She spots me and Trish and does a double take. "Oh. Sorry, I was just looking for a quiet place to . . . I'll get out of here." She rushes out of the room and down the hall.

"Fuck," I mutter.

Trish raises a brow. "Are you two . . . ?"

"No. Nothing like that."

"I want to hate her," she says, staring down the hall where Mia disappeared. "Hate is so much more comfortable than the guilt. But I can't help it. I try to hate her and can only hate myself for what I did."

"What do you mean?"

She shrugs. "It's not like I thought he'd broken up with her. I just thought it was only a matter of time. I think I always loved

Brogan, but she had him under some spell. I couldn't compete, so I played dirty."

"Forgive yourself, Trish. Carrying around this regret isn't going to help anyone. Try to forgive yourself."

She releases a puff of air that's probably supposed to be laughter, and her lips twist into something that's probably supposed to be a smile. It's all so much uglier than the girl she was before the accident. The girl who lost the guy she loved.

"Have you forgiven yourself for that night?" she asks me.

"Of course not."

"Then you understand why I can't forgive myself either."

MIA

He's *free to be with whomever he wants,* I tell myself. But it doesn't feel that way. Finding Trish in the study with Arrow—behind a closed door—felt like as much of a betrayal as the night I walked in on Trish and Brogan.

That's not fair. He's not mine. But tell that to my waking heart.

I go to the nursery to give Katie her bottle and rock her to sleep, and after she drifts off in my arms, I settle her into the crib.

When I got back from Indianapolis this afternoon, everyone was at the house. Again. It seems like they spend more time here than they do at their own homes. And I know for a fact that Mason and Chris just got a new apartment off-campus, and I thought they'd want to spend some time there.

But no. Arrow has the pool. Arrow has the cool theater room in the basement with the state-of-the-art sound system. He has the rec room and the air-hockey table and the always-stocked fridge.

So they're here. And I'm actually starting to like it.

At first it was torture, a reminder of the life I used to have. The life Brogan used to have. It was a reminder of *normal* when it felt like normal was an insult to the man I loved. But now it's the new normal, and I'm starting to feel like maybe it's okay. We don't know how much longer Brogan has, and I'm starting to feel like that's okay, too.

I say a prayer every night that he'll wake up and be himself again so they can start dialysis before it's too late.

The first time Sebastian comes in from the pool, I wave him into the kitchen. He doesn't quite fit in with this group yet. He's more like me than like them. But they're trying to include him. He'll be an important part of the team next year, and for BHU to have another chance at a bowl game, they'll need him.

He steps into the kitchen. "What's up?"

"So, I've been looking at that list." We're alone in the kitchen, but I still check to make sure no one's around to hear our conversation. "And Bailey talked Denny's Garage into giving us a list, too. I compiled the names and have been going through them."

"Okay. Any luck?"

I shake my head. "I keep thinking about that night and what I saw. Did you ever take a criminology class?"

He nods. "A couple."

"You know how they teach you that memory's not static? It's dynamic? So someone can suggest an idea, and you might layer that idea into your memory without realizing it."

"Right," he says cautiously.

"I don't know if that's what's happening, but ever since I saw Coach's name on that list, I've been thinking about what I saw that night. Now when I close my eyes and recall the car driving away, I see a white bumper sticker on the tailgate of the car."

He folds his arms. "Okay."

"I keep thinking maybe it had a streak of red through it. Like a Blackhawk Football bumper sticker. Like the one Coach has on the tailgate of *his* car."

He shakes his head. "I'm telling you, Mia. I worked on that job. I remember it. He hit a deer."

"I know it's ridiculous. I know it, okay? But I have this idea in my head, and sometimes when I get an idea in my head, I just can't make it go away."

"You're talking about my coach," he says.

"I know."

He sighs heavily and turns to look out the back window, where Keegan tosses a long-legged blonde into the pool. "I'll tell you what," he says. "I actually know how I can put your mind at ease."

"You do?"

"If I can prove to you that Coach wasn't involved, will you drop it?"

"How are you going to prove that?"

"You'll see." He grins. "What do you say? I'll pick you up tomorrow afternoon. I'll show you what you need to see, and then you go on a date with me as payment."

I open my mouth to say no and then remember Trish standing in the study with Arrow.

Sebastian is adorable. Well, okay, Bailey would say he's *hot*, and he's definitely got the sexy body thing happening, but he's adorable in that floppy-eared puppy kind of way. His hair's always falling in his face, and he keeps flashing that lopsided smile, like he can't be bothered to bring the other side of his mouth up to meet the first. He's adorable and he likes me and he doesn't confuse the shit out of me.

"It's a deal."

"You didn't need to come today," Mrs. Barrett says behind me. "I cringe to think of what you've been spending on gas."

"It's worth it," I tell her. The truth is, I'm afraid he's going to die before I've said all I have to say, but every time I stand by his side, the words dry up on my tongue. "How is he?"

She steps forward and squeezes my wrist. Sebastian's picking me up from the Woodisons' in two hours, but I wanted to squeeze in a trip to the Barretts' first. Instead of answering my question, she says, "Have you thought any more about singing at the funeral?"

Then again, maybe that's her answer.

I don't know if I'm ready. I've squandered so much time with him. Wasted our last good night together and have been holding my breath waiting for a second chance. Maybe half of grief is just accepting that we don't get one.

I draw in a breath. "I haven't decided."

She gives my wrist a final squeeze. "I'll leave you alone, then."

I watch her leave, grateful that she pulls the door shut behind her to give me some privacy. Suddenly, I know what I need to say.

I take his hand in mine and squeeze. When I close my eyes, he's bloody in my arms again, apologizing with his final words. "I forgive you. For Trish. For refusing to take me home. For all of it." I swallow hard. I've been so busy taking the blame onto myself that I've never taken the time to tell him he's forgiven. Maybe that's what we all need to hear—to believe—if we're going to find some peace. "None of us are perfect, and I never wanted you to be, either. Thank you for loving me."

When I open my eyes, they see a body on the bed that once belonged to Brogan, but he's not there anymore. Maybe he hasn't been for months. I brace myself for another blow to the chest—the kind of grief that steals my breath—but instead I find myself exhaling and then refilling my lungs.

This is what it feels like to let go.

I brush his hair from his face, close my eyes, and say a prayer.

When I get back to the Woodisons', I feel lighter than I have in months. It's not the happy lightness of submitting your last final exam or the giddy lightness of having a crush. It's the weight of a burden lifted from your shoulders.

I'm running late, so I rush to my room to figure out what to wear. My black-and-pink polka-dot sundress used to be my favorite, and I pull it on, step into a pair of flip-flops, and head downstairs to wait for Sebastian.

Arrow's in the living room, and he stands up when he sees me. "You look nice," he says, dragging that slow, hungry gaze down my bare legs. "Where are you going?"

The doorbell rings, and I turn to open it without answering Arrow's question. Sebastian stands there in a pair of low-slung jeans and a fitted black T-shirt. He grins at me and offers me the trio of bright yellow daisies in his right hand.

"For the pretty girl," he says.

I can practically feel the moment Arrow realizes who's at the door. He comes to stand behind me, and it's as if the temperature in the house drops ten degrees.

"Hi, Arrow," Sebastian says, inclining his chin.

I feel a little guilty. This is the guy who's replacing him, but at the same time, this is the guy who will smile at me. Who will give me the time of day without looking at me like he resents my need to hear his voice. I don't know that I want to be with Sebastian, but I need a friend.

"Sebastian," Arrow finally responds. "How are you?"

"Good." He holds up the flowers a little awkwardly. "You?"

"Hunky-dory," Arrow says dryly. "Living the dream."

Sebastian laughs. "Let me know if I can get you anything, okay, man?"

Arrow releases a long, slow exhale and shakes his head. "Don't be that guy."

"What?"

"Just don't be a nice guy. If you want to do me a favor, pretend to be the asshole I need you to be." He turns around and goes to the stairs, leaving us.

"Well, that was awkward," Sebastian says, making a goofy face.

I want to laugh over how ridiculous that exchange was, but I'm too confused by the guy walking away. "Yeah," I agree. I don't want to think about Arrow right now and wouldn't know what to think if I wanted to. I grab the flowers and take them to the kitchen, popping them in a small vase with some water before heading back to the front door where Sebastian's waiting. "You still haven't told me where we're going."

"We're going to Dad's shop," he says. "Come on."

I follow him to his car and he opens the door for me. I turn around as I start to climb in and see Arrow watching me from his bedroom window, his arms crossed, a frown on his face.

Sebastian follows my gaze. "Should I assume he's going to punch me in the face the minute he's no longer on probation?"

"Don't worry about Arrow," I say, climbing into the car. "He doesn't want me." *Our history is too complicated,* I think, but I don't explain that to Sebastian. I don't have the energy to answer the questions that explanation would invite.

Sebastian grunts. "It's cute that you believe that."

I toy with the radio as he drives, and when he pulls into the lot in front of his dad's body shop, I cross my arms and look at him. "You have me curious," I admit. "What are we doing here?"

"You'll see." He unbuckles and grabs a backpack from the

back seat. "Come on. In the back."

I climb out of the car and follow him around to the gate at the back of the shop. He unlocks it, pulls it open, and nods me on through.

A chrome bumper lies in the grass.

"That's Coach's," he says, nodding to it. "I pulled it out of the scrap pile for you this morning."

I step forward, my insides trembling as I near the mangled chrome. "That's it?"

"Yeah," he says. "And Mia, he hit a deer. I know that without doing anything else, but I know you need some kind of closure on this. I took a chemistry class at BHU last semester. It was called the Chemistry of CSI, and they taught us about the chemicals and tests used in some basic crime scene investigations." He slides his backpack off his shoulder and to the ground and pulls a couple of tubes from it. "You're lucky Professor Drew liked me. He gave us the chemicals we need to run the test."

One of the tubes has a long cotton swab in it, and he pulls it out and hands it to me. He crouches next to the bumper and points to the edge. "It's still smeared with blood. No reason to scrub it off when you have to replace the whole part anyway. We'll use this stuff called anti-human serum. You take the sample and put it in this solution. It'll tell us whether it's animal blood or human blood."

"That's a real thing?"

He laughs. "Pretty cool, huh? Go ahead and swab it."

My stomach curdles. I'm not sure I want to know anymore.

What happens if it turns out that it's human blood on the bumper? Do we go to the police from here? And what about Sebastian? Could he live with turning in his coach?

"Calm down, Mia," he says. "I promise it's deer blood."

With a shaking hand, I swipe the wet swab across the dried blood and then hand it to him.

He takes it and dips it into the other vial. "What will happen is that if it's human blood, the solution will react, and if it's not, it won't."

"That simple?"

"The best chemistry is, isn't it?" We stare at the liquid in silence, and it doesn't react. "See? Told you. Do you feel better now?"

I stare at the vial, half expecting it to change. It doesn't. "Thanks, Sebastian." Why was I so sure it was human? "I promise I don't have a personal vendetta against the coach. I just saw his name and couldn't get the idea out of my head that it was his car—that I saw that bumper sticker."

"He hit a deer, Mia."

I nod. Did Sebastian test it himself before he brought me here? Does it matter if he did? The results are what they are. "Okay. Got it. Thanks again for doing this."

"And now you owe me dinner," he says.

"Deer blood to dinner." I laugh at his grimace. "It's okay. That was our deal, and I'm actually pretty hungry."

A few minutes later, we pull up to a casual hole-in-the wall that serves the best Lebanese food.

"This okay?" he asks when he stops the car.

"This is perfect," I say.

We get a seat and both order iced tea and sampler platters, and they bring our food out quickly. I can't get my stomach to settle down from the nervous tremors that started back at the shop, and even though this is probably my favorite place to eat, I just poke at my food.

"Did Bailey lie to me?" he asks.

"I'm sorry. What?"

He nods to my untouched food. "I asked her what kind of food you liked, and she suggested this place. You don't seem very interested in your meal."

"You asked Bailey where to take me for lunch?" Sebastian hasn't been hiding his interest in me, but I thought it was more casual than that. I was convenient. But maybe Bailey was right, and he's been interested for a while now.

He grins. "I wanted to impress you with more than my chemistry skills today." His smile falls away then. "But seriously, are you doing okay?"

"I'm just thinking." I shift and take a deep breath. He's going to think I'm crazy. I should be able to drop this, but I can't. "I have this big list of people who got body work done, but except for my crazy gut reaction about Coach, nothing's jumping out at me. And I know you're right and I should probably let it go, but I have this list and I feel like I should *do* something. What if one of those people is responsible for what happened?"

He puts down his fork and swallows his bite. "Why is it so

important that you find out? You don't strike me as an eye-for-an-eye type. Is it just about revenge? Justice?"

"Honestly?"

"Yeah. The truth."

"I can't stand everyone thinking my brother was responsible. He screwed up. He was a teenager and thought it'd be easier to take care of me and Dad if he was dealing. And I'm not saying it was right, and I'm not saying there aren't other ways to get by, but he wasn't the horrible, hardcore gangbanger the people in this town paint him as. After my mom left, he saw an easy way to make money, and he took it." I take a drink of my tea, hoping to wash down the memory of the disappointment I felt when the police found the meth in Nic's trunk. I was in high school and had always idolized him, and he let me down. But I do believe he learned his lesson, and when he was released from prison, he didn't touch drugs. No using. No dealing. "As long as no one is arrested for this crime, people will go on thinking Nic was dealing again. They'll think this horrible tragedy happened because he couldn't stay out of the game."

"I guess I understand that," he says. "The accident reports weren't any help?"

"Accident reports?" I ask.

He grins. "Yeah. You can get them online—assuming a report was filed."

"I didn't know that."

"I'll tell you what. I'll do it for you. I should have some free time in the next few days or so. You have a lot going on with the Woodisons and Brogan and everything."

"Thanks. That means a lot to me."

"I do want to help you," he says. "I like you, Mia."

I stare at him a long time. "I like you too, Sebastian. But..."

He groans. "I knew that *but* was coming."

This should be easy, but it's not. After months of feeling so little, I'm overwhelmed with emotions that seem to contradict each other. One moment, I'm frustrated with Arrow and confused about where I stand with him, and the next I'm so swamped by grief I can hardly breathe. Brogan is dying, and there's nothing I can do to stop it. Even if I should give Sebastian a real chance, I don't have the emotional energy. "No, it's just that I like you too, but I'm not ready."

He picks up his fork and nods. "Okay, but for now...friends?"

I smile, relieved. "Yeah. Friends would be great. Thank you."

I lie in my room in the darkness and listen to the fall of Arrow's footsteps down the hall.

When I came home from my date with Sebastian, Arrow was out at the pool with Mason, Chris, and a few others I don't know very well. I heard everyone leave half an hour ago, and I've been lying here trying to convince myself not to go to Arrow. I don't care what Gwen thinks. My reluctance to go to him isn't about her. But every time I think about Brogan dying—about putting him in the ground in the same cemetery where my brother is buried—I feel numb all over. I'm scared. I'm the tightrope walker standing on her platform and knowing her net is gone, knowing the only way forward is to take a step.

Arrow keeps telling me I didn't die that night, and I want that to be true, but I'm not sure it is. I'm not sure I'm brave enough to keep going.

With a deep breath and shaking hands, I go to his room and open the door without knocking. He stands by the window, illuminated by the bedside lamp. He's in a pair of gym shorts, his chest bare.

"Did I wake you?" he asks.

Closing the door behind me, I shake my head. "I wasn't sleeping."

"How are you holding up?"

I walk to him. I don't want to talk. And I know I shouldn't, but I take his hand and slide it up my shirt, pressing it between my breasts and against my beating heart.

He draws in a ragged breath and squeezes his eyes shut. "Mia."

I guide his hand down again, lead his fingertips to sweep across my belly and under the waistband of my shorts. Through every inch I guide his hand, his eyes lock on mine, dark, intense, as if he's searching for truth.

"Touch me again," I whisper. I'm reaching out, trying to take that first step. Every inch of me trembles.

He grips my hip tightly and his eyes scan my face, study my lips, then he releases me and steps back. "I can't, Mia." He turns back to the window and buries his hands in his hair. "*Fuck*. I'm sorry. I just can't."

ARROW

This is my fault. I touched her. I lied to myself and touched her when I had no right.

I want to touch her so badly, I can practically feel the slick heat between her legs, but I can't. Not tonight.

Last semester, I tried everything to erase the memory of her from my mind. Pot, meth, alcohol binges, lines of coke—nothing worked, and I was lucky because even though the judge made me go to rehab, I wasn't an addict. Even when I was chasing my next high, there was nothing I wanted as much as I wanted Mia Mendez.

"You . . ." she whispers. "I thought . . ."

It's still true. I can't think of a single thing I want more than her. Especially at this moment when these secrets are too much and my guilt is too heavy. I could lose myself in her. Touching her would chase away the ugliest parts of this world, let me hide from the ugliest parts of myself.

And that's exactly why I can't do it.

"Mrs. Barrett called before I came up." I swallow hard as I watch her moment of mortification melt away. "I'm sorry, Mia."

"He's gone." She wraps her arms around her waist and squeezes her eyes shut. "Shit. I'm sorry I came in here. I'm sorry I . . ." She shakes her head and rushes from the room.

"Mia." I go after her, but she closes her door before I can get there. I lean my head against it and spread my fingertips over the wood. "Don't shut me out." I'm not being fair. I pushed her away, and now I'm asking her to let me in.

"Go away, Arrow. I need to be alone."

Turning my back to the door, I lean against it and spot Gwen just outside the baby's door.

She studies Mia's closed door and then looks at me. "Would you tell Mia that Uriah and I are taking an impromptu trip to Louisville? Mom's keeping the baby, but we'll be gone a few days."

I grimace. "Brogan just died. The funeral will be this weekend."

She sighs heavily. "I'm sorry for your loss."

"Dad should be there. It's not a bad drive. He could come back and—"

"It's not always about you, Arrow."

I clench my fists and bite my tongue. "Fine. Have fun."

She nods and starts toward the stairs, then stops and turns back to me. "Piece of advice, Arrow?" She tilts her head to study my face. "About Mia?"

I don't want any advice from her—especially not now and

especially not about Mia—and I can only set my jaw and stare at her, hoping she'll go away.

Her façade seems to crumble with every second she stares back. No more perfect trophy wife, only a vulnerable young woman. "Don't try to compete with a dead man," she says. "The dead always win. Take it from someone who knows."

MIA

The line at the visitation extends out the door of the Blackhawk Valley Catholic Church and all the way around the block. It's full of college students, football players, coaches, Blackhawk Hills University professors and administration, and residents of Blackhawk Valley who have probably known Brogan from the day he was born. Some of the crowd he grew up with gathers here and there. Some of them make jokes, tell stories, and laugh together while they wait. Others wait in complete silence, stepping forward when they can, pausing when they must. A receiving line of grief.

I keep thinking about what Brogan would think of this line. I think he'd be surprised to see all these people came out for him. I think he'd say, *"Don't you all have something more interesting to do than stare at me? I mean, I'm good-looking, but I'm still a dead guy."*

But in a world full of ugliness, you just have to take the time to say goodbye when you lose one of the good guys. And despite what Brogan thought in those last lucid moments on Deadman's Curve, despite his mistakes and terrible judgment that night, he was one of the best.

Brogan's mom and younger brother stand at the foot of the casket, shaking hands and hugging people as they come by. Mr. Barrett stands at the other end, his jaw working like he has to swallow back tears he's determined not to shed in front of this crowd. Lying in the casket in between is Brogan, half the man he used to be, his cheeks hollowed out, his shoulders narrow, his body a weak imitation of the powerful force it once was.

The funeral is tonight, and I still can't bring myself to promise I'll sing. Mrs. Barrett is being unbelievably patient with me and told me the organist will play either way, but she hopes I'll do the vocals.

Arrow's there, and I'm so relieved to see his face and have his strength so close. He's not Brogan's competition. Not his replacement. Here and now, he's a reminder of what Brogan once was.

Wordlessly, he takes my hand and threads our fingers. Just a squeeze, and then he pulls away. The gesture seems to reassure me it's all right, and at the same time remind me that I have to let Brogan go. *This is what he would want.*

"She asked me to speak tonight," he says, his gaze steady on the front of the room and the overgrown line slowly crawling its way past Brogan. "And I just keep thinking the last time I spoke with Brogan, I wanted to punch him. He wanted to punch me.

I keep thinking, should I really be the one to speak at this guy's funeral?"

I hate that I can't touch him here. I want to curl into him. We should hold each other while we talk about this. "If Brogan could choose, I think he'd say yes."

He grimaces and swallows hard, as if the idea of Brogan making the request hurts him somewhere deep. "You don't understand the irony, Mia."

"I know Brogan," I say. "He'd tell you that a moment of anger doesn't change the fact that you spent most of your lives closer than brothers. Because as much as your fight sucked and as angry as we were with each other, it was a moment among thousands and thousands of moments. Any regrets you have from that night are *nothing* in the scope of your bond."

Arrow stares at some point beyond my shoulder and lifts his chin. His eyes glisten with tears, and I stare with some sick fascination with seeing them fall. He needs to cry—if not for Brogan then for himself and what he lost last night. Maybe privately he's shed as many tears as I have, but I doubt it. Crying is a luxury Arrow would deny himself.

"It's okay to be scared," I say. "No one wants to give the eulogy for someone they were close to, because it's an invitation for everyone to see all your vulnerabilities."

"Brogan would call me a pussy." He releases a puff of air and his lips curl into a soft smile.

"You gonna do it?"

"Yeah. Yeah, I've gotta."

"She wants me to sing," I say.

He levels his gaze on me with no judgment or expectation. "Will you?"

"I don't know if I still can. I don't remember the last time I sang. It was..."

"Before?"

I hold his gaze and nod. "Before."

"I think it's time, then, Mia. Maybe it'll help you let him go." He brushes my hair behind my ear, and the soft touch makes me waver toward him. "You have to forgive yourself. You weren't driving the car."

Pulling back, I stand up straighter. "I'm looking for the person who was."

His face hardens. "What?"

"The police don't care. They haven't even looked. I'm doing it myself. I need to find out who *was* driving the car. Sebastian's helping me."

"Arrow!" Mrs. Barrett calls, waving her hand in the air. "Can you come over here a minute? I want you to meet Brogan's cousin, Eddy."

He nods and looks to me as he steps away. "Mia, we need to talk. Soon."

I don't need another guy telling me that answers won't bring my brother back, but I'm not going to pick a fight with Arrow. Not here. "Okay. You know where to find me."

ARROW

This day has been surreal. Sure, there are the assholes who crack jokes about how "lucky" I am for this day of freedom from my house arrest, and there are the guys on my team who seem to be willing to go to any length to make each other laugh. But then there's Mia telling me she's looking for the person who hit Brogan and her brother. And now there are all these people filling the church pews in front of me, waiting for me to speak.

"Brogan was . . ." My voice cracks and the mic reverberates through the church speakers. I clench my fist and ignore the fact that there are more than one hundred people staring at me and waiting for me to say something that will help make this horrible moment more bearable.

I never cared for public speaking.

When you're a hotshot football player, it comes with the territory. You talk to your team. To the press. You give a speech at high school graduation when they recognize you as the senior athlete of the year. At the draft, you stand behind the podium and say your thanks to the team that took a chance on you.

In December, I thought a potential draft acceptance speech was the scariest thing I'd have to do in the coming year.

Until this. This is hell. I'm supposed to talk to all these people about a man I loved like he was my own brother. A guy who was closer to family to me than anyone else in my life. I'm supposed to talk about the man whose girl I stole and whose life I took.

Fuck. It's my very worst crime, my ugliest sin, and I can't even remember it. I keep waiting for flashes of being in the car, the screeching tires. But I get nothing.

The whole congregation stares at me, waiting for me to speak. I let them wait. I need a goddamn minute.

"Arrow?" Chris asks from the front row. "You okay, man?"

I nod. *I need to tell Mia.*

How can I speak about Brogan when that's all I can think on repeat? *I need to tell Mia. Mia needs to hear it from me.* I have to figure out how I can do that without fucking up Coach's life, how I can tell her the truth without her going to the authorities. If it were just me, it would already be done. I'd be serving my time, and Mia would be hating me as she should. But Coach doesn't deserve to be punished when all he was doing was trying to protect me.

I have to tell her.

Women shift in their seats, and men clear their throats, filling in the silence as they wait.

"We're all here to say goodbye to Brogan," I say, "but most of us don't have a clue how to do that. Putting a man like Brogan in the earth before his life had really begun feels like burying a dream. It feels like choosing the nightmare instead. It feels like staying in the cave, cold and shivering, and knowing that all you have to do to feel the sun is walk outside. So many of us have spent the weeks leading up to this moment talking to Brogan and holding his hand and lying to ourselves that the sun was waiting out there for us. That we could wake up from the nightmare at any minute."

Lifting my eyes, I'm greeted with a sea of my teammates in black suits. These are the men who show no fear on the field, but right now their faces show all the fear I'm feeling. I clear my throat and turn to look at Brogan—maybe the only guy here who doesn't look half terrified.

Looking at him helps me go on. "Part of saying goodbye, I'm learning, is accepting that there is no choice. We don't get to choose the sunlight over the cold inside the cave. We don't get to choose the dream over the nightmare. Part of saying goodbye is accepting there are things in this world that are out of our control."

A sob rises from the crowd. Trish is curled into Coach's chest, and he's stroking her hair. Mia's sitting between Chris and Mason, her face pale, her cheeks dry. She's not even holding a tissue.

"Someone told me that faith isn't about trying to understand why God did what He did. It isn't about trying to make sense of His plan for us. It's simply the acceptance that some things are out of our control and that's *okay*. Maybe that's why Brogan gave us time. He took the slow way out of this world, and we had months to say our goodbyes. Or maybe he just didn't want to let go. This is a guy who was so full of life and so full of love. He and I were like brothers before I even understood what that meant. We liked all the same things. The same teams, the same position in football . . . the same girls."

That gets a few laughs, and I smile.

"I'm an only child—or was until a couple of months ago. Brogan taught me what family is. Family is letting someone make a mistake, letting them hurt you without it changing how you feel about them."

In front of me, Chris meets my gaze and nods. Two rows back, Trish pulls out of her father's arms and wipes her eyes.

"He wasn't perfect. He had a temper. Made rash decisions. Had a selfish streak. More or less, he was the average college guy when it came to his faults. But he didn't expect perfection from anyone else. It made him so easy to love. There were very few things he wasn't willing to give. It was easy to get selfish loving Brogan. He wanted the people he loved to have everything. In seventh grade, I punched him because I found out he kissed Emily Sauer and I had a crush on her. He just smiled at me, lip all bloody, and said, 'Sorry, man. I didn't know. Go get her.' There were very few things Brogan went after in this world that he wasn't willing to give to someone else."

My eyes go to Mia, and she has her hand pressed hard between her breasts, as if she needs it there to hold her heart together.

"Very few things," I repeat. I turn toward the casket. "Buddy, I'm sorry I didn't get out of the way. I'm sorry *I* didn't take the punch now and then and tell you to go after it." I release a puff of air that's supposed to be laughter and look at the ceiling as I bite back a curse. "I can hear him. Like he's right here. I can hear him telling me it's okay. That was Brogan. He'd forgive me. Even if I don't deserve to be forgiven."

My gaze lands on Mia. "I know he'd forgive me. He was always faster to forgive me than I was to forgive myself, but I'm going to try. For him. And you guys should, too. Let go of any of the regrets you had concerning Brogan, because he'd tell you that it's okay. That's the kind of guy he was."

Mrs. Barrett steps up to the podium and puts her hand on my arm before drawing me into a hug. "Thank you," she whispers. "I needed to hear that."

I hug her back and my eyes lock with Mia's. I hope my message got through to her. She's not the one who did wrong, but I know she carries the weight of that night on her shoulders. I know Brogan wouldn't want that.

Mia stands and comes to the stage as Mrs. Barrett releases me. The women look at each other, and Mrs. Barrett gives a sad smile and nods before turning to the mic.

"Now, Mia Mendez is going to sing for us. Brogan always loved to hear her sing."

Mia avoids my gaze and stiffly takes her place behind the mic. I take my spot next to Chris as the organs plays the opening chords of "Amazing Grace," and Mia opens her mouth and sings for the first time since New Year's Eve.

The house is milling with guys from the team who wanted to hang out rather than go home after the funeral, but the only one I want to talk to right now is Coach.

I lock eyes with him and nod toward my dad's study. I don't wait for his response before I head down the hall and wait in there.

Less than a minute later, he joins me, closing the door behind him. "You have a houseful of people, and I'm not going to talk about this now."

"We're going to talk about it. I can't keep this secret anymore. I tried. For you. But you cornered me. You put me in a horrible, unthinkable position by covering it up." God, I wish he'd just understand. "It's too heavy," I say. "I can't hold it anymore."

"Is this about Mia?"

"No." I grimace then shrug. "Yes. Kind of. It's about everyone. It's about doing the fucking *right* thing."

"Arrow, I know you think going forward is the right thing—"

"It is. We can do it together. I'll tell them. We'll explain you were trying to protect me." My voice squeaks. I'm a little boy begging for some attention from his father. "Don't you understand? The only reason I haven't gone forward is to protect you. I didn't ask you to do what you did, and if you hadn't, I wouldn't be carrying around this unbearable . . . *Please.* The truth is the only way I can get out from under this."

He looks over his shoulder at the closed door of the study, as if someone might be standing there listening in to our conversation. "I know you think it's the right thing," he says when he looks back to me. "But it's not. You have to think of the big picture here. You feel a little guilt off your chest, and then what? Everyone you love will know what you're responsible for."

"Would you stop acting like you're doing this for me?"

"Fine, then. I'm not. This isn't about you, Arrow." For the first time in our long relationship, there's derision in his voice when he says my name. "But if you care about *me* at all, you'll keep your mouth shut. I am a father. Trish doesn't have anyone else. Maybe I'm selfish for doing what I must for her, but so be it. Make it about me, Arrow. Shut the fuck up about this *for me*."

MIA

The house is quiet. Too quiet. Suddenly, I wish for the clamor of the BHU O-line gathering around the patio, even Trish's drunken screeches of delight when one of the guys throws her into the pool.

I stand in my room for a long time, lost without the nightly tasks of taking care of the baby, doing the laundry, and preparing Uriah's meals.

There's a chill on my skin that feels like New Year's Eve, and I know if I let it, it'll take over, and I'll stand here—shivering my way to numbness.

It's dark outside. It's dark inside.

I want to pull the curtains wide and open the windows and let the humidity of the Indiana summer seep into the room. I want it to wrap me up. I want the sticky air to cling to me. To hold me here so I can't get sucked back there. I need the heat to remind me the chill is only in my head. To prove to me that night has passed.

I go to the window and pull it open, leaning my head against the screen. *Breathe in. Breathe out. Breathe in. Breathe out.*

The night had an end, but I've trapped myself inside it and pretended there was no way out. The night of the accident was a cliff, and I let myself believe there was nothing beyond it. Because I was too afraid to jump.

I close my eyes and listen to the sounds of him getting ready for bed. A drawer opening, the rustle of clothes as he changes, the click of a lamp.

A rush of heat climbs up my neck, warms my cheeks. The thought of Arrow climbing into bed in cotton briefs. His strong legs between the sheets. His bare chest. His big hands.

I'm alive.

I press a hand against the wall. Heat swells in my belly and swirls to a tight knot between my legs. I squeeze my eyes shut, but the backs of my lids are painted with the image of him with his hand between my legs, and my mind is full of the sound of his breath against my neck as he slides his finger inside me and tells me I'm beautiful. His fingers slip over me. Heat pools in my belly, and that coil pulls tight between my legs.

I want to go to him, tell him he's the one I want, tell him that today when I sang, I let go.

There's a knock on the door, but I don't turn as it creaks open. The only other person in the house is Arrow, but this house could be full of people and I'd know that it was him standing behind me. When he's close, I feel him like the beat of my heart.

"Are you okay?" he asks. His voice is low, husky.

Slowly, I nod.

"Are you *okay*?" he asks again.

"I'm alive," I say softly. Maybe it's the first time I've actually believed it. The sticky air on my skin, the heat of summer curling the tendrils of hair at the nape of my neck. "I'm alive."

"Fuck, Mia." He doesn't come closer.

I wait, staring out into the dark night, watching the reflection of the moonlight bounce off Arrow's car and remembering the night at the lake, jumping into the water wearing nothing but starlight. He doesn't come closer.

"Mia?" I turn at my name. He's in nothing but a pair of boxers, and my gaze lingers on his strong, bare chest. "We didn't get a chance to talk after the funeral. I wanted to check on you. Are you doing okay?"

In my stomach, butterflies flurry from side to side. "No."

His face falls and he steps forward. "What can I do? Anything?"

Taking two steps toward him, I draw in a long, slow breath. "What are you offering me, Arrow?"

His breath catches, and his eyes rake down the length of me and back up. "Anything I have."

"I don't want to be alone." It's a simple sentence, and I realize it's what I haven't allowed myself to admit during these months of grieving.

"Then you can sleep with me." He's so matter-of-fact. So sure that he can hold me and never cross the line I so badly need him to cross.

"I don't want to sleep with a man who doesn't want to touch me, Arrow." I release a dry laugh. "But I only want to sleep with you. And there's the rub."

"Mia . . ." He takes a step forward before stopping himself. "If you think I don't want to touch you, you have it all wrong. I've even told you . . . sometimes touching you is all I can think about."

My breath catches at that thought—Arrow imagining how he'd touch me. "You think about it?"

His gaze drops to my mouth before returning to meet mine. "I think it might bother you if you knew how much. Or if you knew that touching you has been my primary fantasy since the day we met. Even when you were his, my imagination always made you mine."

My body seems to hum at his confession, a taut string on a cello rubbed long and low with the bow. Stepping forward again, I bring my hands to my shirt. I undo one button then the next then the next and his eyes follow my fingers. My hands drop to below my navel as I release the last between his eyes and my bare flesh. I let the shirt fall from my shoulders and slide my hands beneath the waistband of my skirt to push it from my hips.

The phrase *turned on* gains new meaning. I've been walking around shut down until he came home and turned me back on. Right now there's nothing that could make me feel as alive as his eyes on me, and I have it.

He's staring at me. His eyes ask a thousand questions. The

thrumming pulse in his neck and the accelerated rise and fall of his chest give me all the answers I need.

I step closer, and my nerves are no fight against my need. Another step. His eyes skim over my breasts and over my simple black satin bra. Another step. Now I could reach out and touch him.

I take his good hand and press it against my chest. "I'm alive."

He drags his bottom lip between his teeth and nods. "You are. And so beautiful."

I trail his fingertips over my bra and down over my stomach, bring his hand back up, and guide it to cup my breast. He doesn't resist but he doesn't initiate a single touch. I lead his hand to explore my torso, the dip above my hipbone, the curve of the bottom of my belly, the hardening swell of my nipples.

He stares at me with parted lips and pupils so wide there's nothing but a thin line of honey brown left of each iris.

He squeezes his eyes shut, and I press his hand flat between my breasts so he can feel my beating heart. "I didn't die that night, but until you came back into my life, I wasn't living. Every breath hurt until it didn't hurt at all. Until I felt nothing. You make me want to breathe when before I just wanted any excuse to stop."

He slides his hand out from beneath mine and lifts it to cup my jaw. I lean into the heat of his touch, and he lowers his parted lips to skim over mine in a movement that is less kiss than it is sharing air. Tilting his head, he follows a path over my cheekbones and down my jaw, then shifts his hand aside to give my neck the same treatment.

I draw in a ragged breath and another. "Arrow." His parted lips skim over my collarbone, and I shudder. "Touch me. Please. I let go today, and I'm alive and free, and I can't think of anything I want more than for you to show me what you think about when you imagine touching me."

He lifts his head and looks into my eyes, and I don't know what he sees there, but it must be the answer he needs. His hand slips off my jaw and behind my back to release my bra. He watches it fall to the floor then dips his head again, barely skimming each breast with his mouth before he sinks to his knees before me and hooks his thumb under the band of my panties.

His touch is life. Heat. And every cell in my body feels like a blooming flower craning its neck to be closer to the sun. I slide my hand under the lace.

"Don't." I freeze at his words, and he nods. "Let me take my time." Gazing up at me from his knees through those thick, dark lashes, he looks less like a lover and more like a man at worship. "Let me love you, Mia."

At the sound of my name on his lips, I shudder. The muscles between my legs tighten in a pleasure and ache so intense, I sway toward him without meaning to. He gives each leg the same torturous treatment he gave my breasts—a skimming of his lips. A tease. He's sampling me like wine, and I want him to swallow me whole.

With nothing more than the slight pressure of his fingertips, he leads me to turn so my back is to him. I feel him at the backs of my thighs, the wet heat of his breath followed by lips so soft my knees buckle and he has to tighten his grip on my hip to help me steady myself. Then slowly, so slowly I want to beg, his lips follow the path halfway up the back of one thigh and then the other. He's not kissing me, but his lips move against my skin, and gentle puffs of air lead his mouth one aching centimeter at a time, as if he's whispering his way to the top of my thighs.

Only when he reaches the lace of my underwear does he finally use that hand at my hip to draw my panties down. They drop to the floor, and I step out of them, but before I can turn, his hand returns to my hip, his grip more aggressive than before. This time his mouth is open—hot, wet, and firm at the top of my thigh. He sucks, and I cry out. In pleasure. In pain. In desperation. He releases, then sucks again harder—marking me and ruining me in ways that go far deeper than this skin.

When he pulls back, my skin feels cold where his mouth was. He turns me slowly and rises to stand in front of me, releasing my hip and holding his good hand up for my inspection. His fingers tremble like every inch of me, inside and out.

"Do you see what you do to me, Mia?" he asks, and a surge of power rushes through me. "Do you understand why I can't walk away from you, even when I should?" His eyes are heavy with lust, his words laced with something else entirely—that desperation I've gotten used to seeing. That fear of hope.

Instead of letting my heart crumble for him, I focus on his shaking hand and bring it to my mouth. I press a kiss against his open palm. "I don't want you to."

His hand finds my jaw again, then his fingers thread into my hair. He tilts my head to the side, studying my face.

I suck on his bottom lip and push his boxer briefs down over his thighs. His hips buck toward me, and I'm filled with such a rush of power, practically dizzy with it. I find him between our bodies and wrap my hand around his length. He gasps against my mouth. It takes my breath away to be this close. To touch him like this.

He cups my breasts, squeezes, teases one nipple, then the other, until I'm making sounds I don't recognize—moans, whimpers, pleas for more. He lowers his head and draws me into his mouth sweetly, sucking softly. I tunnel my fingers through his hair and let my head fall back as the heat takes over my body like liquid that starts at my fingers and toes and fills inch by inch inward. I'm nothing but heat, and the need to be more, to feel more, pulls low in my belly and presses against the muscles between my legs.

He guides me to lie back on the bed and follows me, resting on his elbows and framing my face with his hands. When he settles between my legs, I gasp and swallow hard. We've been here before. Done this before. And yet this is all new. We're both bare tonight, our excuses left behind in the back seat of his Mustang. Our defenses have been left at the gravesite where we watched Brogan lowered into the earth.

He shifts his hips, stroking against my entrance. His neck strains and his jaw tightens. "You're sure?" I lift my hips in answer and he pulls away. "I'll be right back."

He leaves the room and returns with a condom. He stands

beside the bed and rolls it on before lowering himself back onto me. When he slides into me, I wince, and he stills before retreating.

"You were a virgin that night." He grazes his knuckles over my cheek and swallows. "I wish I'd known."

"I was afraid you wouldn't touch me. Afraid I'd never have the courage again." I lift my hips. He gasps as he sinks deep.

"Christ, Mia. It's—"

"I know."

I stroke down the side of his jaw, trail my fingers over his shoulders and chest, stopping to press my open palm against his beautiful beating heart. Something changes in his face. He drops to his elbows, trapping my hand between our bodies and burying his face against my neck.

He trails kisses along the side of my neck and over my shoulder while he moves inside me, and he seems so sad. Like this isn't the beginning of something new but the end of something treasured.

"Roll over," I whisper.

He rolls to his back and watches me with awe-filled eyes as I climb to straddle him.

"Watch me."

"I couldn't take my eyes off you if I wanted to." He skims his hand down my chest and over my stomach and lower to find the sensitive piece of me where our bodies meet. My back arches and I move my hips faster. I'm so full. So aware of every touch. *Alive.*

I rock into him, letting him fill me and stroke me, and when my muscles coil and squeeze, I hold his gaze for as long as I can, feeling the pressure build until I liquefy and explode, and he comes with me.

Bringing me to rest against his chest, he knots a hand in my hair and I count his slow, ragged breaths.

I am alive, but today killed Arrow a little. Maybe I'm not the only one who needs answers about that night. Maybe answers will bring Arrow peace as well.

I squeeze my eyes shut. Tomorrow Sebastian's going to get me the police reports. I'll follow every clue I can until I find the truth.

PART VIII: BEFORE

New Year's Eve, the night of the accident

ARROW

It's New Year's Eve, and I'll be fucking glad to say adios to the year from hell. I shouldn't feel that way. Not everything about this year sucked. Football was good, so good in fact that Coach wants me to enter the draft this spring—take an offer while I'm hot, because next year's never a sure thing. But everything with Mia leaves all that in a shadow of loneliness and frustration that makes me feel like a fool.

You know how I want to spend my New Year's Eve? I want to spend it with Mia. Just the two of us in my car by the lake. I'd let it idle for hours so we could sit in the back together, watching the stars twinkle across the ice.

Instead, I volunteered to help set up for the party at West High School. There's a big initiative to keep students off the roads on New Year's Eve, and the high school is hosting an overnight party as part of the effort. I don't have to be there all night, but I promised to help set up the food stations. I'm borrowing Coach's

SUV so I can pick up the ice and root beer keg, and I should be done by nine, ten at the latest.

I pull on a hooded BHU sweatshirt and shove my keys into my pocket to head out the door, but when I step into the common space, I hear a weird sound from Brogan's room and stop. It sounds like someone crying. A girl.

"This is the last time," Brogan says. "I mean it. This is a mistake I'm not making anymore."

"What makes her so much better than me, huh?" the girl asks. The voice is familiar, but I can't place it.

Brogan murmurs something I can't make out.

"You never complained when my mouth was on your dick," she says, and I know I should leave but I'm frozen in place, rage dripping into my blood like so much potent poison.

There's a sharp crack—like an open palm across a cheek. "Fuck, Trish." Brogan groans. "That hurt."

"Good. Do you understand that if I walk out that door, I'm not coming back? When she breaks your heart, you're on your own."

"I love her."

The bedroom door swings open, and Trish storms through. She spots me and pauses only briefly before charging out the main door and slamming it behind her.

When Brogan steps into the common area, he has a damning case of bedhead and is buttoning his jeans. He doesn't notice me at first, his eyes on his fingers, but I just stare at him with everything I feel—anger, frustration. *Hatred.*

I swallow hard. I never thought I'd see the day that I'd feel anything like that toward Brogan. Not for a second. But I don't know any other word for this blackness clawing at my gut.

As if he suddenly senses my presence, his fingers freeze on the last button and he slowly raises his head to meet my eyes. His jaw goes slack as mine tightens.

"How much of that did you hear?" he asks.

"Enough."

He grimaces. "Listen, it's not what it looks like."

"Does Mia know you're fucking Trish?"

"She probably wouldn't care. It's not like she's doing it."

I step forward and plant both hands against his chest, shoving him hard. He stumbles back, only stopping when his shoulder hits the doorjamb. "What the fuck is wrong with you? You have everything—*everything*—and you're throwing it all away on some easy lay."

He pushes me, and I stumble back. "*I* have everything? Look who's talking! You have no idea what it's like for us mere mortals. You have money for anything you need. You have fucking NFL scouts salivating for a chance to get you on their team."

"I'm not talking about money or football."

He takes a step closer and sneers at me. "Oh, you want to talk girls? You sit there judging me for not being the perfect boyfriend when you could have any girl you want."

"That's not true." I'm not even sure why I said it out loud. Maybe because I'm sick of pretending. Maybe because after years of feeling guilty for having so much more than my best friend in every single way, I want him to understand that he has more in the only thing that matters. He has Mia.

His lips curl into a smirk. "Right," he says slowly. "It's not. Because she chose me. Even when you *fucked* my girlfriend the first chance you got, she didn't want you. She chose me."

I swallow hard. "She told you?"

His nostrils flare and his face contorts in a grimace. "No. You just did." He points to his chest. "But I knew. You two think I'm stupid or something, but I knew the second I saw you in her doorway with those flowers. I saw it all over your face and all over hers."

I shake my head. "I didn't touch her until after she broke up with you."

"But you sure didn't miss a beat when the opportunity presented itself, did you?" He puts both palms flat against my chest and shoves me.

"You don't fucking deserve her." I catch myself as I stumble back and charge at him, shoving him into the wall. "She doesn't deserve someone who's going to fuck around on her."

"*I* am her fucking boyfriend, Arrow. She chose me, and *she* gets to decide what she does and doesn't deserve."

"Fine. I'll tell her what I heard between you and Trish today, and then you can see what she thinks she deserves."

"She chose me. And you won't tell her, because your fucking ego couldn't handle knowing that you're her second choice. You want her so goddamned much, but you don't want to be the guy you were that night. You don't want to be the one who picks up the pieces. And if you tell her, that's all you'll ever be."

I clench my fist and back up a step and then another before grabbing my keys off the end table. "Fuck you, Brogan."

I leave the dorms and operate on autopilot. Before I have a chance to clear my head enough to think about what I'm doing, I find myself at Mia and Bailey's apartment, my hand poised and ready to knock on the door.

I drop my hand and step away before I can knock.

The door swings open, and Bailey stands there, her coat zipped to her chin, her purse thrown over her shoulder. She startles when she sees me, then cocks her head and frowns. "Can I help you?"

"I . . . um . . ."

Bailey rolls her eyes before turning into the apartment. "Mia! Someone's here for you." When she turns back to me, she studies my face. "You decide what you want," she says quietly, "and then you fight for it."

I wonder how much she knows about what happened in October, but before I can ask or respond in any way, she pushes past me down the hall and to the stairwell.

Mia appears at the door in front of me. "Arrow? Are you okay?"

I open my mouth then close it again. *"Your fucking ego couldn't handle knowing that you're her second choice."*

He's right. Fuck him. But he's right. I don't want to be the guy she's with because the one she wanted screwed up one too many times.

I swallow hard. "I have to help out at the high school for a few hours, but after..."

Her forehead furrows as she studies me, waiting for me to spit it out.

"Do you have plans for tonight?" I'm so lame. So fucking lame I want to stab myself in the eye with the nearest sharp object. And I can tell just by looking at her that she has plans.

She looks gorgeous. She always looks gorgeous, but tonight she looks like an angel. She's dressed in white, a little dress that shows more leg than it covers, with a tiny sweater on top that covers her shoulders and her freckles. She's wearing makeup and her hair is down around her shoulders. My stomach knots. She's definitely going out tonight, and of course she has plans. Brogan would make sure they had plans for New Year's Eve.

"Okay, so you obviously already have plans." I lick my lips, not sure how to go about this.

"I do."

Since the day I met Mia, she's had my heart in her hands, and every day that I deny that, it just hurts me more. "Cancel them. Whatever you were going to do with Brogan tonight, don't do it. Be with me instead."

Her brow wrinkles with concern. "What's wrong, Arrow? You look upset."

I drag my fingers through my hair and tug on it. *You deserve so much better than this.* "Mia, I'm in love with you."

MIA

My heart. Oh God, my heart. "Don't say that."

"What do you want, Mia?" He lifts his arms, palms up. Anguish pulls at his mouth, contorting his attempted smile into a frown. "Do you not see it? Have you really been oblivious all this time to how much you mean to me? How special you are to me?"

"You're important to me, too." The understatement is a betrayal to how I really feel. I fell for Arrow that first day. He smoothed that shiny purple leaf in his fingers and offered it to me as a gift, and I was never the same. "Arrow, I want us to be friends."

He drags a hand through his hair and spins away, as if he can't handle the sight of my face anymore. "I don't."

The night goes quiet. Maybe the frogs and owls are as shocked by his words as I am. "What?"

When he turns back to me, grief twists his features. "I've

tried, Mia. For over a year now, I've tried to be your friend and nothing more. But I don't want to be your friend. That's not what you are to me. It's not enough."

"Don't do this," I whisper. "Don't look at me like I'm something to you."

"I'm sick of ignoring this ache in my chest when I see him with you. I'm sick of pretending I don't need to be more than that guy you fucked up with once. You're not *something* to me. You're *everything*."

"Don't." My voice cracks to match my heart. "You don't understand. We can't be together."

"Why not?"

"Because our parents—"

"I don't care if your dad hates me. We'll work it out. I'll win him over. Can't we just—"

"We can't."

"Then look me in the eye and tell me you don't have feelings for me. Tell me our night together didn't *mean* something to you."

I hold his gaze and open my mouth, but I can't force the lie out.

"Why?" he whispers. "What is it that's keeping you away from me? I'll leave you alone. I won't bring it up again. I just want to know why."

I want to lie to him, but the only way past this is with the truth. "Because my mother had an affair with your father. She left when my dad found out and started making threats."

His face goes blank—whitening. I did that—I pulled the

drain on all his hope. "What? When?"

I swallow hard. "Nic says it went on for at least a year before she left town." His lips move slowly as he mentally positions the timeline, and I can't stand here at the edge of this cliff and wait for the end of anything he and I could be, so I help. I push. "It would have been your freshman year in high school, and the summer before your sophomore year."

His face contorts as he clings to confusion to dodge the pain. "But my mom..."

His mom was at home dying that year. The cancer was taking over her body and his father was screwing my mother.

His nostrils flare and his eyes narrow in on me. "How long have you known this?"

"I'm sorry," I whisper.

"Fuck it, Mia, you *knew*?"

I stumble backward. I've seen Arrow angry, but he's never looked at me with anything short of kindness and affection. Until this moment. "I know what your mother means to you. I didn't want to hurt you."

He lets out a puff of air that might have been a laugh if it weren't filled with so much disgust. "That ship's sailed, Mia. All you've ever done is hurt me." He shakes his head and backs away. "From day one."

ARROW

I drive too fast to Coach's house. I let my car fly over the hills on the back roads, my stomach pitching into my chest when I go airborne at the crest of each hill. Up and around Deadman's Curve, I race toward the setting sun, wishing I could disappear into it.

I take the turn onto Coach's road, my back wheels spinning in the gravel as I over-correct and fly through the dust down the county road to his house.

I tear into his driveway, skid to a stop, and press my forehead against the steering wheel. I open my mouth and make myself breathe as I count the lashes to my heart.

I told her I loved her, and she said she wanted to be my friend.

My father was fucking her mother while my mother was dying, and she knew. *She knew.*

Throwing my head back against the seat, I smack the steering wheel, and the horn blares into the country silence.

Coach wanders out of his garage, one hand on his hip, the other wrapped around his hunting rifle.

I climb out of the car, and he arches a brow. I know that look. It's the look he gives players who show up to practice late. It's the look he gave the QB when he fumbled the ball on the five-yard line. It's the look that says, *"Calm down, figure out what's wrong, and fix it."*

"He was having an affair," I whisper. "While Mom was dying, Dad was having an affair."

"Shit," he mutters. He leans the gun against the side of the garage and wraps his arms around me. He's a big guy, taller than me and broader, and I tuck my head into his chest and let myself hide from the world for the count of three ragged breaths before backing out of his arms.

"My world is fucked." I press my palms against my eyes and wipe away the moisture. I'm not going to cry like a fucking child over my father. He doesn't deserve it. But Mia...

"It's not," Coach says. "I know it feels like it, but it's not. Now who told you this?"

"Mia Mendez." I draw in a long, slow breath, steadying myself against the pain saying her name brings. I just want to be fucking numb. "Dad was fucking her mom. And Mia knew. She knew, and she didn't tell me."

Coach puts his hand on my shoulder. "Is this really about your dad, or is it about Mia?"

I lift my eyes to meet his. "Both." I rub my palm against my chest. "It hurts so much."

"Take a breath. You need the car still?" He holds my gaze, his eyes stern. "You take a breath and fulfill your commitments. You can wallow later."

I swallow hard. "Right. Of course."

He puts the keys to his SUV in my hand and nods. "Commitments first."

"Right," I whisper. "I'll be back in an hour or so."

"Take your time. And slow down on that road out there. Killing yourself isn't going to solve a damn thing."

MIA

"God, you're beautiful." Brogan grins, as he rakes his gaze down the length of my body.

"Thank you." I'm still shaken from Arrow's visit, and suddenly my choice of outfit feels slutty and inappropriate. I don't want to show myself off for Brogan. I'm not his anymore. I haven't been since that night at the lake. Brogan's been trying so hard that I felt like it was my turn to try. But I can't shake the look on Arrow's face when he left.

"All you've ever done is hurt me."

"Are you ready, then?" Brogan asks.

I shrug into my coat and grab my purse off the hook by the door. "Where are we going?" I ask, as I step into the corridor and close the door.

His lips quirk into a smile. "You'll see." He holds out his hand, and when I take it, he squeezes and pulls me close. He lowers his mouth to hover over mine and whispers, "Unless you don't want to go anywhere. We'd have your apartment to ourselves. I could be persuaded to spend the night in."

I can't let my conversation with Arrow ruin tonight, so I force a smile. "I want to know what you've been planning."

"Feel like singing tonight?"

I take a breath. "Yeah. That sounds great."

I close my eyes as Brogan leads me around the dance floor. I want to be present in this moment, and I'm failing.

He put so much thought into tonight. He drove us to Indianapolis and we had dinner downtown, and then he took me to a bar down the street with an open mic and a busy dance floor. We ate, we danced, and I sang—pouring all my heartache from my earlier conversation with Arrow into my favorite ballads. Every detail was planned for my benefit, and I can't stop thinking about Arrow. Should I call him? Text? Apologize?

What exactly would I be apologizing for? My mother's decisions? My decision not to tell him when I first found out? Or would I be apologizing for letting him fall in love with me? For *wanting* it, despite myself?

Brogan pulls back and frowns. "What's wrong? You're upset about something."

I swallow hard. "Arrow came to my apartment earlier. I'm sorry. I won't—"

"Arrow?" His frown turns into a snarl. "Are you fucking kidding me?"

I step back. There's so much anger in his voice and face. I don't think I've ever seen him like this before. It scares me a little.

"Jesus, Mia. Nothing happened. Arrow's overreacting."

"What are you talking about?"

"You know Trish. She likes to make a scene. Arrow had the wrong idea."

I step out of his arms. "Trish?" I don't have to add *the one I caught sucking your dick,* because that's all right there in the way I say her name.

"What did he tell you? Jesus, I swear, I was ending it with her. Cutting it off. I love *you*, and I couldn't—"

"I thought you said nothing happened."

"Nothing that meant anything." He grimaces. "I'm making a mess of this."

I stare at him, but all I can think is that this should hurt more than it does. Finding out that my boyfriend cheated on me *today* should hurt more than Arrow's anger about our parents. But the ache of this revelation feels a lot more like a bruised ego than a broken heart.

"Say something," he whispers.

"I want to go home."

"No, come on. Let's stay and have a good time. I want to hear you sing again."

I shake my head, grab my purse from the table, and head to the car. He takes so long to join me that I'm heading back toward the building when he finally emerges from the restaurant and hits the button for the automatic locks. I climb into the car the second the locks click.

"If you aren't okay to drive, I will," I say when he gets into the driver's seat.

"I'm fine." He jams the key into the ignition, and the silence between us is angry and tense as he drives back to Blackhawk Valley. At first, I think it's gonna be okay. He's hurt, and I'm mad, but he's gonna take me home and this horrible night will be over. But then his driving becomes more erratic, and as we reach the hills at the edge of the city, he swerves every time a car comes toward us in the other lane.

The gray sky opens and sleet covers the windshield, and the next time he swerves, a tire slips off the side of the road, making us fishtail.

"Brogan, pull over," I say, gripping the dash. "Jesus, are you drunk?" I look over and know it's true. His cheeks are flushed, and his eyes are glassy. He only had a couple of glasses of wine at the restaurant. "Is that what you were doing while I was waiting for you to come out to the car?" I ask. "You were in there *drinking*? Do you want to kill me?"

He yanks the wheel and pulls off the shoulder before throwing the car in park. "No, I don't want to kill you, Mia. I was having a couple of drinks and trying to calm down so I didn't have to go back home and beat the shit out of my best friend."

I want to smack him for putting this on Arrow. "It's not Arrow's fault you can't keep it in your pants."

He squeezes his eyes shut and smacks the steering wheel. "Can we just slow down and figure this out?"

"There's nothing to figure out. I'm breaking up with you. This is *over*."

"I love you," he says. "How can you sit there and act like that means nothing? I've been so patient for you. Waiting when you weren't ready."

"You're going to make this about sex? Like that excuses you?"

"Not just sex. Arrow."

"No." I shake my head. "Don't bring him into this."

"But isn't it? Hasn't it always been? You think I don't see the way you look at him?"

I hold out my hand and am shocked to see it so steady when my gut is churning. "Just give me the keys so I can drive us home." We're off the side of the road at the top of Deadman's Curve. The sun is gone, and our headlights cast out into the darkness that seems to go forever.

I reach for the door handle, and he hits the locks. We used to joke about the child locks being activated in this car, but right now it's not funny.

"I'm not going anywhere until you talk to me." He reaches behind my seat and pulls out a bottle.

"What are you doing?"

He unscrews the cap and drinks. It smells like rubbing alcohol it's so strong. "Just having a little fun on New Year's Eve."

"Let me drive, Brogan. Please. I don't want to fight with you while you're drunk."

He shakes his head. "You have to make me believe we shouldn't be together. If I let you go again, I don't think I'll ever get you back. Make me believe it, Mia!"

I set my jaw. If he wants a hit in the gut, I'll give it to him. "I slept with Arrow. The night you and I were broken up."

His lips curl into a snarl, and he takes another drink.

"I'm not trying to hurt you, Brogan." What a lie. I want to hurt him. I don't like being trapped in this car. I hate being made to feel like a hostage. This isn't healthy, and he's getting drunker by the minute. This isn't the man I know.

He takes another swig. "I thought you were saving yourself for marriage, but you were only saving yourself for him." He offers me the bottle, and I shake my head. "But it doesn't matter. We love each other. We can get through this."

"No. I don't want to pretend that we're this happy couple anymore. If that were true, you wouldn't be sleeping with her." I move as fast as I can, reaching across him to hit the button for the automatic locks and then reach for the door.

Before I can open it, he wraps a hand around my arm and squeezes too tight, making the skin throb beneath his fingers.

"You're hurting me."

"Don't go." He loosens his hold on my arm but doesn't let me go. "Promise me you'll stay here until we figure this out."

I take a breath. He's not acting like himself. I can't reason with him. "Okay," I say, "but we have to stay here. You're too drunk to drive."

He looks out the window and nurses the bottle.

I surreptitiously fish my phone from my purse and type a quick text to my brother.

Deadman's Curve. Brogan's red Jetta. Come get me. SOS.

Brogan swings around to look at me right as I tuck my phone away. I fold my arms and promise myself Nic is on his way. I'll sit here and talk to Brogan, and soon enough Nic will be here and everything will be fine. Maybe if I can calm him down, Nic could drive Brogan home, too. He's in no shape to drive himself and I can't leave him here.

Everything is gonna be fine.

I whisper the sentence to myself on repeat, but I don't believe it. It feels like everything is spinning out of control. Like tonight is the beginning of the end.

ARROW

Two a.m.

"Wake up."

My eyes are gritty and my head aches like every member of the BHU drum line is in there pounding on me. I squeeze my eyes shut again, trying to block out the pain.

"Arrow. Wake up."

Coach.

Where the fuck am I? I pry my eyes open again, and Coach stands over me, leaning into the car down and shaking my shoulder.

I scan my surroundings, and everything tilts sideways. Everything's blurry, and I fight through the cobwebs in my brain, trying to remember what happened tonight. The fight with Brogan. Then Mia. There was a party at a house off-campus, and I told Mason I'd swing by before returning Coach's car. Then Trish grabbed me. She promised she could make me forget Mia, and that sounded so damn good. After that . . . shots. Too many shots. And then . . . ?

"Get out of the car and come inside."

I blink at the steering wheel under my hands, and my stomach pitches. Why am I in the car? "How did I get here?"

"You drove." He mutters a string of curses after that, curses that feel directed at me and that I probably deserve, and I follow him into the house, fear tapping at my conscience and doing its part to sober me incrementally.

I sink onto the couch, my head spinning as I wait for a lecture. I hear water running in the kitchen. The squeak of the pipes as he turns off the tap, and then he shoves a glass of water into my hand.

"Drink."

Sitting up, I bring the glass to my lips and take a drink. My stomach rolls when the water hits it, and I put the glass down and close my eyes. I just want to sleep.

Coach shakes his head and presses the glass back into my hand. "Drink the damn water first."

I drain the glass against the protests of my stomach, and I swear I'm in that horrible drunken limbo where I'm still not sober but the hangover has already started, that half-conscious land of nausea and sleep as Coach leads me up the stairs, down a hall, and to a bed. The world goes black.

Five a.m.

I wake with a start. I'm gonna hurl.

I roll over, trying to bury the pain in my head into the pillow, and realize I'm sharing a bed with Coach's daughter. Trish. She must have come in here and climbed in beside me after I passed out.

She's asleep and huddled under the covers. She draws up a knee, and her toes skim my calf.

More memories from last night flash through my mind—Trish laughing with me. Dancing. Licking tequila off her cleavage. The images are bright and loud against my headache, and I just want them to go away.

"*Dad's here.*" Her whisper, hot and suggestive against my ear. "*I promised him I'd be home for the ball drop, but I'll be in my bed after that. I'd rather not be alone.*"

I hear something and realize it was my phone that woke me. I pull it from my jeans and blink at the screen.

Mia Mendez.

Beside me, Trish mumbles something in her sleep. Mia's calling me, and Trish is curled against my side.

I decline the call with a swipe of my finger and silence the phone before closing my eyes and letting sleep pull me under again.

Six a.m.

Trish clings to me in her sleep, her hand wrapped around my arm.

I hear people talking downstairs, then the sound of footsteps up the stairs and coming down the hall.

The bedroom door opens slowly, and Chris walks through, wincing when his eyes land on me. "I thought you might be here." His eyes flick to Trish and back to me, and he shakes his head.

"How'd you know?"

"Pictures on Facebook of you two all over each other."

Facebook. Which means everyone's going to know I spent my night with Trish. Mia's going to know.

I expect a lecture, or at the very least that look of disappointment Chris has mastered so well. He finds my shoes on the floor and tosses them onto my chest.

"Come on. We've gotta go."

I sit up and wince when the movement sends pain jackhammering through my head. "Where?"

"To the hospital." His eyes scan my face, and even hungover and miserable, I recognize the grief in his eyes. "There was an accident."

My gut lurches. "Mia?"

"Brogan." He swallows and shifts his eyes to the wall. "It's not good."

I hop out of bed and slide on my shoes. This doesn't feel real and I'm not sure it is, but I follow Chris wordlessly to the door.

Trish rolls over in bed. "Arrow? Where are you going?"

"He'll call you," Chris says. "Come on."

My feet aren't steady under me. My brain is a bunch of floating pieces in my skull. With every step down the stairs, I almost anticipate the floor falling out from under me. I'll fall and then I'll wake up.

Brogan. It's not good.

We hit the base of the stairs, and I turn instinctively toward the TV. Coach is on the couch, staring at the screen, transfixed.

"One man dead and another critically injured this morning after a hit-and-run accident on Deadman's Curve."

I turn to Chris, and he nods. "Dead?" I ask.

"Mia's brother didn't make it," he whispers. "Brogan . . . we don't know about Brogan yet."

Coach turns away from the TV and his eyes lock on mine like he's trying to tell me something.

"Sorry about showing up at your door at this hour, sir," Chris says, his Texas accent thicker this morning. It does that when he's tired.

Coach inclines his chin. "Arrow will meet you outside, son. I need to talk to him for a minute."

Chris cuts his eyes to me.

"I'll only be a sec," I promise.

He nods and closes the door behind him as he leaves.

"Police are investigating, trying to find the owner of the dark SUV responsible for the accident," the woman on the TV says. "If you know anyone, please call the anonymous tip line listed on the bottom of your screen."

Coach stands in front of me, and I get that out-of-body feeling again. Like nothing is happening as it should and everything is fragmented. "You got here before midnight, and you snuck into Trish's room."

I blink at him. "What?"

"If anyone asks. You got here before midnight and snuck into Trish's room to be with her."

"How did I get here?"

"You drove."

"The police will arrive any minute. I hit a deer at the end of the drive this morning." He shakes his head. "Stupid, really, but I was distracted because I saw your Mustang in the driveway and I knew you were with my daughter. Just went out for a drive to clear my head, and the stupid deer ran in front of me."

"You've had too much to drink."

"I have to find someone who can drive the Cherokee back to your dad's."

Trish grinning against my mouth. "And then you know where to find me."

Trish pressing her lips to my cheek, lifting her phone, and snapping another picture.

The ground shifts under me. "Coach?"

"Tell me you understand."

I shake my head. "What happened?"

"You're a good kid." His eyes fill with tears, and I've never seen him like this. Not when I took our team to the state championships. Not when his wife died. Never. This is a man who doesn't cry. "Everyone makes mistakes, and I won't let this one destroy your life. Let me fix it."

Out front, I hear the pop of gravel spitting out from under tires.

"If I—" I try to swallow, but I can't. There's too much fear in my throat. Too much confusion and horror.

"No, Arrow. It's done. It's taken care of."

Footfalls sound on the front porch, and then three sharp knocks at the door.

Coach swipes at his eyes. "It's *done*. Go to the hospital. Brogan needs you." He crosses to the door and pulls it open. "Thanks for coming out," he tells the officer. "Just saw on the news what happened last night."

The officer waves a hand. "Not much we can do about that."

"You know what Mendez was like," Coach says. "Makes you wonder if it wasn't just a matter of time before one of his rivals took him out."

"Just too bad Barrett had to be collateral damage." The officer shakes his head somberly. "Where's the deer?"

"Put her in the garage. Hope you don't mind. She's a beaut. Hate for her to go to waste." With one final look at me over his shoulder, Coach leaves, taking the officer to the garage.

When I find my way to Chris's car, my insides are trembling and I can't make them stop. I'm so afraid the truth is written all over my face and Chris will know, but he's in his own world.

I pull my phone from my pocket and see a dozen missed calls and texts. I punch the number for my voicemail and hold the phone to my ear.

She's crying. *"Arrow, it's Mia. Something terrible happened. Brogan. My br-br-br— We're at the hospital. So sorry. So, so sorry."*

"Oh, shit. Pull over."

Chris yanks his car to the shoulder, and I barely get the door open before I heave the contents of my stomach onto the ice-glazed grass.

When we get to the hospital, half the team and dozens of our friends fill the waiting room, but my eyes instantly pick Mia out of the crowd of faces. Her white dress is stained with blood and her face is pale.

"How did I get here?"

"You drove."

Her eyes lock on mine, and I want to cut myself open right there. Spill my guts onto the floor so I don't have to live with this pain and horror and ache inside me. Her brother is dead. Brogan might die.

"Everyone makes mistakes, and I won't let this one destroy your life."

I look away, find a seat, drop my head, and try to pray that this nightmare will end.

PART IX: AFTER
May, four months after the accident, the day after Brogan's funeral

ARROW

My first thought when I wake up to a gun in my face is that the police have come and they're here to finally arrest me for what I did.

My second thought is that I never locked the door or activated the alarm last night. I was on my way down to do it when I came into Mia's room.

"Get *the fuck* away from my daughter."

The gun shakes. It's no more than an inch, maybe two, from my face, but I can't bring myself to confirm that it's Mia's father on the other end. I can't get my eyes off the barrel of the gun that is way too fucking close to Mia's head.

Slowly, I release her, sit up in bed, and raise my hands, never taking my eyes from the barrel of the gun.

"Daddy?" Mia sits up beside me. "Daddy, put that down!"

"They told me—down at the bar—they told me my daughter was living with the Woodisons. They told me, and I told them they were fucking liars."

"Daddy, put the gun down."

"He took my daughter. He took my daughter from me and made her into a liar. You said you were living with Bailey."

I stand, keeping my hands raised by my head, palms out. I have the distant thought that I'm glad we put on clothes before we fell asleep, minimal as they are. Mia's in a T-shirt, and I'm in my boxer briefs. "Mr. Mendez, this is between you and me. Let's go downstairs. We'll make some coffee."

His hand shakes harder, and the scent of whiskey is so potent it rolls off him. "I don't want your fucking coffee. You can't talk your way out of this."

"Daddy!" Mia says.

He sniffs and clears his throat. "They told me my daughter was living with the Woodisons, and I told them they were liars." He swings on her, the gun going with him.

She gasps to find it pointed at her head. "Go ahead," she says, her voice hard now. "I know I'm no use to you anyway. But killing me won't bring Nic back."

"Don't you dare speak my son's name to me. You're here, whoring yourself like your mother did."

"Daddy—"

"They think they can take whatever they want just 'cause they have all the money, but *you let them*."

Footsteps sound down the hall. *Boom. Boom. Boom.* "What the fuck are you doing in my house, Mendez?"

My dad's home.

"You think you can come into my house wielding a gun like some kind of maniac?"

I hold my breath. Dad steps forward and pulls the gun from the man's hand as if it were nothing more than a toy.

"Get out," Dad says. "Before I call the cops."

"I hate you." Mia's father shakes and spits the words. His face blooms red. "I hate you so much."

"I know you do," Dad says. "But it doesn't give you the right to bring a gun into my house. If you'd like, we can have the authorities weigh in on that. But I think you'd rather they not know you were here this morning. I think, given your track record of drunk and disorderlies, you'd rather they not know you broke into my house and put a gun in my son's face."

"You seduced my wife and stole my daughter."

Uriah clicks the safety on the gun and folds his arms. "You tell yourself whatever you need to, old man. But maybe your daughter's just trying to keep your lights on, keep you fed. Maybe she's here because somebody has to make money so that you—piece of shit—don't wither away and die. Maybe she's just trying to pay her way through school so she has a fighting chance at a life better than the one you'd have her lead."

I didn't give Dad enough credit. I figured he had no idea what her reality was, but he's known all along. He's never as clueless as he lets on.

"And I'm not speaking to you about Isabella," Dad says, referring to Mia's mother. "Get out of here, Mendez."

"Gimme my gun back."

My father laughs. "You think I'm an idiot? Now go."

With one last look at Mia, and betrayal all over his face, her father turns and walks out the door, and we all hold our breath. We listen to his slow, heavy tread as he makes his way down the stairs.

Mia stares at my father. "I'm sorry. I'm so sorry." She grabs a pair of jeans off the floor. "I'll take him home. I'm so sorry," she says as she rushes out the door.

I start to follow, and Dad grabs my arm. "House arrest, remember, son?"

"Mia!" I call, and I hate how trapped I feel. I should be with her while she talks to her father. I should talk to him myself. But what would I say? *I'm in love with your daughter, and by the way, I killed your son.*

She stops in the doorway. "It's okay. I'll be fine."

All I can do is watch her leave. I listen to her steps down the stairs and then the click of the front door.

"I thought you were in Louisville," I say, without turning to my father.

"I came home for a quick meeting this morning," he says. "Why wasn't the alarm system on? Did you even lock the fucking door? How did that man get in here?"

I straighten. Dad and I don't talk. Not *to* each other. We talk around each other, about each other, but I feel like he hasn't looked at me since he joined us at the hospital on New Year's Day. But he's looking at me now, and there's disgust all over his face. I'm in nothing but my boxer briefs, and I feel exposed.

"It's my fault," I say.

"And you being in Mia's bed this morning? Is that your fault, too?" When I open my mouth to answer, he holds up a hand. "And her sleeping in your bed before? Is that your fault, too?" He drags a hand through his hair and exhales heavily. "Jesus, it's a good thing Gwen isn't here. She'd lose her mind."

"I'm sorry I didn't lock the door. Please don't blame this on Mia." *Don't fire her. Don't take her from me.* God, I want to beg it. But it's selfish, and when I tell Mia the truth, she's not going to want to be here anyway.

He sighs. "She does her job and she's good at it, so I haven't said anything, but he was your best friend. Did you forget that?"

I back up a step. "Don't pretend you know what we're going through."

He narrows his eyes and points a finger at me. "You think you're the only one who's ever lost someone they *loved*?"

"I think Mom was *dying* in your bed and you were fucking around with Mia's mom." It's the first time I've admitted that I know, but he doesn't look surprised, only resigned.

"It's not the same," he says, his jaw hard.

"How? Mom wasn't even *dead*, and you were screwing someone else."

Now he's the one to take a step back, and his face softens. "It's lonely to watch the woman you love die. It makes you feel helpless. Powerless. But Isabella Mendez made me feel like a man again when that was what I needed most. She comforted me. But I'm guessing you know all about a beautiful Mendez woman giving you just what you need."

"It's not like that with Mia."

"You've been sleeping with her."

"But it's not just sex." I swallow hard. "I love her. I've loved her..." I drop my head and stare at my bare feet. "Always."

"And you think I didn't care about Isabella? That I'm just an old asshole who fucks around on his dying wife? Sometimes we love the people we shouldn't exactly when we shouldn't." He tilts his face to the ceiling and draws in a long breath. I've never seen him like this. Vulnerable. *Human.*

"Then *how* is your story so much more forgivable than mine?" I ask, and when the question slips from my lips I realize just how much his reaction to the last few months hurt me, just how much I needed him to swoop in like a worried father and not judge like a disappointed employer.

He steps forward and places a big hand on my shoulder. "Because you're *better* than me. Don't you get that? I was lonely and grieving for a woman who was still breathing. I'm not proud of what I did, but you're *better* than me. You're not the one who does drugs or gets in trouble and needs his dad to call in favors to keep him out of prison. You've always earned what you had. Proven yourself. I didn't know what to do with a son who couldn't handle grief when I could never handle it either."

I close my eyes and focus on the weight of my dad's hand on my shoulder. The day of my mother's funeral, I stood by his side as people walked by to pay their respects, and he kept his hand on my shoulder. It grounded me. Reminded me I hadn't lost my whole family. His quiet sign of strength helped me find mine, and it does the same now.

When I open my eyes and meet his steady gaze, I say, "I was driving the car that hit Brogan and Nicholas Mendez."

The blood drains from my father's face. "Don't say that."

"I was driving the car. I don't remember it. Not at all. But Coach found me in the front seat of his SUV after midnight. There was damage to the front. He'd seen the news so he put two and two together." Dad stumbles back, and I take a breath. "He covered it up. He was trying to protect me, but I couldn't live with myself."

Dad shakes his head. "Don't say that out loud again. You understand? Never say it again. Don't speak of it."

I can't make that promise now. I never should have made it the first time. "I'm so sorry."

"Who knows?" he asks, and I feel like I'm watching him age before my eyes. He seems to shrink into himself, the wrinkles around his mouth and eyes suddenly more prominent.

"Trish was in the car. She remembers it. And then Coach knows. He was trying to protect me, but I hate that he did." I take a breath. It feels so damn good to have said it aloud. "I wish he hadn't."

"Mia?" he asks.

I shake my head, and guilt knifes through my gut. *I made love to her before she knew the truth.* I need to tell her. I have to find a way.

Dad's phone buzzes, and he curses when he looks at it. "I'm

late for my meeting, and then Gwen will cut off my balls if I don't get back to our suite." He slides his phone back into his pocket and his shoulders sag. "But I can stay if you want me to. I'll get out of the meeting, make up some excuse for Gwen."

"No. Go on. I need to think anyway."

"Promise me you won't do anything rash," he says, and when I just look at him, he adds, "At least not until after we have a chance to talk this out together. I lost your mom." His voice grows thick and weakens until he has to swallow to finish. "I can't lose you, too."

I nod. "Then we have to find a way to make this right."

MIA

Dad's silent on the drive back to his trailer. He took a cab to the Woodisons'—thank God for that moment of good judgment. Since I met Arrow, I feared the day my father would learn how I felt for him. I let that fear dictate my choices, and now that it's happened in one of the most mortifying scenarios imaginable, I'm ashamed I let it rule me for so long. But more than that, I'm ashamed I've passively accepted my father's addiction.

Parking the car in the gravel in front of his trailer, I cut the engine and take a long, slow breath. "I'm not my mother," I tell him.

He lifts his chin. There are tears on his cheeks. "You're just like her."

Kids play in the empty lot across the street, laughing and chasing each other with water guns. It could be a picture from my childhood. "I work for the Woodisons, true, and I've fallen for Arrow, but I'm not her. I didn't cheat on my husband or leave my family behind. I took a good job with a wealthy family so I could pay for my school and take care of you."

"You let him ruin you."

He still won't look at me, and I swallow back the hurt. "If you think my only value was in my virginity, then I guess you're right." I take another deep breath and watch the kids play, their bare feet flying through the thick green grass. "I'm really smart, Daddy. I know you know that, but you never would admit that it mattered. And I sing. I'm good at it, and it makes me feel alive. I'm a lot more than an unmarried girl who gave up her virginity to a sweet boy who made her feel special."

"I know that." His voice is low and quiet. "Why do you think I wanted more for you than to be their servant?"

I press my palm to my chest and squeeze my eyes shut. "There's no shame in working your way to a better life. I'm proud of the work I do. I don't want to do it forever, but that's exactly why I'm working so hard. So I *can* have better down the road."

When he finally turns to look at me, another tear slides down his cheek and slices through my heart. "I'm so sorry." He scrunches up his nose and draws a breath in through his teeth. "I panicked. I never should have gotten my gun. Don't hate me. You're my Mia. I can't lose you, too."

My eyes burn and the world goes blurry for the heartbeat before the tears start rolling. My dad's a lazy, misogynistic drunk, but that doesn't change the fact that I love him, and I've needed to know that he loves me too.

"This can't go on." I reach over the console, take his hand, and squeeze it. Tears thicken my throat. How is it we can know something for years, but it only seems real when we finally say it out loud? "You've got a problem with alcohol, and we need to get you some help."

"I'm fine," he says. His lower lip trembles, and he looks so much older than his fifty years.

"No you're not, Daddy. You haven't been fine since Mom left. And it's time to do something about that. It's time to sober up."

He holds my gaze and shakes his head. "I already tried AA. Nic had me going before he . . ." He squeezes his eyes shut and exhales slowly. "It didn't work."

"Let's get you to bed," I say, because I don't want to argue. Not today. I promise myself I'll try again tomorrow, but this morning my heart aches too much to carry on like this.

I get him in the house and tuck him in, then I search for liquor bottles—under the bed, behind the toilet, under the sink—and dump everything I find. I clean the kitchen and tidy the living room and kiss my sleeping father on the forehead before I leave.

When I go out front, I see Sebastian's car at his grandmother's trailer and decide to tell him that Dad's promised to stop drinking.

The screen creaks and rattles as I knock.

"Come on in," Sebastian calls.

I step into the trailer and smile at the scent of chocolate chip cookies. The trailer is almost identical to Dad's, though this one's been better maintained, and where Dad's feels small and cramped, this one feels warm and cozy. This one reminds me of how Dad's was before Mom left—always a blanket on the back of the couch and the smell of cookies in the air.

Sebastian sits at the kitchen table with a manila folder in front of him. The folder is open to a thick stack of papers, but he's holding a single page and staring at it like he's trying to interpret hieroglyphs.

"What is that?"

Sebastian's head snaps up. "Mia. I didn't know it was you."

I step forward, and he drops the paper on top of the pile and closes the folder.

"Nothing." He steadies his gaze on the wall behind me.

"Is it about the accident? Are those the police reports you said you'd get me?"

"I didn't know you'd be here. I wanted to look through them first." He grimaces.

"Let me see it. Let me see the one you were looking at when I walked in."

"*Mia.*"

"You found something, didn't you? You figured it out."

Standing, he unzips his backpack and slides the folder inside. "Let this go, okay? Nothing good is going to come of digging any further than you have." He pushes through the screen door, and I follow him onto the front porch.

"It's Coach. Emmitt Wright hit Brogan and Nic."

"Shh." He does a quick look around us to make sure no one heard me but we're alone. "Stop talking. Right now. Just stop this while you're ahead."

"He did it." I know it's true, because I can see it in Sebastian's eyes—that horror, that need to protect someone who's protected him. I imagine I'd see the same thing in Arrow's eyes in this situation. He'd feel trapped by the truth. He'd be torn between his innate sense of justice and the man who's been all but a surrogate father to him. He'd be a mess, and—"Oh my God. It was Coach, and Arrow knows."

"Coach hit a deer." Sebastian stands and throws his backpack over his shoulder. "His car was damaged because a doe jumped out in front of his car on New Year's Day morning. He even filed a report. Let this go."

"You'd already tested the blood, hadn't you?" He was too sure, too confident when he took me to the shop. "You knew something was off about the accident long before I started raising questions, and you'd already tested the blood."

He shakes his head and turns away from me, heading toward his car. "Let it go."

"I'm not going to stop, Sebastian," I say, my feet crunching in the gravel as I follow him. "I'm not going to let this go. I can't have the whole world believing my brother was responsible for what happened that night. Keep it to yourself if you must, but I'll find out eventually anyway."

"Fine." He yanks his backpack open and pulls the folder out of it. "Take it, Mia, but I don't want anything to do with this. Do you understand?" He climbs into his car and pulls away.

I take the file to my car and sit in the driver's seat before opening it. The accident report for Emmitt Smith is on top. When

I first scan it, I don't see anything that would upset Sebastian, but then the words jump out at me. *The officer noted the deer had been shot prior to the collision.*

Why would Sebastian be so upset to see the deer was shot before Coach hit it? Maybe it was injured and that was why it ran into the road.

Or maybe the deer was a cover-up.

I drive to the BHU football facility and park in the side lot next to Coach's Cherokee. I stare at it for a long time.

If the deer was a cover-up, he wouldn't have scrubbed the underside of the car or put deer blood there. Even if he took it through a car wash, there's a good chance trace evidence would remain.

I know what I need to do.

ARROW

I'm totally naked when Mia rushes into my room. I'm just out of the shower and my skin is still damp, my hair still wet.

She throws the door shut behind her and wraps her arms around my neck, presses her body against mine. She rises onto her toes to kiss me and threads her hands into my hair.

"Mia," I say against her mouth. "What are you doing?"

She reaches a hand between our bodies, unbuttons her jeans, and pushes them from her hips along with her panties. "Arrow." My hand is fisted at my side and she takes it, opens my palm, and guides it down her body, over her stomach and between her legs.

I don't know what's gotten into her. This is nothing like last night. This is frantic. This is the greedy kind of lust that isn't ever about sex at all. She's looking for escape, and I give it to her.

I cup my hand between her legs and drag my open mouth down the side of her neck. She arches into me, the cotton of her tank brushing against my chest.

"Arrow, please." She lifts a leg and wraps it around my hips, trying to pull me closer. She's still half clothed, and she rubs herself against my cock.

"Mia, slow down."

"It's over," she says, lifting her eyes to meet mine. "I know who did it."

At those words, all the blood in my body goes cold, and at the same time, I want to pull her closer. I want to put my mouth over hers so she can't say it out loud, to silence her and protect our last seconds together.

I step away.

"Arrow." There's so much sadness in her eyes. "I need to say goodbye."

"What do you mean?"

"Make love to me one more time. I have to do something, and I . . . Please. Just let's take right now. This moment. Because when I . . . I have to do what's right, and you might never forgive me."

Those words are a fist to my heart. "I could forgive you anything, Mia."

"One more time. Please."

"No." I take another step back. "Talk to me first."

She squeezes her eyes shut. "I have to turn him in. I'm sure it was him and I have to . . ."

What's she talking about? What does she think she knows? "Who?"

"Coach."

One word that says she knows more than she should. "Mia—"

"Coach was on Deadman's Curve on New Year's Eve. *Coach* hit Nic and Brogan."

I should have told her the truth before. I should never have waited. But no choice seems right when each means someone gets hurt. Or worse. "Mia—"

"I *have* to turn him in. There's still blood under the car. Not deer blood. Human blood, Arrow. I climbed under there myself and took a sample to the lab at BHU. I got the call this morning. Coach told the police he hit a deer, but it's not deer blood. He did it, and I have to turn him in."

I shake my head, my mind running too fast and in too many directions. "You *don't*."

"Everybody's been talking. You've heard them. They've been running their mouths about my brother for months. They think this was Nic's fault."

Where do I start? "Slow down."

"I knew how you'd feel." She folds her arms and draws in a ragged breath. "That's why I wanted to say goodbye. I owe it to my brother. He'd cleaned up, and they all ran their mouths like he hadn't. I owe it to him and everything he did for my family. I need to tell the police who was responsible for what happened that night."

I want to pull her into my arms and hold her one last time. Because she was right when she burst in here. Everything changes after this. I could kiss her, hold her close, and taste her lips one last time before she hates me. I don't let myself. "It wasn't Coach."

"I'm sorry, Arrow. I know how important he is to you. But we're talking about my brother, and I just . . ." She starts pacing, her arms wrapped tight around herself.

I have to grip the bed to keep myself from wrapping her up in my arms, to keep from begging her to forget whatever it is she knows. It had to come out, I realize that now, but I wish it didn't have to happen like this. "It wasn't Coach," I repeat.

"I wish he hadn't covered it up. It was dark, and they were fighting in the road like freaking idiots. I have to do this for my brother. Everyone thinks he was involved in drugs again, but he wasn't. He was clean. I have to turn him in."

"Mia . . ."

She stops pacing and stares at me like I'm not hearing her. "I'm telling you there was blood under that car that doesn't belong to a deer. It's human blood. I had the lab at BHU test it." She puts her hands in mine, and I have to pull away, otherwise I might bring them to my mouth, kiss her fingers one by one, trail kisses up her arms and along her jaw.

"I don't want to let you go," I whisper. "Every time you're almost mine, I have to let you go."

She frowns at me, and I know I'm not making sense. "I'm not asking for your permission, but I'm hoping you can understand why I have to do this."

Her shirt's damp from when she was pressed against me, and she takes my hands again, squeezes my fingertips in her palms, so desperate for the permission she says she doesn't need.

"Coach wasn't driving the car," I say. "I *know* he wasn't the one driving that car."

"How would you know that? You were drunk with Trish. The pictures were all over Facebook. How would you even know . . ." Her flushed cheeks turn pale, and every ounce of blood that drains from her face makes me feel smaller, more powerless. "Arrow?"

"I wanted to tell you." Everything feels like an excuse now, and I don't know how I can explain the claustrophobic hell that is being trapped from doing the right thing. Regret has gotten me nowhere, but if I could wipe my existence from Mia's life to save her the pain I see on her face right now, I wouldn't hesitate.

She drops my hands and backs away. One step. Two. She tilts her head first to one side and then the other, and narrows her eyes. It's as if she's suddenly realized I'm not the man she thought I was. Instead I've been standing in front of her all this time and she's trying to comprehend how she never noticed that I'm a monster.

"I wanted to tell you, but I knew you'd want to go to the police." More excuses. There's no good way to say this. There's no way to soften its ugliness. "I knew how you felt about your brother's reputation. Coach was just trying to help me. He didn't want one horrible mistake to ruin my life, and I couldn't ruin his by confessing."

"How . . . It was Coach's car. You were . . ."

I sink to the side of my bed and hang my head. Worse than regret is looking back and still not seeing the right path. Everything after waking up parked in Coach's lawn felt so out of my control, and everything that mattered before I can't remember. "I'm so sorry. You can hate me. *Please* hate me. I hate myself."

She shakes her head and takes another step away from me. "You told me to let him go. *You* told me. How could you? For *that* I could hate you, Arrow."

It's a knife twisted in my gut, and all I can do is hand her another. "He wasn't Brogan anymore. He was trapped in that body, and you know he wouldn't have wanted that."

"I don't . . ." She meets my eyes and shakes her head as if she still can't quite bring me into focus. "Arrow?"

"I wanted to turn myself in." I shouldn't explain. I shouldn't try to excuse it. But this is Mia, and no one else matters. This is Mia, and I need her to understand. "I want to do it. *Every. Fucking. Day.* But I couldn't. Not without hurting Coach. He covered it up trying to protect me, and turning myself in would have ruined him."

"They're *dead*, Arrow." Her voice is shrill, nails on the chalkboard of my heart. "This isn't someone's football career or someone's chance at a scholarship. Two men are dead because of . . ." She lifts her eyes to mine.

I take the knife she's poised and shove it the rest of the way in. "Because of me. They're dead because of me."

She crumples to the floor. "No. You're wrong. You're protecting him. This cannot be the truth."

Nausea wraps me in its sweaty fists. I want to go to her, but I can't. I'm everything that's making her hurt right now. "Mia, every day I've woken up knowing I ended my best friend's life, that I killed the brother of the woman I love, and I couldn't even come clean about it. That's my hell. That's my punishment for taking those keys and driving when I had no business behind a wheel."

"You kept driving." She swipes at her wet cheeks as if she's angry with her tears. "I watched that car. It hit them and it skidded to a stop, and then it just kept driving. How could you do that?"

I never knew I could. "I don't know." God, it hurts. Showing her the worst of me. Watching her tremble on my bedroom floor and knowing I'm to blame.

I spent the whole spring semester sabotaging my own future, trying any way I could to make *someone* punish me for *something*, anything. Seeing Mia like this is the unnecessary reminder that I deserve so much worse than I got. "I don't remember anything. The worst fucking thing I've ever done, and I have no memory of it at all. I was drinking. I was with Trish. I was pissed at Brogan and pissed at you." I shake my head. Months later, the fragments from that night still form nothing but the fractured edges of a thousand-piece puzzle. "Everything happened so fast, and I don't even remember..."

She shakes her head, and I know I'm talking too fast, giving her too much to process. She looks at me. "You made love to me, Arrow."

I swallow. "I know."

"You were *inside me* with this disgusting secret."

"Yeah. I'm a piece of shit, Mia." I hang my head. I'm not strong enough to keep facing the hatred in her eyes. "I'm a piece of shit."

She grabs her pants off the ground, stands, and steps into them, yanking them up her legs. Shaking hands on the buttons, she turns to the door. "I have to go."

"If I could have figured out a way to turn myself in without Coach getting in trouble, I would have done it. You have to believe me."

She stops and turns back to me. "Don't you understand? He *should* be in trouble. He did something terrible, too. He covered up the murder . . . the death . . . the . . ." She squeaks and bites her bottom lip.

But I never wanted to ruin his life, too. I'd already destroyed so much, and I couldn't be responsible for more. Even now, even with Mia's anger filling the room, I can't figure out how I could have made another choice without destroying someone else. Maybe I should have said that I made Coach cover it up. Would they have believed me? "I couldn't live with myself. I couldn't turn myself in and I couldn't stand to look at my own reflection, so I had to find a way to get in trouble—to take some sort of punishment—without hurting anyone else and without telling the truth. They took away football and gave me fucking house arrest."

"That makes it okay?" She's still not looking at me. Her hands are clenched at her sides and her voice shakes hard. "You got your punishment and now you can just, what? Let it go?"

"I lie in bed at night and I can't breathe because I know what I've done. Brogan lost everything. I wanted to suffer the same, and if I thought killing myself would bring him back, I would have done it months ago."

She flinches as if I struck her. "I'm not saying that I think you should have."

I push off the bed and stand in front of her. Her face is blank and hopeless, like some asshole's been beating on her and she's given up. That's my fault.

I need her to understand. I can take any punishment. I can give up my freedom and my life, but I need her to understand. "Then *you* were here, Mia. And suddenly I needed to live." Bile rises in my stomach at the memory of her vacant expression as she waited on my family. "I needed to stop punishing myself for the same reason I couldn't come forward after Coach covered it up." I press my palm to the ache in my chest. "I'd already ended two lives. You were the walking dead. I had to wake up and wake you up, because I couldn't handle the thought of a third life ending because of what I did that night. I couldn't change things for Brogan. It was too late for him, but if I could save you, if I could wake you up, it would have been . . ."

She cocks her head to the side. "So you fucked me to soothe your conscience?"

I nearly double over from the pain of that accusation. "I know. I'm a piece of shit. But I'm a piece of shit who was trapped in a corner, just doing what he thought he had to do."

"I have to do this." She rushes from the room, and I move to go after her and stop.

I'm so ready to be done with these lies. I'm so ready to be released from this purgatory.

All I can do is get dressed while I listen to the sound of her junky old car pulling down the drive. Jeans, a T-shirt, maybe my last outfit outside of jail. I miss the emptiness I felt before I returned, the numbness that got me through the months after the accident. Because right now I feel everything. Ugly. Hurt. Angry. But mostly I just feel the wake of her hatred, so intense it threatens to plow me over long minutes after she's gone.

All I can do is sit and wait for what happens next.

MIA

I drive on autopilot and park the car in the lot. This weather reminds me too much of the night of the accident. The rain falls in thick swaths I could hardly see through on the drive here.

I let the windshield wipers run even after I put the car in park, finding some odd comfort in the rhythmic *whoosh whoosh* of their dance.

I keep waiting to wake up. I feel like I've been living the last four months of my life just waiting to wake up.

That's not entirely true, though. There were moments when I was alive. Awake. Moments when he was touching me. Making me smile.

How could he have kept this secret?

Yanking the keys from the ignition, I stumble out of the car and toward the only place I could come after what I learned this morning. As much as I told myself the police station was the right place to go, I'm here instead.

The whole drive, I kept thinking, *I should go to the police. I should do what's right.* But I couldn't make myself do it.

I walk through the rain past the tall monument statues and to the modest plot in the back where my brother is buried. I drop to my knees in front of his gravestone and run my fingers over his name etched into the granite.

I've been wishing for a way to clear his name, and now I have the opportunity.

Brogan didn't die because my brother was mixed up in drugs again. He died because some irresponsible college kid drank too much and got behind the wheel. Such a cliché. Such an old story.

Rain and tears mix to blur my vision, but I don't feel like I've been able to see clearly since the day I met Arrow. As much as I miss my brother and want to bring him back, as much as I wanted someone to blame for the horrible thing that happened to him, and as much as Arrow's story leaves little doubt as to who's responsible for everything we lost that night, Nic was the fucking idiot throwing punches in the middle of the road on a pitch-black night.

"I can set the record straight," I tell my brother's grave, but I can't hear myself over the pounding of the rain on the gravestones around me. "You worked so hard to stay clean, and they should know. But if I do that, I'm choosing your reputation over Arrow's life."

Is it any wonder Arrow spun out of control the way he did? This is a man who's always done the right thing, and Coach cornered him into keeping a secret he didn't want to keep about a horrible thing he can't even remember doing.

Nic never gave a shit about his reputation. That was me. *My* pride. *My* insistence on the world knowing my brother wasn't the scum they believe he was. I know without a doubt Nic could forgive me for staying quiet. He understood secrets better than most. But why does that have to be a choice?

I'm drenched, and I stand with every intention of going to my car and driving to Bailey's apartment to get a hot shower. Instead, I find myself at Brogan's grave. Yellow barriers surround the fresh mound of dirt, and being blocked from his grave breaks something inside me. It's just all too much.

Brogan would know what to do. He was my voice of reason. I just wish he were here to tell me what I'm supposed to do next.

ARROW

"I think Crowe's gonna be good," Chris says between bites of pizza. He and Mason showed up a few hours ago and they've been here ever since, making themselves at home and unknowingly distracting me from obsessing over Mia. Not that it's working, but it's better than being alone.

"You could paint a thunderstorm with sunshine and rainbows," Mason says.

I've only been half paying attention, and I look up. I don't want to hear them fighting over whether or not my replacement is good enough.

The rain's still coming down, and thunder claps over the house. Out the window, a zigzag of orange cracks open the middle of a gray-black sky.

"You guys, will you go?"

They both stop talking and look at me.

"What?" Mason asks.

"We'll get out of your hair," Chris says.

I shake my head. "It's not that. I want you to go find Mia." I look out at the rain again, the weariness in my gut growing. "I just need to know she's okay. Don't tell her I sent you."

"Yeah," Mason says.

"Of course," Chris agrees, pushing his plate aside and standing.

"Anywhere we should look?" Mason asks.

"We'll start at her dad's trailer," Chris says. "I bet she's there."

"Then we'll go to Bailey's," Mason says.

"Of course you want to go there," Chris says.

"Fuck you, I'm trying to help."

I hold up a hand. "Stop. Start at the cemetery." Another clap of thunder booms over the house, and suddenly I know without a doubt that's where she is. Bailey was telling the truth about her not being there. Mia wouldn't have wanted to face her dad while she was so upset. And the police would have been here by now if she'd gone to the station. Should I be grateful that she didn't? But if she doesn't, we're both trapped in the hell of knowing this horrible secret. "Start there," I say. "If she's outside, talk her into getting out of the rain. But if she's not there and you find her safe inside somewhere, leave her alone. All I want is to know she's okay."

"Yeah," Mason says. "We'll let you know what we find."

"Thank you."

I pace the long wall of windows in the family room while I wait for them to return. I know they'll find her at the cemetery.

I just know. Like the night she caught Brogan cheating on her, I stayed in my room because I knew she was coming. I've always felt that connection to her—like our souls are hardwired together, no matter how much I try to let her go or tried not to care when she was with Brogan. Our connection is some cruel cosmic joke.

I don't know how long it takes. Minutes pass. The sky grows darker, the storm louder.

I'm on the front porch when Chris's car tears up the drive and parks behind my Mustang.

Mason climbs out of the back and scoops Mia into his arms. She presses her face against his chest and away from the rain as he carries her to me. She's drenched to the bone, and her clothes are smeared with wet earth. Her hair is matted and clotted with mud.

"We found her at the cemetery," Mason says, transferring her to my arms. "She was lying on Brogan's grave. They have barriers around freshly filled graves for a reason, but apparently she didn't care. She was just lying in the mud on his grave."

This is my fault. I did this to her. I took her brother. I took Brogan. And now I've broken Mia. The realization makes me hold her tighter.

Chris meets my eyes. "She told us to bring her to you."

She's shivering now, and I wonder if it's the first time all day she's realized how cold she is.

"I've got you, Mia."

She wraps her arms around my neck and clings to me.

"Need help?" Chris asks.

"No. I've got this."

He nods. "Okay."

"Call us," Mason says. "Let us know that she's . . ." He stops before saying *okay*. Mia is not *okay*, and everyone knows it.

"I'll call you later," I say.

I don't bother waiting for them to go. I turn into the house, close the door behind me, and carry her through the living room, through my father's bedroom, and into the master bath.

I sit her on the edge of the tub and run the water to warm it. She's shivering full-force now. Every part of her shakes, from her shoulders to her hands to her toes.

"I need to warm you up, Mia."

She nods and puts her hands to the buttons on her shirt, but they're shaking too much. I do it for her, ignoring the ache in my heart that demands I hold her close and tight. I pull the shirt from her shoulders and take off her muddy canvas sneakers. She lifts her hips so I can pull her jeans down and off her feet.

I check the water to make sure it's warm enough, and she climbs into the tub. In nothing but a bra and panties stained beige from muddy water, she draws her knees into her chest and wraps her arms around them.

I sit on the edge of the tub behind her and draw her between my legs. Turning the spray nozzle to the softest setting, I start the process of rinsing the mud from her hair.

"I'm sorry," she whispers.

The words are a dull blow to my heart. "You have nothing to apologize for."

She squeezes her eyes shut. "Then why do I feel like I'm drowning in regret?"

I swallow hard and focus on the task at hand. There's so much mud clotted in her hair, and I keep rinsing, watching the brown water circle the drain. I rinse until it starts to clear, then slowly work shampoo through her long locks. She lifts her chin and leans back into me as I massage the suds into her scalp.

When her shivers have stopped and the water runs clear of dirt and shampoo, I turn off the water. My jeans are drenched and my shirt is soaked across the front. I yank off my shirt to get it out of the way and reach for a towel to wrap around Mia's shoulders.

"I'll clean the tub later," she whispers.

"Mia."

"I'll clean the tub later," she says, her voice stronger now. "Because it's my job."

I shake my head. I'm not going to argue with her about this now. I just want to get her in bed, get her warm, and know she's safe.

I lead her up to her room, leaving a trail of footprints behind me. I find a sleepshirt and a pair of underwear and hand them to her. She gives me her back as she pulls off her wet bra and panties and puts on the dry clothes.

I pull the covers back and lead her into the bed, but as I draw them over her, she shakes her head. "Arrow?"

"Yeah?"

"Please don't leave me. I'm so tired of hurting all alone."

I draw in a ragged breath before nodding. I shuck off my wet jeans and toss them over the back of her desk chair before climbing into bed beside her. She rolls to her side, and I pull her back against my front and hold her as tightly as I can without hurting her.

"Brogan would have done the same," she says. She finds my hand at her waist and squeezes my fingertips in her palm. "What Coach did to try to protect you . . . had their positions been reversed, Brogan would have done whatever he had to do to protect you. It still would have been wrong, but he loved you. He wouldn't have wanted your life to have been ruined by one mistake."

I don't know what that means. I don't know if it means she understands but she still has to go to the police, or if it means she plans to carry this secret, too. All I know is that right now she's in my arms, and I thought I'd never get to have her here again. I know she's safe and dry and warm, and the dirt from my best friend's grave isn't knotted in her hair. All I know is that whatever she decides, the only sure thing I have is this moment. So I take a breath and I accept it for the gift it is.

MIA

"You choose *everything*, Uriah. You chose that we stayed in this house. You chose that your delinquent son would serve his house arrest with us when I wanted nothing to do with him. You even fucking chose that we got married in Vegas instead of giving me a real wedding. You're not choosing this. Her father brought a gun into my house, and she's fucking your son. You don't think you're next? You don't think she'll spread her legs fastest for the one with the most money?"

My door flies open and Arrow walks in, his jeans unbuttoned and slung low on his hips, a towel in his hand, his hair still dripping from his shower. Apparently he's been listening to Gwen scream, too. Not that we could miss it at the volume she's carrying on.

I woke up to an empty bed and Gwen shouting. I guess they got home earlier than expected.

He stares at me and shakes his head. "Don't listen to her."

The thing is, I don't even care that she thinks I'm a whore. She had no idea what I've been through and why I've made the choices I have.

"You think I don't know about her mom?" Gwen shouts. "That I don't know you denied me and used your dying wife as an excuse when you were fucking the trash?"

Uriah's voice is a series of low murmurs, and though I can tell he's been weighing in on this conversation, I have no idea what he's said to his wife.

Arrow squeezes his eyes shut. "Jesus, Mia. I'm sorry."

"Either she goes or I go," Gwen says. "And that prenup might keep you from doing right by me, but my lawyer will make damn sure you do right by your daughter."

I grab my suitcase from the closet and put it on the bed. I can't do this. I can't tear apart another family. Maybe Arrow was driving the car, but I'm the reason Brogan was on that road. I'm the reason my brother showed up, and I'm the reason they were fighting instead of going home.

"What are you doing?" Arrow asks, as I open a drawer and pull out a stack of clothes. I ignore him and take them to my suitcase. "She'll get over it, Mia."

"It's time for me to leave. I've been unprofessional."

"Jesus, Mia. I . . ." He turns toward the sound of Gwen's heels as they grow closer on the wooden staircase.

She throws the door open and scowls at Arrow before leveling her angry gaze on me. "I'm done," she says. "You think I'm not a fit mother. You think I can't do this on my own."

Have I really been so bitchy? Do I come off as if I think I know how to raise her daughter better than her? "I never said that."

"There are plenty of people who'd be thrilled to have your job. Who I could pay a whole hell of a lot less because Uriah doesn't have some irrational sense of guilt toward them."

That's a slap in the face. I pride myself on making my own way, but they don't pay me like they do because I work hard. My paycheck is about Uriah's guilt. It shouldn't hurt—shouldn't matter—but it does.

"I'm not fighting with you, Gwen." What could I say anyway? That I deserve that check? I'm not sure it's true. That I haven't been sleeping with Arrow? At this point, everyone seems to know I have.

"I am," Arrow says. "She's the best fucking nanny you're going to find around here. She does everything for you and she *loves* Katie. What are you—"

Gwen holds up a hand. "Get out of my face. This is about *my* baby. This is about *my* baby's life."

"Are you sure?" Arrow asks. "Because it sounds like it's about your petty jealousy over a woman who hasn't lived in this city for almost six years."

I still at Arrow's words. He's defending me. I don't want to compare him to a dead man—it's not right, and it's not fair—but Brogan always found a way around defending me to his mother.

"I've had enough," Gwen says. "Mia, you are out of here." She turns on her three-inch heels and leaves the room.

Arrow opens his mouth and goes to follow her, but I reach out and squeeze his wrist before he can say anything else. "Just let it go."

His jaw works, but I know he won't say any more because I've asked him not to.

I don't have that much here. I don't have much in general. I've never been the kind of person who was big on *things,* with a few exceptions.

I gather my belongings, fold my clothes, pack my suitcase, and slide my textbooks into my backpack. The last thing I get is my dancing fairies painting from the bottom drawer of the desk. I still remember the night he gave it to me. I was so touched by his thoughtfulness, and something else, too. My skin prickled, and it felt like all those little fairies were dancing up and down my arms, connecting me to Arrow with thousands of invisible currents. It wasn't just that he remembered my story; it was that he understood how important it was to me.

"You still have that?" Arrow asks.

I skim my fingers over the painting's textured surface, and those same chills come back. Will I ever meet anyone I feel as deeply tied to as him? "Of course. It makes me think about my mom. About the good times." I lift my eyes to his and see all the questions there. I don't know where we are. I don't know how I'm supposed to go forward—how I'm supposed to live or breathe knowing that the man I love killed my brother and the man I . . . loved. "It makes me think of you, Arrow. It was the sweetest gift I've ever been given."

"I don't want you to go," he says softly. His eyes are so sad, and I draw in a sharp breath because I've somehow forgotten. Living here, working here, I got to see Arrow all the time. It was so easy to forget that he was on house arrest. But if I don't have an excuse to be here, when will I see him? Nights sleeping in his arms will be a thing of the past. Talking to him in the darkness an old luxury.

I force a smile. "It's for the best. I'll be okay."

"Mia—"

"I'll be okay. Bailey will take me back, at least temporarily, and I'll find another job. It's not like I'll be living on the streets." Avoiding his gaze, I zip up my suitcase and do one last look around the bedroom to make sure I haven't forgotten anything. I feel Arrow's gaze on me with every move I make. "I think that's everything."

"I'll help you load up your car."

ARROW

I lift the suitcase into the trunk and close it. Mia's hands are tucked into the pockets of her jean shorts and her eyes are cast down to the ground. Yesterday's rain is gone, and the sun brings out the light brown highlights in her hair.

"You can do better than this job, Mia." I can tell from the look on her face that her employment status is the least of her problems. That today, any worries of whether or not she'll be able to transfer to BHU are buried beneath bigger worries.

I understand what that's like. When something that once mattered seems inconsequential in the face of the nightmare you've woken to.

"I'll make sure Dad gives you good references," I say. It's so lame. If I could, I'd weave together a big, bright future for her and hand it over wrapped in a bow. She's been stuck in the quicksand of my mistake for too long. "There are a couple of board members who might be interested in a good nanny."

"Arrow," she says softly, and I want to pull her into my arms so badly it hurts.

"I won't tell anyone your secret," she says.

I suck in a breath and hold it to trap my rage. It's not her job to free me from this burden, but I hoped she would. But mostly I want to rage because I know now she carries it too, and I don't want that for her. "Don't do that for me. Don't hold it for me."

She tilts her face toward the sun. "I'm not doing it for you."

I shake my head. "I'd forgive you anything. I'd understand if you felt like you needed to—"

"Arrow, it's done. I know you'd have gone forward and done the right thing if Coach hadn't cornered you into keeping the secret. And I'm sorry for the ugly things I said yesterday. You didn't deserve that. You've suffered enough. I forgive you," she whispers, and those words hurt more than I'm prepared for.

I look away, shocked by the dull force of it. "Don't do that. I don't *deserve* that."

She puts her hands on my face, her palms along my jaw, her fingertips in my hair, and turns me to look at her. "I forgive you, and I hope you'll do whatever it is you need to do to forgive yourself. Do it for Brogan."

"Fuck, Mia . . ."

The sun shines in her eyes. In a different life, maybe we'd be enjoying this beautiful day together—holding hands and sitting on the dock and watching the light reflect off the water. Then I'd pull her into me and kiss her, smell the sunshine in her hair as she whispered my name against my neck.

That's not the fate we were given, and as she looks up at me, I realize I've had that image of us together from the day we met. I've never been willing to let it go. Not when me being a Woodison stood between us; not when Brogan stood between us. Not even when I sat in the hospital, willing my memory of New Year's Eve to come back, or when Brogan was in surgery fighting for his life.

How different would our lives be today if I'd been able to let it go? If I hadn't shown up at her door and told her I was in love with her? Would Brogan still be alive?

Part of my mind has always believed Mia was mine and has held on to the hope that we could make it work. Someday. Somehow. All of this could have been avoided if I hadn't so stubbornly held on to that belief.

"That day that we met," I say. "I think about it a lot. About how we seemed to click, but then you wanted nothing to do with me."

"It seemed like such a big deal then." She gives a sad smile. "I thought it was a terrible day to have met this sweet, amazing guy and find out he was a Woodison." She exhales slowly and wraps her arms around her waist. "What I wouldn't give to go back there and have that be the biggest problem in my life."

I turn away because I can't look at her and say what I need to say. "If I could go back, I never would have taken that first walk with you."

She laughs a little uncomfortably. "What happened to wishing you'd kissed me?"

I stare at the ground and shake my head. "If I'd let you go, if

I'd let you be with him without the questions of whether or not he made you happy, without being the one to catch you when he hurt you, without showing up at your door to tell you I was in love with you . . . everything would be different. Everything." I lift my head and force myself to meet her eyes. "You kept trying to tell me we couldn't be together, and I didn't want to see it."

"What are you doing?" Her voice wobbles on the question like a novice on a tightrope.

"You could never be with him completely because I stood in the way. And you've never been able to move on since because of me." I shove my hands into my pockets so I don't grab her and hold her tight. "I'm letting you go. I'm telling you I don't want you to carry my regret and my mistakes around in your heart. I need you to figure out how to live your life without me in it."

"Don't do this, Arrow."

"I thought it was my job to help you lead your life, to help you wake up. But it was another excuse to be selfish. Another way I could avoid letting you go."

"You're my friend," she says, a little desperately. "There's no reason we can't always be friends."

"Except there is. You'll always look at me and remember what I've done. We'll never be together without the past wedged between us. You deserve better than that." I take a step forward, toward her upturned face, closer to her parted lips. I don't know how to shut off the magnetic pull between us, but I make myself stop and take two steps back, two steps away from temptation. "You have too much beauty to hide from the world. I can't stand here and tell you that I hope you fall in love with Sebastian, and that I hope he's the one who can make you happy. I'm not that good of a guy to say those things. But if I don't think about the specifics and I step back a little, all I want is for you to be happy. All I want is for someone to fill in the empty places in your heart the way you did mine from the beginning."

"Arrow?" She drags in a choppy breath, and I look up to see tears welling in her eyes. "You're breaking up with me when all I want is to be your friend."

"If I don't, I may as well have killed you that night, too. I've brought you nothing but pain."

"Arrow . . ." She opens her mouth and closes it again, and I realize I'm holding my breath, hoping she says she loves me too much to let me go.

That's not why I'm standing out here. That's not why I'm doing this. But I wait, half of my heart praying she'll let me set her free and the other half waiting for the miracle.

"Is this goodbye?" she asks.

"I want you to live, Mia. I want you to *sing*. Don't come here anymore. I'll only keep you in the past. I'll only weigh you down."

She swallows hard and swipes tears from her cheeks with the palm of her hand. Then, without arguing or agreeing, she climbs into her car, and I step onto the porch and watch her drive away.

MIA

I drive straight to Bailey's apartment. She opens the door seconds after I knock and pulls me into her arms.

"You having a hard time, sweetie?" she asks.

Mason's sitting on the couch, his jean-clad legs stretched out in front of him and crossed at the ankle. His chest is bare, and he's leafing through a magazine. When he looks up and sees me, he puts down the magazine. He grabs his shirt from where it was draped across the back of the couch and pulls it over his head. "I'll give you two some privacy." He steps into his shoes and cocks his head at Bailey. "Call me?"

She gives him a noncommittal smile and opens the door wider.

"Right." He grimaces and heads out without another word.

"What was that?" I ask. "I thought you two weren't sleeping together anymore."

"We weren't," she says, pulling me into the apartment and

closing the door. She shrugs. "Funerals make me sad. I needed something in my life that wasn't sad, and Mason in my bed is very much *not sad*."

I'd love to indulge in a heart-to-heart about her love life. I'd love to give her a little lecture about how Mason's a really nice guy who deserves more from her.

I stare at her, and she rolls her eyes. "It's just sex, Mia."

I'm selfish today, so I don't push it.

She grabs two glasses from the cabinet and sets them on the counter in front of me. She uncorks a bottle of red wine and fills them both nearly to the brim. "Do you want to talk about it?" she asks, lifting her glass. "Or do you want to just hang out and have me pretend I'm not dying to know what's going on between you and Arrow?"

"What do you mean?"

"Mia, Mason told me about last night. About finding you in the graveyard and you asking them to take you to Arrow. Which is some really sad-ass shit, by the way, and if Mase hadn't all but stolen my keys, I would have come over to be with you." She sighs. "And even if he hadn't told me, it's all over your face every time you look at Arrow. He came home, and you started to . . . I don't know, *care* again. Before, you'd been looking at the world through glazed eyes, and Arrow snapped you out of it."

"I'm in love with him."

She wraps her arms around me and nods into my shoulder. "I know that, sweetie."

"I thought I might be able to move on if I knew who was

responsible for the accident. I thought that would help me get there."

She nods again. "I know that, too."

I open my mouth then close it again. If I'm scared to tell my best friend—a girl I trust more than anyone—the truth about what happened that night, how did I think I could go to the police? "The truth is supposed to set us free, and in my mind that meant maybe Arrow and I would have a chance. I was wrong."

She pulls back and nudges my glass toward me. "Drink."

With my eyes on her, I obey. It's wine the way Bailey likes it best: sweet and cheap.

"Tell me what's up with Arrow. Is he screwing around with Trish? Mason told me she'd been over there a lot. She's a hot mess. I think she might be a cutter. Did you see those marks on her arms when she was at the pool?"

I shake my head. I don't want to talk about Trish. "Remember when I told you I thought there was a chance Coach was the one driving the car, but Sebastian proved he wasn't?"

"Yeah?"

"The police report for the accident said the deer was shot, and I thought it might have been a cover-up. So I decided someone needed to check under the car."

"Oh, no," she says.

"Yeah. There was blood under the car. Real blood."

"Coach," she says, as if she's trying to wrap her mind around it.

"Not Coach," I answer. "Coach's *Cherokee*."

She wraps her arms around herself and backs away, as if she's not sure she wants to hear anymore.

"I told Arrow I thought it was Coach, and he told me . . . the night of the accident . . ."

She tenses her shoulders, shielding herself from the blow. "He'd borrowed Coach's SUV. I never thought about it before, but I remember seeing him. He was helping to set up for the high school lock-in." She meets my eyes and shakes her head.

All I can do is nod.

The color drains from her face all at once, and she spins around to the sink and throws up.

I've been so selfish—so caught up in my own grief that I never stopped to think about how hard the last few months have been on Bailey. I wasn't the only one who lost someone I loved that night. Bailey lost Nic. I may not have approved of the way she loved him or the fact that she wanted to be with him, but she did. She's been so quiet about her grief, so selfless in supporting me through mine because she knew I was dealing with losing my brother and Brogan all at once.

She turns on the tap and scoops handfuls of water into her mouth, then she just hangs her head over the sink. I wrap her in my arms from behind and rest my forehead on her back, letting her sobs move through me, and when she calms, I give the rest.

"He said he wanted to turn himself in but couldn't because Coach covered it up, and he didn't want him getting in trouble, too."

Bailey sinks into the stool beside me and studies her wine.

"God, it's so obvious now, isn't it?"

"What do you mean?"

She shakes her head. "The drugs. The fights. He wasn't himself after the accident, and we all thought it was grief, but he was ruining his life on purpose."

"I told him I was going to the police. I told him I was turning him and Coach in. That's where I thought I was going when I got in the car."

"You can't turn him in, Mia," she says. "His life will be over."

"I'm not going to."

She closes her eyes, exhales slowly, then pops them open. "Mia, is he sure he was driving that night?"

"Yes. He doesn't remember it, but Coach found him in the car and woke him up."

She grabs her keys. "Come on."

I put down my wine and follow her out the door. "Where are we going?"

"To get answers," she says. "We don't have the full story."

Five minutes later, Bailey knocks on the door to Mason and Chris's apartment, and I shake my head. "I don't know if we should be doing this."

"Yes, we should," she says. "We need to find answers, and that's why we're here."

"But maybe Sebastian was right. Maybe nothing good can come of digging up information from that night. If we don't want people to look at Arrow and find out what happened, we shouldn't ask too many questions."

"We don't *know* what happened," she says. "Nobody does. Just be cool. It's fine."

Chris opens the door and sees Bailey. His eyes go wide. "Hey! Mason's in the living room." He seems surprised to see her here. He seems to have some opinions about Bailey's relationship with Mason, and he's not alone.

"Thanks," she says. "But I'm not just here for him, ya know. You're my friend, too."

"Mmm," Chris says, unconvinced. "Okay."

We go to the living room and find Mason sitting at the TV with a PlayStation controller in his hands, some military game with lots of gunfire on the screen. He looks up and sees Bailey, does a double take, and then turns the TV off.

"Hey." He puts the controller on the cluttered coffee table. "What's going on?"

"Can't I come and hang out with my friends?" she asks. "You guys show up at my place all the time. What's the difference?"

Chris clears his throat. "No, *we* don't."

"Shut up," Mason says to Chris. Then to Bailey, "It's cool. You can come over anytime you want."

"Mia got fired this morning," Bailey says.

"Bailey!"

"What? It's not like it's a secret."

I sigh. "My pride or something, okay?"

"Ouch," Mason says. "Why'd the old man fire you?"

Bailey opens her mouth, but I shoot her a look and she closes it again. I don't really need her talking smack about my dad to these guys.

"It's complicated," I say.

"Complicated?" Chris asks, "Or Gwen didn't like you sleeping with Arrow?" Bailey and I both spin on him, and he holds up his hands, palms out. "I'm not judging! I just know she doesn't like your relationship. It's pretty much all over her face every time she sees you two together."

"I'm not *sleeping* with Arrow," I say. Then I grimace. "I mean, not anymore. Exactly."

Bailey moves toward the kitchen. "It doesn't matter. But speaking of people who are sleeping with Arrow—"

"Or not sleeping with him," I say.

"Yeah, whatever." She rolls her eyes. "What do you all know about him and Trish?"

"Oh, man," Chris says, turning away from us and busying himself stacking dishes from the drying rack in the kitchen.

Mason shakes his head. "I don't want to get into that. She's a hot mess. A live grenade ready to blow."

"A live grenade? You play too many video games," Bailey says.

Mason lowers his voice and points his thumb toward the hallway. "And she's sleeping in Chris's room."

Bailey and I both turn to stare at Chris.

"Not like that," Chris says. "He's right. She crashed here last night. Showed up at our door drunk—maybe high. I don't know what she's doing. She started going off about her dad, and we took her keys so she couldn't drive home. I gave her my bed and slept on the couch."

Bailey looks at me, then back to Chris. "What did she say about her dad?"

He slides a stack of plates into their spot in the cabinet and shuts the door. "Normal daddy-issue stuff. He's a selfish asshole. He's made her life hell." He shakes his head. "I don't know. But I *do* know that the last thing I need is for Coach to catch his daughter at my house, high on God-knows-what. I'd have taken her home myself if she hadn't threatened to slit her wrists if I did. Someone needed to keep an eye on her."

"Do you guys remember her and Arrow being together on New Year's Eve?" Bailey asks.

"Who could forget?" Mason mutters.

I have goosebumps and that uneasy tightening in my chest and stomach. I always feel like this when we talk about that night. It's as if I'm standing on the side of the road again, the sleet slicing at my cheeks.

"Do you remember when they left together?" Bailey asks. "Who was driving?"

"They left together?" Mason asks. "I didn't see them go."

Chris frowns. "He could hardly stand up straight. Trish had Keegan help her get him into the car. It was crazy. Arrow never drinks like that. Or at least he didn't before the accident."

I draw in a ragged breath. *She had Keegan help her get him into the car.*

Someone knocks on the door, and Bailey and I look at each other.

"I'll get it," I say.

I pull open the door, and Sebastian pushes past me into the apartment. "I've been looking everywhere for you. What did you say to him?" he asks. He looks like shit. He's always so composed, and today his eyes are bloodshot and his skin is sallow, like he hasn't slept in a week. "What did you say to Coach?"

Bailey and I exchange a glance. We're both still processing what Chris said, and I just want Sebastian to leave so we can talk about it more. *Arrow wasn't driving. It wasn't his fault.* But I need to know for sure before I go back to him, before I tell him he can stop hating himself for a night he can't remember.

"Mia!" Sebastian growls. "What did you *say*?"

I pull my gaze away from Bailey and return it to Sebastian. "What are you talking about?"

"About his car. About the accident."

Mason hops off the couch. "Coach was in an accident? Is he okay?"

"On New Year's Eve," Sebastian says, not sparing Mason a glance but continuing to skewer me with his gaze. "You said something to him. I told you to let it go."

I shake my head. "No, I didn't."

Chris walks toward us. "New Year's Eve?" He looks from me to Sebastian and back to me. "The dark SUV?"

"Are you sure, Mia? Because—" Sebastian drags his hands through his hair. "Fuck. You don't understand what a good guy he was. He's family to his players. *Family.* And he meant that and more to so many of us."

"Coach didn't have his SUV that night," Chris says, and now

he's searching my face, too. All these people looking at me when I don't have the damn answers.

"Talk, Mia!" Sebastian says.

Bailey steps forward, scowling at Sebastian with her arms folded across her chest. "Stop shouting at her." He's easily twice her size, but she's coming at him like she'll take a swing if she needs to.

"What's going on?" Mason asks.

Sebastian sets his jaw and turns his gaze to the floor. "I have a friend at the station. Coach just turned himself in for the hit-and-run on Deadman's Curve."

Bailey and I draw a sharp breath at the same time.

Sebastian collapses onto the couch, elbows on his knees. "You were right," he mutters. "I knew that damage didn't look like it came from a doe, but I didn't want to believe it. Goddammit, you were right."

I spin when I hear a bedroom door open in the back hallway and Trish comes out, her T-shirt falling off her shoulder, her eyes bleary. "My dad turned himself in?"

Sebastian drags his hand through his hair. "I'm sorry, Trish."

"That fucking asshole," she mutters.

"Coach wasn't driving his SUV that night," Chris repeats.

"Arrow thinks he was," Bailey says.

"Bailey!" I shake my head frantically, as if she could take the words back.

"That's why he's been such a mess," she continues in a hurry. "Arrow can't remember that night, but someone made him think he was driving." She turns to Trish now and stares her down.

"Keegan had to help him into the car," Chris says, and we all turn to Trish. "I watched him load Arrow into the passenger seat. You were driving." His voice is deadly soft, and I'm not sure she can hear it.

As if all her bones dissolved, Trish crumbles to the floor. "I was so scared. I didn't know what to do, and Daddy told me to go to my room. I shouldn't have been driving."

I draw back. She did it. There's no more guessing or speculation. She did it. Arrow's been torturing himself for months because she and her father made him believe he was guilty.

"Dad asked me if Arrow had been passed out the whole time," she says, rubbing her arms. "When I said yes, that Arrow had been passed out since we left the party, Dad told me he'd *take care of it*. I didn't realize how buzzed I was until I came over that hill. It was dark, and the sleet made it hard to see, and I shouldn't have been driving."

"You killed Brogan," Mason says. He steps toward her, hands clenched at his sides, and Chris grabs him before he can go further. "Get out of my fucking apartment."

Trish wraps her arms around her knees and rocks herself back and forth. "I'm sorry. I'm so sorry. I was scared, and I didn't know what to do, and Dad said he'd take care of it. He told me to go to bed, and when I woke up the next morning, the cops had already been there to file the report on the deer, and he'd already made Arrow think he'd been driving." She looks so pathetic, so utterly destroyed that I can't hate her like I want to. Hate would be so much easier than this mess.

My head snaps up. "Sebastian, did you tell Arrow that Coach is at the station?"

"I went to his house first," he says. "I was looking for you."

Bailey stops pacing and looks at me. "Oh no."

"Arrow knows Coach turned himself in." I'm already grabbing for my phone and punching in Arrow's cell number. "Voicemail," I tell Bailey when Arrow's message clicks on.

"What did Arrow say when you told him?" Bailey asks Sebastian.

He shakes his head. "He said he had to do something and he . . ." His frown deepens. "He got his keys and got in his car and left, but he's on house arrest."

Bailey rushes over to me and wraps me in her arms.

"Where would he have been going?" he asks.

I squeeze my eyes shut and open them again, like a child trying to wake from a bad dream. "The police station."

ARROW

When I pull up to the police station, I'm trembling. I want to be this brave guy who isn't scared to do what needs to be done. But even though I'm anxious to unload this weight from my shoulders, I'm terrified.

Coach is right. They'll make an example of me. They'll compare me to that *affluenza* kid, and my life will be over. My dream shattered on Deadman's Curve.

But I'm ready to be free of this terrible secret, and the second Sebastian told me Coach had turned himself in, I knew it was time.

I don't know what Coach is telling them. I don't know if he's throwing me under the bus or trying to take the blame himself—lie and say he was driving the car. But it doesn't matter. If he's turning himself in, it means I get to finally tell the truth without his fate weighing on my conscience.

I turn off my car and squeeze my eyes shut. I should have

done this sooner. I should have insisted.

I swallow hard, pocket my keys, and climb out.

When I step into the station, the officer who arrested me for possession looks up from his desk.

"You're supposed to be on house arrest," he says.

Not far away, Coach stands with another officer, who's pointing to the back hallway.

"I'm here to turn myself in," I say.

"No, you're not," Coach says. "You can't confess to a crime you didn't commit."

"Just because I don't remember—"

The doors to the station burst open, and Mia and Bailey rush in.

"You weren't driving!" Mia shouts.

Bailey nods frantically, and Trish steps through the doors and stands at my side. She's a mess, her eyes red, her face wet with tears, her hands full of tissues.

"They're telling the truth," Trish says. Her voice shakes, but she stands firm.

"Don't try to protect me," I say.

Trish squeezes my arm. "You never drove that night, Arrow. You weren't behind the wheel even once after you started drinking. You were passed out in the passenger seat." She steps forward and wraps her arms around her waist. She meets the eyes of the officer standing by me. "I was the one driving." She turns to me, her face falling. "I'm sorry I let you believe that it was your fault."

"Trish." I shake my head. "You didn't—" I look to Coach, who's avoiding my gaze. "I was in the driver's seat. When you woke me up. When you found me in your yard..."

He lifts his eyes to mine, and I see the truth right there. "I moved you to the driver's seat," he says.

That doesn't make any sense. If he was trying to protect me, why would he put me there? None of this makes any sense. "You were trying to protect me. Right?"

Trish squeezes my arm again, hard. "He was trying to protect *me*, Arrow. I was driving, and he was trying to protect me."

I'm frozen, but I feel as if I'm falling. Even when things were at their worst, when it felt like the whole fucking world was constructed to ruin me, my one constant was that at least there was Coach—someone who, right or wrong, loved me enough to take drastic actions to protect me.

Trish looks at the officer, takes a breath, and says, "I'm here to turn myself in for the hit-and-run accident that killed Nicholas Mendez and Brogan Barrett. My father covered it up and made Arrow think he did it, but I was the one driving the car."

MIA

"I can't imagine what you're feeling right now," Bailey says, as we pull into our old trailer park. "Because personally, I feel like I've been sucked dry. What a fucking insane day."

"No kidding." I scroll through the dozens of group texts between Bailey, me, and the guys on the team. The responses to everything that went down today run the gamut from anger toward Arrow for months of silence, to pity for me, to some rather unpleasant suggestions as to what Coach's punishment should be.

After the officers took Arrow, Trish, and Coach back for questioning, Mason and Chris showed up at the station to give their statements about seeing Trish drive the Cherokee, and Bailey and I were told to leave. I didn't want to, but Bailey reminded me that my dad might like to know the truth about what happened that night.

"Oh, for fuck's sake," she says as she parks the car. "And today just got a little more interesting."

I pull my eyes away from my phone and follow her gaze to the front steps of Dad's trailer. When I see her standing there, my heart squeezes so hard in my chest it brings tears to my eyes.

"Do you want to leave?" Bailey asks. "Because you've had a shit day, and you don't need to deal with this right now. I can tear out of here and hide you at my apartment until she leaves." She puts her hand on the gearshift, ready to pop the car into reverse.

Mom's eyes meet mine, and she gives a soft smile. Her hair is swept off her shoulders and tied at the back of her neck. Standing there in her yellow tank top and frayed jeans, it's as if she never left.

To this day, she's the most beautiful woman I've ever met, and despite all the anger and resentment I've directed her way in the last six years, there's no one I'd rather see right now.

"It's fine," I tell Bailey. "I'll talk to her."

Bailey frowns, grumbles something under her breath about masochism, and reaches across me to open my door. "I'll be at Mom's trailer if you need me, okay?"

I nod. "Love you, Bail."

"Love you, Mee," she whispers.

I close the car door and head for my mother.

Mom tucks her hands in her pockets as I walk forward. "Hi, Princess Mia," she says. She comes down the steps and worries her bottom lip between her teeth just like I know I do when I'm nervous.

I don't reply in any way but to wrap my arms around her and hug her tight. Because sometimes a girl needs her mom. "I missed you."

I know it's a silly thing to say when she was here in January for Nic's funeral. It's probably a little weird that in all the times I've seen or talked with her since she left when I was fifteen, this is the first time I've said it. Maybe it's not a fair thing to say when she tried to convince me to come back to Arizona with her and I refused, but after what I've been through in the months since the accident, I just need her to know.

"I miss you every day," she says, stroking my hair. "Your father tells me you're going to BHU next fall. He said you're the smartest girl in town."

I chuckle against her shoulder. That's my father. Everything in hyperbole. I pull back so I can look at her. "Why are you here?"

"Your father called me." Her smile falls away. "He told me he has a drinking problem, and he wanted a loan to check himself into an in-patient rehabilitation program. He said he wanted to do it for you."

"I could have given him the money," I say, looking over her shoulder to the dark and quiet trailer. Is he already gone?

"It was the least I could do, Mia." She swallows hard. "How long has he been like this? I suspected when I saw him at Nic's funeral, but we were all a mess and I . . ." She shakes her head. "Why didn't you tell me he was drinking? I would have come home."

"Nic and I thought we could handle it." It didn't seem like

a secret at the time, just something she didn't need to know. Or maybe part of me felt like I was punishing her by not sharing the details of our lives and keeping her in the dark about the hardest parts. I didn't want to need her after she left us so easily, and neither did Nic. "You didn't want to be here, so we didn't tell you anything that would make you feel like you needed to come back."

Her face crumples like tissue paper. "Baby . . ." She closes her eyes and composes herself.

I wait until she opens her eyes before I speak again. "I know about your affair with Uriah Woodison."

She folds her arms, and I recognize the defensive stance. I'm just like her. "I didn't want you to know." She drops her gaze to the ground and digs the toe of her white sneaker in the dirt.

"I needed you." I'm surprised to hear myself admit it and more surprised to hear my voice crack on the admission. It's been years, and I made it. I survived my teen years without my mom to wipe away my tears and hold my hand. It shouldn't matter anymore. But it does. "Why did you leave?"

She lifts her head and studies me. "I wanted you to be better than I was. Uriah, he wanted me to stay in town. He said he'd take care of us if I left your father, but he was still a married man, and you know what people would say." She drops her arms from around her waist and turns her palms up in a shrug. "I was ashamed and thought the best penance was to leave. You wouldn't have to be the daughter of the whore. You were always so smart. I didn't want my mistakes to follow you."

They did. Even when she was gone, they were here, haunting me. They were the reason I didn't give Arrow a chance that first day we met. They were the reason I got back together with Brogan when it should have been over. The reason I couldn't admit to myself that I loved Arrow. But I don't tell her any of that, because I know it will hurt her, and sometimes love means keeping secrets.

I guess I'm a lot like her after all.

"Dad?" I ask, nodding toward the trailer.

"I checked him into the clinic this morning. He said he wanted to be sober and gainfully employed next time he saw you. I told him you would be proud of him."

I stare at her—at the eyes so like the ones I see every time I look in the mirror, at the freckles she tells me are from her German grandmother—and I feel another piece of my safety net lock into place beneath me. After months of walking this tightrope of my life vulnerable and blindfolded, it's a relief. "Thank you for taking care of that."

She smiles and points to the trailer. "I made some cookies. Would you like to come in and have a couple? I'd love to talk more." She shifts and wrings her hands in front of her. "I'd really, really like to know about your life. More than you tell me in a ten-minute phone call."

My heart squeezes and I take a step forward, knowing it'll be okay if I fall. "Cookies sound great."

ARROW

It's hours later before they release me from the little room at the back of the station. There were questions and more questions. There were lectures and guilt trips. The police asked me about what I remember from that night so many times that I'll probably be reciting it in my sleep.

They made Mia and Bailey go home. I'm told that at one point, Chris and Mason showed up to give statements of their own about that night, but they were gone before I finished.

Dad came with his lawyer, and they got filled in on everything. The look on his face when he realized I hadn't been driving, that I wasn't about to face years in prison . . . it was good for me to see. He has trouble talking through his feelings, but his expression in that moment told me everything I need to know.

"Can I go home now?" I ask on my way back up front.

The officer who's spent most of his day with me nods. "If you want. But if you're willing, Mr. Wright has asked to have a few words with you."

I stop in the middle of the hallway.

"He's in there," the officer says, pointing to another room.

All this time, I'd valued Coach more than my own damn father. But today I learned which of the two really puts me first. "No thanks," I say. "If that's okay, I'd rather not talk to him right now."

"Not a problem," the officer says. "It's understandable."

"Thank you."

I leave the station, climb into my car, and drive home.

It's surreal, driving home when you thought you'd be spending the night in jail, and as betrayed as I feel over what Coach did to me, that's nothing compared to the weight that's been lifted from my shoulders. My albatross thrown into the sea.

When I pull into the drive, Chris's car is parked up front beside Mason's. For almost five months, I've prepared myself to lose my friends if the truth ever came out. Today, even when Trish confessed and explained I wasn't at fault, I still wasn't sure how they'd feel. But here they are, letting me know before I can even worry about it that they've got my back.

I find the two of them in the living room huddled in front of the television.

Mason grabs the remote and turns up the volume. "Coach is about to give a press conference."

Dad walks into the room from the kitchen. He looks to the screen and then to me before coming to stand by my side.

It's a live feed from in front of the courthouse, and Coach

Wright steps in front of the microphone.

"Today," Coach says into the microphone, "I'm officially resigning from my position as the head coach of the Blackhawk Hills University football team. It's a position I've been proud to hold and a group of young men I've been blessed to lead, but I'm no longer fit to be their guide." He unfolds a piece of paper and smooths it flat on the podium. "On New Year's Eve, I got the phone call every father fears. My daughter had been in a terrible accident." He swallows hard. "But the difference between my call and the one Mr. Mendez and Mr. and Mrs. Barrett were getting around the same time was that my daughter was okay. She was physically unharmed. And she was home—calling me from the front yard where she'd parked my SUV."

Dad puts his hand on my shoulder and squeezes, and I'm so damn grateful to have him here by my side. I take a deep breath and listen to what the coach has to say.

"She was in a panic because she'd hit two boys on Deadman's Curve. Every father wants to believe he'll do the right thing faced with a moment like that one. And I told myself, as I went outside and pulled her out of the car, that I was doing the right thing."

"Like hell you were," Chris mutters from the couch.

"She'd been drinking," Coach continues. "She shouldn't have been driving. But I knew what she'd face if she turned herself in.

"Her friend Arrow Woodison was passed out in the passenger seat. In a misplaced sense of fatherly duty, I decided I'd cover up what my daughter had done, but I had a choice to make about Arrow. To further remove my daughter from the crime, I pulled him into the driver's seat and let him stay there for almost two hours before I woke him and told him he'd driven there. I proceeded to take a series of steps to cover up my daughter's crime. I shot a deer and smeared its blood on the damaged front end of my car, then called the police to file a report that I hit the animal to explain the damage to my Cherokee." He draws in a long, slow, ragged breath and lifts his tired and tormented eyes to the camera. "And when Arrow woke up, I told him he'd been driving the car that hit those boys."

A barrage of questions surge from the audience and his pause is filled with the *click click click* of cameras.

Mason looks over his shoulder at me and my dad. "I can't believe he's saying all this in a press conference."

"I'm sure his lawyer is shitting himself," Dad says.

"Why not just say he's stepping down and be done with it?" Mason asks.

Drawing in a long breath, Chris looks at Mason, then steadies his gaze on me. "Maybe he needed to be heard. I think it's brave."

Coach starts speaking again, and we return our attention to the television. "I committed a horrible crime when I covered up what my daughter did. And I knew I'd have to live with that. What I wasn't prepared for was to live with the guilt of two young people who'd have each done the right thing had I not been there steering them in the wrong direction. I watched my daughter turn into an alcoholic, a cutter, a young woman who'd rather experiment with drugs than live in the moral hell I'd trapped her in."

"Jesus," Mason whispers. "I didn't know she'd gotten that bad."

"We didn't want to see what we didn't understand," Chris says. He shifts his gaze to me and grimaces. "And that goes beyond Trish."

Coach takes a long, deep breath. He looks like he might disintegrate into tears at any moment. "I watched Arrow Woodison, a man who was like a son to me, take up drinking and drugs and throw away his football career while he tried to punish himself for a crime he didn't commit." He wipes the tears off his cheeks. "When you make a decision like that as a father," Coach says, "you tell yourself you're acting out of love. The truth was, I was acting out of fear. I was afraid for my daughter, and I was afraid for myself and how lonely my life would be if I lost her. If I'd truly been acting out of love, when she called me and said, 'Daddy, I've been in an accident. I think I need to call the police,' I'd have listened to what happened and agreed. Then I'd have stood by her side while she told the truth and did what was right. But I've let fear lead my whole life for the last four months. I can't apologize enough for what that did to my daughter and what it did to Arrow, who was innocent in all of this."

Dad's hand tightens on my shoulder, and I realize he too has tears streaming down his cheeks. I wonder if he's half as overwhelmed as I am. I'm swamped in relief—the final shackle of this hell being unlocked.

"I know an apology will never be enough," Coach says. "But I want to give it anyway. So that when this community sees my daughter in court or sees Arrow in the streets, they can understand the part I had to play in all of it." Clearing his throat, he folds his paper and tucks it back into his pocket. "That's all. Thank you."

Dad squeezes my shoulder one last time before excusing himself, and Chris and Mason turn to me.

"We should have known there was something more going on with you," Mason says, his voice thick.

"What can we do?" Chris asks.

I shake my head and gesture to where they're sitting on the couch. "You're already doing it." The front door opens and I look over my shoulder to see Dad stepping outside. "I should go talk to him."

"We'll be here," Chris says.

Mason offers his fist and I bump mine against it. "Thank you, you two. You have no idea what this means to me."

I find Dad sitting on the front porch smoking a cigar. I close the door behind me and he nods to the chair beside him. I take it but shake my head when he offers me a cigar.

"You've had quite a day," he murmurs.

"I'm sorry about everything, Dad." I lean forward, propping my elbows on my knees. "It never even crossed my mind that Coach would have lied to me like that."

"I'm glad the truth came out." He releases a mouthful of smoke. "It has a way of doing that."

"I guess it does. Eventually."

"Gwen left today." He says it as if he's telling me there's

leftover spaghetti in the fridge. "Don't look at me like that. She wasn't happy, and everyone knew it. She thought she wanted the grumpy old man for his money, but it turns out I'm not worth it. She tried to forbid me to go to the station to help you, and you can imagine how well I handled it." He sighs heavily. "Anyway, she took Katie and went to her mom's."

"I'm sorry, Dad."

He shrugs. "Me too, but I'm not sorry she left. Just sorry we weren't right together." He takes another puff and leans back in his chair. "I miss your mother."

I swallow hard. Other than our anomaly of a conversation yesterday morning, Dad and I don't have talks like this, and we definitely don't talk about Mom. "You do?"

"She was my heart." He swallows hard. "Love like that is rare, but assholes like me fuck it up anyway."

"I don't want to fuck it up with Mia," I say, studying my hands. "I love her."

"Then be with her." There's something comforting in how simple he makes it sound.

"I keep pushing her away. I don't know if I get another chance at this point."

Dad stamps out his cigar, stands, and pats me on the back. "Then you should go to her and beg for one. That's what your mom would tell you. Life's too short."

I yank on the pant leg of my jeans to show him my ankle monitor. "House arrest."

"I think you can figure this out, son."

I swallow hard, both hopeful and terrified at the prospect of holding Mia in my arms again as soon as today.

He opens the front door and then stops. "Ask if she'd be interested in coming back. Katie will be with me half the week, and I'll need help around here."

And I need her. "You have to give her a raise."

"Already done."

"And have her sit with us at family meals, and hire someone else to cater your parties. No treating her like the help."

"Understood."

I nod. "I'll ask her, then."

Dad goes into the house, and I pull my phone from my pocket and dial my probation officer.

MIA

I am wrung dry and I am filled up.
I am confident and I am terrified.
I am lost but I know exactly where I am.

Bailey lies beside me in the grass across from Dad's trailer. From under the big maple, we stare up at the sky, watching the stars twinkle through the leaves.

"You have room for one more?" a deep voice asks from our feet.

My heart skids to a halt and then accelerates again all before I can take a breath. *Arrow.*

"Holy shit," Bailey mutters. She props herself on her elbows. "Aren't you on house arrest?"

"I told my probation officer what happened today and that I owed some apologies." He looks at his watch. "I have an hour."

Bailey hops up and brushes her hands on the back of her jeans. "I'll just get out of your way, then." As I sit up, she winks at me and then strolls away.

Arrow takes a step toward me, but before he's close enough to touch, he stops and shoves his hands into his pockets. "Gwen left Dad."

"I'm sorry," I say.

He looks over his shoulder toward the house. "You know, I think it's okay. I think he was sick of falling short on making her happy."

I shake my head. "That's where they went wrong. It's not his job to make her happy. It's hers."

He gives a sad smile. "Yeah, someone told me something like that once."

I lean back on my elbows and study the starlight through the broad branches of the old maple tree. "She was wise." I swallow hard.

"Do you remember when you told me about your mom? About the fire and the sun?"

My stomach twists. I tried so hard to justify ignoring my feelings for Arrow. "It was just a metaphor." It was a false binary that didn't work in a world where two guys who were best friends were both so important to me.

"I like metaphors," he says, sinking to sit in the grass beside me. "But that one's never worked for the way I feel about you. I don't want to be your fire or your sunshine."

I can't pretend to look at the stars anymore. I turn to look at his face and see he's watching me. "You came here to tell me again that you don't want me in your life?"

"I didn't say that. It's just not the metaphor I like. It's too simple to describe what I feel for you." Reaching over, he brushes my hair behind my ear. "You're not the hot, burning fire, because you're there even after a long, hard rain." He swallows and takes a breath. "You're not the sun, because you're there in the darkest night." He traces my lips with his thumb.

"Arrow . . ."

"You can't be the wind—beneath my wings or otherwise"—he laughs and then his smile falls away as he traces his thumb down the column of my neck—"because you keep me warm during the deepest winter." He closes his eyes, lifts his hand from my neck, and clenches his fist.

"Are you okay?"

He opens his eyes again and gives me a crooked smile. "I'm not done, but I really fucking want to kiss you right now."

The butterflies in my stomach burst into raucous applause. "That would be okay with me."

He strokes my cheek, and traces my lips again. "I need to finish first."

I bite back a smile. "Then hurry, because now that I know how this conversation ends, I'm pretty anxious to get through it."

His gaze lands on my lips for what feels like a thousand desperate beats of my heart before he meets my eyes again. "For a long time I thought you were gravity. Always there. Always pulling me your way. But that can't be it either, because you don't pull me down. You lift me up when there's no reason I should be able to stand."

My stomach twists in knots of hope and worry. Of love and insecurity. I've spent too much of my life not saying what needs to be said. When Mom left, I didn't tell her how much that hurt me. When Dad reacted to Nic's death as if he'd lost his only child, I didn't take away his booze and tell him he still had a daughter who needed him. I can't be like that anymore. "Arrow, you pushed me away when I wanted to stand by your side."

He slides a hand into my hair and scoots closer. His mouth is a breath from mine; each word could almost be a kiss. "But that's exactly it. You're too important to be brought down by me. To me, you're *everything*. And this morning when I told you I wanted you to be free of me, know that I meant exactly that. I've never wanted to be free of you, only the other way around."

I shift and our lips brush. The contact is electric, and I want to do it again and again, but I make myself back up an inch. I'm going to try to say this without hiding behind analogies, a lover of metaphors stripping bare. "It's always been you. And I know you think you need to free me because our past is complicated, but I'm here to tell you that if I'm free, if I can *choose,* I'll be right by your side. Because I love you."

He exhales slowly, then slides his hand behind my neck. "I love you, too. You are the most important pieces of my heart."

When he finally kisses me, I melt into him.

ARROW

One week later...

The sun is shining and my friends lounge around the pool, lazy thanks to full bellies and warm sun, and Mia's in my arms. Mason cooked us burgers on the grill, and Chris cleaned up after, insisting that Mia gets her share of domestic duties through the week.

I used to lie in bed trying to rewrite the past in a way that would mean Brogan would still be with us. But after everything that's happened during the past week, I've begun to accept that I don't get a redo. What I get is today. What I *know* is that in a world that has proved to be too cruel to bear during some moments, other times prove to be impossibly perfect.

It's a good day to be stuck at home.

Chris wipes down the table a final time before sinking into the chair next to mine and Mia's. "I heard they lifted your on-campus suspension. Does that mean you get to play next year?"

Mia tilts her face up to mine, and I press a kiss to her grinning lips before I answer. "I'm finishing my house-arrest sentence. My lawyer thought he could get it reduced, given the circumstances, but I broke the law, and I'm going to finish it. But BHU has said I can return to classes in the fall, and I'll be able to do that within the terms of my house arrest. And when my sentence is over, I'll be back on the field."

On the other side of us, Mason pulls off his sunglasses and grins. "Hot damn."

I shrug. "I'm not saying I'll start. There'll be some stiff competition this year."

"You'll start," Mia says, rolling her eyes. "You'll totally start."

It's so good to be here—with Mia and my best friends and waking up to days where football matters again. I tighten my arms around her and bury my nose in her hair.

"Would you two get a room already?" Keegan grumbles.

"Shut up," Bailey says. "They're fucking adorable. And at least *someone's* getting some." She tosses a pseudo-irritated glance in Mason's direction.

Mason lifts his palms. "You know my terms."

Keegan blanches and scrapes a hand over his face. "I don't understand you, Mase. She's *hawt*. Like H-A-W-T *hawt*." He grins at Bailey. "If you need someone to keep your bed warm, I have no terms and no conditions."

"And no chance," Bailey says, and we all laugh.

Chris looks at his watch and groans. "I have to head, guys.

I've gotta catch my plane."

"Tell your mom we said happy wedding," Mia says.

Mason smirks. "Gonna hook up with a bridesmaid?"

"At my *mom's* wedding?" He gives an exaggerated shudder. "The bridesmaids are my aunt Cindy and my soon-to-be stepsister, so thanks, but I'll pass."

"The stepsister's the one who's coming back with you?" I ask Chris. "She's staying with you and Mason for the summer, right?"

"I hope she's hot," Keegan says, and Bailey elbows him in the side.

"She's a hot mess is all I know," Chris says. He points at Keegan. "And the whole reason Mom asked me to have her stay with me is to keep her *out* of trouble—got it?"

"Y'all are no fun," Keegan mutters.

"Have a safe trip, Chris." Mia steps out of my arms to hug him. "We'll see you next week."

Everyone says their goodbyes, and after I throw a few pointed looks at Bailey, Mason, and Keegan, they get the hint and leave as well.

"Finally alone," I whisper in Mia's ear when they're gone. "Want to go upstairs and get naked?"

She presses a finger to her lips and pretends to think about it. "Hmm. I was thinking about washing my hair tonight."

I tickle her, and she jumps away from me and runs inside and toward the stairs.

"You'd better run," I call after her. I chase her up and catch her at the top, collapsing on top of her where the light from the second-story foyer window casts a warm glow.

She rolls under me and grins. "I guess you caught me. I'm all yours."

"Finally," I whisper.

I lower my mouth to hers and slide a hand up her shirt. She moans under me, and I close my eyes and feel the heat of the sun on my back, the softness of Mia under me, and I take the moment and all that will follow for the gift they are.

THE END

Thank you for reading *Spinning Out*, the first book in The Blackhawk Boys series. If you'd like to receive an email when I release Christopher's story in book two, *Rushing In*, please sign up for my newsletter. If you enjoyed this book, please consider leaving a review. Thank you for reading. It's an honor!

SPINNING OUT
Playlist

"Say Something" by A Great Big World
"Something I Can Never Have" by Nine Inch Nails
"Rolling in the Deep" by Adele
"You Ruin Me" by The Veronicas
"When You Find Me" by Joshua Radin
"Stay" by Rihanna
"Fast Car" by Tracy Chapman
"What Now" by Rihanna
"By the Grace of God" by Katy Perry
"Grace" by Kate Havnevik
"Lay Me Down" by Sam Smith
"Dark Times" by The Weeknd, featuring Ed Sheeran
"See You Again" by Wiz Kahlifa, featuring Charlie Puth
"Lay It All on Me" by Rudimental, featuring Ed Sheeran
"Jealous" by Labrinth

Love Unbound
by LEXI RYAN

If you enjoyed *Spinning Out*, you may also enjoy the books in Love Unbound, the linked series of books set in New Hope and about the characters readers have come to love.

Splintered Hearts (A Love Unbound Series)
Unbreak Me (Maggie's story)
Stolen Wishes: A Wish I May Prequel Novella (Will and Cally's prequel)
Wish I May (Will and Cally's novel)

Or read them together in the omnibus edition,
Splintered Hearts: The New Hope Trilogy

∞

Here and Now (A Love Unbound Series)
Lost in Me (Hanna's story begins)
Fall to You (Hanna's story continues)
All for This (Hanna's story concludes)

Or read them together in the omnibus edition,
Here and Now: The Complete Series

Reckless and Real (A Love Unbound Series)
Something Wild (Liz and Sam's story begins)
Something Reckless (Liz and Sam's story continues)
Something Real (Liz and Sam's story concludes)

Or read them together in the omnibus edition,
Reckless and Real: The Complete Series

Mended Hearts (A Love Unbound Series)
Playing with Fire (Nix's story)
Holding Her Close (Janelle and Cade's story)

Other Titles
by LEXI RYAN

Hot Contemporary Romance
Text Appeal
Accidental Sex Goddess

Decadence Creek Stories and Novellas
Just One Night
Just the Way You Are

ACKNOWLEDGMENTS

I'm so grateful to have a supportive husband who believes in me and my work, who understands why my stories mean so much to me, and who makes the sacrifices necessary when I need to work sixty hours a week to get a book done.

I'm surrounded by family who supports me every day. To my kids, Jack and Mary, thank you for making me laugh and giving me a reason to work hard. I am so proud to be your mommy. To my mom, brothers, and sisters, thank you for cheering me on—each in your own way. I'm so grateful to have been born into this crazy crew of seven kids.

This book is for my nephew Kai, whose absolute passion for football made me fall in love with the sport so many years ago. Kai, you might notice I stole some of your friends' names randomly for the book. As the characters are obviously not based on your old friends, this is merely a nod to the bond you all formed playing ball together. That kind of friendship isn't easy to come by, but it's the kind I like to give my characters before I drag them through hell. I'm proud of you, kid. Even if you did try to break my nose with your mom's cell phone when you were three.

I don't think I'd be able to keep my sanity if it weren't for my friends. You encourage me, you believe in me, and, when necessary, you pass the vodka. A special shout-out to Mira, whose calls save me from meltdowns and who understands that #livingthedream comes with really effing stressful moments. To

Kylie and the entire CrossFit Terre Haute crew, for teaching me to love picking up heavy things, which is, incidentally, a much healthier stress management tool than ice cream. To Annie for believing in me since I was seventeen and wore the identity "writer" like a badge of honor.

To everyone who provided me feedback on Arrow's story along the way—especially Annie Swanberg, Heather Carver, Mira Lyn Kelly, and Samantha Leighton—you're all awesome. Thank you for believing in my ability to tell this story when I was having doubts.

Thank you to the Terre Haute Police Department for answering my questions. I know they seemed weird and you didn't buy for one second that it was research for a book, but four call transfers later, you gave me the information I needed. Thanks for that and for the chuckle.

Thank you to the team that helped me package this book and promote it. Sarah Hansen at Okay Creations designed my beautiful cover and did a lovely job branding the series. Rhonda Stapleton and Lauren McKellar, thank you for the insightful line edits. Thanks to Arran McNicol at Editing720 for proofreading. A shout-out to all of the bloggers and reviewers who help spread the word about my books. I am humbled by the time you take out of your busy lives for my stories. You're the best.

To my agent, Dan Mandel, for believing in this book *years* ago and staying by my side through tough career decisions. Thanks to you and Stefanie Diaz for getting my books into the hands of readers all over the world. Thank you for being part of my team.

To my NWBs—Sawyer Bennett, Lauren Blakely, Violet Duke, Jessie Evans, Melody Grace, Monica Murphy, and Kendall Ryan—y'all rock my world. I'm inspired by your tireless work and always encouraged by your friendship. Thank you for being a part of this journey.

To all my writer friends on Twitter, Facebook, and my various writer loops—especially to the Fast Draft Club and the All Awesome group—thank you for keeping me company during those fourteen-hour work days.

And last but certainly not least, a big thank-you to my fans—the coolest, smartest, best readers in the world. I owe my career to you. You're the reason I get to do this every day and the reason I *want* to. I appreciate each and every one of you. You're the best!

~**Lexi**

CONTACT

I love hearing from readers, so find me on my Facebook page at facebook.com/lexiryanauthor, follow me on Twitter and Instagram @writerlexiryan, shoot me an email at writerlexiryan@gmail.com, or find me on my website: www.lexiryan.com

Printed in Great Britain
by Amazon